RAVAN AND EDDIE

Kiran Nagarkar is the author of the critically acclaimed novels *Cuckold* (for which he won the Sahitya Akademi Award), *God's Little Soldier* and *The Extras*, a sequel to *Ravan and Eddie*. His first book, *Saat Sakkam Trechalis*, written in Marathi and translated into English as *Seven Sixes are Forty-three*, is considered a landmark in post-independence Indian literature. His novels have been translated into German, French, Italian, Spanish, Portuguese as well as Marathi. Nagarkar has also written several plays and screenplays, both in Marathi and English.

Ravan and Eddie is slated to be published as an e-book by The New York Review of Books under their new imprint, NYR Orignals.

Praise for *Ravan and Eddie*

'(*Ravan and Eddie* is) one of the wittiest, bawdiest, most perceptive books in contemporary Indian English literature.'

– **Prem Panicker,** *The Sunday Observer*

'Kiran Nagarkar is totally unpredictable, and reading his books is like taking a roller-coaster ride for the imagination...(His) use of language recognizes no barriers, and flows over through and around the reader, engulfing him in a torrent of fantastic images... (His) lively imagination is like a force of light, touching now this problem, now that. His digressions are perhaps the best part of the book.'

– **Usha Hemmadi,** *The Indian Express*

'This is the hilarious story of Ravan, a Maratha Hindu, and Eddie, a Roman Catholic, growing up to adolescence on the different floors of the CWD chawl No 17 in Bombay... Nagarkar writes so honestly and effectively that he has brought out the smell of the fish and the urine of the chawls right into our drawing rooms.'

– *The Tribune*

'*Ravan and Eddie* compels attention. The sheer power, vigour and imaginative lusciousness of the narration possess a stunning visual quality.'

– *The Telegraph*

Ravan and Eddie

Kiran Nagarkar

HarperCollins *Publishers* India
a joint venture with

New Delhi

First published in India in 1995 by Penguin Books India

This edition published in 2012 by
HarperCollins *Publishers* India
a joint venture with
The India Today Group

Copyright © Kiran Nagarkar 1995, 2012

ISBN: 978-93-5029-325-6

2 4 6 8 10 9 7 5 3 1

Kiran Nagarkar asserts the moral right to be identified
as the author of this work.

This is a work of fiction and all characters and incidents described in this book are the product of the author's imagination. Any resemblance to actual persons, living or dead, is entirely coincidental.

All rights reserved. No part of this publication may be reproduced,
stored in a retrieval system, or transmitted, in any form or by any means,
electronic, mechanical, photocopying, recording or otherwise,
without the prior permission of the publishers.

HarperCollins *Publishers*
A-53, Sector 57, Noida, Uttar Pradesh 201301, India
77-85 Fulham Palace Road, London W6 8JB, United Kingdom
Hazelton Lanes, 55 Avenue Road, Suite 2900, Toronto, Ontario M5R 3L2
and 1995 Markham Road, Scarborough, Ontario M1B 5M8, Canada
25 Ryde Road, Pymble, Sydney, NSW 2073, Australia
31 View Road, Glenfield, Auckland 10, New Zealand
10 East 53rd Street, New York NY 10022, USA

Typeset in Adobe Garamond 11/13.85
InoSoft Systems Noida

Printed and bound at
Thomson Press (India) Ltd.

Acknowledgements

❖

In 1978, a well-known director of serious Hindi films approached me to write a screenplay for him. He and I met a few times to discuss a detailed treatment of the screenplay but the as yet untitled project did not persuade him to think of me as the great new hope of Indian cinema. I think he saw clearly that our minds worked differently, that after a point I would always rat on my earnestness with something farcical, bawdy or self-deprecatory.

The film director may have dropped my two heroes and their story but I owe *Ravan & Eddie* to him. I fell for these two guys who did not know how to give up on life. Within a year I had not just finished a longish screenplay in English on them (four and a half hours: any takers?) but had written close to seventy pages of a novel in Marathi on them.

Other more important things intervened: the problems of making a living and other minor preoccupations.

In 1991 I took a few months off and got back to *Ravan & Eddie*, this time in English.

I had not realized what a pleasure it would be to thank those who have helped get this book together. I wish to thank Nancy Fernandes who has typed and re-typed the repeatedly corrected versions of *Ravan & Eddie;* Rani Day who helped Nancy decipher my illegible, tiny scrawl; Anita D'Souza who took time off from work to key in more corrections; Neal Robbins whose generosity I would not know how to pay back and who sat late into the night to type in a missing chapter and reformat the book; Susan Daruwala Robbins who didn't just read the manuscript a couple of times but was kind enough to opine on whole new chunks at very short notice; Tulsi Vatsal who read through the manuscript and helped with critical corrections with a saint's patience while I made myself as unpleasant as possible and treated her helpful suggestions as if they were bent on destroying the fabric of the book; Daljeet Mirchandani, whose greatest asset is an open mind that never stops growing, with whom I've shared good and thin times, who would never dream of reading a novel, but has been a friend of Ravan and Eddie without knowing them; a special thank you to David Davidar who took time off from being the book's publisher to edit it.

One

❖

It must have been five to seven. Victor Coutinho was returning from the day-shift at the Air India workshop. Parvati Pawar was waiting for her husband on the balcony of the Central Works Department Chawl No. 17 with her thirteen-month-old son Ram in her arms. Night-shift from tomorrow. The thought that he wouldn't be able to see Parvati Pawar for a whole month depressed Victor. Every day he resolved to talk to her as she stood on the balcony of the fourth floor as if she were waiting for him. Shouldn't be difficult to break the ice. They had so many things in common.

Your son and my daughter are almost the same age. Maybe they were born in the same month? Who knows, maybe on the same day. Was your son born at six in the morning? What a coincidence. So was our Pieta. Are you still breast-feeding him? My wife Violet insisted that Pieta switch to solids when she was eight months old. Screamed the roof down for a whole week. You must have heard her, of course. Wants attention all the time. Your son is exactly the opposite. So well-behaved. Isn't that so, Mr Well Behaved koochi poochi moochi? Your carbon copy, that's what he is. Same big eyes, long eyelashes. A fine forehead. The same peek-a-boo smile. Though of course he doesn't have your pomegranate breasts. Pom-pom, pom-pom, may I squeeze them? Victor could have talked to Parvati for hours. But who was going to translate his Konkani or English into Marathi for her? Frankly, if he'd had the guts, he could have managed well enough in his broken Hindi. They could have discussed the two babies forever, comparing their sleeping habits, their temperaments and tantrums, the first word they uttered. Speak up, Victor, talk, say something, anything, he would tell himself as he eyed Parvati's back on the fourth-floor landing. Go to it, Victor. Be a man. Go down on your knees, go on. Tell her how much you love her, confess, confess, confess. Tell her you cannot live another day without her. Tell her that she has begun to invade your dreams. Tell her you love your wife, it's nothing like that at all, nothing physical; it's just that you're going out of your mind lusting for her. Call her on the phone, never mind if she doesn't have one, neither do you. Install one. Write her a letter. Tell her you are a lonely man in love with a lonely, lovely woman. Accost her in the corridor, meet her in the market and buy cabbage and chillies with her, join her at the Maruti temple, accompany her to the flour mill, ask her to fly away with you to the Andaman islands. Victor, Victor, Victor, you're no Victor but a born loser.

How was Victor to leap across the abyss that separated the fifth floor from all those below? A couple of times in the past when Parvati had turned around and seen him, he had missed a step or looked the other way and hurried upstairs. Last chance, Victor, today's your last chance, he tried to prod himself into action with every step forward. When he was standing right under Parvatibai, he realized how much in the realm of the impossible his wishful thinking was. He looked up. What he saw made him feel faint. His eyes singled out Parvati's breasts. It was an ample bosom. There was so much of it and so high, that although Parvati was not wearing a low-cut blouse, a whole lot of it could be seen. It was like a cold, restful glass of fresh lime with honey for a weary hitch-hiker. An altar at which the lame and the halt could become whole again. A place to soft-land those new planes Air India was buying. It went up and came down with pleasurable regularity.

Victor's hands shot up and waved to Parvati's son. 'Come, baba, come. Come, come.'

Parvati and her son were watching a pariah dog at the corner of the chawl scratching its ear with brisk, obsessive strokes of its left leg. When she finally noticed Victor, she was mystified by his gestures.

'Come, come baba, come.'

Parvati was delighted with the attention her son was receiving. She pinched Ram's chin and tried to steer his gaze to Victor. But the boy was mesmerized by the scruffy dog. Parvati's breasts pressed softly against the child as she transferred him from her right arm to her left to give him a better view of Victor. Victor felt he was witnessing a small miracle seeing them released in front of his eyes. He beckoned to the boy with renewed vigour.

'Come, come.'

Finally, Parvati's son saw Victor waving at him. Little bubbles of happiness burst out of the child's mouth. He screamed and pulled at Parvati's ears. Victor sensed a shadow flicker above Parvatibai's head. He looked up. His wife Violet and their daughter Pieta were in the balcony of the floor above. There was a strange confluence of revulsion, envy and rage in Violet's eyes. Victor's hands flopped and came back to his sides. And the remaining two come-comes broke off half-heartedly.

Parvati's son bounced excitedly in her arms. Yes yes yes, he wanted to play with Victor, see the dog scratch himself, watch the game of kabbadi kabbadi, get on to a double-decker bus and sit at the very front with the wind in his eyes and hair. He stretched out his arms and leapt.

Those who saw Victor said later that his eyes seemed to be blazing, it was as if they had caught fire and the flames were flaring in every direction. When she recalled the incident in the years to tome, Parvati's comment had two words of English, as befitted the seriousness of the occasion. Heart and halt. Mazhe heart halt zale. But despite her cardiac arrest she had enough presence of mind to scream preternaturally. Even today people in the chawl across point to a break in the monumentally solid wall of their building and tell you it's Parvati's crack.

Parvati's son went overboard and along with him almost three-quarters of Parvati stretched out precariously over the balcony. Victor's hands went up again. What he saw was a vision of the child Jesus. The sun was behind the boy like a stellar halo. He had thrown his head back and was laughing. His arms were wide open. How can anyone, Victor wondered, how can anyone but the God-child trust someone so completely?

Nobody could have said with any certainty whether Victor's hands shot up for Parvati's foolish son or for Parvati. And later, it became a little difficult to get Victor to talk about the matter. Despite the hurtling impact, Victor didn't let go of the boy. His hands held Ram under the armpits. He patted the child on the back and set him gently on the ground. Victor then sank down beside him, his eyes turned towards the sky, and lay down quietly on the road.

Tearing down, skipping stairs, her petticoat getting caught in her toes, somersaulting to the landing, her hair streaming behind her, Parvatibai ran out of the chawl. Her son was playing with Victor's shirt collar. She picked him up and felt him all over. Then she kissed him five hundred times in five hundred places. Her eyes fell upon Victor. His mouth was still a little ajar and the air of surprise had not faded altogether. Clasping her son tightly to her breast, Parvatibai bent forward and put her hand solicitously on Victor's forehead. Victor's wife, nine months pregnant, waddled down the steps and saw her. Holding Pieta with her left arm and rowing the air back with her right, she walked directly to her husband.

'Get up, Victor.' Her voice was brusque. Victor was unmoved. Parvati, knuckles cracking against her forehead to banish the evil eye from her son, was keeping up an endless patter. 'My baby, my sweet one, my honeybun, barely a year old and you want to leave your mother, aren't you ashamed of yourself? Talk to me, baby, what would I have done if something had happened to you? Your father would have eaten me alive. Khandoba was merciful, that's why you were saved. And because of my prayers to Saibaba last night.' With a sleight of hand that was breathtaking, and without opening a single button of her blouse, she flipped out her larger-than-the-dome-of-the-Sanchi-stupa right breast and pressed it into her son's mouth.

Violet couldn't take it any more. From where she stood, she could see Victor's eyes glued to this shameless exhibition of motherly love.

'Stop it, Victor. Get up,' she hissed in Konkani.

Frankly, Victor should have got up by now. But he didn't budge.

Violet bent down. 'I hate you. I hate you.'

No response. Violet placed Pieta beside her husband. She tried to get hold of the collar of his shirt but her belly came in the way. She sat down and shook Victor by the shoulders. His head swung back and forth like a cloth doll's.

'Stop playing the fool—' She stopped suddenly and strenuously tried to ignore a thought worming its way into her mind. But it was no use. Victor's inebriated head fell forward on his chest. She laid him down carefully and looked blindly at the people who had gathered around. She suspected that they were whispering something about Victor and her. Her finger pointed at Parvati's son.

'Murderer, murderer,' Violet said in a hoarse voice. Parvati was quick to grasp that the woman was saying something damaging about her son in a foreign tongue.

'Kya, kya, what, what?' The only language they had in common was Bombay Hindi.

'Yes, yes,' Victor's wife hissed.

Parvati put her son down next to Pieta.

'What's this yes yes? Say what you want to clearly. In a language I can understand.'

Violet either would not or could not forsake English. 'Murderer, murderer.'

Parvati's son climbed on to Victor's chest. 'Murdererrrr, murdererrrrrr,' he screamed gleefully.

~

The next day at four o'clock a funeral van came and stood where Victor had lain. In fact, he was still lying down, with both his eyes and mouth a little open as if he had not yet got over his surprise. But instead of looking at the open sky, he now stared at the black roof of the van. Black suit, white shirt, black shoes and black tie, Victor was all dressed up and ready to go. His hands had been crossed like swords on a wall. Glittering one-foot-high square poles, joined together by heavy brass chains with diamond-shaped links, cordoned off the coffin on three sides.

Behind the funeral van Father Agnello D'Souza was trying to comfort Victor's wife. Crying had exhausted her. Her sobs sounded dry and heartless but he continued to do his duty. 'Nobody's fault, Mrs Coutinho. You can't blame anyone for Victor's death, not even that child. Who can stop you when your time's up? You have no choice but to go. And those who are gone, go straight to our Lord.' How ennobling it was to see the priest assuage Violet's grief. The Hindu families watched this moving spectacle from a distance and felt privileged to be a party to it.

Violet held Pieta in her arms. Behind her, their close relatives stood in neat and decorous lines, two to a row. Victor's brother, his mother, his eldest and middle sister (the youngest was in Madagascar), and the sisters' husbands were followed by Victor's friends, people from the Air India workshop and Catholic neighbours from the CWD chawls. The men wore black ties and black jackets, the women black dresses. Victor's brother will wear a black ribbon on his shirt sleeve tomorrow when he goes to work. Victor's mother will be in black for a whole year. Death will make his relatives special. They'll nurse their sorrow for a year and exhibit it with deliberate modesty. They will talk softly and expect to be treated with deference. Wherever they go, people will lower their eyes, give them right of way and remember the departed man in whispers.

Father Agnello D'Souza made the sign of the cross over Victor. The Catholic community assembled there sang a beautiful and solemn psalm along with him.

The Hindus on the ground, first, second, third and fourth storeys of the CWD chawls felt left out.

Two fellows from the funeral parlour arranged dozens of bouquets, wreaths and crosses on and around Victor. White lilies; red, white and yellow roses; and the cool, soothing and delicate green leaves of ferns. On each flower-arrangement was the name, signature and address of the sender and a poetic message. It was not quite clear who the message was addressed to. God? The dead man? The people who were left behind?

'Gone to Jesus forever. Remembered on earth every day.' 'Snatched from us. Folded in God's bosom now.' 'The Lord giveth. And the Lord taketh.' Signed Gilbert Rodriguez, wife, and family; Errol D'Souza, Mr and Mrs Quentin Aranha, Julian Fonseca and the Fonseca sisters, Mr and Mrs Paul Monteiro, Michael Pereira and Mom, Sebastian Veigas and family, Joachim Castellino, Cajetan Figuereido, Peter Menezes, wife, mother and fly, Ozzy Braganza and family.

The last wreath was from the Catholic Brotherhood Club of Air India. It was a huge floral aeroplane. On its white ribbon was a legend in red: 'May your soul fly to our Saviour Jesus Christ.' They tried fitting it into the van but the span of the wings was too big. It was Paul Monteiro who finally suggested a solution. 'Why don't you tie the plane to the roof of the van?'

In the future, whenever there was talk of wreaths and decorations, the magnificent floral arrangements at Victor's funeral were recalled with awe. The van looked like the bridal bed in a fairy-tale and Victor was the prince. It was just a matter of minutes before the incredibly lovely princess in white came and kissed Victor on the lips and the two of them flew into the sunset on the Air India plane.

The Hindu boys and girls and their parents from the neighbouring chawls gazed in wonder at the indescribable beauty of a Catholic funeral. Truly, even if you were born a Hindu, it was worthwhile dying a Catholic. How much pomp and glory and solemnity there was in Christian death.

Suddenly all hell broke loose. The earth rocked and the heavens swayed. The people at the funeral looked shattered. Even Father Agnello D'Souza was speechless. Were these the voices from the Tower of Babel?

Loudspeakers placed in Parvatibai's windows were blasting the entire neighbourhood with the Satyanarayana rituals.

Parvatibai had hired a Brahmin priest to offer thanks to God for the miracle that had saved her son from certain death, and he was giving her her money's worth. Those ancient buildings, the CWD chawls, stronger than the pyramids in Egypt, even they shook like onion paper. The Catholic mourners were pounded and assaulted by the indecipherable cacophony. How uncouth and vulgar it sounded. Trust these Hindus to celebrate on such a sad and tragic occasion.

Even the Hindu neighbours had no way of figuring out what the priest recited, though it was in their mother tongue, Marathi. He didn't give a damn about the meaning of the words, the feeling behind them, the poetry of the language or the complex manoeuvres of the plot line. He had no thought for metaphysical implications nor time to translate them in terms of everyday life. He was telescoping words, sentences, paragraphs, hurtling through chapter after chapter. He was vomiting all over the place, choking on his own breathless mess. What came forth were huge boulders and sharp and clangorous bits and parts of iron pistons and bridges and girders.

The Brahmin priest communicated his frenzy to Parvati's child, Ram. The baby became frantic. He bawled and howled as if poison from a scorpion were rising in his veins. Parvatibai tried to pacify him with toys, her inexhaustible nipple, and the shira with bananas that was meant for the god Satyanarayana himself. The boy was beginning to respond to Parvati's array of baits. He was almost quiet when the priest looked at his watch and realized that he had barely twenty-seven minutes to make it to his next assignment, the engagement of a Chitpavan Brahmin girl to a Deshastha boy to be celebrated in much more affluent surroundings. In his haste, he poured too much ghee into the flames of the makeshift brick altar and the whole house was engulfed in smoke.

That did it. Parvati's son couldn't breathe, he couldn't see his mother and he found the smell of the burning ghee overpowering. He was frightened. He went berserk. Parvati picked up the spatula with which she was stirring the semolina in a gigantic pot and whacked the brat's buttocks. 'Who do you think we are performing this Satyanarayana puja for, you stupid fool? What do you think this Brahmin priest is doing in our place? Now, are you going to stop bawling this minute or shall I shove that rolling pin down your throat and shut you up for good?'

Parvati's son invented a whole new octave and managed to drown out the voice on the loudspeaker.

'You got away without a scratch yesterday, Ravan, but if I hear one hiccup or burp or even the slightest sound out of you now, I'll throw you down with my own hands.' Parvati caught hold of the boy's right leg, walked to the window and dangled him outside head down. The eyes of all the mourners on the ground turned to Parvati. She shook the boy like a rattle, above the crowd.

Victor's wife moaned. She went into labour. Her legs caved in first. Then her body folded up. Father Agnello D'Souza leaned forward and placed his ear close to her mouth to find out what she was muttering. But she had nothing private to impart. With a superhuman effort she took a deep breath, pointed her finger at Parvati's son and tore open Father Agnello's ear-drum.

'Cain. Murderer.'

~

'Did I hear you wrong? You didn't call him Ravan, did you?' Parvati's husband Shankar-rao asked above the din in his home.

'I did too.' Parvati turned to face her husband while her son was still hanging on for dear life outside the window.

'Don't you ever call him that, not even in jest.'

'From today his name's Ravan,' Parvati said with a flatness that made Shankar-rao realize that they had come to some kind of turning point in their child's life.

'He's been Ram since he was born. He'll remain Ram till he dies.'

'He nearly died yesterday, isn't that enough for you? Such a beautiful baby, such a sweet and innocent look in his eyes and a name like Ram. No wonder someone put nazar on him. No. The only way we can ward off the evil eye is to call him Ravan.'

'Over my dead body. Have you lost your mind, can't you tell the difference between gods and demons any longer?'

'I would rather that he was a live devil than a dead god.'

Shankar-rao was screaming by now. 'Which mother will want her daughter married to a villain called Ravan?'

'Makes no difference. From today his name's Ravan.'

'Wait till he grows up and tries to abduct every Sita in town. You'll regret it.'

'Mark my words. Every Sita will be chasing my Ravan.'

'Call him what you want, he'll always be Ram for me. The boy will curse you all his life,'

~

Something snapped in Violet. She blanched and the blood drained out of her face. Her right hand clutched at her belly and kept feeling around it.

'It's coming,' she said and swooned. Father D'Souza was acutely embarrassed by the investigations of Violet's hand. A little bemused, he looked around self-consciously. People ran hither and thither. Violet didn't seem to have any intention of getting up.

'Who's coming?' Father Agnello D'Souza sounded puzzled.

'Jesus Christ!' Violet's mother shook her head in disbelief.

Father D'Souza hurriedly made the sign of the cross. 'This is blasphemy, Mrs D'Silva. You are jeopardizing the very soul of your son-in-law by taking the Lord's name in vain.'

Violet's mother ignored the threat to Victor's eternal soul. 'Father, help me lift Violet.'

'Why, what's happened?'

Violet's mother lost patience. 'Because I'm telling you to.'

Father D'Souza put one arm under Violet's back and the other under her knees and lifted her awkwardly. He had not realized she was going to be so heavy. She was sweating profusely. Father D'Souza found her skin unnaturally cold. A particularly vicious wave of pain twisted her body and distorted her face. The breath from her open mouth fogged his glasses. Under the slithery black silk Father D'Souza was keenly aware of Violet's flesh.

Violet's mother had got into the van and was pointing to the long seat parallel to Victor's coffin. 'Here. Put her here.'

Father D'Souza pushed aside a few of the wreaths and laid Violet gingerly on the seat beside her mother and hurried out.

'Get back in, Father,' her voice pulled him up short. 'Sit down. I'll need your help in the hospital.' Violet's mother placed Violet's legs across his thighs. Soft silk killing his will power softly. A mysterious black mist that brushed against him and got under his skin and drew him deeper and deeper into the vortices of hell. There were evil spirits moving restlessly in it and scorching his five senses. How it felled him, that lucent black. Father, oh my Father, why hast thou forsaken me?

'Hospital? Why do you want to take Victor to hospital?'

'Violet is about to have a baby.'

'No please. Please, Mrs D'Silva, I beg of you. You go with her.'

'Father, behave yourself,' Violet's mother said sharply. 'In times of crisis, you too have some duties and obligations.'

'All is lost,' Father D'Souza muttered to himself. A horned pit viper had got hold of his soul and was leering wickedly as he gobbled it up. It was a tight fit in there and his soul was being pumped into an endless tunnel of serpentine guts. The snake wound itself around the tree of knowledge and spiralled up. Father D'Souza heard his soul crack and crumble. As it was crushed, he got a fleeting glimpse of the snake. It was still smiling. It had Victor's face.

Violet's mother got up, closed the door of the van, walked back and opened the glass pane between the driver's compartment and themselves.

'Driver, take the van to the J.J. Hospital. Fast.'

'My orders are to take the funeral van to the cemetery, madam. Nowhere else.'

Violet's contractions began to come fast and without pause. She arched her back. Whatever was inside her belly was in a state of turbulence and turmoil. It couldn't seem to make up its mind whether it wanted to stay put or break out. She was grinding her teeth, her nails went deep into Father D'Souza's arms and stayed there. They would have to cut Violet's fingers to free Father D'Souza from her.

'Thank you, oh Lord. Your wisdom and mercy are truly infinite,' Father D'Souza said as he slowly came out of the fog of piercing pain in his arm. 'Do what the lady says,' he told the driver in a voice that would brook no opposition. 'Hurry. The lady's going to have a baby.'

The van came to life instantly. People in India are still respectful of funeral corteges. They got out of the way. And a good thing it was they did, because the driver of the van was willing to run them over. This was sacrilege. He was sure that his boss would sack him on the spot if he discovered that his solemn van had doubled as a maternity ward. He tore through red lights, wove in and out of the traffic. The passengers were flung all over each other and at times Victor seemed to rise out of his coffin. Father D'Souza looked straight out of the glass panes of the rear door. The whole of Bombay seemed to be out on the road. There was a festive air about the place. Surely it was not an extension of the thanksgiving puja at that Hindu boy's place below Victor's house. Then it hit Father D'Souza. In the rush of events, it had slipped his mind that it was independent India's first Christmas Eve. Violet screamed, Violet panted, Violet collapsed, but he did not hear any of it.

'It's all right, Father,' Violet's mother told him as they entered the hospital gates. 'Violet's got a baby boy.'

'Praise the Lord.'

Two

The Hindus and Catholics in Bombay's CWD chawls (and perhaps almost anywhere in India) may as well have lived on different planets. They saw each other daily and greeted each other occasionally, but their paths rarely crossed. Ravan and Eddie too went their separate ways. It was not just a question of different religions and cultures, they shared neither a common colonial heritage nor a common language. India won independence from the British in 1947. The tiny state of Goa, tucked into a pocket of the subcontinent, was a Portuguese colony till 1961. When the Catholics from the CWD chawls went home to Goa, they needed a Portuguese passport. Their children went to 'English-medium' schools run by Catholic priests and nuns in Bombay. They learnt Marathi, the local language of the region, under duress for a few years and tried to forget it as quickly as possible thereafter.

At home, they switched unconsciously to Konkani. Their parents, who were educated in Goa, spoke and wrote fluent Portuguese. The Pope and Rome were important to them but the most devout event of their lives was kissing the toe of the miraculously undecaying body of Saint Francis which had rested in the Bom Jesu Church in Panjim, the capital of the colony, for over three hundred years. They celebrated Christmas but they really let their hair down at the Carnival in Goa.

There was prohibition in the state of Bombay, as it was known then. In Goa, wine and booze, both the local and foreign brews, were available dirt cheap. You drank for fun and sang and danced without reason. Goan Catholics were born and bred in India but their umbilical cord stretched all the way to Lisbon. Practically all the Hindus at the CWD chawls spoke Marathi or a dialect of it. Almost all of them went to Marathi municipal schools where the second language was English. English, the language of the former colonizer, was still the key which opened doors and gave you special privileges. But it was taught so badly and feebly in vernacular schools that it retained the status of a perpetual hurdle.

~

Parallel worlds can only meet in a geometrical Utopia called the horizon. Then where did Eddie learn to speak Marathi like a native? And how did Ravan discover the sin of Cain? How did Hinduism bring those mortal enemies, Eddie and his sister Pieta, closer? What made tae kwon do part of Ravan's physical vocabulary when hardly anybody in India or the West had heard of the Far Eastern martial arts?

Perhaps the answer lies in subtle undercurrents; in phenomena or vibrations so tenuous that no instrument can record them. If history is the teeter-totter dialectic between heroes or villains and social forces, then chance, the stray remark and the accidental encounter are often the underrated instruments which shape and reshape the contours of individual lives.

In front of Chawl No. 11 were open grounds. On the left were an Indian gymnasium, a small Maruti temple, a sand-pit with three swings and a see-saw. The empty space changed character depending on the season and occasion.

During the Ganapati festival, an icon of the god sat here under a cloth shamiana to the accompaniment of fourteen hours of blaring and cracked film music, with a break at 12 noon and 8 p.m. for aarti and other rituals. Come election time, local leaders gave speeches here. Once in a while the chief minister or a big name from Delhi would come and the grounds would be packed. But most of the time it was a playground. The boys played cricket and games like kho-kho, hu-tu-tu or kabbadi-kabbadi as it's called now, seven tiles and gilli-danda, games that hardly anyone remembers today. Sometimes the Christian boys got together and played football.

The space in front of the gymnasium, it was generally recognized, belonged to the Sabha, a volunteer organization of Hindu revivalists, of white shirts and flared khaki half-pants fame. 'All are welcome. Come one, come all,' Lele Guruji, the head of the Mazagaon branch of the Sabha, told Parvati when she decided to enroll Ravan, as he told every mother who wished to recruit her son in the Sabha brigade. Needless to say, in the all-encompassing 'all' of Lele Guruji, there was no room for Muslims.

Parvati had no idea of the political sympathies of the Sabha and it certainly wasn't Ravan's idea to save India from non-Hindus. Parvati's objectives were pragmatic. Keep the boy out of her hair and out of trouble. He had taken a bet of four annas with a boy twice his age that he could break three panes from his own kitchen window with three successive throws of the tennis ball with which they played cricket. He had lost the bet because, when he came to pick up the ball after the second hit, Parvati sliced it open with a knife and was willing to do the same with his head. The older boy had come up to collect his dues but had instead to part with eight annas in damages because, as Parvati said, 'At your age you should have known better.'

There were barely seventeen members in the Mazagaon branch of the Sabha. Once, when Ravan showed some resistance to attending the Sabha sessions, Parvati hauled him along to Lele Guruji. The Guru looked genuinely puzzled as he listened to Parvati's plaint. 'Now why would you want to stay at home when you can help build a great Hindu nation?' he wondered as he lifted Ravan off the earth by the narrow edge of his ear. It was a stunning experience. Ravan felt he had been shot in the head by a million pin-point pellets that exploded in undreamt-of colours like Republic Day fireworks. He was not overly keen to repeat this exercise in levitation.

Putting on the white shirt and khaki half-pants (never called shorts) was a ritual as complex as a samurai initiation. First, the loincloth. You tie the strings around the waist at the belly button while the tail of the loincloth trails on the ground. Ensure that it's at the dead centre of the cleavage of the buttocks. Now pick it up, bring it forward between your legs and pass it under the knot at your navel. Heave. Tighter and tighter. Can't breathe? You're joking. Looks loose even from this distance. Haul, heave, pull, and then pull some more till your testicles have ascended all the way into your brains. Now pass the band of cloth over your crotch once again and tuck in the remainder as tightly as you can at the back.

Your balls may be pinched, smashed, squashed and crushed but this home-made jock strap will make sure that you'll never get hernia. Put on your vest and your shirt. Pick up your half-pants. The relationship of the bottom of each leg of the pants to the waist is as precise as the ratio of the circumference of a circle to its diameter. The flare is 7.19378345267 times the waist. Put the left leg through the left khaki pyramid, then the right leg through the other pyramid. Tuck in the shirt, very tight please. Don't want to see a single crease in it at the waist, do we? Okay, button up and buckle up. All set? Good. Now just before you step out, shove your hand under the pants, get hold of your shirt and pull. Go on, keep at it, the idea is to use your shirt to lever your half-pants up to your rib-cage, preferably all the way to the neck. As soon as you reach the grounds, shove your hand in again and hoist the recalcitrant pants. This is the only way they can defy gravity. Any time there's a break in the exercises, or your sister-in-law or Lele Guruji himself comes over to talk to you, pull. Even when you grow up and become Shakha Pramukh and are talking to an assembly of distinguished guests, don't forget, yank up the pants.

'Attention,' Lele Guruji barked, and fifteen youngsters, five to a row, came sharply to attention. Each boy stood a precise arm's length from his neighbour. On the right, resting on the ground beside each child soldier for Hindutva, was his six-foot wooden staff. Time to bring one's right hand smartly to one's chest and say Jai Hind before going home. Instead, Lele Guruji said 'at ease' and followed it up with a 'sit down'.

He looked into the distance. The all too solid and numerous CWD chawls obscured his view, but he saw right through them into every boy's soul.

'Every day you reiterate your loyalty to our cause. You swear that you have faith in our religion. But faith is a torch. Unless you light torches in the hearts and souls of others, our flame will waste and die. Our Sabha desperately needs new blood.'

This was puzzling. Why was the Sabha bloodthirsty?

'Hindutva is an infinite ocean. But in the last few years, especially after the death of the great martyr Godse, the ocean is retreating.' Ravan got the picture now. Hinduism was an ocean of blood but there was a hole at the bottom, so you had to keep filling it. 'It is your bounden duty, it is your dharma to enroll at least one new member in the next ten days. Anyone who does so will get a magnificent calendar with a picture of the goddess

Bhavani presenting her sword to his royal highness, Chhatrapati Shivaji Maharaj.

'But even this is not going to be enough. Our leaders have sent a special message to us. For centuries, Muslims, Catholics and Protestants have converted Hindus. It is time we turned the tide. What we need is a wild bushfire that spreads across the country and brings back the lost souls to Hinduism. Anyone who enrolls a non-Hindu in our Sabha will get a Wilson fountain-pen. And the new member will be given not only a Wilson fountain-pen and ball-point set but also a beautifully illustrated and abridged copy of the *Stories from the Mahabharata and Shri Krishna's Life* in Hindi, English or Marathi. Go into the world and light fires, the fires of Hinduism. Jai Hind.'

Did Lele Guruji know what he was doing? That ten- and fifteen-year-olds, like forty- and fifty-year-old adults, may pick only the out-of-context vivid phrase and act upon it? How many of Lele's pupils became arsonists must remain a matter of conjecture. We must disappoint you and inform you that Ravan didn't. But the mixed and muddled metaphors of his Guru and the temptation of a Wilson fountain-pen which school would only permit him to use a nib and holder had a fiery effect upon him. He would convert, yes, he would be a missionary such as the world had never seen. Having resolved upon a vocation, the question was: whom was he to convert? What better place to start than home? No point letting go of the calendar. After all, Lele Guruji hadn't said it was an either/or proposition. He would win both the calendar and the Wilson fountain-pen.

'Dada, I need to talk to you about an important matter.' His father was lying on the only bed at home in the living-room with his face to the wall. If anybody had asked Ravan what his father did, he would have said, 'He lies in bed with his face to the wall.' He had done that ever since Ravan could remember.

From the occasional outbursts of his mother, Ravan had gathered that there was a time when Shankar-rao Pawar had had a job. He had been a weaving operator in a cloth mill, moved on to an ice-factory as loader, had done a stint as a car mechanic's helper and then been a dark-room assistant in a photographer's studio.

'Why don't you work like a man?' Parvati would scream at her husband every few months.

'What's the point, I always end up resigning. Mark you, I've never been sacked. I've always walked out.'

'Every man I know works. Nobody sits at home.'

'You should have married them. You know so many of them, God knows how intimately.'

'You watch your tongue now. My own husband saying such awful things about me.'

'Why shouldn't I? You don't treat me like your husband. You don't let me come into your bed.'

'Is this any way to talk in front of a child? Besides, I would if you were a man and earned a living like one.'

Ravan couldn't figure out why Parvati asked his father to mind his language. He rarely swore. He certainly hadn't just now. Unless bed was a swear word.

He had the strange sense that when his parents argued about work, or anything else for that matter, they always ended up where they started. No gains, no losses. Back to square one. His father still called him Ram. Parvati called him Ravan. If they called him Ravan in school, it was because Parvati had taken him over for registration. Was he Ram or Ravan? Good or evil? Black or white? He had no idea. He didn't mind being either. His name was a source of taunts and baiting in school and in the chawls but even good, solid, decent names could be distorted and lent themselves to wit, rhyme and scatology. 'Eat shit Dixit.' 'What the fuck, hard luck Deepak.' He would have liked to have made everybody happy by calling himself Ram-Ravan or Ravan-Ram, but both his parents found the hyphenated conjoining offensive.

~

His father wasn't sleeping, but if you wanted him to respond you had to repeat whatever you said.

'Dada, I need to talk to you about an important matter.'

'If it's fees, talk to your mother. If your school principal's rusticated you, I'm sure you deserve it. Talk to her but I doubt if it will help. Frankly if it's anything important, might as well catch her ear. You know I don't count in this house.'

'It's about some work.'

'Not you too, you brat.' His father got out of bed with unfamiliar alacrity, but Ravan sprang out of his reach. 'Don't you tell me how to lead my life.'

'Not work work. It's got to do with the future of the Hindu nation.'

'Is that what you woke me up for, Ram?' He was very angry now. 'Well, you know where you can shove the future of the Hindu nation?'

'Where?' Ravan asked not so innocently, for he had a feeling that this was a rare occasion and his father was going to use some choice phrase. But before Shankar-rao could reply, his mother was out of the kitchen.

'Don't you dare, don't you say a word against our Hindu religion.'

~

No, Ravan had to admit that recruiting his father was not a wise move. How foolish of him. Why hadn't he thought of it earlier?

There was a candidate, no, a house full of candidates right next door. The Dixits. The mother and four daughters, like his own mother, had to be disregarded unfortunately since the Sabha, at least the Mazagaon branch, didn't admit any women; but between the Dixit father and sons, the tally was a goodly seven. And there was no doubt that you couldn't get a more eligible family than the Dixits. They were the only ones apart from the Monteiros who flew the national flag on Independence Day.

Should he talk to the youngest Dixit and then work his way up, or just talk to the boss man and leave the rest of the clan to follow? Caution, he counselled himself, best to talk to Chandrakant who's my age and my friend but choose a time when the father's around and casually direct some of the heavy stuff I have to say in his direction.

Ravan chose the occasion astutely. Five of the children and Ravan were playing not-at-home, the most popular game of cards in the CWD chawls, while Mr Dixit read *The Times of India*.

Chandrakant narrowed his eyes and looked at his older brother like a policeman collaring a thief.

'All right, Ashutosh, it's about time you parted with the four aces you've been hoarding. Let me have them.'

'Not-at-home,' Ashutosh yelled gleefully.

'Chandrakant, the Hindu nation is in danger. Only you can save it.'

The effect of his words was beyond his wildest expectations. Without looking at Dixit Sr, Ravan knew he had got his full attention. He hadn't just lowered his newspaper, he was taking off his specs.

'Me?' Chandrakant asked in wonder and awe at discovering such unsuspected prowess.

'Not just you. You and your entire family. The infinite ocean of Hinduism is drying up because Muslims, Christians, and,' the word Protestant was too difficult and new for him, 'Parsees are converting Hindus to their religion. We need to light a fire to convert...'

Ravan heard a rumble. He had never before heard or seen a volcano but he knew in his guts that this was it.

'Sala, you bloody murderers of Mahatma Gandhi, yes, yes, you, don't pretend to be so surprised, you murdered the Mahatma, you have the gall to come to my house and preach the gospel of the Sabha? Five times I have been to jail. I left school to follow Gandhi and save our nation and now you want to destroy everything that we stood for and built? Out, out.'

The whole building, Mazagaon, Bombay city seemed to resonate with that cry. 'Don't you ever, ever step into this house. Chandrakant, if I see you talking to this boy again, I will strangle you with my own hands.'

Three

✦

Ravan spotted him from the balcony. He was ambling along. Come on, come on, how can you drag your feet on your way home? On your way to school, yes, that I can understand. But coming back ... You must either hate home or you need to have your head examined.

Now he was climbing the stairs, one step at a time. What's wrong with this fellow, still at the first landing? My father—and you can't get older or slower than him—has more spring in his step than our friend here. Okay, here he comes at last. Ravan quickly hid himself in the passage.

'Eddie, Eddie.'

Eddie stopped and looked for the faceless voice. Who could be calling him from the fourth floor, or from any one of the first four floors, for that matter? As Ravan materialized from the shadows, Eddie froze. So did Ravan. It was the first time he had formed his lips around that name. It felt, tasted, smelt and sounded alien. Had he uttered a forbidden word? Had he ventured beyond the point of no return? The two boys stared at each other. They were neighbours. They had run into each other almost every day for years, but they had never before looked closely at each other's faces. Eddie's sharp, straight nose and broad forehead, Ravan's large, perfect oval eyes, his left ear noticeably lower than the right one. Yet the shock and the surprise of the encounter were such that both boys would be hard put to assemble the separate features into a recognizable persona the next day.

Eddie made the first move. He shot up the remaining stairs to his floor.

'Eddie, listen.'

'What?' Eddie looked down from the security of his own floor.

'You don't know what you're missing.'

'What?'

'A brand-new Wilson fountain-pen and ball-point pen. And a story-book with beautiful coloured pictures.'

'What do you want for them?'

Ravan couldn't figure that one out. 'What do you mean?'

'What do you want in exchange for them?'

'Nothing.'

'What do you take me for? A fool?'

'All you've got to do is come to our Sabha meeting tomorrow. And our master will give them to you.'

'Just like that?' Eddie asked scornfully.

'Yes. And he'll give me a Wilson pen too. Will you come?'

Eddie shrugged his shoulders and looked bored. 'I've got better things to do.'

～

That evening Ravan did the unthinkable. He put on his white shirt and khaki half-pants, left home and didn't go to the Sabha. He didn't know where he was going, but it didn't matter. He kept asking himself a question that philosophers had asked for centuries. 'What is the point?' He was disillusioned and disheartened. Where was he going wrong? Was he failing the world? Or were the people around him letting him down? He had given it his best shot and yet he had nothing to show for it.

He had reached the Byculla bridge. A local train swept past without stopping at the station. Like a sponge being squeezed, the people on the platform shrank back. There were commuters hanging from the bars of the carriage windows. Some stood precariously on god alone knows what between compartments. Every once in a while a trousered leg or an arm swung wildly but hurriedly got back to its owner when a signal pole or the support of a bridge rushed past. The sides of the train were bulging with the pressure of the people packed into it. (How many passengers does a Bombay 'local' hold anyway? Twenty-five thousand? Thirty? Forty?) Any moment now that speeding solid iron shell was going to split open and thousands upon thousands of bodies were going to be flung all over Bombay, all the way to Borivali and Virar, some falling into the Thane creek, others into the Arabian Sea.

Almost by rote, Ravan had stuck his head into one of the diamond-shaped openings in the gridiron of the bridge. This was, after all, one of the most exciting places in the universe. Besides, the riot act as written, read and practised by his mother said that he was never to go to the bridge alone. But Ravan's heart was not in it today. His eyes took it all in but there was neither wonder nor mystery in what he saw.

He needed to do a post-mortem on the fiasco of his enrolment drive. He sensed uneasily that he had not used the right words, perhaps he had spoken them at the wrong moment or in the wrong order. Was his tone of voice a little too excitable, not solemn enough? Perhaps his face lacked authority, was he gesticulating too much or too little? Somewhere in the universe there must be a gesture and a set of words that would persuade people to do what he wanted them to do. Every situation, even the most intractable, was poised to go either way; it was always touch and go. But if you had the right combination of pauses, silences, thoughts, animation, stillness, words, you could not only communicate anything you wanted, you could get the results and responses you needed. There were people like that, he was sure about it. He was not one of them, at least not at this point in time.

On his way back home, he stopped at St Sebastian's School and Church. The light was beginning to fail. In the vast public grounds which the school for all purposes treated as its own, the football players were taking off their shoes but a game of cricket was still in progress.

Ravan watched the batsman take the bowling apart. Then the bowler hit pay dirt. One of his deliveries sang in the air like that fast train under the bridge. Suddenly, just as the batsman lifted his bat to swing at it, it turned an invisible corner and took off all three stumps. That ended the game and Ravan wandered off to a strangely dressed group of people at the other end of the field.

They reminded Ravan of his own Sabha, the way they had spaced themselves. There were about thirty of them, all a little older than him. Must have been between twelve and seventeen. In front of them stood their teacher, just like Lele Guruji. But there the resemblance ended. All of them, including the teacher, were in white. They wore loose white trousers that stopped at the calves and a white jacket tied around the waist, with a white belt knotted on the side. Ravan had never before seen a workout like this. Their arms and legs shot out wildly but always in unison. Their hands chopped the air, described arcs over their heads, they leapt, they kicked in mid-air, but the weirdest part of it was that they accompanied every action with a sound so alien and abrupt, it was like a missile aimed at him. Without meaning to, he tried to dodge it physically.

But if Lele Guruji was strict, unsmiling and a pain in the neck, this teacher was the sourest man he had ever seen. Nothing pleased him. He found fault with everything. He walked in and out of the cluster of boys with a cane that flashed and stung every defaulting limb. But it was not the cane that bothered Ravan, it was the distress and displeasure that the slightest imperfection caused the man.

'You are at least fifteen to twenty years younger than I am. But all of you are made of plywood. I want willows. You think this is Pee Tee, you clowns, imbeciles, cretins? We are talking about mind control here, the total subservience of the body to the disciplined mind. Instead, what I get is apoplexy, your limbs thrashing around like the severed tails of geckos before they too lose the spark of life. Arseholes, now look and see if you can respond to poetry for an instant. You won't be able to appreciate it longer than that.'

He rose into the air. Six feet above the ground his body became parallel to the earth. He hung there motionless. Then a shoulder turned, the body crouched in mid-air spun around like a silk veil, a leg seemed to disengage from that body-ball, it became a projectile, there was the sound of air being slit into two perfect halves in Ravan's ear and the tip of the right toe brushed the seven upright hairs on Ravan's head. At that very instant the body rose to meet the heavens again, became an arrow that climbed, then split at the crotch as the arms unfurled and let out a howl of damnation on mankind. He landed lightly, his feet eighteen inches apart, arms akimbo in front of Ravan.

'What do you think you're doing in my class, ghati? Go back to your Sabha.'

There was going to be hell to pay when he got back, but that didn't worry Ravan overmuch. He was still distracted. Why had that man, who he was sure could fly, who had done that incredible and glorious trick in the air, been so hostile and offensive?

Ravan tugged hard at his shirt from under his half-pants the next day, and was out of the door when his mother called out.

'Ravan, come back.'

'What is it?'

'Pull my sari down at the back.'

'I'm running late. Lele Guruji will make me sit in the evening after class and do penance.'

'Thirty seconds won't make a difference.'

'It will.'

'You've already wasted, a minute. Tell that Lele you were straightening out my sari.'

It was a routine that Ravan was familiar with. So were the protestations. The starched sari which his mother wore while going to the temple or on special occasions always stuck awkwardly to the back of her petticoat. It was his job to pry it loose and pat it down.

'See, how much time did it take?'

'An hour.'

~

Was that sari responsible for what happened at the Sabha? If Parvati had delayed Ravan a little more, would his life have been different? Would he have been spared the dreadful discovery that was to haunt and affect his whole life?

'That's two penances. One big one for playing truant yesterday. And another for not being on time today. Mussolini, the great leader of the Italians, conquered Abyssinia and many other countries. With his friend Hitler, he nearly won the Second World War. But do you know what is considered his greatest achievement even today by many scholars and historians? He made the trains in Italy run on time. He who knows the value of time will never be left behind. Do you know why the British conquered us and why we will never make any progress? Because like you, Ravan, Indians have never been on time.'

If you were late you were the recipient of this homily, a whack between the cortex and the neck that made you reel like a drunkard, followed by a pinching of the arm that was Lele Guruji's original contribution to the vocabulary of punishment. He caught a bit of your flesh and a chunk of biceps between his index finger and thumb and dug in till the muscle fibres separated into individual stinging strands of fire that spread in waves and made your earlobes burn and brain wilt. It was always the right arm unless you happened to be left-handed. Corporal chastisement was followed by spiritual disciplinary action. You copied a couple of chapters from the Gita with a hand that shook as if your bloody pumping heart had got trapped in the upper arm.

That was the small penance. What was the big one going to be? Ravan stopped in his tracks. The Mazagaon Sabha was assembled in full strength, with everyone sitting in the lotus position. A makeshift dais had been erected. Appa Achrekar, the elderly firebrand and legendary hero of the Sabha, was there along with three other local Sabha leaders. What was going on? How could he have forgotten it? Today was Founder's Day, and he was an hour late. Well, might as well beat it, instead of being humiliated in front of all these big shots. Ravan turned his back on the ceremonies and then turned round once again. Who was that boy on whose shoulder Appa Achrekar had laid such a loving and paternal hand? I'll lie down and die. Eddie.

'There's a famous story in the Bible about a father and two sons, both of whom he loved dearly. The older boy was a fine, dutiful and obedient son. A dependable sort, one on whom you could always rely, just like our Dharmaraj. The younger one was lovable and wild. One day the father and sons were in the fields supervising work when the younger son turned to his father and said, "I'm leaving, Father." "My son, it is not yet eventide. Only at the end of a hard day's labour are you entitled to rest and relax." "I'm leaving you, Mother and the farm, Father." "What has got into you, my son? Where are you going?" "I'm going to see the world, Father. My feet grow smaller working the same field. My eyes are going blind seeing the same old people every day of my life." Then his brother spoke up. "Go if you must but bear this in mind. Only he who toils is entitled to the fruits of his toil and of this land. If you leave now, do not come back and demand your share." The younger brother laughed and poked his older brother in the ribs. "Fear not, my brother, I shall not covet your land or your cattle or grain. They bore me fearfully." "And why will you covet my land," the brother asked, "when you have already taken half of everything that our parents own?"

'Years passed without a word from the wandering son. The older son toiled without pause. More and more his parents came to depend upon him. He fulfilled all his obligations as an older son should. And then one day they saw a dot at the very edge of the horizon. "Who could it be?" the mother asked her son. "It is a shadow, Mother, it will pass as a cloud in the sky." But the shadow grew bigger and bigger and the word spread like fire in yellowing grass. It is the young master, he has returned. And even as the shadow grew bigger, the father ordered a feast such as the town, nay, that part of the world had never seen. And the shadow now was so big and close it fell upon the older brother. "Wherefore do you rejoice, Father, in the return of a son who abandoned you, and prepare unimaginable feasts for him, yet never say a word of thanks to the one who stood steadfast and loyal all these years and looked after you?" "We'll not just celebrate and feast for the next few weeks my son, but all that we have is his who has come back." "And what is my reward, Father?" "Duty well done is its own reward, my son. Surely you did not love us for gain and rewards. Thanks be to the Lord. For there is no greater joy for parents than to see their prodigal son return to the fold." And so saying the father and mother put their arms around the younger son.

'Eddie Coutinho is our prodigal son. How many centuries have passed since he and his people were converted and left us? I have lost count. But he is back amongst his own and we rejoice at the return of our prodigal.

'Mark my words. Eddie will not just bring honour to the Sabha with his valour and devotion, in a couple of years he'll become the Prefect of the Mazagaon branch and before long one of our great national leaders.'

At this point Lele Guruji got up hastily and, handing a packet to Appa Achrekar, whispered something in his ear.

'To celebrate this occasion, Eddie, the Sabha wishes to give you a Wilson pen and ball-point set, though I must tell you that I do not approve of these pens and ball-points for children. And here's a fine illustrated book, *Stories from the Mahabharata and Shri Krishna's Life*. Give him a hand, my friends.'

Amidst the thunderous applause they failed to see the comet, that had watched the proceedings transfixed, spin into orbit and race straight to the dais. Ravan was behind the chairs now; he put his hand in the rear loop of Lele Guruji's half-pants, yanked him back, threw him off balance, and stood in front of Appa Achrekar.

'Where is my prize?'

The closely tonsured, white-haired, gaunt leader who had not feared the might of the British empire, had shot but not killed a particularly vicious deputy police commissioner in pre-Independence times and been sent to the Andaman islands for life-imprisonment, looked at Ravan through glasses made from soda water bottle bottoms but couldn't make sense of the raging, wild anger shaking before him.

'Is this another non-Hindu?' Appa directed the question at no one in particular.

Lele Guruji had regained his balance. He had not eaten children of ten yet but he was about to make a start. He got hold of Ravan's collar along with the thin flesh at the back of the boy's neck and began forcing him to retreat.

'No, Appa. This is a nobody. What do you want, Ravan?' One flick, a flip of the tail of a whale and Ravan had shrugged him off.

'My Wilson fountain-pen.'

'What fountain-pen, you ass? What have you done to deserve it?'

'I brought Eddie.'

'Sambhaji Satpude got him. And he's already been given his reward.' Lele Guruji's hand was tightening its grip on Ravan's neck while dragging him off the stage. But he had underestimated the strength of the boy. Ravan was not fighting for his life, he was fighting for his honour.

'I talked to Eddie and persuaded him to join us. Ask him,' Ravan hollered at the top of his voice.

The world stood still. And the two boys were alone on it. Time forgot to tick the seconds off. A voice like an oiled whip cracked across Ravan's back. The welts would never disappear from his soul.

'He's lying. Why would I talk to him? He murdered my father.'

And now Ravan was alone, truly alone, and the loneliness seared and shrivelled him as if the sun had suddenly withdrawn all heat from the earth. Everyone was looking at him. Appa, Lele, the other youngsters, the people on the road, the CWD chawls, the mercury lamps, the men and women in England, the Red Indians his teacher in school had talked of, the stars that you could not see but were there. They looked at him in horror, wonder and dismay. And yet Ravan, son of Parvati and Shankar Pawar, the ten-headed monster and evil incarnate had only one question to ask.

'When?'

Ah, the moment of truth. What god in his madness and wanton cruelty had ruled that we must confront it?

'Ask your mother.' What turned Ravan's soul to ice was the certainty in Eddie's voice. He would ask for proof all his life, but the only proof that mattered he had already heard. He wasn't aware of the tears, but there was acid scooping inch-deep tracks in his face.

'I didn't. I swear to you, I didn't. I've never even seen your father.'

But what was the use of protesting when he knew the truth? In the distance he heard Appa Achrekar asking Lele Guruji, 'What is the boy doing in our Sabha? Get rid of him immediately.'

As if Ravan wanted to continue in the Sabha or be counted among the living.

Four

❖

Evenings were the quietest time in Ravan's home. His father went out at 5 o'clock after a long siesta, three hours at the minimum. Teatime was 4.30 and at five he walked to the corner to pick up the evening rag, *Bittambatmi*. He knew his priorities. Work was anathema; as for the rest, he was willing to make adjustments. People may have sniggered at him because Parvati wore the pants in the family but who had gifted her the pants anyway? In return, he got three meals daily, tea, snacks, clothes, betel nut to chew, pocket money for the evening paper, two movies a month and, most important of all, peace.

Sex was a grey area. Parvati was not just a fine-looking woman, there was a sexual charge in her, an animal magnetism, to use the current popular magazine phrase, that she was completely unconscious of and that drove some men insane and others to asceticism and flagellation.

It was this innocence that women never forgave her. Manu, the ancient law-giver and misogynist was right, they told themselves. Women were a curse but Parvati was a catastrophe. How could she be so ignorant of the effect she had on others? It was a crime. You had to merely look at their husbands, somewhere in the middle distance, to see their members rise in outrageous rebellion, and sunder their jock straps. How their dicks howled, shrieked and bellowed at the sight of her. Tarts were better. At least they did it for a living.

Time and circumstances had taken their toll on Parvati. Besides, she hardly ever stepped out. But she was still a pain in the groin when she was not sweating. Fortunately for Shankar, she sweated. Incessantly. She was a non-stop, squelching, slushy mess. Her hair sweated, her neck, ears, hands, arms, breasts, the small of her back, her buttocks, her thighs, her heels and toes sweated. She wiped herself with the end of her sari and, when that was dripping, with the middle, back and sides of her sari and petticoat. If she stood in one place, in front of the three jumbo stoves in her kitchen, for instance, the sweat dripped from her thighs and calves and formed puddles under her. Time and again she wrung out her clothes but it was a losing battle. She was so wet all day long, everything became transparent. All that remained impenetrable was the shape of her bra and the line of her home-made panties.

And yet, on some nights when she was not thawing feverishly, Shankar-rao would be beside himself and on top of her. Once in a while she let him. Mostly, however, she turned over and lay on her breasts and face. This made him furious but it also drove him crazy. When she stood to put the string of flowers on the miniature gods in the tiny altar in the kitchen, he could see her arse from where he lay in bed and couldn't decide between her breasts and her buttocks. All he wanted to do was assault her, mount her from behind as she lay motionless for fear of waking up Ravan. But she had a way of tensing her back, buttocks and thigh muscles that gave him no purchase, and if he persisted, all he could show for his efforts was a battered and bruised limb. He would quietly get up, open the tin in which his wife stored papads, pick up the notes hidden at the bottom and walk out of the house.

A man who had little use for time, Shankar was nevertheless obsessively conscious of it. He might as well have been a nail on the wall as far as Parvati was concerned, and she often took him for granted or forgot that he was a member of her household; but come 4.25, and she knew it was wise to make him his cup of tea. Because if it wasn't on his bed at 4.30, he became vile and vicious and reminded her of all the goods and artefacts her parents still owed him. After he had pronounced that her father and mother were mother-fuckers, he couldn't think of anything which would top that observation and kept repeating it till Parvati lost all control over herself and threatened to jump from the window. Poor Parvati, it never occurred to her to tell him that she would throw him out of the window instead. Or more to the point—out of the house, physically and literally.

A Harangue on Poverty

For have you not wondered why Ravan's home did not fold in on itself many years ago? How do you think Parvati fed her son, husband and herself? Where did she get the money to buy food, pay the rent, send Ravan to school, replace the panes in the windows that Ravan broke, buy clothes? Who paid the electricity bills? Maybe she was born with a gigantic silver ladle in her mouth, maybe Shankar's grand-uncle had left him real estate in South Bombay, maybe Parvati ran a numbers' racket. Who knows? Life goes on. You have to take the good with the bad. Everything that happens, happens for the best. No need to be superior and look down on platitudes and cliches. What would we do without them? How else would we bear with such admirable fortitude the trials and travails of others?

In India, as in other poor countries, we have a line that is invisible and abstract and yet more powerful and pervasive than anything the West or the Japanese have invented. It is called the poverty line. Above the poverty line are three meals a day. Below it is a spectrum that stretches all the way from 2.99 to zero meals. As familiar as a clothes-line, most people in India spend their entire lives trying to reach out beyond it. It is their greatest aspiration. If you are fortunate, if the gods smile and you are lucky, you may get a glimpse of it. You can't see the line, you can't touch it, and five hundred million people are trying to get to it. But if you brush against it, sink your teeth into it, grow your nails, scratch at it as if you were trying to gouge out the eyes of a man who had tried to rape you, take a breath, deep but quick, and hoist your right leg. No grip, no toehold, no thin end of the wedge, no chink in the armour, just the transparent give of air, what patent nonsense, you knew that all along, you twit, get that leg out, flail, rage, fume, fight, you've torn your right thigh, it's a bleeding, gurgling and bubbly mess, whole chunks of it are flapping red and merry in the air, that's fantastic, that's glorious just so long as your leg is pinned and pierced into the barbed wire of that line to the big time. You've made it. Because, if one is to believe what they tell us, there are houris and TVs and videos and musk and the seven heavens, not to mention full bellies, on the other side of that line.

As for the rest of the five hundred million, maybe the poverty line is so far away and so high they never get to see it. Or if they do, they tell themselves it is a mirage.

~

What in god's name was the matter with Parvati? Why did she sweat so obscenely and voluminously? A hormonal problem, an endocrinological imbalance, a hyperactive sweat system, maybe she drank too much water, maybe she was just a nervous person? Why not come right out and say what her neighbours assumed: her sweating was a direct consequence of being oversexed. What do you expect, all that garlic and onion are bound to send the libido through the roof.

Those, of course, are the facts, the true scientific causes behind Parvati's excesses. It may however also be mentioned in passing that after Shankar gave up work for higher pursuits, Parvati spent twelve hours a day in front of three monster kerosene-stoves, cooking lunch and dinner for fifty bachelors or at least quasi-bachelors. They had left their wives, farms and homes behind in the coastal villages and hinterlands of Maharashtra and come to Bombay in search of work. Some stayed four to a room, some shared the same space with ten or twelve others. Still others occupied a room in shifts. Parvati supplied them meals. The food was not the greatest, many complained incessantly about it and swore to terminate the arrangement at the end of the month. Parvati's answer to them was, 'We eat what you eat.' The food was hot when it was filled into the tiffin boxes at nine in the mornings and six in the evenings, but tepid or cold by the time it got to the mills, factories and workshops where Parvati's clientele worked.

You paid for a month's meals in advance. You missed your payment on the 30th (27th for February), and your tiffin box didn't turn up the next day. Every once in a while someone who had not got his box came over and threw a tantrum, made a scene or cried his heart out at Parvati's door promising to pay within two days or a week. Often Shankar intervened on behalf of the defaulter. 'I know him. We worked together at the Sapna Leather Works (or The Royal Cotton Mills or Graphix Printers). He's a good man, he'll pay. Send him his food tomorrow.' Parvati always acquiesced in her husband's wishes. 'I will,' she said, 'if you start working from tomorrow.' That seemed to end the argument, at least as far as Shankar was concerned.

If the client grew abusive and violent, Parvati would look to her husband for help. That was in the old days, but her foolishness became obvious to her soon enough. She understood that there was always help at hand. Its beginning, middle and end was herself, Parvati.

~

After the tiffin carrier man picked up the dinner boxes at six, the house would quieten down. Parvati would then go shopping for vegetables to the Byculla wholesale market. You couldn't get fresh vegetables cheaper anywhere else. She could have sent the elderly woman whom she had hired the previous year to help with the peeling and chopping. But there was a fine line between economical and rotten and the old woman invariably transgressed it. The tomatoes she bought were either overripe and squashed or had fungus turning both the seed and red flesh black. She seemed to pick cauliflowers that had more stem and leaves than flower. And she had a predilection for okra, one of Parvati's specialities, that were so tumid and dry they wouldn't cook even in her brass pressure cooker.

Besides, there was one other factor. Any minion was bound to come to an understanding with the vendors about prices and margins. There were slim profits in Parvati's business and the key to them lay in the shopping.

They called her the mother of fisherwomen at the vegetable market. When it came to bargaining or a squabble, you could cross words with a Bombay Koli woman only at the gravest risk not just to your self-esteem but to your person. Parvati did not supply fish to her clientele, but she had mastered the technique of Koli women and made some radical improvements on it. The vendors at the market loved and hated her. She knew everybody by name. Something about her, not just her looks or sex, made them confide unwisely in her about women troubles, troubles at home, good times, who was cheating whom, who had got into debt, who was planning to run off with the neighbour's daughter, who was paying exorbitant interest. They asked for Parvati's advice and she gave it freely. Often it turned out to be sound counsel, but it meant that she knew your little secrets and would not hesitate to use them if you gave her cause.

If Parvati came into her own, it was in the market. She chatted with the vendors, asked after their wives, children, parents and second cousins, got spicy bhakarwadis for them, she humoured them, she scolded them. For coughs and colds she brewed home-made concoctions that tasted of green grass mixed with horse-manure. The vendors' taste buds revolted and their stomachs retched in dry paroxysms, but the phlegm came unstuck and they told her that she was the guardian witch of the Byculla market.

Parvati was born to be Superintendent of the Byculla vegetable market, if not the Governor of the Reserve Bank of India or the Finance Minister of the country. She could make two ends meet and have a bit left over. There was nothing underhand about her. But she was a wheeler-dealer at heart. Bargaining was in her blood. She instinctively knew how to give in on small matters and gain the big advantage. Anybody who dealt with her came out feeling cleansed, heroic and on top. She could scream but you could always out-scream her. She made the vendor taste victory and that made him generous. When both parties feel good after striking a deal, the prospects for future business are bright.

Parvati took Ravan to the Byculla market a couple of times, but he hated it. Lorries were parked three deep and stretched to the end of one's vision and beyond. Hundreds of bent men, parallel to the ground from the waist upwards, carried loads of vegetables that were bigger than those on the trucks. They wobbled and tottered and couldn't walk in a straight line. When one of them hobbled past him, Ravan hugged Parvati and sank his head into the folds of her sari. The floor of the market was filthy and slippery with vegetable debris. Parvati told him to watch his step, but a banana peel was stuck to the sole of his right sandal. Every time Ravan moved, his foot slithered and he would have broken a couple of bones if Parvati hadn't held his hand tightly.

The vendors sat on raised platforms with stack upon stack upon stack of brinjals, cabbages, spinach, potatoes, onions, beans, pumpkins, melons, bananas, carrots, green beans and cucumbers on either side of them. But there was life under the platforms too, where the reserve stock was kept. Ravan was transfixed by a dwarf at eye level who was burrowing in a hole underneath. No, not a dwarf but a man on his haunches whose duck feet paddled him in and out of the dungeon. On his way out he brought forth an oversized, tumescent jackfruit in his hands. Ravan had never seen anything so large and malevolent. It was breathing, you could see its pregnant belly swell up and deflate. The man on his haunches raised the living, deformed fruit and yelled, 'How many more?'

Scores of shoppers with overloaded bags and their coolies with big, flat baskets piled high with the day's shopping collided with each other in the narrow passages between the rows of open shops. They were unaffected by the subterranean drama. The vendor on the platform grabbed the fruit. It was so heavy he nearly fell over. 'Another fifty,' he shouted and stood up on a stool and balanced the jackfruit on a pile that seemed to reach the ceiling. They were all breathing, those jackfruits. The pile expanded, Ravan could hear them inhaling. Then slowly they shrank back. The stench of the ripened jackfruit was buzzing in his head. It made him feel faint. He didn't know what he hated more, their stink or their yellow-green prickly texture. They were hard and misshapen and made of stone. Any moment now they were going to come crashing down and he would be buried under them. Parvati was going to look for him for days but wouldn't recognize him because his skin would become hard and yellow-green and spiky and his insides would be pale gold and smell sickeningly sweet.

Parvati cut him open with a butcher's knife. It was her favourite fruit. It reminded her of her childhood and her mother's home and carefree days. The suppurating yellow smell made her sigh in ecstasy. She gouged out his soft, pale, voluptuous, gold fruit-flesh. She gorged herself to her eyes all day long and dug in for more. Then she threw him up. She vomited for days and weeks and months till she became nothing but a transparent collapsible shell. She was pale and lay dying in her own filth. The men and women who were shopping crowded around her and looked down, way down into the well where she lay. It was her last breath but she was trying to say something. They couldn't make out what she was saying but Ravan understood her. 'More. Just a little more jackfruit.'

~

Ravan's father Shankar knew only two postures, the foetal position and a prostrate one in which he stretched out on his back. He practised the first for about eighteen hours a day, when he lay curled on his side in bed, with his face to the wall. Over the years the bed had begun to resemble a hammock. The web of steel springs that stretched under it from end to end was about six inches from the floor in the middle. The slightest variation in pressure and position made the bed squeal anxiously. Shankar had no problems living with the creaking. Every nine or ten months when the springs began to sound like cats in heat, Parvati poured coconut oil into a cup and oiled them. Then for a few months the bed's protestations were muted.

Ravan thought that his father was born in striped shorts and a short half-sleeved vest which he rolled halfway up his chest because of the heat.

When he was not in bed, he was sprawled on a grandfather armchair. It had a cane back and the length of the arms could be doubled by extending the flat boards under them. Shankar lay on the chair, his legs resting on the lengthened arms, his head collapsed to one side and the newspaper held in front of him. It was an effort to read the paper but this was one task which he did not shirk. He read the tabloid with the concentration, unease and intensity of people who have to pick out letters to form the harder words and are not too sure of their meaning.

Bittambatmi was the highest-selling paper in Bombay. The name *Bittambatmi* meant every bit of news and that's what it had, so long as it was sensational, gaudy and mostly fabricated. The schematics, if anyone bothered to study them, were always the same. Three rapes or near rapes, one of which was a confession by the rapist, the second an emotionally charged and suggestive account from the victim and the third a mere news item. Murders, contraband hauls and gang wars were headline stuff. The second page was the police beat, the third a review of the criminal cases in the courts and excerpts from the memoirs of police inspectors, customs officials and lawyers. The fourth was devoted to astrology, miracles, rebirths, two-headed babies, triplets with one conjoined set of lungs, and a column where Auntie Lalan sternly answered or deflected readers' queries on every conceivable weakness, failing and sexual aberration. Of late, the paper had been taking a high moral stand on wife-burnings and abuse but managed to spend the greater part of its time and space instructing its readers on exactly how to proceed in such matters.

While his father read about a man who lured women to his home, kept them chained for months and raped them repeatedly, Ravan did his homework on the floor. There were eleven problems in arithmetic that he had to solve and after almost an hour he was still on the first. He did not really have any difficulty with them; it was just that he had not even looked at them. Were memories dreams or dreams memories? And were there memories that the mind did not remember? Was it possible to do something while one slept and not recall it? Then how come Eddie, who was younger than him, remembered something he did not? Was it possible to access someone else's memory without that person's knowledge? When had he killed Eddie's father? And how? And why? Was he leading two lives and did the one not know of the other? Did his parents know that he was a murderer? Were they keeping mum because he was their son? And it wasn't as though this was a solitary accident. He seemed to be adept at killing though he couldn't recall the second murder either. Mr Dixit obviously had very clear memories of his killing Gandhi. Did he kill Eddie's father first or Mahatma Gandhi? Or did he commit both crimes on the same day? It was all very puzzling. Lele Guruji said that Nathuram Godse killed Gandhi and had become one of the great heroes and martyrs of the Hindu cause. They had hanged Godse. What about Ravan? Would they be coming to get him one of these nights? Are you hanged twice if you commit two murders? If they hanged him, would he too become a hero and martyr? Or was it something more complex than that, since he had killed Eddie's father which both Lele Guruji and Appa Achrekar disapproved of? Had his father's paper *Bittambatmi* carried the news, a blow-by-blow account of how he had done it? Done them? Did Godse fire the first shot? Or did he? Where was the gun? And Eddie's father, had Ravan shot him or stabbed him with a knife? And what if his parents didn't know anything about his past either? What would happen when they discovered it? Would they throw him out? What a question. Who would harbour a murderer?

~

The previous year Parvati had bought a ceiling fan and had it installed in their living-cum-bedroom. When she got back from the temple and after the meal boxes had been dispatched, she brought out the vegetables that needed to be cut for the next day and sat under the fan next to Ravan. As she sliced the long green beans, she hummed a song from *Baazi,* a film she had seen a couple of years earlier. Usually, Ravan interrupted her to tell her that the words she sang were not in the song she was trying to sing and could she possibly refrain from singing because there were limits to tunelessness and she was breaking every one of them? She thought he was bloody cheeky but in this one instance she loved it. Because if you sang badly, Ravan couldn't resist telling you and would instantly show you how the tune went and what the words were. And he never sang a couple of lines but the whole song.

What Ravan meant to her, Parvati would never be able to say and would not want to either. But when he broke into song, she sat agape in wonder, amazement and pleasure. Did you hear his voice? Would you believe he was just a child? He held nothing back, he put everything he had into it. It was a voice as open, as guileless as he was. It reminded her of the blue sky in her village. It was blue blue, it was dense, it was higher than the sun and it danced. It reminded her of the wind on the hill in her village and the green that stretched forever. It brought back the river to her, the big, vast and deep river that flowed so quietly, you thought its waters were still. Where did he get that voice from?

And how did he learn the words when they had no radio (she was going to buy him one as soon as she had collected enough money), and how did he hold a tune, every nuance of it and how come he was utterly, utterly unselfconscious?

She deliberately hummed some more but there was no response from him today. She had been watching him for a while now. He did his homework regularly and she was not one to bawl him out because his mind had wandered. But something was amiss today. She had not seen him so unnaturally still before. It was as if he wasn't there.

'What's the matter, son?'

She had touched a mansion eaten through by termites. The whole edifice of Ravan Pawar (eight years and two hundred and thirty-seven days old, black hair, widow's peak, trusting eyes) crumbled before Parvati. There was no sound to his tears.

'You never told me I killed Eddie's father.'

Parvati was speechless. He didn't need reconfirmation but there it was—her silence, the sudden throb of memory in her eyes, the flash of rage that ignited her tongue.

'Has that Violet woman been talking to you?' So his mother knew and so did Eddie's mother. They had an understanding, a pact of silence.

'You didn't kill him. He almost killed you.' He had never seen her so angry. But he was not deceived.

'How come I'm alive and he's dead?'

Parvati's hand flew out and hit Ravan hard on the cheek.

'Don't you ever say something so terrible.' She drew him to her. He resisted but she wasn't aware of it. She clasped him to her breast and kissed him all over his face as if this was the last time she was going to see him. 'May all your ill-wishers die this minute. I got you back from death. No other mother has been as fortunate as I. I don't intend losing you now.'

Five

'I've got so much homework, multiplication, division, geography, history, English. I'll have to sit up late tonight.' Coming as it did from Eddie, this was such a novel sentiment, it was almost revolutionary. Violet was impressed. Was he turning over a new leaf? Or was he being his usual mendacious self? He hated studying and homework.

Whether the liberties Eddie often took with the truth indicated a creative flair or were just plain hogwash depended on your point of view. Violet thought the future boded ill. This was the stuff of which hardcore criminals like that unmentionable devil with the unmentionable name on the fourth floor were made. Every lie would plunge him deeper into the fiery pits of hell. But to turn a blind eye to sin was also a sin, especially when the sinner was your own son. Besides, timely punishment was a lesson and a deterrent. She was not very hopeful, but there was a chance that it could change his ways and save him from damnation.

Victor, Victor, the bell in her mind had chimed every single day and sometimes every minute, how could you have died on me? The thought of betrayal had shrivelled her brain. It had become small and hard and craggy like the seed of a peach and it rattled all day and sometimes through the night. Black was her colour. She wore black every day of her life. Her eyes were black and there was black around her eyes. Her hair was black. (Even when it turned grey in her late fifties, she dyed it black so that there was no break in her mourning.) To her dying day she would not stop mourning for a man she could never forgive. But more wearying than the gong in her head was the bitter, sour taste in her mouth. It had changed her features and coloured everything she did.

Neither Eddie nor his older sister Pieta would ever get used to that bitter, sour odour. It assailed them, and even today took them by surprise when they got back from school or play or from the grocer's or wherever they had gone. It was not bad breath. Mr D'Cruz from the corner room on their floor had that. You held your breath and you put as much distance between him and yourself as your lungs and your legs would let you if he happened to pass by or, worse still, open his mouth.

No, the smell that emanated from Violet had nothing to do with halitosis. It was the smell of pain, of unshed tears, of dour rectitude, of implicit faith in Jesus and not knowing why he should deal her such a cruel blow. Anyone who came in contact with her, passing contact, was touched and trapped by it. Even dear, ineffectual Father D'Souza, who tried to please everyone and was wracked occasionally by doubts that God was not overly pleased with his performance, dreaded Violet's visits. She never complained. She bore it all stoically but God help you if you forgot her everlasting grief.

Her mouth was a slightly askew bloodless blue line and her eyes warned you not to put too much faith in your good fortune for that too would pass. Like a kidney stone growing inside her, she nursed her grievance. It was the rock on which she built her life. She was aware that CWD Chawl No. 17 was not the most congenial of places in which to bring up her children. But that only reinforced her inexhaustible sense of being wronged. Where was he, the father of her children? She was the mother, God's chosen vessel for softness and for gentling Pieta and Eddie. It was her husband Victor's task to be stern and chastise the children. He should have been the rock instead of her. It was he who should have disciplined Eddie when he said he couldn't go to school because he had a clot in his left tentacle. She clipped him on the jaw and sent him off. When he failed in three subjects out of eight, he said he had haemorrhoids in his brains which was why his eyes were bloodshot and he couldn't see clearly during his arithmetic, history and geography exams. She thrashed the daylights out of him that day and every whack of the cane drew a welt on her soul.

When these terminal illnesses failed to move his mother, Eddie shifted ground. 'No school tomorrow,' he told his mother one day with tears in his eyes. 'An Ambassador car ran over my schoolteacher and broke his kidney waters. He's in hospital dying.' Kidney was a word Violet understood. She let him stay at home but went to school to check, just in case. She didn't like Mr Lobo. He looked like a bulldog. The children were frightened of him. So was she. 'I don't quite understand your question,' he said, his voice neutral. 'As a woman you should be familiar with the phrase "breaking water". Men do not. At best or worst, depending on your point of view, men will break wind, though that is not their exclusive privilege. These children, I will not call them fiends because you are a mother and may take offence, may have broken my spirit and my heart but my kidneys, I assure you, are as yet unbroken. You may also have noted that despite your son's fervent prayers and wishful thinking, I am not dying, school is not closed, no damage has been done to any car and class was in progress till you came with your solicitous enquiries about my well-being. As for your son, Madam, I can only recommend, mind you, there's no obligation, as there is none with the directive principles of the constitution of our nation either, that you break a leg of that perpetually prevaricating son of yours who would see me in hospital or, if he had his way, in a morgue.'

Violet went home and followed Mr Lobo's advice, to the letter, well almost. Eddie, she knew, was her cross. She bore him as she had borne him on the day of his birth with equal amounts of dignity, resignation and resentment. She suspected that Mr Lobo had been trying to humiliate her with his superior attitude and his highfalutin language. If she had had any say in the matter, she would have had a chat with the principal, Father Giacomello, and had Mr Lobo dismissed.

But in truth, Violet's anger was against herself. She knew her son and his shams and his ploys and yet she'd been taken in. He was making a fool of her and nobody did that with impunity. He had his father's charm and the ability to spin a story which she knew was not really different from easy virtue. If she didn't look out, he would go his father's way. As always, her own mother who adored Eddie and cracked up every time he pulled a fast one, and Pieta who couldn't stand the sight of her younger brother, begged and pleaded with her and ultimately wept silently while Violet caned his calves till the flesh broke in an attempt to flagellate herself.

~

Eddie sit up and study the whole night? Pieta did that when her exams were approaching. Any pretext was good enough to keep her up all night to study. But Eddie? Violet made the sign of the cross and went down on her knees. Why were Violet's prayers always delivered aloud? Weren't prayers a matter between you and your Lord? Maybe elsewhere. The essence of life in a chawl is that everything is public property. When you are constantly in each other's hair, it's almost impossible to get the lice out of your own hair without picking a few out of somebody else's. You get used to a larger audience. You can't always see them but you know they are listening, so you make sure that your stage whisper projects into the last row. Besides, with Violet, prayer was a report to God. He was omniscient but it was best to play safe and keep him informed. Prayer was also a way of letting the children, especially Eddie, know that she knew what was going on and what the score was. 'Lord, is he pulling my leg? If he's not, if he's serious about studying let it not be for a day but forever. You know he has a sharp mind. All those medical terms he uses, he should make a fine doctor. You remember the day he came home with slight fever and said he had got typhoon and, of course, I disregarded his words and that nearly cost his life for he had diagnosed his condition correctly and it was typhoid or at least para-typhoid. If only he applies his mind. Let's have a fair exchange. Let him become studious and it's OK with me if Pieta manages to scrape through. She's the one who's had her heart set on becoming a doctor since childhood. Where's the money going to come from? And you know what happens to these overeducated girls. Men don't want to marry them. You took away Victor. Now give Eddie an early start. I'll slave away for another fifteen years as I have done these past seven or eight. Then let Eddie take over. Make him a heart surgeon like Dr Oliviera Cabral of Panjim. Make him the most famous Catholic heart surgeon in India. He'll make us wealthy and happy.

'I'll go to Mahim Church this Wednesday and the next eight Wednesdays and lay a wax brain at Mother Mary's feet. No, he has enough brains. It's application he lacks. I'll make a table of wax with a book on it. Do not disappoint me, Lord.'

His mother's prayers gave Eddie pause. Did his mother know that this was another of his tricks? His sister certainly did. Liar, she had hissed at him when he made his announcement. Was Violet telling him to pull himself up by his bootstraps? And what was this thing about becoming a heart surgeon? He hated doctors. Do you know what they did when they were drilling your teeth? No more, they said and went ahead and drilled some more. Won't hurt, their family physician Dr Carvalho told him before giving him an injection for his inflamed tonsils. Brother, did it hurt. Even his mother, his very mother who never had a word of sympathy for him, said that Dr Carvalho had not replaced the set of needles he had inherited from his father's practice. Short of taking a hammer and hitting the plunger in the syringe on its head, the doctor did everything possible to ram the blunt needle into his buttock. It wouldn't go in at the bulging centre of his left rump, so he tried again at another spot. Despite his hoarse throat, Eddie screamed blue murder and kicked and recoiled. The syringe fell like an arrow to the ground. Its path was perpendicular. The needle had taken a 'U' turn. You could go fishing as soon as you stuck a live fly into it. The syringe itself was shattered to twenty seven thousand glinting, refracting, radiant pieces of kaleidoscopic quartz.

Dr Carvalho was six feet four inches tall. In his perfectly hairless head were a long nose, sad, docile eyes and the ruins of his teeth. When he opened his mouth you felt awed. What terrible battles and wars had been fought here. The hordes of Genghis Khan about whom Eddie read in his history book had gone on a rampage for eleven nights and eleven days and razed the temple to the ground. Not a single tooth was left intact. Instead there were delicate broken pillars and shards in nicotine yellow and brown, and frail grey where the destruction was still in progress. Dr Carvalho had to lean forward to bypass his paunch and look down on Eddie. Before he could say anything, Violet interrupted him. 'I'll pay for it.' 'Indeed, you will,' Dr Carvalho said, 'but it was one of my father's syringes. Now I have only two of them left.'

The compounder came in and held Eddie's feet in a vice while a shamefaced but determined Violet held his head down as if she wanted to bury it in the hard wooden divan whose once-green rexine cover had become almost black. It was murder. Might as well have plunged a spear into his heart. But that was nothing compared to whatever it was that Dr Carvalho was trying to inject. It felt as though he was trying to introduce solid concrete into his flesh. For weeks Eddie's bum was hard as stone. You could have built the Qutab Minar on it. No, thank you. His sister Pieta, forever pious, over-zealous and prim and the darling of her teachers, that living fraud and the bane of his life, was welcome to become a heart surgeon. She was made for it. Won't hurt at all, she would say as she sat next to her patients and yanked their bloody hearts out.

~

He could see the corner of the story-book in its purple wrapping paper with the red ribbon in his school bag. It had taken a superhuman effort not to unwrap it when it was presented to him but he didn't want to share it with anyone. He had rushed home and in a flurry of exaggerated activity had hidden it in his school bag.

He had it all worked out. Prepare the ground by making a lot of noise about how much homework had to be done. That would please his mother and shut up his dearly detested sister. Granna was hardly ever a problem. After dinner, while Pieta was doing her three-minute brushing routine and his mother was cleaning up and putting things away, he would quickly remove the shining gift wrapping, place the *Stories from the Mahabharata and Shri Krishna's Life* in his history book, it was the only one large enough to accommodate it, pull out the flap and supports of the folding table which served as his writing desk and sit down to a long and happy read. Just the thought of stories of strong warriors and duels, heroes and blackguards made him feel giddy. There was homework of course and it was wanted for the first class he had at nine in the morning, but really, you couldn't do everything at the same time. He would think about it tomorrow. Get up early in the morning or cajole Roger into letting him copy his answers.

Trust his mother to throw a spanner in the works by bringing God into it. He resolved the problem quickly. He would do one half of his homework, make it one-third, that would make God and his mother happy, and then he would look after his own happiness.

He was not the fastest reader in the world, and things were slower than normal today because of all those strange names like Vichitravirya and Bhishma and Amba and Dhritarashtra and Pandu. It took him time to get into stride. As a matter of fact, he was on the verge of giving up when he turned a few pages and saw the picture of a boy hardly older than himself practising archery in front of the statue of a bearded, old but powerful man. The legend underneath it read: 'Dronacharya refused to teach Eklavya. So he made a statue of the guru and became the greatest archer till...'

Why did Dronacharya refuse to teach Eklavya? How come Eklavya didn't tell the fellow to go jump instead of making a statue of him. And how does a statue teach you anyway? Eddie was curious by nature but it was the 'till' with the three dots that hooked him for good.

It was Granna who gave him his love for stories. His mother had told him and Pieta bedtime stories when they were little, but they were the most boring tales you could imagine. Eddie always felt that she had wrung out all the juice from them.

Granna was different. She often told the same stories as his mother, but she drew them out forever till Eddie and Pieta went out of their minds wanting to know what happened in the end. 'Oh, you want to know the end, why didn't you say so, I would have told it to you at the very beginning.' She was capable of it, both the children knew that. Granna was a great mimic apart from being a superlative actress. When she wanted to kill a story, she told it exactly as their mother would, voice, pitch, words, tone, the pauses, the forgetting of crucial parts, punch lines. The children would be in splits. Even Violet who hated anyone poking fun at her would smile.

One evening, as had happened numerous times before, their mother brought a story halfway and then looked blank. 'I don't remember the rest of it. Why don't you tell them since you fancy yourself such a spinner of useless tales?' she asked Granna. 'I know you're dying to. Always filling their heads with nonsense.'

'Me? I don't know that story. Which is why I was listening to it with such interest.'

'Don't lie. I heard that story from you when I was a child. And you've told it to the children fifty times if you've told it to them once. No wonder Eddie can't tell the difference between lies and truth.'

'You were such a lovely child, Violet, with such a sweet temper. When you grew up you were the belle of our town. Two months before the carnival, the parents of at least thirty boys would come around to ask whether you would dance with their sons. Some said you were Greta Garbo, others thought Olivia de Havilland looked like you, still others insisted you were the twin of Myrna

Loy. Your father was flattered. I was not. I thought you were more beautiful than all those three Hollywood queens put together.'

What was Granna talking about, who were these beauties his mother was supposed to resemble, and anyway why had she changed the subject and brought up all this rubbish? He looked at his mother. Her face had softened, her mouth had relaxed and there was a faraway look in her eyes. When she leaned forward, her hair came loose and hung like a fine black veil around her head. It was amazing, this power his Granna's stories had to transform, not just people but inanimate objects like chairs, doors, houses, even the quality of the light and the air.

'Do you remember when the Governor came to Vasco to inaugurate a manganese plant nearby? Your Aunt Lilly and Uncle Osmond, who were invited to the Governor's ball because he was the deputy municipal commissioner, insisted on taking you along. You wore an emerald green sleeveless dress that came to your ankles and almost transparent green gloves which rose above your elbows?'

Eddie saw light flowing from his mother's face. It hung around her like a halo. The tension in her face had gone. All the lines, including the line of her nose that made her seem hard, unhappy and grim, had shifted a little. He couldn't quite put his finger on it, but it was as if her face had turned to clay and some artist was reworking it with swift but minimal strokes to bring out the fragile beauty of her person.

'It began to pour and soon there was a traffic jam in that small place. Your uncle was already at the municipal hall but your carriage and the Governor's car almost collided, and in that lightning and thunder and crush of people and rain, your carriage driver lost control and the horse reared. The Governor asked his ADC to bring the horse under control. Do you remember the ADC?'

'Go on,' Violet said, 'don't stop.' Eddie and Pieta looked at each other. It was their pet line. Violet had never used it before.

'His name was Mario de Lima Leitao. When you got back you said he was the handsomest man you had ever seen. He was dressed in navy whites trimmed with gold braid. Many medals hung on his jacket front. He was drenched to the bone by the time he quietened the horse. He went back to the Governor's car and the driver gave him an umbrella to escort the Governor and his wife, Dona Lucinda, into the hall. The Governor asked his wife and his ADC to proceed and he himself came to your carriage. You and Aunt Lilly had your own umbrellas, but you hesitated to get out of the carriage because the ground was squelchy and there were rivulets of rushing water everywhere and you didn't want to ruin your clothes. The Governor gave you his umbrella and said, "Open this, it's much bigger and will keep the rain out." As you opened the umbrella, he held you by the waist and carried you in his arms to the hall. He turned back for Lilly but she had already gone.' Granna paused.

'And then?'

'You know the story better than I do. I wasn't even there. It's all hearsay for me.'

'And then?' Violet's voice was imperious.

'Well, nobody could believe their eyes. They were appreciative of the Governor's gallantry but they were, I think, taken aback if not a little unhappy that you were the object of so much attention. Your father was, after all, nothing but a clerk in the railways. You were lovely and people had never ignored you but that day you were Cinderella.

'Mario de Lima Leitao sent for another uniform from the D'Sa residence where he was staying with the Governor. All night he danced with you except when the Governor tapped him on the shoulder and asked, "May I?" They said even the Governor's wife was upset with her husband for ignoring her.'

'And then?' This time it was Pieta who chipped in.

'Nothing. Fairy-tales too come to an end. Your mother came home and the Governor, his wife and the ADC went back to Panjim the next day.'

'That's not the end.' Violet was hot and flushed and her eyes challenged her mother.

'Are you sure you want me to go on?'

'Yes.' The children were as firm as Violet.

'Lieutenant Lima Leitao wrote to your father saying that, with his permission, he wished to visit us for just one day. Your father was perturbed and delighted and puzzled. But he wrote back to the Lieutenant to say that he was welcome and hoped that he would stay with us.

'To cut a long story short,' it was a phrase that Granna had never used before, 'he came and asked for your mother's hand.'

Pieta and Eddie gasped. They looked at their mother in awe. Was this woman whom they called Mamma, really the same woman who had swept both the Governor and his ADC off their feet? Eddie gingerly held Violet's hand. She did not let go of it.

'Is all this true?' Pieta could not contain herself.

'Of course not,' Granna kept a straight face but her eyes gave her away, 'just a pack of lies. There was just one problem. He was leaving within a week for Portugal with the Governor whose term in the colony was over.'

'Where did he stay?' Pieta, who had her mother's liquid eyes, asked in wonder.

'I don't remember,' Granna said.

'You don't remember?' Pieta asked in disbelief.

'What do you expect at my age? It's not important.'

'Where did he stay?' Pieta turned to her mother. Violet was lost in thought and didn't seem to be in the mood to answer.

'Oh, shut up.' 'Shut up' was a forbidden phrase in their house, but Eddie was sure that no one was going to pull him up for using it today, even if Pieta protested violently. 'Then what happened? Mamma married him?'

'Silly,' Pieta's scorn would have demolished lesser thick-skulled souls, 'then how would Papa be our father?'

'Your mother's father said, "This is all very sudden and we really don't know how to react."

'"I understand your dilemma, Mr D'Silva, but what choice do I have? I do not know how many years it will be before I return. Perhaps I never will. Except to visit you and my parents."

'"My daughter will be seventeen, the Thursday of next week. It is unfair to put the weight of perhaps the most important decision of her life on her shoulders at such a young age, and that too at such short notice. But however difficult it may be, she is the only one who must choose her future." He turned to me and asked, "What is your feeling, Inez?" and I, who always talked nineteen to the dozen, was speechless. All I could say was: "What can I say?"

'Then your grandfather looked at your mother and said, "I'm not shirking my duty, Violet, but it would be unfair both to you and the Lieutenant, about whom we hardly know anything at all, if I tried to sway you either way."

'Your mother was young but she carried herself like a queen. At her age she had more poise than I have today. "These are unusual circumstances, Lieutenant Lima Leitao, and I have no choice but to give a quick answer. May I have till the morning?" Lieutenant Lima Leitao was courtesy and graciousness itself. He looked at your mother and said, "Of course. I leave at 9.30 sharp tomorrow morning. I trust you will have word for me by then."

'He smiled then for the first time. Oh, what a smile it was. I was willing to sell my soul to the devil to be young again and be courted by the Lieutenant. He was boyish and disarming but underneath it was the bedrock of confidence that no one could have the audacity to refuse him.

'Later that evening, Lieutenant Lima Leitao asked your grandfather's permission to go out for a walk on the beach with your mother. I doubt that Mr D'Silva had faced a more difficult situation in his life. Like everybody else in our town, he was an orthodox, conventional man. He had never been exposed to conflict. What will people say was not a question that occurred to him until he heard of the excessive chivalry of the Governor and his ADC to Violet. It was out of the question. What was it that made him shake his head in refusal but say yes? He had already abdicated the responsibility of choosing a husband for his daughter. Did he not owe it to her to let her have the chance of understanding this man a little better before she refused or accepted him? Perhaps we were all a little overwhelmed. It was impossible to say no to the Lieutenant who was used to getting his way. "You may go for a walk in the mango orchard after dinner. Mrs D'Silva will chaperone Violet."

'It was a moonlit night. There was a restless wind blowing. The mango tree is a strange one. It hoards darkness. We walked together for a few minutes, then I fell back. Violet turned round and called out to me, "Mamma." The two of them hardly spoke to each other. They became invisible when they entered the pools of bottle green. Then suddenly the light caught the starched white of his uniform and I could see them for a few minutes before they disappeared again. I walked to the beach in front of the house and sat on the sand. How far was it to Lisbon from here if I drew a straight line? I thought it would be rather nice to cross the seas and visit a new country to see my daughter.

'The next morning, breakfast was on the table by seven thirty. There was oatmeal, eggs and bacon and sausages, milk, tea, and coffee, pineapples and bananas. There was all manner of talk except what was on everybody's mind. Every once in a while one of us stole a look at Violet. She had worn a severe white dress. The only touch of colour was the ruby pendant around her neck which my grandmother had given me. I believe for once the Lieutenant's self-assurance was a trifle forced. Violet on the other hand was the very picture of poise. You would never know whether she had slept soundly or stayed up all night. She was the perfect hostess. "A little marmalade? I made it myself this summer. Is this coffee strong enough for you?"

'Finally, that interminable breakfast ended. Violet placed her napkin on the table and looked the Governor's ADC in the eye. "Lieutenant Lima Leitao, you have done my family and me the honour of asking for my hand. We appreciate this, especially in the light of the fact that you have to make arrangements to leave for Portugal within the next six days. It is difficult and futile to speculate how things may have turned out had we had a normal courtship. Suffice it to say that my answer under the circumstances is no. This decision is mine and mine alone as are the reasons behind it. We wish you all the very best in your career and life. Godspeed."'

'Oh Mamma, why, oh why?' Pieta was close to tears.

Eddie was struck by the sudden chill in the air. It emanated from Violet. Yet the change had been wrought by his Granna. What strange powers did a story have that it could make you happy and elated one minute and depressed and dissatisfied the next? What kind of weapon was it that it could blow hot and cold not just alternately, but simultaneously? He could feel the lines around his mother's mouth and eyes harden once again.

He hated her for going back to her old self. And he blamed his grandmother for it. Why did she have to continue? Why could she not have stopped halfway even though Pieta and he, and tacitly even his mother, had begged and pleaded and forced her to go on.

He looked at Granna. She was sitting still. She looked tired. In his incoherent and inarticulate way, Eddie realized that his Granna had gone on because she wanted Violet to live through it again. Where did his father figure in all this?

Violet looked defiantly at her mother. 'The reasons are mine and mine alone,' she said.

~

Around ten when his mother stopped sewing, Eddie quickly closed the story-book and placed it under his history text. He could have read on, but what if his mother came over to tell him to go to bed and spotted it? Even that he could handle with a quick shuffle. What worried him was that, despite his growing interest in the book, he might doze off and be caught red-handed. No, he wasn't taking any chances. He raised the two books to his face casually, breathed deeply. There was no question about it, the scent of the new pages gave him a high. He slipped his hand in randomly. The page felt smooth and glossy, must have opened on a page with an illustration. He wondered if, with practice and time, his fingers could tell who or what they were touching, a kind of tactile vision.

'I thought you said you were planning to sit up late at night.' His sister Pieta was going to have a field day needling him the next few weeks. He was glad to see that his ploy had worked. The next second Eddie was regretting his cockiness.

'What have you got in your hand? Behind the history book?' That witch had X-ray eyes and a hound's nose. If only he could rub chilli powder in her eyes and nose, twice a day, no, make it thrice. Too late now. She was advancing on him.

'Leave him alone, Pieta. Stop poking your long nose into everything.' Thank God for Granna.

Eddie hurriedly shoved the books into his school bag, turned his back to his mother, screwed up his eyes and waved his tongue at Pieta.

'Did you see what he did? He's making faces at me, Mamma.'

'Enough. I don't want another word out of either of you.'

Six

❖

If you want to know the people of the CWD chawls and how their minds work, you must first understand the floor-plan of the chawls and the amenities it offers.

Think of a plus sign, now extend its horizontal arms ten times on either side. This is the main passage or corridor on each floor. On either side of the corridor arm are ten rooms. That's twenty rooms to the left of the vertical stroke of the plus sign and twenty on the right. The short vertical houses the staircase and a balcony with a concrete parapet where Parvati stood the day Ravan took his first leap into the world.

Each room was twelve feet wide and twenty-four feet deep with a wooden partition separating the drawing-room-cum-bedroom-cum-study, library, playpen or whatever from the kitchen which doubled as dining-room, bedroom, dressing-room, and bathroom (a tiny four-foot x four-foot washing space with a tap was cordoned off on one side with a two-foot wall on which were stacked pots of water). Each room was home to one family, nuclear or extended. It is uncommon to have only two people staying in the one long but partitioned room. The average is between six to eight. Patriarch and wife, sons and daughters-in-law and grandchildren.

Forty families shared the corridor and did much of their living there. In the afternoons the women cleaned the rice or wheat, combed their daughters' hair or left the papads to dry on a thin piece of cloth; some evenings you'd see a game of cricket in progress here; this was the venue for the annual carrom tournaments and at nights the corridor became a dormitory for many of the children and adults from the floor.

But we are straying away from our floor-plan. At the end of the long arms were the mini dhobi-ghats, the place where the women or the help would beat, bully and wash clothes on a pitted black stone. Beyond this washing area were the common toilets.

There were solid old British brass taps above the flat black stone which decades of washing had almost worn smooth. Every once in three or four months some housewife who couldn't bear to look at the dull and unwashed brass, scrubbed them with tamarind. Within minutes the glint and gold would be back in them. In the toilets there were neither water cisterns nor chains. The flushing arrangement was a push button one. You pressed a brass knob, the springs were rusty and you had to lean hard on it, and even then there was no guarantee that a jet of water would leap out into the toilet pan. The giant cast-iron water-storage tanks, both for the homes and the toilets, were all stockpiled on the terrace of each chawl. The British engineers who had designed the water supply set-up some seventy years ago had done a good job. Despite heavy use and maltreatment, the system still worked. All that the tenants had to do was to wait and pray for water.

The Great Water Wars

They should have killed for water, the men and women of the CWD chawls. People have been known to kill for less: religion; language; the flag; the colour of a person's skin or his caste; breaking the queue at a petrol pump.

One of these days they may get around to it but so far Ravan, Eddie, their mothers and the tenants at the CWD chawls haven't committed murder in the name of water. Though God knows there have been times when they were close to it. There have been words, nasty, bitter, venomous, corrosive words; genealogies have been traced, incestuous sexual acts involving mothers, brothers and sisters invoked in swear-words; hostilities have been declared, words have led to physical fights. Frictions have festered; attitudes hardened and prejudices led to Pavlovian reflexes of bellicosity and at times it's been touch and go.

The causes have almost always been the same: supply cannot meet demand. Planning and execution have met the needs of the population figures of a decade or two earlier. Rains are an act of God in India. And God as we know is a law unto himself. He is not responsible, neither is He accountable. That is the essence of God: He gives with two hands and takes away with eight more. Why else would Indian gods and goddesses have several pairs of hands?

The nature of the municipal water tap is feudal and bureaucratic. It replicates and clones the Almighty's manners and moodiness but never his generosity since its power is entirely derivative. It is a middleman, its patronage disburses what does not belong to it. The only way it can experience and feel power is to exert it erratically and often. Hence it is not enough that it calls the shots, it must perforce leave you in the dark. You are at its mercy. You are grateful for its bounties and contrite for its seasons of drought.

The unstable tyrant of the family in the CWD chawls is the man of the manor. Drunk, sober, employed, jobless, taciturn or gibbering, his word is law. His wife sustains and not infrequently supports the family and is more than happy to give her husband all the credit if only he will allow her to carry on with her work. But despite the boss-man's pretensions and the wife's sacrifice and self-effacement, the prime mover of life is water. You snapped out of anaesthesia, interrupted coitus, stopped your prayers, postponed your son's engagement, developed incontinence, took casual leave to go down and stand at the common tap, cancelled going to church because water, present and absent, is more powerful than the Almighty.

You left the tap open before you went to sleep. When the water sputtered and splattered at three, four or five a.m. and sometimes not at all, was when your day began. You cursed and cribbed and filled up every vessel in sight and tried to zip through a bath and if there was still a trickle left, woke up the children and gave them a speed bath that was more an act of the imagination than an exercise in cleansing. If it wasn't already six, you stumbled back to a twilight sleep where nameless fears and forebodings, all of them waterlogged, crawled and rose in phantasmagoric shapes from the floor of your subconscious and left you tepid and perspiring.

There's a water tap in the bathroom of every house in the CWD chawls, in the four toilets at the end of the left and right wing of each floor and the two common wash-areas opposite.

If the tanks on the terrace run out of water—two or three days at a time is not unusual—you are forced to troop down to the public tap. There's one for every two chawls. There's no law on the subject but the idea is to share the water amongst the four hundred and eighty families who live in the two adjoining buildings. There is no court of appeal but by and large almost everybody adheres to the unwritten protocol.

'Those people' as the people on the ground floor were called in the CWD chawls, the three hundred or so families whose very shadows polluted the others had a couple of separate taps just as six taps were reserved for all the Catholics. When the water was short or if the papers gave notice that there was going to be a water-cut the next day, the untouchables were shooed away from their taps and water filled from them after the first woman in the queue perfunctorily threw a few drops in the direction of the brass nozzle of the faucet to make it clean and usable.

The municipal tap is the original cornucopia. It is plugged into the mains and supplies water twenty-four hours of the day. Twenty-four hours, as you know, is a flexi-time concept in our country, and can stretch anywhere between three to four hours. That's on the good days. The timings are fixed. When the water comes, you know it's come.

On any given day, there were anywhere between a hundred to two hundred and fifty pots waiting in queue. What a sight it was. Two thousand years of brass and copper craftsmanship. Long, slender necks, wide bodies, broad butts, svelte torsos, short-chinned stodgy tankers, tightly corseted, narrow-bottomed, prissy mouthed, there was no end to their shapes and sizes. Despite the perpetual water shortage, they shone like flares from newly sunk oil wells. That was thirty years ago. The brass and the copper have been replaced by cheap, exuberant plastics which the sun denudes of all colour and turns grey and anaemic within three or four months.

The women came down, stood by their pots and buckets, chatted, compared notes on which ration shops had sugar and kerosene, went back to their homes to feed their babies and send their children to school, returned, untied their hair and knotted it tightly at the back with effortless and casual grace, adjusted their saris and waited.

Hours passed.

The lead pipe went into a spasm, recoiled and kicked and threw an epileptic tantrum as if it were made not of lead but rubber. It made threatening noises, coughed and cleared a thirty-metre-long throat, vomited seventeen drops of brown tepid goo, withdrew, brooded, went dry. Wring the neck and length of the pipe all the way back to Tansa lake and it won't yield a drop of water for the next fifty years. It shuddered. A quake, 7.5 on the Richter scale, shook it. It lashed out, the jet of water a venomous fist of fury that sent the copper pot under it skittering for shelter.

The response to the sight of flowing water is desperation, a frenzy of pointless activity and loss of sanity.

There were fights every day over water, but that didn't make them any the less interesting. A good scrap was liberating, especially when someone else was doing the fighting. It always made you feel mature, objective and wiser. How foolish people were. What utterly ridiculous and petty things they fought about. It took all your self-control sometimes not to egg them on and join them and see some blood spill. No question about it, it was a great spectator sport, so long as you weren't at the centre of it. And frankly, sometimes it felt great letting go, standing there arms akimbo, saying the most God-awful things and believing that you were alone against the world, after all, look how your adversary for whom you had done so much, put her up for the nights when her husband had pulverized her and she had nowhere else to go, was repaying you. Well here goes, you kicked her water-pot, it keeled over and all the water drained away, she would have to go and stand at the end of the queue all over again. Look out, she had pulled your head down and thrown you back till you were sitting on your butt, you were not going to take it lying down, besides for some reason best known to them, a few other women had joined the fracas, you didn't know who was on whose side but that didn't matter, hell, this was a free-for-all, if you didn't take the offensive, you were dead.

One of these days, it may be tomorrow or twenty years from now, the municipal tap in the CWD chawls is going to run dry while the forty-seventh woman is still filling her pot. The remaining two hundred and nineteen women will complain as usual and go back with empty pots hoping that they can stretch the water in the drums in their kitchens till the next day. But on that day Mrs Rele, Mrs Pathare and Mrs Ghatge saw the knife-grinder walking into the CWD chawls compound with his unwieldy grinding wheel slung over his shoulder and brought their knives down to be sharpened. Did the sun shine in Mrs Ghatge's eyes or did a fly buzz too insistently around Mrs Rele's face or was it that Mrs Pathare didn't like the colour of Mrs Rele's eyes? All we know is that Mrs Pathare plunged her yet-to-be-sharpened knife between Mrs Ghatge's third and fourth ribs. Mrs Ghatge was thrown off balance but managed to bring down her meat-cleaver on Prabha Salunke's head and open it up as if it were a coconut. It was Prabha's engagement tomorrow. More knives appeared, all you had to do was scamper up to your kitchen and rush down. That day blood flowed freely in the CWD chawls.

Water. Blood. Is there a difference?

The water wars had started. It had taken a long time but the CWD chawl women had finally begun to understand the value of water.

～

Ravan had nothing to do. He was discovering what it meant to have time on his hands. He was irritable, edgy and resentful. He had a grievance against the world though he didn't know what it was. He wanted to get even with total strangers, passers-by he had never seen or met before. He wished to pick a quarrel and beat up someone. Anyone. He realized this was unreasonable and also not very wise. It might turn out badly. They may end up beating the shit out of him. As he stood at the entrance of his building, his hands stuck deep in his pockets, he could see his old and ex-closest friend Chandrakant Dixit playing gilli-danda with six or seven other boys. Chandrakant lifted the gilli in the air with a wooden stick and bounced it up and down with effortless dexterity as if it was a ping-pong ball rather than a piece of wood. He could have gone up to Chandrakant and asked to be included but he knew what his response would be. He could have approached some other boys who were playing a local version of cricket where you pitched a tennis ball at the batsman instead of the stone-hard, skull-breaking cricket ball, and bowled under-arm and not over-arm as adults did, for fear of shattering the glass windows in the chawls. But the game was already in progress and had the feel of a closed circle.

He had to bite someone soon, sink in his teeth viciously and tear off an arm or a head before this bottled-up and unfocused dissatisfaction exploded in him and he went out of his mind. Maybe it was too late. Maybe he had already gone mad. He remembered Shambhoonath Pissat.

∽

Shambhoonath had run away from his village because he had heard that in Bombay there were double-decker buses, buildings that were over ten storeys high and an everlasting sheet of water that stretched all the way to the sky. Shyamjeebhai Valji Patel Grocers and General Merchants in Chawl No. 11 had employed him on a temporary basis. 'We'll try you for a week and see how you shape up,' Shyamjeebhai had told him over two years ago but the probation period showed signs of being like the sea that Shambhoonath visited every Monday at Chowpatty, his only day of rest in the week: it seemed to go on forever. 'When will you make me permanent?' Shambhoonath had asked Shyamjeebhai several months ago. Shyamjeebhai had whacked him under the ear and in return asked him a question to silence all future questions on the subject. 'Do you want to keep the job or not?'

Shambhoonath's hours were not fixed. He worked weekdays from seven in the morning till Shyamjeebhai put his pen down after writing up his accounts at night. That could be at nine or eleven at night or one in the morning. Shambhoonath was not unhappy. The question of happiness had not crossed his mind. He was given two cotton shirts and khaki shorts during Diwali. The shirts were always ill-fitting and he had to tie a string around his waist or leave the buttons above his fly open, depending on whether the shorts were loose or tight. He got a bar of washing soap now and then and it sufficed to wash himself and his clothes. He was given breakfast and two meals every day and a salary of ten rupees a month.

Shambhoonath had one friend, the cobbler's dog, Tiger. On his day off, Shambhoonath often took Tiger for a walk around the block. When his master was not looking—this was rarely the case except when Shyamjeebhai went to the toilet—he would pick up the lid of one of the fat glass bottles and throw a biscuit to the dog. A few months ago Ravan's neighbour, Mr Dixit, noticed that Tiger was behaving strangely. He was restless and irritable. He was foaming at the mouth and he could neither eat nor drink.

Mr Dixit was a conscientious man. He called the Ward Officer in charge of infectious diseases at Mazagaon and informed him that there was a rabid dog loose in the CWD chawls. When the Ward Officer did not turn up the next day, Mr Dixit went over in person to the municipal office.

That Sunday afternoon, two men came by in a closed municipal van and got out with iron muzzles and gunny sacks. They were thin and weedy, the younger one smoked a beedi while the older man chewed tobacco. Their untucked shirts almost completely concealed their shorts. They were scraps of human beings and should have looked harmless. But even the children knew that they were the gods of death, Yama senior and junior. They asked street-vendors and shopkeepers to close shop and told mothers to take their children home and lock the doors.

Ravan watched from the kitchen window. It was amazing how many stray dogs there were despite the fact that the vendors had shooed their favourites away. The two men separated. The older man had a funny, sideways gait, it was impossible to tell he was moving. He was next to a dog before the creature knew it and had clapped the muzzle with the long handle over its mouth. The younger one pulled the jute sack over the animal. The surprise and the sudden darkness made the dog immobile for a moment. They walked back to the van, the older man opened the rear door for an instant while the other let the dog slip out and into the van. In about an hour and a half they had rounded up nine strays. But the sick dog was nowhere to be seen.

The two men waited. They sat on their haunches. They were in no hurry. They knew the dog was around. Silence stretched like a brittle trampoline across the chawls. There were parents and children peering out of every window. The dogs in the van had sensed that something was amiss. They stood up on their hind legs and watched through the tiny grill without barking. Someone started to play a record on a gramophone but it was instantly switched off.

Ravan got restless and asked his mother if he could go out. She didn't bother to answer him. He persisted. 'Sure, you want to be bitten and become a rabid dog? They'll put a sack over your head and take you away.'

There was a bark, a ragged, scrawny bark that amplified the silence. The men did not move. Tiger slunk in from the corner of Chawl No. 21. His sense of balance was precarious, his hind legs looked ready to give, his eyes had a mindless anger in them. He saw a pool of water overflowing from one of the gutters and he froze and reared. It wasn't clear if he had seen his reflection or was terrified of water. He bit sharply into his flank and drew blood. The older man was beside him. His arm telescoped out and the muzzle docked into the dog's face. His companion was slipping the gunny sack over Tiger when Shambhoonath called, 'Run, Tiger, run.' The dog faltered and sank on his hind legs. His head slipped out of the muzzle. He rose unsteadily. Perhaps his mind cleared and he remembered his friend. 'Run, Tiger, run,' Shambhoonath yelled with renewed urgency. Tiger looked mean and vicious and full of an insane anger. He leapt at the younger man and toppled him over. The dog was almost atop the sprawled man and going for his throat when the back of the steel muzzle made contact with Tiger's head. There was a sound of bone cracking and the dog flopped. The young man lay screaming even after the dog was removed and thrown into the van.

Shambhoonath missed Tiger and talked about him to all the customers who would listen.

'There was nothing wrong with him. If Mr Dixit had not reported him, he would be fine and right here with us. Do you think they killed him? He was such a nice dog. He never asked for anything.'

'Shut up and go back to work,' Shyamjeebhai snapped at him.

Five weeks later Shambhoonath's moods began to swing unpredictably. He was running a fever and he was either depressed or manically talkative. He answered back, told Shyamjeebhai that he was leaving if he didn't get a raise immediately and an hour later apologized abjectly. He became delirious.

Once again it was Mr Dixit who diagnosed the symptoms as rabies when he was at the grocer's to buy betel nut on his way home from the office. Shambhoonath yelled that he was dying of thirst but when he tried to drink water, his throat muscles went into a violent spasm and he couldn't swallow.

Mr Dixit spoke to Shyamjeebhai and told him of the danger and threat that Shambhoonath posed to everybody in the chawls.

'How can it be rabies?' Shyamjeebhai queried Mr Dixit. 'Tiger never bit Shambhoonath.'

'It's not the rabid dog's bite but his saliva which carries the virus,' Mr Dixit explained to the grocer patiently. 'You must take him to the doctor now and admit him to the Haffkine Institute. This is urgent, Shyamjeebhai. It's more than that, it's a matter of life and death.'

'No need to get agitated, Dixitbhai,' the grocer assured Mr Dixit. 'I will ask my son to take Shambhoonath to Doctor Atre right away. You go home and rest your mind in peace. Everything, you'll see, will turn out for the best.' That night Shyamjeebhai threw Shambhoonath out and locked the doors of his shop.

Two days later Shambhoonath returned from wherever he had disappeared. Shyamjeebhai locked him in the storeroom behind his shop for fear that Mr Dixit would see him. The grocer needn't have worried. Mr Dixit had gone off on a seven-day tour of duty inspecting mofussil schools. Shambhoonath Pissat screamed for food, screamed for water, screamed to be let out, and screamed for pity and help. Ravan waited for the two men to return.

'Will they kill him?' he asked Parvatibai as he lay in bed.

'Of course not.' Parvatibai patted him a little too hard on his head in an attempt to convince herself and put Ravan to sleep.

On the fourth day, there were no words to Shambhoonath's scream but it had become much louder.

'Why don't they kill him?' Ravan asked his mother that night. She didn't try to answer.

It was late afternoon the next day. Shambhoonath bit through the cords tied around his hands and feet, unlocked the door at the rear of the storeroom and began running wildly in the CWD grounds. His eyes were red and his lower jaw hung unnaturally open. He made odd noises and his movements were erratic. There was nothing human about him. He had become some strange animal that was full of hate and fear and would never be brought under control. Young men, women and children ran helter-skelter and screamed louder than him. Shambhoonath's jaws snapped at the empty air with a force that could have bitten off heads. Suddenly the grounds were empty. There was not a sound but Shambhoonath's breathless panting. He scanned the buildings and the sky. His head moved jerkily. There was a rage in him and he did not know what to do with it.

Ravan sensed something was wrong as he walked in from the road between Chawl Nos. 3 and 4. His school bag fell down but he was not aware of it. He was fascinated by Shambhoonath to the point of being paralysed. Shambhoonath watched Ravan with hooded eyes, wondering if he was going to move. He looked away pretending he had lost interest, and then charged at Ravan. Ravan was struck by the reaction of the various dogs which hung around the CWD chawls. They were all petrified and had their tails between their legs, as if they too were trying to disown Shambhoonath. Ravan thought that he heard his mother yelling his name. There was a note of demented urgency in her voice. Shambhoonath too seemed to have heard it. He stopped still and gazed at Ravan. Ravan felt an overwhelming wave of pity for Shambhoonath. He was so terrified and alone. Parvatibai was screaming at Ravan now, telling him to run, run. Shambhoonath stood undecided, panting and snapping his mouth. The two Yamas were now standing behind him. They threw a fishing net on Shambhoonath. Shambhoonath fought for his life, fought for air and fought, Ravan thought, so that he could be overpowered and put out of his misery. The old man and his companion dragged Shambhoonath for fifty yards and bundled him into the same van that had transported Tiger. Shambhoonath stared out from the grill of the window in the van. He could see Ravan. His jaw snapped one last time before he disappeared.

~

'Will you play with me, Ravan?' Shobhan Sarang asked Ravan as he stood indecisively, wondering how he could break up the gilli-danda game Chandrakant and his friends were playing. He was ready to bite her. Those two men would have to come and throw the fishing net on her and take her away. She had a soft, uncertain smile. Did she know? Know about him and the murders? It didn't matter whether it was a child, cat or the help in the house who crossed Ravan's path. Everything boiled down to those two questions. Talk to me. Tell me. Look me in the eye. Do you know? What do you know?

Was Shobhan Sarang taking pity on him? Was she putting him on or trying to inveigle the details of his infamy from him? Why else would she want to play with him? She was at least ten years older than him. She had always been friendly, but there was something distinctly suspect about the timing of her invitation. And what could she play with that club-foot of hers? She tried to cover it up by wearing her sari long but that didn't fool anybody.

'Why should I play with you?'

'Be... be... because I am alone and not doing anything.' She did not have a stammer but she sometimes tripped over the simplest words. It was as if the stutter was meant to divert attention from the limp.

'Do you know I can bowl over-arm?'

'Really, that's something, isn't it?'

'I can get all those fellows playing there out within two overs. And score a century.'

'You must be a real asset to your school cricket team.'

Was she making fun of him? No, she seemed genuinely impressed.

'What game could you play with your...' Ravan stopped himself in time but Shobhan completed the sentence for him.

'With my club-foot?'

Ravan looked away. Why was he behaving so crassly? Was she going to cry now?

'I can play hop-scotch.'

'I'll give you a handicap. I don't want you to think I'm unfair.'

After half an hour it looked as if it was Ravan who needed a handicap.

'Shall we go to my place now? I'm a little tired.'

'If you want to. I was just about to turn the game around and beat you.'

'I know.' Shobhan smiled gently. 'I made shankarpalya this morning. Do you like them?'

'They're all right.' Ravan tried to sound offhand. He was sweating after all that exertion. He pushed the hair back from his forehead and involuntarily put his hand under his shorts and pulled his shirt down. Shobhan was not sweating, the hair from her long and thick plait had not come undone, and it looked as if she was wearing a newly starched and ironed sari. But her cool composure and reserve could not conceal the club of her foot. It was encased in a black leather pouch with laces and a heel. It was like a fist instead of a foot, but she could put her weight on it as easily as Ravan could on his.

They climbed the stairs. She had to clutch at the banister to bring the defective foot up. Ravan made it a point to stay ahead of her. He was intent on proving to Shobhan that he could get the better of her.

Shobhan produced a wicker stool from under the bed and asked Ravan to sit. Ravan wondered how the Sarang clan fit into the place. They had the same amount of space he and his family had. Maybe they took turns sleeping, or perhaps all of them slept standing up. They were, not counting the parents and grandmother, nine sisters, that's excluding the sister who had died some years ago and one brother who had left home four years ago and not bothered to come back.

Shobhan went into the kitchen to get the sweets. Her sister Tara, Ravan had no idea where she figured in the chronology of the Sarang family tree, was standing in front of a small mirror on the wall and applying Afghan Snow on her face. Didn't she remember what had happened a couple of nights ago? How could she not? Some of the sisters were sewing, two were cleaning rice and dal, one was reading a mystery novel. Tara caught Ravan staring at her and turned around to put big daubs of the Snow on his cheeks. Before he could protest she had rubbed it all over his face. 'There,' she said, 'you look like a film star now.' He was revolted by its gooey texture. Poor Ravan. It would take him half a dozen years before he grew up and learnt of the magical properties of that pearly and glutinous unguent. Perhaps he never would be enlightened.

A Short Digression on Snow

To be fair is to be God's chosen. Fairness was more precious than immortality, nirvana or moksha. It was on a par with virginity. It was more desirable than all the treasures of the Mughal emperors and the inspiration of the poets. Admittedly, not more sought after than wealth and power, but just as potent and indispensable. For truly what are wealth and power without a fair skin?

There is no doubt about it. There is justice on earth. Justice and a sense of fair play are at the root of reincarnation. Those who walk the righteous path in their previous life are born fair. It mattered little if you were plain as whitewash and had a sick haemoglobin count of 2.7. If you were fair, it was obvious you were beautiful. The rest of humanity was condemned. To be dark was to have committed original sin. (Even our gods had to undergo colour shifts. Since black would not do for humans, how could Lord Krishna be permitted to be dark? They turned him blue.)

Then the House of Patanwala invented Afghan Snow. A patina of Afghan Snow could never never substitute or pass for fairness but for those of us who are deprived, discriminated against and desperate, Afghan Snow was till the early 1960s the next best thing to being fair. It was second skin and second nature. It was inconceivable to leave the house without smearing it on your face. It filled craters and levelled the mounts of acne. It stood out like barium in an X-ray plate of the lower abdomen. It was so effective and noticeable, even the fair of complexion would not dream of being seen without it. It was every man and woman's Phantom of the Opera, the Kathakali mask that made you larger than life. It was your public persona. Without it you merged and disappeared in a grey mass. It gave you presence. It was society's stamp of approval. But, most important of all, it made you acceptable to yourself. Truly, artifice alone could now vouch for the real thing.

Nobody knew what the secret of Afghan Snow was. It had a glittery sheen on it and it transcended the gender-gap long before unisex came into fashion. It cut across caste and class barriers. Men and women, young and old, sank their index and middle fingers into a bottle of Snow (the label outside showed perennial snow-capped mountains supposedly from the Hindukush ranges in Afghanistan) and returned with a gob of the silvery butter and rubbed it into their faces. Having prepared the ground, it was time to overlay it, as Tara was doing just now, with Himalaya Bouquet, or if you could afford it, Cuticura toilet powder.

~

Ravan tried to wipe the Snow away with his hands. His face still felt sticky. He pulled out his shirt and scrubbed his cheeks hard with it. Tara was laughing at him. Had she really forgotten their last encounter? It was barely a fortnight ago. Maybe it was nothing special at all and he was making too much of it. But he remembered the surprise on her face. It was as if she had wanted him to be struck blind at that moment.

He had got up in the middle of the night with diarrhoea. The alarms to wake up the chawls' men and women to fill up water hadn't gone off yet and it was a long time before the milk vans would come. 'Didn't I warn you not to eat so many shrimps? Did you listen?' His mother woke up briefly, delivered her routine remark on such occasions and went back to sleep. Ravan stumbled out grumpily and walked towards the end of the corridor where the toilets were clumped together. Suddenly Tara and that boy from the ground floor of Chawl No. 22, who was doing a mechanic's training course, the one they called Shahaji Kadam, unlatched the door of one of the toilets and stepped out. Why were they using the toilets on Ravan's floor and not on their own? What was she doing with that man anyway? Didn't she know nobody spoke with the people from the ground floors of Chawl Nos. 7, 11, 22, 23 and 29, neither the Hindus nor the Catholics? It wasn't a taboo or anything of the sort, you just didn't. Full stop. You gave them as wide a berth as you could.

Two people in the same toilet at the same time, it didn't make sense. He was obviously three-quarters asleep and hallucinating. But Ravan realized that the expression in Shahaji Kadam's eyes could not be a figment of his imagination. It was not that of a thief caught in the act, or of a pariah dog cornered by the squad from the municipality. It was that of a man relieved to find that his days of fear and terror were over. He stood there waiting for summary judgement and execution of the sentence. Both he and Ravan waited in an agony of indecision until Tara pulled Shahaji away with a laugh. 'He's sleepwalking. He won't remember a thing.'

~

'Don't you want to be a film star? Dev Anand, Dilip Kumar, Premnath and now Ravan Kumar?' What was it about Tara's laughter that made him feel uneasy? He did not know how to respond to her. He wanted to be in her company and touch her but didn't know whether or not his hand would be singed.

'I hate you. I hate you,' Ravan told her venomously.

'I think your boyfriend wants to snap my head off, Shobhan,' Tara said.

'Has she been teasing you, Ravan?' Shobhan was quick to come to his rescue. 'Stop it Tara.' She put the plate of shankarpalya on the floor next to him and held out a glass of milk. 'Take your time. Tara's going out. Drink your milk after you've had the sweets.'

Tara put vermilion on her middle finger and drew a perfect circle in the centre of her forehead without looking into the mirror.

'How do I look Ravan?' Would she never stop laughing? 'Won't I make a lovely bride?'

'If only someone will marry you.' Mr Sarang walked in. 'You or any one of the women in this house. Frankly, I don't mind if a single man takes the lot of you and opens a zenana just so long as you are off my hands.'

'I do mind.' Mrs Sarang stood in the door of the partition between the kitchen and the front room.

'Then I'll leave it to you to find them husbands. We can start with Ravan here.'

Ravan knew Mr Sarang well. He was often the conductor of the BEST electric tram which took him to his municipal school. When the tramcar service was discontinued he was shifted to a bus on the same route. He was an absent-minded man whom the children from Ravan's school harried and harassed till he started to scream and rave. They crowded him, all fifty or a hundred who had boarded the tram and clamoured for tickets while preventing him from moving. That way half of them could get off without paying their fares. Ravan never managed to do this because Mr Sarang knew him by name and they stayed in the same chawl. 'Nine and a half?' he would ask Ravan. 'But you were nine and a half yesterday too and the day before. You should be at least eleven today. Didn't they teach you how to count? You'll be a grown man with children and you'll still tell me I'm ten and demand a half ticket.'

'And pray where are you going, Miss Tara?'

'To see *Albela*. Sandhyarani's bought a ticket for me.'

'Are you sure this Sandhyarani whose name you've been quoting rather often in the last few weeks is a respectable girl and not a man?'

'Yes it's a boy and I intend to elope with him.'

'Just don't come back, that's my only request.'

Tara left.

'So, Master Ravan have you got a ticket? You can't expect to get a free ride in the Sarang household while I'm around. Shobhan, has he bought a ticket?'

'Oh, Father, stop it.'

Ravan couldn't figure out how Mr Sarang could joke and laugh. One of his earliest memories was of Mr Sarang standing in the open space of the chawls with his daughter Meena in his arms at six in the morning. Parvatibai had pulled Ravan back from the kitchen window before he could see Meena's limp form but Mr Sarang's words rang out loud and clear. He was crying uncontrollably and saying, 'Why did you take her away? My innocent, sweet Meena? Don't you have a heart? I'll never forgive you. Never. I'm washing my hands of you. You are of no use to me.' Mr Sarang's outpourings subsided. Ravan was confused. Was Mr Sarang talking to his dead daughter? If her death had upset him so much, why did he say he would have no truck with her? 'Why is he angry with Meena?' he asked his mother.

'He's not. He's angry with God.'

'Why?'

'Because God took her away.'

'Will he take you away too?'

'Better me than you,' Parvati said with grim determination. Mr Sarang was off again.

'Oh, Meena, where have you gone? I could do nothing for you. The doctors said it was late, too late by the time they found out. What kind of doctors are they? Why are they doctors if they don't know their job? What if it had been their own child? How can I live without you, Meena? Every breath I take will remind me of you.'

Ravan never forgave Mr Sarang for crying and frightening him so badly. His pain and loss stuck in Ravan's belly like shrapnel that no surgery could remove. Did he have to bring the dead

Meena home from the hospital and make a show of his grief? Thanks to Meena, he and every other child in the chawls had to have an anti-diphtheria injection. He was five and he was sure he was going to die just like Meena. It was Shobhan who took him to the municipal dispensary and buried his head in her breasts because he didn't want to look at the injection and kissed his arm where the doctor had given him the shot so that it would not hurt.

Mr Sarang was a liar. He had forgotten Meena and forgiven God because even now he was garlanding the portraits of Shankar, Rama, Krishna and Dutta on the wall.

'How come you're the only son, Ravan? As a matter of fact the only child?' Mr Sarang peered closely at Ravan as if the question had been bothering him a long while. Ravan looked nonplussed.

'Is your father planning to have any more or not?'

Mr Sarang waited for an answer.

'I don't know.'

'Odd. Your mother is obviously not barren since she begot you. And your father looks like a man in good health and you are living proof that he's a capable man. Then how is it that you don't have any more siblings? Most puzzling.'

'Leave him be, Father,' Shobhan interrupted her father. 'The poor child doesn't know what you are talking about.'

'It's unfair, that's what I say. People who have less children should pay a sur-tax to support the excess children of others. What sin have I committed that I have so many? Just look at them, no room to move. Can't get a single one married. Sharada was the only exception. See Suman there, she's thirty-three. Who's going to marry her? Savitri's thirty-one, maybe thirty-two. A few more years and her menopause will start and she'll require full dentures. Yamuna, twenty-nine but not a sign of a husband. All of them darkies, who's going to look at them? All that Snow they slap on can't make them fair or attractive. Your ticket, Master Ravan? Kindly buy your ticket. There are no free rides in the world. I can barely feed this brood on my salary. Where am I supposed to get the money for their dowry? It's a vicious circle.'

'That's enough, Father.' Shobhan had a soothing effect on her father. 'Go and wash your feet and I'll make you a cup of tea.'

'Tell me, Master Ravan, do you have any ideas on the subject? My Mrs and I produced one beauty, one really fair and lovely girl but she's even more of a problem than the others. Don't know who begot her, the misshapen, club-footed wretch. See my feet, is there any defect in them? None, right? Mrs, come here.'

'Let it be now,' Mrs Sarang spoke from inside the kitchen. 'I'm cooking.'

'I said come out this instant. We have an impartial observer here. Let him be the judge.'

Mrs Sarang came out wiping her hands on her sari. She looked resentful but could not deny her husband his catharsis.

'Pick up your sari.'

Mrs Sarang shook her head.

'Only up to your ankle.' She did. She had done it a hundred times before.

'The best pair of ankles in the CWD chawls. Walk.'

'He's seen me walk.'

'Walk. He's young, he may have forgotten.'

Mrs Sarang walked back into the kitchen.

'Perfect equilibrium, wouldn't you agree, Master Ravan? Vision 20:20; 20:20 feet and legs. And then look at this gargoyle.'

Shobhan stood still.

'Show him,' Mr Sarang screamed. Suman, Yamuna, Savitri and the rest of the sisters did whatever they were doing a little more intently.

Shobhan picked up her sari and showed her pouch-bound right foot.

'Take that bloody sack off, the one that costs me half a month's salary and show him the whole fucking mess, the twisted bones and the knotted, revolting skin around it. Let him see the beauty and the beast all in one and let him tell me how I'm supposed to marry off such a loathsome creature. Show him, I said show.'

'I don't want to see, I don't want to.' Ravan ran and clung to Shobhan.

Mr Sarang started to bash his head on the bars of the window. 'What kind of father am I? I can't get my daughters married, so I humiliate them to hide my shame. I am going to kill myself. Yes, I am. They'll stay spinsters but at least they won't be tortured and disgraced by their own father.'

He was bleeding now, the blood from his forehead was flowing freely. Mrs Sarang came out and drew him away. She made him sit on the bed and applied cold compresses to his head.

～

Ravan became a regular at the Sarang home. Shobhan and he played hop-scotch and marbles. He taught her and her sisters how to spin a top and use a catapult. Shobhan taught him noughts and crosses, a game that he lost 239 times out of 240 on an average day. The last one was usually a draw. Ravan's grades improved. Shobhan sat with him while he did his homework and helped him out when he was foxed by a sum in arithmetic or a question in geography. They played cards: not-at-home, bluff and rummy.

He introduced them to carrom. They bought a carrom board. In the summer holidays, they played non-stop. Sometimes Mr Sarang would join them. Even Mrs Sarang who was busy in the kitchen the whole day tried her hand at it. Ravan fought vehemently with Tara when she surreptitiously picked up a card from the discards piled up in the middle or innocently dispatched her own pieces down the pockets of the carrom board with some delicate fingerwork when no one was watching. She would burst into fake tears rather than admit to finagling. She and Ravan often came to blows.

Tara was Ravan's area of darkness. She confused him. His feelings about her were in a state of constant flux. She teased and needled him unceasingly, mussed his hair, asked him whether he would have her as his girlfriend and when he said 'no', she told him she would commit suicide by leaping off the two bottom steps of Chawl No. 17 because he was the one and only man in her life and if he didn't care for her, there was no point living. She hid his shoes. When he asked for a glass of water, she poured it down the back of his shirt and shook her head sorrowfully. 'How could you, Ravan? You are a grown-up young man. How can you still wet your pants.' He would pray that she would not be at home when he visited the Sarangs and yet if she was not there, he would be restless and ask a dozen times when she would be back.

She was his secret passion, his puppy love, his infatuation and he was her go-between, messenger and alibi. He took her messages to the twilight zone, the ground floor of Chawl No. 22, and occasionally tramped up to the garage at Byculla, where Shahaji Kadam trained and worked, for last-minute changes of plans.

Shahaji Kadam, now there was an enigma. Ravan had checked him out surreptitiously and sometimes frontally. He had scrutinized his face, his legs, his feet, his hands, his ears, his back. He was often black with grease but so were most of the mechanics at the Byculla Automobile Repairs and Maintenance Works. But when he had cleaned up and shaved and went to a movie with Tara he looked like any other man; actually he looked better than a lot of the lean and hungry specimens from the CWD chawls because he worked out at the Telang Gym every morning. It was true he sweated a lot but so did Ravan's mother. Then why did almost everybody avoid him and his people? He would have liked to have asked his mother but she was not exactly the fount of knowledge, and her view of the world was rooted in commerce. Does he want meals? Noons and nights or both? Can he pay?

Who and what and why were Shahaji and his people untouchable? It had taken a lot of doing but Ravan had touched Shahaji when he took him for a long ride on a motorcycle. Ravan had put his arms around his waist just as Tara did. He was for real all right, a solid wall of muscle. He always had a different car or bike when he and Tara went out to the movies or to Malabar Hill, the Gateway of India or anywhere else for a ride. She never met him anywhere near the chawls, at least not in daylight. They fixed the location of an assignation in advance and trysted there. Did Shobhan know about Shahaji and Tara? Tara said it was their secret, Ravan's, Tara's and Shahaji's.

Seven

What had made Eddie join the Sabha? There were of course mercenary considerations, no denying that. A Wilson pen and ballpoint laid out on purple velvet and anchored in an ebony black plastic box with thin black elastic bands was no mean temptation. Had he known the contents of the stories, the book alone would have sufficed. But when the offer was made, he had no idea what the Mahabharata was, nor could he guess that he would continue to flip through its pages almost every day long after he knew the stories by heart.

The fact is, Eddie, born of Catholic parents and a confirmed and practising believer in the sacrament of our Lord Jesus Christ (granted, he would have been as devout a Muslim, Sikh, Jew, Zoroastrian, Buddhist or Hindu had he been born in any other sect or denomination), was favourably disposed to joining the Sabha. He would have been surprised if you had told him that its inspiration was Hinduism. He would have been completely befuddled if you had added that while Muslims were suspect and unwanted in the Sabha's paradigm of India, minorities like Christians and Parsees were welcome so long as they subscribed to Hindu pre-eminence. Like most other Catholics, he would have found it enlightening to learn that the Sabha was meant to be a group dedicated to the service of the nation.

The Sabha was of considerable interest to him because of the six-foot wooden staff and what could be done with it. He had seen them wield the staff, especially the teacher, with such dexterity, fluidity and prowess, that he had stayed glued, watching them for hours from the window of his kitchen, the balcony on the landing and on his way back from school. The Sabha boys would be locked in deadly combat, one wooden staff crossed and pressing down upon the other, when suddenly, as if at a predetermined signal, they would disengage, whirl around, throw their staffs into the air, catch them and swing them with such speed that you could barely see them till they were once again sparring, whipping, connecting and clashing.

Eddie grasped the principles of the wooden staff within a couple of months. Technique took longer, but he practised for long hours by himself and with his colleagues. The objective was clear enough. You fielded the assault of your opponent by presenting the broadside of your staff, recoiling and then taking the offensive. But how did you anticipate which way he would swing and bring down the staff? A slight miscalculation and your flank was exposed and ribs cracked. Or if you didn't leap aside in time, your head was split open. Ironically enough, the secret of the staff and its attraction lay in the suggestion, but conscious absence, of violence. It was like a dance fraught with danger. It was physical chess. The better you anticipated your opponent's game plan and were also conscious that he was changing it in response to your own moves, and the more swift and alert and seized of the dynamics of the combat you were, the greater the likelihood of your being safe.

There was no denying the discrimination at the Mazagaon Sabha branch. Lele Guruji was more attentive to Eddie, he watched and coached him continually. Only the older boys were allowed to exercise and practise with the staff but Eddie was adamant about learning to use it. Rather than lose him, Lele Guruji spent time teaching him after class. Eddie too put in much more effort than the other students. He was like a dog. He wanted Lele Guruji's approval and encomiums daily, so he worked harder than all the other boys, not just at the staff but at everything else.

He was fascinated by the traditional Indian-style gymnasium. Its centrepiece was a sandpit in which stood a ten-foot high wooden pole called the malkhamb. It was a foot across at the bottom and tapered to a mere four inches at the top. Young men and boys with well-oiled bodies gripped it and glided up effortlessly. Months and years after Eddie mastered the art, he couldn't get over the wonder of the strange chemistry between the column and the human body. Technically, you cupped your feet and hands around the pole and pushed yourself up. But it was like rising out of the deep. With just a flip of the toes and a little fingerwork you shot up. En route you did some incredible acrobatics. Head down or sideways, you twisted and wrapped yourself around the pole. You let go of your hands, your body arched out, your legs zipped through the air and came full circle. Atop, you stretched out parallel to the earth, wheeled around and almost disproved the laws of gravity.

The accent was never on building muscles for their own sake or pumping iron. Muscle tone, suppleness, deep-breathing were all that mattered. Eddie did surya-namaskars, the stunted and utterly inadequate version of which the West calls push-ups. He did baithaks in which you rapidly squatted on your haunches and stood up. They looked easy—all those exercises did—but do them twenty times and you were flat out for the next week or two. He did pranayam, the system of breathing that is at the heart of yoga, and he practised on the parallel bars.

Outside he worked on the lezhim with his new-found peers. Lezhim was the part of the exercises Eddie enjoyed the most. It was nothing but a wooden stick and a chain with steel discs on it. But if you held it right in both your hands and performed in unison with the other members, it created its own compelling percussive patterns and the rhythms meshed into a heady dance that gradually turned hectic without losing its sinuous grace or exhilaration. At the end of the session, he sat down with the others for a fifteen-minute bowdhik. This should have been the most tedious part of the class, but Eddie's arrival had transformed the guru as much as the pupil. Lele Guruji's sermons had always bored his class but that had never bothered him. But let Eddie's attention wander and the master was in a panic. If Eddie stopped coming, Lele would be in hot water with the authorities. But in fairness to Lele, it must be said that he didn't just want the boy to stay, he wanted to inspire him. The battle was not for Eddie's body, it was for his soul. And Eddie's attention, he discovered by chance, was up for grabs if you could spin a tale.

A kind of intellection had always been a key part of the Sabha dogma and doctrine. The teacher dwelt on abstractions, theory and cerebral rigour and, alas, more often than not succeeded in alienating his youthful audience. The dropout rate was directly in proportion to the dryness of the bowdhik.

Lele Guruji's stories, to his amazement, had turned all his pupils into avid listeners. Attendance and numbers, albeit only Hindu, swelled. Lele Guruji ransacked his mind for stories and when he had scraped the bottom, discovered the Central Library.

History was stories, literature was stories, the Puranas were stories, biographies were stories and so were the Mahabharata and Ramayana. One day, almost accidentally, Lele stumbled upon the trick of turning geography and philosophy into stories and vice versa. Without knowing it, Lele, the tyrant and bore, had become magician and pied piper.

~

'What is the hurry, Ravan-rao?' Mr Tamhane's voice struck like a fist-sized hook in Ravan's back.

You don't need an afterlife to pay for your sins. You pay for them here and now. Ravan had been in no hurry till he heard his name being called out. Did he really think that he would get away with what he had done to Mr Tamhane's son? He could hear Mr Tamhane closing in on him.

Ravan remembered the manic glee he had felt seven days ago, maybe it was ten. He was standing at the balcony on his floor, watching the world go by: Chandrakant Dixit was pretending to be Shivaji and embracing Sanjay Rawate, whom he had persuaded to impersonate the great Afzal Khan, and was dismembering him just as the Maratha king had done with steel claws. Shambhoonath's replacement Narottam was whipping up a blizzard of dust beating the doormat at the grocer's with a stick borrowed from one of the Sabha boys. Mr Sawant who had retired from his job at the Municipal Corporation twenty years ago was taking his evening constitutional, and the unattainably beautiful and serene princess, Eddie's sister, Pieta Coutinho, was returning home. Wait a minute, that head peering out from the balcony on the second floor, wasn't it Anant Tamhane's, no, couldn't be, what would he be doing in Chawl No. 17, damn, I'll cut my heart out and lay the bloody, palpitating thing in front of the next petrol tanker, it is the one and only Anant Tamhane rolling the spittle in his mouth and taking aim at Pieta. It was Anant Tamhane's favourite game. He would stand in the balcony of his own chawl and spit on unwary passers-by.

Ravan had been one of his victims and was willing to do almost anything to get back at him.

Ravan mustered all the saliva in his mouth and dropped the spit bomb. It landed and splintered on Anant Tamhane's thin, long head. He was screaming shrilly, summoning his father and mother from Chawl No. 23 and craning his neck up to see who had dared pay him back in his own coin.

Ravan thought he had escaped detection by hurriedly pulling his head back but the long and skinny arm of the law had caught up with him.

Sadashiv Raghunath Tamhane was five feet five inches tall but looked much shorter because of his stooping shoulders. He had high cheekbones, darting fish-eyes and a pinched straight nose that gave the impression of being hooked. His skin was sallow and his face sagged. Even when his mouth was closed he seemed to be cackling with his thin, crisp lungs. Ravan saw him sitting on the topmost bough of a leafless banyan tree looking down disapprovingly at the world below.

Mr Tamhane was a man of infinite faith in the depravity and crookedness of his fellow man. He suspected everybody of the very worst and refused to be disappointed when he was proven wrong. All goodness was a front, a feint, an expedient retreat before a person showed his true colours. He couldn't have chosen a more fulfilling career. It confirmed his worst fears about the human race. He was a clerk at the Metropolitan Magistrate's Court at Marine Lines. Every day there passed in front of his eyes an endless procession of petty thieves, hit-and-run drivers, indigent blackmailers, violent drunks, unsuccessful kidnappers, wife-beaters, extortionists, closet sodomites, pimps and prostitutes, down-and-out racketeers, forgers and counterfeiters, greenhorn delinquents, vernacular pornopeddlers, quacks, babas, hoaxers and spiritual swindlers with wandering hands, false prophets and fraudulent water-diviners, exhibitionists, peeping toms, failed suicides, shoplifters and con men. He enumerated their offences and dilated upon their criminal psychographics at such length and with such sour pleasure, his lips stayed open at all times in a rictus of distaste.

~

Under Indian Penal Code Section 407, Clause 3C, Your Honour, the defendant was caught red-handed spitting on the head of a mere innocent. The defendant may be of the same age as the plaintiff but I urge you, Your Lordship, to look at his previous record. In the annals of the most heinous crimes, you will not come across a criminal so hardened and beyond redemption as this child of the devil himself. He first killed an unborn son's father in the prime of his life and widowed a wife and orphaned a lovely girl barely one year old, and then with Nathuram Godse, he shot and murdered Mohandas Karamchand Gandhi, a.k.a. the Mahatma. There is no punishment on our planet, nay, in our universe, which is commensurate with his unmentionable deeds and yet we must make do with what we have. I beseech you My Lord, think not of Anant Tamhane as my son but as the flower and future of India and the trauma he has suffered at the hands of this nasty, short and brutish Ravan, King of Ceylon and evil incarnate. Jail him your honour, not just for life and without parole but put him behind bars, and do not release his bones even after he is dead and gone, for his crimes are such that an eternity of incarceration is not enough.

Ravan waited to be handcuffed. Mr Tamhane was prosecutor, judge, jury and executor, and he was about to take Ravan into custody. Running away wasn't going to help. It would only confirm his guilt and besides Mr Tamhane's posse of policemen would drive up in their blue-black vans, comb the CWD chawls and pin him down to the ground with bayonets.

~

'Ah, Master Ravan Pawar, do tell us of your assignations with Tara Sarang.'

As always he had got it all wrong. Mr Tamhane didn't know or didn't care about the blob of spit fizzing on his son Anant's sparse head of hair. He was after bigger game. Oh God, how did he know that Ravan had touched an untouchable, not just once but thirty, maybe eighty times and... and, Ravan couldn't get himself to say the words, and hadn't washed himself clean after each occasion. He knew Mr Tamhane did, though if one is to be absolutely factual, he screamed his meagre lungs out warning untouchables and their shadows to steer clear of him and so did Mrs Tamhane and Anant. What did he do, Ravan wondered, when he travelled by the local Harbour branch of the railways to office daily and discovered that an untouchable was not casting a shadow but was standing and sweating copiously next to him? Did he jump from the train, or did he throw the offending body out and then excuse himself from his Lordship's presence and go and have a bucket bath in the court premises? Incidentally, were there bathrooms in court houses and did they have water all day long? Come to think of it, nobody else in the chawls made such a song and dance about an untouchable shadow. Oh sure, the old-timers shrank into themselves but it was a covert, surreptitious act, the same as when you happened to pass by a leper.

'Who would have thought that the notorious Ravan, ten-headed abductor of the beautiful consort of Shri Rama, Princess Sita herself, is a closet Shri Krishna?' Ravan could feel Mr Tamhane's leer stick to his back like black tar.

Had the man lost his marbles? Had the Court clerk gone completely bananas? Ravan had no doubt about it. Mr Tamhane had obviously taken leave of his senses.

'I know the gopis beckon,' Mr Tamhane had caught up with Ravan, 'but can you not delay the dalliance in the groves of Brindavan a little, Lord Shri Krishna? Tarry a while and share with us poor mortals, lascivious tales of your thousand and one nights at the Sarang household. And pray, do tell us which of the nine hundred and ninety-nine positions invented and expounded by the great master of concupiscence, Vatsayan in his all-time classic, *Kama Sutra*, have you been practising?'

'My name's Ravan, not Shri Krishna and what gopis are you talking about?'

'You can no longer fool us, you've been discovered, you are the blue god, Shri Krishna, under the guise and name of Ravan. As to the gopis, the dear shepherdesses, there are at least nine of them in the Sarang household. Doubtless a trifle overripe but luscious and full of juice, nevertheless.'

He had been called all kinds of names, he had long since been resigned to that, what do you expect with a name like Ravan. He had heard them all, good and bad, mostly bad, there was nothing, absolutely nothing new that anybody could say to him, nothing that would hurt or surprise him. And yet here was this disagreeable and dried-up old man whose prurient insinuations and strange revelations made Ravan feel dirty and left him speechless. He was sure Mr Tamhane was mocking him despite his straight face but he was hard put to understand the nature of the joke and the lewd suggestions in his words.

'Mighty tales of your insatiable sexual appetite, of all-night gambolling and cavorting, of endless lascivious adventures and frolicsome lechery have reached the four corners of the world. Will you marry all nine of the Sarang girls on the same day or will it be on consecutive nights? I have heard that good old Sarang, the girl-making machine, is heaving a sigh of relief. Are you going to take over from where he left off? Will you have a dozen, make it a double dozen daughters from each of the Sarang beauties?' Mr Tamhane shook his head sadly. 'We'll all have to vacate the CWD chawls to make room for your brood.'

～

Ravan tucked the peacock feather in his head-band, tied the yellow silk sash around his waist and scampered out with his flute. He was the first one up and he wanted to wake up the whole world. He reached the grassy knoll where he and his friends played. The river was a swollen dark welt on the land. Not a cow mooed or moved. His friends the cowherds were lying haphazardly, still asleep. He closed his eyes and formed a hole with his lips which he fitted over the one in his flute.

This is what he liked most, waking up a still life. He breathed softly into the flute. The air grazed and rubbed its back against the walls of the reed and a deep, hollow sound like wind in a cavern came forth. The first tentative notes grew in number and strength and became a song of creation that echoed from mountain top to mountain top. The birds in the trees shook their feathers, cleaned themselves and trilled. The river Yamuna slipped out of the vice of night and caught silver fire from the sun as it flowed down boisterously. The wind yawed and yawned and bumped into the cowherds. They woke up with goose pimples and found newborn calves sucking frantically at their mothers' teats. Where were the milkmaids, they wondered, as they tried to drag the young ones away. If they didn't come soon the whole of Brindavan would have to go without milk today. But they underestimated the power of Ravan's song. You could hear the bells on their anklets long before you saw them. There they were, Savitri, Shobhan and Tara, Kausalya and Ragini and the other sisters. Their hips swayed and their skirts swirled. But instead of milking the cows, they formed a circle around Ravan and began to do the ras-leela dance.

'Stop it, Krishna, stop playing,' the boys swore at Ravan. 'If you don't, the girls won't milk the cows.'

'That's between you and them.' The rising sun shone over Ravan's blue skin naked to the belly button till it matched the turquoise blue of the peacock feather in his head-band.

'No one will marry you once you are seen with this philanderer, Krishna,' the boys warned the girls. 'Your parents will skin you alive. Come away and milk the cows. You know very well who will complain about you if he doesn't get curd for dinner this evening, the very same Krishna for whom you are willing to risk your name and your honour.'

Those foolish boys might as well have asked the Sarang girls to stop breathing. Of course they didn't listen. Ravan could barely conceal his joy. He accelerated the pace of his song. The cows were standing ten deep watching the duet between Ravan's flute and the girls' feverish dancing. The birds came and sat on the branches of the trees. Those who couldn't get a place sat on the horns of the cows and watched bewitched. Even the simple cowherds forgot to crib and bitch and wondered what the results of the mad competition would be. Faster and faster the girls pirouetted around Ravan. It was a giddy sight, all those bright coloured skirts swirling madly, long plaits flying in the air and the clipped accelerating beat of the wooden sticks striking each other. Which of the Sarang sisters would fall in a dead faint first?

Ravan seemed to have forgotten the world, his eyes were closed and his flute was a song that would never cease. And yet with infinite grace and care, he brought his song as well as the girls to a stop.

Savitri was the first to garland him. 'You are mine today and forever,' she said. It was only when Kausalya, Ragini and Sumitra put strings of mogra flowers around his neck that he realized he was married to the girls. It was Tara's turn. She pulled him close to her with her garland and whispered, 'You are mine, Krishna, only mine, today and forever.' Shobhan was last. 'How did you dance, Shobhan? Nobody would have suspected that you have a club-foot.' Shobhan's answer was simple. 'I can do anything for you. I'm yours, Krishna, for now and for always.'

That night Ravan took his wives home.

'Your father can't support one woman and you think you can look after nine, you polygamist?' Parvatibai asked him.

'What's a polygamist? And you don't have to worry. I don't have to do a thing. They married me, they are going to support me, Ma.'

'Over my dead body. No son of mine is going to live off his wives.' Parvatibai slammed the door in Ravan's face.

He took his wives to the Sarang place. Mr and Mrs Sarang were waiting for him at the door. Mrs Sarang was wearing a green nine-yard sari and the diamonds in her big nose ring sparked like silent flashbulbs. She lit a lamp, circled it in front of Ravan's face and put a dot of crimson powder on his forehead. Mr Sarang embraced him. He handed him a package, gift-wrapped in red foil.

'Open it, open it,' he beamed. Ravan pulled the ribbon gently and the knot came undone. Inside were BEST bus tickets of every denomination. 'You and your new family can travel a whole year anywhere in Bombay with them.'

Ravan was overwhelmed. He touched his father-in-law's feet and tried to enter the room.

'What are you doing?' Mr Sarang asked him sharply.

'Coming home.'

'Do you think I got rid of my daughters so that you could bring them back to stay with me? Don't you ever show your face to me.'

Just for one night, Ravan thought in desperation, we'll stay in the toilets for one night and look for another place tomorrow. He tried to make his wives comfortable but all night long they were disturbed by men and women who wanted to use the facilities urgently. It was as if everybody in Chawl No. 17 had eaten shrimps and had got the runs. It was odd but even the people from the Catholic floor were coming down in droves.

At 2.30 a.m. there was a cryptic knock on the door.

'Tara,' a voice whispered, 'Tara, open the door, it is me, Shahaji Kadam.'

Ravan looked at Tara. Even a blind man could have seen that she was in two minds and the mind wanting to go to Shahaji was far stronger. Ravan bolted the door and told Tara to stay where she was. Shahaji kept knocking and begging for another half-hour, the pest, but Ravan was unmoved.

He was woken by a twittering and cheeping of birds. There were at least a hundred babies clambering all over him.

'Whose are these?' he asked in a panic.

A chorus of voices answered him, 'Yours.'

He looked at his wives in disbelief. 'Who'll look after them?'

'God gave them to us. He'll look after them,' they said.

He saw them clearly for the first time. They were an odd lot. If they had not been his own, he would have said they were a horrid combination of chicks and dwarfs. They craned their necks to look at him and they kept saying the same thing over and over.

'Daddy food. Daddy biscuits. Daddy bread. Daddy basundi.'

'Why are they making such a racket?' Ravan asked his wives.

'They want to be fed.'

'Why don't you?'

'Try feeding all hundred of them.'

Tara undid her blouse. Before she had exposed her bosom, the babies were all over her. They fought furiously for her nipple. One managed to get to it. There was a terrible cracking sound. His beak broke and hung limp. Her breasts were made of stone.

In the morning the rent collector handed Ravan a notice. It was curt.

'You are illegal tenants. Get out or by tomorrow you'll be charged with unlawful occupancy.' It was signed: Mr Tamhane.

The next day when Mr Tamhane came to evict him, Ravan was crouched in the far corner of the toilet. He didn't know what he was doing wrong but those bird-children seemed to have increased exponentially.

'Open the door, Shri Krishna,' Mr Tamhane ordered him.

Ravan would have liked to obey the court's orders but stepping down would have meant trampling at least fifty or sixty of his children.

'Daddy food, Daddy food, Daddy food.'

The cacophony got on Mr Tamhane's nerves. He was incensed by Ravan's recalcitrance. He ordered the bailiff to pull down the door. It was a mistake. Thousands of little babies, wave upon wave of them, burst out and inundated the passage and the corridors. Mr Tamhane was flung back and submerged within seconds. Nobody heard from him again.

There was an exodus the next day. Ravan saw his mother leaving. She was carrying a mattress and a primus stove. There were thousands of others with her. The Dixits, the Monteiros, the Ghatges, the Labdes and the Bhoirs, Eddie and his family, they were all running for their lives pursued by his hordes. Whoever stumbled did not stand a chance. His children ate him or her.

When the last of the tenants had disappeared, they turned upon Ravan.

~

'Where have you been, Ravan?' There was no accusation in the voice, just concern. 'You haven't come home for over a month now. I have been up twice and left a message with your mother. Didn't she tell you?'

Ravan would not look at Shobhan.

'Didn't she?' Shobhan was perplexed.

'She did.'

'You don't feel like coming any more to our place?'

Didn't Shobhan ever get hurt? How come she was always calm and caring and just a fraction distant so you never knew what went on in her mind?

'I've missed you and so has everyone else. We haven't got the carrom board out since you disappeared,'

'They call me names and say nasty things to me.'

'Who calls you names?'

'Mr Raikar and his wife, Mr Lele, especially Mr Tamhane. And all the boys in the chawls. Even Eddie from the top floor.'

'What do they say?'

'That I am Shri Krishna and the Sarang sisters are my harem of gopis. They ask me where my peacock feather is. Mr Tamhane's son Anant wanted to know whether I had stolen your clothes while you were bathing. Eddie Coutinho told one of his Sabha friends to ask me how long you and I had been married.'

'They are jealous of our friendship and they want to break it. You'll ignore them, won't you?' Ravan nodded his head eagerly. The Sarang sisters were the only friends he had left. 'Come tomorrow and have dinner with us. I'll cook something special for you.'

~

Ravan was feeling a trifle uncomfortable but he had no regrets. He had overeaten and he wasn't sure when the buttons at his waist would pop out and fly. How could he have stayed away from them so long? They were his family. Parvatibai was his mother and she protected him like a tigress protecting her cubs. But she was always busy, cooking, marketing, cutting vegetables, keeping accounts. She tried to make conversation with Ravan, ask him what had happened at school, what the new teacher was like, she washed his clothes and carefully put them under his father's mattress so they were creased just right, but no conversation of theirs lasted more than a couple of minutes. As for his father, there were times when Ravan forgot that there was such a person. There were no dramatic ups and downs in their lives, no laughter and crying and reconciliations. Mr Sarang was wrong. It was terrific to have so many children. A large family was a world by itself. If you had one, you didn't need anybody else.

The game of bluff was in full swing. Everybody, even Mrs Sarang had joined in. There were loud cries and hysterical laughter. Mr Sarang was a little low-key but he had been caught out twice and was sure to be planning some new strategy. Ravan was chewing the fat paan Shobhan had got for him. His mother never allowed him to eat one.

'Just for today,' Shobhan had said and smiled, 'because you are back among us.'

'The lings of sharks,' Ravan announced with his mouth full of betel leaf, saliva and loads of masala: cardamom, freshly grated coconut, finely cut betel nut, fennel and rose-petal preserves, the whole concoction dipped in some cloyingly sweet yellow syrup.

'What?' Mrs Sarang asked him. 'What did you say?'

'Re bings of larts.' Ravan enunciated each word lucidly.

'Ma, forget him.' Tara shook her head in disgust. 'He's sozzled. He's eaten so much and now his darling Shobhan's given him a paan, he's out for the count.'

'He's not. I can follow every word he said.'

'Is that so, Shobhan? Well, what did the Prince of Darkness say?' Tara asked Shobhan.

'Three kings of hearts. Ravan swallow the juice. You can't hold it forever.'

'Shall I play?' Savitri asked tentatively.

Tara interrupted her. 'No, it's my turn.'

'No, it's not.' Mr Sarang's voice was unusually shrill and querulous.

'It is, Father,' Yamuna tried to reason with him.

'Four kings of hearts.' Tara looked around defiantly daring someone to contradict her.

'She's lying. The bitch is always lying.'

'That's the idea, Father.' Yamuna was exasperated at her father's obtuseness. 'You can always call her bluff.'

'I am calling her bluff.' His voice was a manic screech now. He knocked the cards out of Tara's hands. 'Pretending to go and see movies with Sandhyarani. As if I don't know who Sandhyarani is. Shall I tell them, shall I tell them, you bitch?'

'Not today, Father.' Shobhan held Mr Sarang's hand gently. 'Not today. It's my birthday.'

'The izzat of our family is at stake and you talk of your bloody birthday, you cloven-hoofed goat. Do you know who she has been seeing on the sly?'

'I know. We'll talk about it tomorrow.'

The old man went berserk after that. 'You knew, you knew she was seeing Shahaji Kadam, that untouchable slime from the ground floor and you kept quiet? Oh you bitch, how could I have fathered such a traitor?'

'Shall we discuss this later, Father? We have a guest with us, little Ravan.'

'Some guest. I'm going to take little Ravan's hide off. He's been stabbing his hosts in the back all these months.' Mr Sarang pulled Ravan up by his collar. 'Tell them, tell them, you bastard, how you've been running back and forth carrying messages for them.'

Mr Sarang's hand came down like a wrecking ball but it fell on Shobhan. She had her arms protectively around Ravan.

'Why didn't you tell me, you slut?' Mr Sarang's attention flitted from one person to the other.

'Because of all your nine unmarried daughters, she alone had found a man and I rejoiced for her.'

'Do you want her to go around with a bhangi?'

'Wouldn't make a difference to me whether he's a sweeper or a mechanic, so long as she's happy.'

'I know your game. Nobody will look at you, so you want to ruin the lives of your other sisters.'

'That's not true. She's never wished anyone ill.' Tara had finally found her voice. 'I met him on my own. I love him.'

'Love? Love? Is that what's made you three months pregnant?'

'He wants to marry me, Father, and I want to marry him and have his baby.'

'And what happens to my other daughters? Who will marry them once they discover that we have a Mahar, an untouchable, sorry, a neo-Buddhist, isn't that what one calls them now, among us?'

'We are all going to die spinsters, Father, because there are just too many of us and you haven't got the money to bribe a caste-Hindu to take us off your hands.'

Mr Sarang's leg rose in the air. It slammed into Tara's belly. It was a powerful kick. Tara staggered and then fell back.

'Don't please.' Ravan crumbled. 'I want to marry Tara.'

'No daughter of mine is going to live with an untouchable: Never.' He kicked her again, a little harder, if that was possible. When Shobhan tried to pull him away, he threw her against the wall. A slow, red pool was forming under Tara.

Eight

Eddie's double life was almost second nature to him by now. What was it that prompted him to keep the Sabha part of his life a secret? How do we know even as children what is taboo? There was no law against reading story-books during leisure time in Eddie's house. Then how had he sensed that the Mahabharata stories would not find favour with his mother? The Sabha had never been referred to in his home. It is doubtful if Violet knew that it was called the Sabha, let alone what its programme and agenda were. Coming right down to it, nobody on the fifth floor ever mentioned the Hindus in the other four storeys.

Gut feeling, instinct, the atmosphere in his home, his Catholic upbringing, call it what you will—and no explanation will ever be sufficient—Eddie kept his secular Hindu incarnation separate from his Catholic life.

He got four annas every week as pocket money. With that and the two rupees twelve annas he had left over from the money Granna had given him on his last birthday, he bought a red loincloth and two pairs of khaki half-pants. The loincloth he washed daily after class and hung up on the latch of the locker in the corridor of the gym. The half-pants he washed every Saturday with soap he filched from home.

Chawl No. 11, where the gym and the Sabha corner of the open grounds were, was not in Violet's direct line of vision had she stood in the kitchen window and looked out. But even if it had been, Violet had no interest in what was going on outside. She had looked out once, a long, long time ago, from the balcony on her landing and lived to regret it. Once in a while, Eddie saw Pieta walking past in the distance but neither she nor any of his Catholic neighbours had reason to pass by the Hindu Gym.

The one person who watched him, Eddie preferred to think he was spying on him, was Ravan. At such times Eddie went into overdrive. His chest filled out, he wielded his staff with exaggerated zeal and on a couple of occasions almost hurt himself. He yelled Jai Hind louder than everybody else and gave Ravan sidelong glances filled with contempt. But Ravan's visits were aimless, a matter of habit and for lack of anything better to do.

~

How many times had he seen the picture? Yet every time he was about to flip the page, he stopped, mesmerized. There were ten other pictures of Lord Krishna in the book. The child Krishna standing on an unsteady pile of vessels and stealing curd from a clay pot hanging from the rafters on the ceiling. Krishna at eight years of age smiling mischievously from the branches of a tree while maidens bathing in the lake below pleaded with him to return their clothes. The same child Krishna holding up Mount Govardhan on the tip of his finger and protecting his people from the deluge. Shri Krishna invisibly frustrating Dushyasan's attempt to disrobe Draupadi in the presence of the august elders in Dhritarashtra's court.

There were four or five others, all of them favourites. But the killing of Shishupal was in a class by itself. It was the only one where you saw Shri Krishna as an active warrior. Shishupal was an evil man who had committed every crime under the sun. The patience of God is great. Besides Shishupal was family, Krishna's cousin. Krishna gave him plenty of rope to hang himself by. He swore that he would not touch Shishupal till he had committed a hundred sins. Hundred was a big number. Besides, who was keeping count? No one. Except Shri Krishna. Years passed. Suddenly one day, Shri Krishna appeared before Shishupal, his eyes glittering with a light even brighter than the halo around his head. Shishupal realized that his time was up. In the picture he had begun to reach for his sword and Krishna was smiling. There was a serenity in Krishna's face that was breathtaking, it was also a face that was strong, decisive and unforgiving. 'Ninety-nine crimes, yes. A hundred, no.' Even as he spoke, he let loose his sudershan chakra, the missile disc that spun at phenomenal speed around his little finger. In the illustration the chakra had already severed Shishupal's head which was lying on the floor and was arcing back.

Jesus was and always would be Eddie's Lord God. There was never any doubt about this in his mind. And yet what was that thought that had slipped through his mind like a fish out of a net? Oh Lord God, was he committing sacrilege? Was his cup of sins brimming over? He shut his eyes tight but the thought darted through again. Was it the devil, was his soul lost forever, the perdition that Father D'Souza always talked of, whatever it meant, had it claimed him already?

Why didn't Jesus ever laugh or play a practical joke? Did he never have any fun in life, not even a day of it? Why was he always so glum and long-faced? Did he never have a fist-fight as a child? Did he ever throw a stone at a clay-pot hanging high from the ceiling, knock a hole through its bottom and drink buttermilk from it? Oh, he knew Jesus was stronger than the strongest but why was he not tough and muscular. Why was he so goody-goody? Now that the dam had burst, he might as well spill it all.

He remembered his first communion. The day coincided with his birthday. His mother had always sewn his clothes but they were school uniforms or daily wear. She was a seamstress. She was at her sewing machine from ten in the morning till eight at night, sometimes even later. But they were mostly women's clothes, dresses, tops, skirts. This time, for his first communion, Violet had become far more ambitious. She had sewn him a white silk shirt with a frilled front and a pair of soft and glossy white trousers made of some material called satin duck.

He had seen a white peacock in the zoo at the Victoria Gardens. Its long feathers and tail trailed behind, a little ruffled and tacky. The monsoons were imminent and under the darkening sky, right there in front of his very eyes, as if someone had pulled a string lever, the peacock's feathers fanned into a shimmering white orb. It picked up its right foot, held it up daintily for a few seconds and then walked towards him. The whole magnificent edifice of taut and snowy lace undulated in fluid waves as it tensed and relaxed. Eddie wasn't quite sure why he felt a little faint and breathless with the beauty of it.

He felt like that peacock on the day of his first communion. All around him was a tremulous glow of electric white. Everyone's eyes, he was convinced, were on him even though there were eleven other boys and girls walking towards the altar with him.

Now it was his turn. Father Agnello D'Souza dipped the thin white wafer in the wine in the polished silver chalice and placed it lightly on Eddie's protruding tongue. That wave in the peacock's feathers was building up in him. It rose and it rose till it was higher than the stone steeple of St Sebastian's Cathedral. The body and blood of Jesus Christ. Not real. Just make-believe. Symbolic, Father D'Souza had said. He felt worse than a cannibal, eating and drinking God. The wave gathered itself to a towering height, pierced the heavens and broke. His vomit had spattered all over his shirt and Father D'Souza's embroidered, gold and silver chasuble.

Whenever Eddie went for the sacrament of the communion he gagged, his intestines churned and he choked. He could never get over it. The Romans had killed Jesus almost two thousand years ago, that's twenty times hundred, and they were still drinking his blood and eating his body and forcing him to do the same.

After that first communion, Eddie could never touch meat. Whatever the vices he was to develop later, he would never become a drunkard. He would wake up at night screaming in utter terror that someone had slipped the Host in the bread or a little wine in the cold kokum soup. Even his mother, who had never forgiven him for the fiasco in church, was shaken by the depth of his despair though she had no idea when and where and how it came to be.

He lay with his eyes shut tight, his fists balled up into his wrists, his mouth clenched lipless as they tried to open his lips and force the wafer down his throat. Then he asked the one question he knew he could never ask: was it not possible to commune with God without spilling his blood any more?

~

His eyes were still shut when lightning fell and burnt a hole, a cavernous hole in Eddie's back. He was slammed awake so abruptly, he nearly threw up and fell out of his chair. His mother was blabbering like a demented woman. But that was the least of his problems. She had planted such a singeing slap on his back that the imprint of all the five fingers of her right hand stood out in relief on his chest.

'Idol worshipper.' Eddie could barely decipher her hysterical words. 'Where did you get this satanic book? Did that Hindu boy, the devil himself, give it to you?' She was beating him like a woman possessed, slapping him, boxing his ears, pulling his hair.

'It's a story-book, Mom, that's all.' Shouldn't have opened his mouth. She was outraged by that simple statement.

'It's a passage to hell lined with thirty-three million Hindu gods and goddesses. Wait till I talk to Father D'Souza.' She grabbed the book and stared at the technicolour miracles Shri Krishna was performing.

'Give me back my book.'

Violet walked into the kitchen and flung it out of the window. It was so unexpected an action, Eddie ran past her and stretched out across the window to grab it. It sped down five storeys and landed with a little muted thud. The binding came undone and a couple of sections detached themselves from the rest of the book. Shri Krishna's sudershan chakra was still on its flight back. Oh, to recall the missile and send it spinning to his vile mother.

He straightened up, walked to the door and unlocked it.

'Don't you dare leave this room.'

Eddie opened the door. Violet was screaming now.

'That's it. I don't ever want you back in this house.'

Granna came and took his hand and drew him to her.

'You stay out of this, Mother.'

'That's enough, Violet.'

~

Ravan had taken to going to the St Theresa's School grounds near the Byculla bridge. He was afraid of the teacher's temper but the memory of the man floating weightlessly kept coming back to him at odd times, and every evening he found himself hanging around St Theresa's School pavilion.

It took him seven days to ask but finally he accosted the man as he was leaving the large one-storeyed stone building with the sloping roof that housed the gym, the tae kwon do room and all the sports equipment of St Theresa's.

'Will you teach me?' The words came out frightened and indistinct.

'Are you from St Theresa's?' the teacher asked.

'No.'

'Speak English?'

'What's that got to do with teaching me?'

'In this place I ask the questions. Do you?'

'No.'

'It's a hundred rupees for six months. You've got that kind of money?'

'No.'

That settled matters. Ravan started to walk away.

'It's seventy rupees for the 5.30 classes in the morning.' The master spoke to his back.

Seventy, hundred, a thousand, it was all the same, where was he going to get the money from? Ravan shook his head and kept walking.

∼

'I'm going to the St Theresa's School gym from tomorrow. Will you wake me up in the morning?'

'What time?' Parvati asked.

Ravan was sure his mother knew that he wasn't attending the Sabha any more, even though Lele Guruji had not sent an emissary or a note saying that her son had been chucked out of class for good.

'Five o'clock. The master is going to teach in English.'

'That's nice, isn't it? You'll become strong and healthy and get to learn some English on the side.'

~

The clock in the tae kwon do room said 5.28. But all the students were already there. They had changed into the white on white suit and were warming up. At 5.30 they had fallen in place. Ravan craned his neck over the window-sill to see what was going on.

For a while he stood still and watched the boys exercising. It began to drizzle. He couldn't contain himself for long. He started to mime whatever they did. It seemed easy till you started to do it yourself. Within minutes he was drenched. He had made up his mind that he would imitate every action and gesture but not the staccato sounds they let out. Before he knew it, he too was barking. It came naturally. The one didn't seem possible without the other.

His timing was a little off. His 'huh' was a fraction of a second later than theirs. He shut up for some time but he had the feeling that the master was aware of his presence. It was pouring now.

'What the hell do you think you are doing?'

Ravan was so engrossed he hadn't noticed the peon from the gym. It was the fourth day and he was getting the hang of things. Bloody careless of him. 'Just watching.'

'You think this is a free show? Mr Billimoria is not running charitable classes. You want to learn tae kwon do, you pay for it. Otherwise get the hell out. Sala, bhag.'

'Learn what?'

'What?'

'Learn what did you say?'

'Tae kwon do. Don't even know what you are learning?' This time he pushed Ravan.

I told you to remain in the dark, Ravan muttered to himself, did you listen? Now stay out for good. But five minutes after the peon left him, Ravan was back.

~

It was raining pretty hard when Ravan left home. By the time he was halfway to the St Theresa's grounds there were gale winds that broke every single rib in his umbrella. The storm drains and the gutters were completely choked. The water from the bridge came racing down. In a matter of minutes the road was flooded and the water had risen to his calves. The wind howled and keened. And the rains crashed down as if the sky had caved in. Monster raindrops pelted him like hail. You could hardly call them raindrops, they were sheets of swirling dark glass with ragged ends.

He was fond of the rain and getting wet in it was one of the high points in his life but the thunder unnerved him today. It bombarded him from all sides and left him light-headed. Lightning pulsed through the sky and lit up the hairline fractures in it. It rolled on the tar road and slithered off it onto the crossed grill of the railway bridge about a furlong away.

As Ravan reached the maidan, there was a shivery sound of tinfoil in his ears. It made the eardrum resonate to its own frequency and jangled his nerves. His fifth or sixth step into the field and he began to get an idea of what it must mean to be caught in quicksand. His foot felt weightless as it sank into the tall grass and kept going into the squelchy earth. When he tried to lift it, there was a sucking hiss in his canvas shoe and he was trapped. He would have to dislodge the whole earth to get his foot out. There it was, that erratic vibration in his ear again. He trudged on. He knew there was no way that the class would be held in this cyclone but it became a matter of honour for him to make it to the gym.

He suddenly understood what the sound was. The wind was lifting off the corrugated tin sheets nailed to the sloping roof of the Mazagaon Cricket Club next to the St Theresa's gym and sending them hurtling across the open grounds. Now he was truly frightened. He tried to run and duck the missiles of death which whizzed past him. They were birds of prey and they were playing with him in that vast and abandoned field. But the running didn't take him far since his feet got caught in the quagmire under him. Exhausted, he stood still and watched this sound and light show with the flying objects. He saw a monster sheet headed straight for him. He was felled violently to the ground. He was sure he had been decapitated when someone lifted him in both arms and sprinted to the gymnasium.

Mr Billimoria opened the lock of the tae kwon do room with his keys and switched on the light. He brought out two towels from one of the cupboards and handed one to Ravan. Ravan was not sure what to do with it.

'Open it and dry yourself.'

Ravan followed Mr Billimoria's example, stripped himself to his underwear, vigorously rubbed himself dry and tied the towel around his waist. Mr Billimoria went to the cupboard again, took a tae kwon do suit off a peg and slipped into it. He took another from a neatly folded pile on the shelf and handed it to Ravan and proceeded to light a kerosene stove. He showed Ravan how to tie the belt and asked him to bring over two stools from the corner. 'Sit,' he said and handed a mug of tea to Ravan. 'Feel better?'

Ravan nodded. There was a smile on Mr Billimoria's face. 'What were you yelling when you opened your arms in the field?'

Ravan kept mum.

'I know you were defying the emissaries of death but I couldn't catch the words.'

Ravan looked positively embarrassed.

'I prayed to God not to kill me because my mother's going to make my favourite dish, puranpolis, today.'

'Do you realize you would be dead if I hadn't knocked you flat when I did?'

'Yes.'

'I like puranpolis too. Get me some tomorrow.'

Ravan nodded his head again.

'Now that you are here, we might as well start classes. You will come here every day at 5.15, not at 5.23 or 5.25 as you've been doing. Change into this suit and do warming-up exercises till 5.30. Classes are held every day barring Saturdays and Sundays and go on till 6.30. You will not be absent except for a month in summer. My class is not free. Tell your mother to pay me whatever she can afford every month.

'I know Hindi but I will speak to you in English. That way you will pick up the language and the other boys in the class won't act superior.'

~

You could count the number of black belts in India on the fingers of one hand in those days. It was a long time before the Bruce Lee craze would hit the world and karate become a household word. There were few institutions in the country which taught the Far Eastern martial arts in India. Mr Billimoria had done a bit of judo at Fergusson College in Poona when studying there. Later he went to Hong Kong to develop contacts in the region for his father's business and switched to tae kwon do. His Korean masters taught him that tae kwon do was like a Zen discipline, a matter of mind dominating the body.

Ravan was to win many prizes in tae kwon do competitions over the years, but as his master often pointed out, that was not of much consequence. He grasped the message of tae kwon do intuitively. It entered his bloodstream. Perhaps it steadied him in later life so that, however much he was rocked, he always regained his centre of gravity. Perhaps.

Ravan's mind did not always triumph over matter. His hit-rate would have averaged the same as most people trying to muddle along in life. But for the first time he felt a sense of belonging. He believed in his master. At a time when the guru tradition was on its last legs in India, he had found his guru and his guru had found the ideal pupil.

Ravan would have done almost anything for Mr Billimoria. That Mr Billimoria did not ask him for the moon, sexual favours or to smuggle contraband is not relevant. If he had wanted any or all of them, he would have taken them as the guru's prerogative. It was the guru's mind that took precedence over the pupil's mind and matter. What it did for Ravan was to make him aware of perfection and to hunger for it. Whether that consciousness would make him a master-craftsman or an artist is a grey area. One thing was certain. A journeyman he would not be.

He practised. Not night and day but as often as he could. The neighbours in the chawl had always kept their distance from Parvati. Now they were convinced that she was either possessed or doing black magic. Ha! Ha! Ha! It was half a derogatory laugh and half a hiccup. Obviously, her voice had turned hoarse and masculine as she blew hard and gustily into a brass pot over the years, inviting the Goddess Amba, who rode a tiger and brandished a sword in her hand, to take charge of her mind, body and soul and do with them as she would.

Ravan drove his mother up the wall. On more than one occasion she would have liked to stab him, strangle him or throw him out of the window.

Ravan's aim was not always very good, at least not in the early years. On one occasion his foot went straight into the rice that was cooking on the kerosene stove. The bubble on it was the size of a decent balloon. Parvati could not contain her joy. She was a great believer in deterrence. He lay there writhing in pain and sizzling agony while she delivered her homily. 'That will teach you a lesson you will never forget,' she told him without making any attempt to commiserate with him. She was wrong. The boy was undeterred.

When his foot healed, he almost succeeded where his mother had failed all these years. He nearly ejected his father from the house. Ravan's contention was that if you moved when he was in action, you not only begged to be hurt but, more to the point, upset his timing.

It started out innocuously enough. Ravan asked his father to stand still, just stand still, okay, while Shankar-rao was transferring himself from his armchair to the bed. Shankar-rao must have been thinking of the news in *Bittambatmi* that day: about the man who pickled the fingers and toes and other limbs of his victims and stored them in the fridge, because how else could you explain his tacitly acceding to Ravan's request? Ravan circled his father, his hands aiming, unfolding, doing figures of eight over his father's head and all the while continuing to stalk him; he then flung himself sideways into the air as he let out a piercing scream. Did his father move, dodge his head, step back half a centimetre, blink his eyelids? These are academic issues. Shankar-rao's specs were lying smashed on the ground and he was bent over double. He didn't say a word because he couldn't. His diaphragm had climbed up and stuck to his throat. His testicles had grown so big, it was a wonder he wasn't floating into Eddie's house.

The weight of the silence in the outside room finally bore down on Parvati. She came out of the kitchen. She went back. She returned with a glass of water with sugar in it and tried to feed it to Shankar-rao. He flung it away with his left hand but brought the hand back to his groin in a hurry.

'I told him not to move. He moved. What do you expect?'

Ravan was as usual keeping a clear line of defence but there wasn't much conviction in it.

Shankar-rao spoke after forty-five minutes. They were his last words on this planet. At least they sounded that way. 'Either he goes or I go.'

That put an end to Ravan's war-games at home. For once he had penetrated his father's habitual torpor and for a while, it was chancy for him. He couldn't risk it again. From now on he decided to go to his gym after school and practise there.

~

Later on, much later when Eddie and Ravan were grown-up men, Eddie would ask: What happened to us in school? Were we border-line average students? Even they pass, maybe we were just dullards? Or were we stupid? Why did we fare so badly?

There were other questions that gnawed at Eddie's peace of mind from time to time and exasperated him because he had no answers. But today was not such a day. Today he was not an underachiever.

It was the twentieth anniversary of the Mazagaon Sabha. Leaders from all parts of Bombay and a couple from the Central Committee were gathered to celebrate the occasion. They were seated on a raised platform under a festive shamiana. As Lele

Guruji would have put it, everything was going like clockwork. The loudspeakers crackled occasionally but at least this time the man from whom they had hired the electrical equipment was making sure that there was no dog-whistle feedback from the amplifier interrupting the speeches.

After *Vande Mataram,* the Sabha anthem and welcoming speeches, there were various competitions: running, yoga, wrestling, malkhamb (they had dug a deep hole in the ground and fixed the tapering ten-foot wooden pole in it with concrete), the fights with the wooden staff, the lezhim dance. There wasn't an item in which Eddie did not participate. The loudspeakers called out his name to pick up a prize in almost every category.

It was time for the elocution competition. Two boys spoke about Veer Savarkar and his exploits; another about Nathuram Godse and his last thoughts before he was hanged and martyred in the noble cause of Hinduism. One of the older boys recited a soliloquy from the play *Manapaman.* As usual there were three or four boys who dealt with Shivaji and how he founded a Hindu kingdom in Maharashtra and his great escape from Agra where the mighty Mughal emperor, Aurangzeb, had kept him under house arrest.

It was Eddie's turn. He looked far and wide so long that even Lele Guruji began to get worried about his favourite student. Just as the audience's restiveness was about to become a murmur, Eddie said in a quiet and natural voice as if he was speaking to a friend on the phone, 'This is Sanjay speaking.' Eddie was thirty seconds into his speech before the elders or anybody else understood that this was the Sanjay from the Mahabharata, telling Dhritarashtra, the blind father of the hundred Kaurava princes, how the father and mother of all wars was shaping up.

Eddie's strategy was simple and one with which every Indian could identify. He was the commentator of a cricket match. He observed the ultimate game, the game of life and death itself and told it as it was. His voice was a supple instrument. It reflected the tensions, the speed, the sudden drama, the heroism, the betrayal and the sorrow of the war. One minute he was with Arjun's son Abhimanyu, the teenager who knew the secret of penetrating a military maze so complex that even the greatest warriors did not know how to negotiate it. Then he was with the Kauravas, struggling with Karna to heft his chariot wheel out of the churning mud in the battlefield. Even from the great distance that separated him from his arch rival Arjun, Karna could tell that Lord Krishna was urging Arjun to shoot, to shoot now, before Karna's deadly arrow pierced his heart and the battle went to the enemy.

And now Eddie was back with Abhimanyu who had reached where no man had, the very core of the convoluted circular formation; but here he was trapped by his own incredible skill, for while he knew how to penetrate the human maze he had no idea of how to get out. And the arrows fell upon him like sheet upon sheet of rain till there was not a millimetre of unpierced skin left in his youthful body.

The bell rang and Eddie withdrew from the mike. There was such a tense silence, he thought something had gone wrong. Had he hurt their sentiments, had he gone too fast, had he lost them because they were bored? He looked at his peers, the young boys with whom he exercised and wrestled and laughed and competed. Had they heard the bell or not? He saw their mouths open. All right, so he had messed up, but what were they waiting for? For him to say sorry? He realized how tense he was. His palms and feet were cold, something that had not happened even when he was on the malkhamb or trying to flip his opponent so that he would land with his back on the floor.

It was a strange sensation this, his blood seemed to be racing while everything around him had slowed down. He saw Appa Achrekar take forever to get up. Was he going to denounce Eddie? Appa brought his hands together, he was clapping ever so slowly, then the others on the stage were on their feet and so was the audience and everyone was clapping. Appa smiled and said, 'And then?'

Lele Guruji was beside him now. Eddie was his prodigal son and he loved him dearly. Ravan would not have believed the change this one pupil had wrought in Lele Guruji. Lele's wife and children, who had been trained by Lele to be almost bereft of all emotion in personal dealings and who had become as dry and desiccated as cinder over the years, were a little ashamed of the warmth and friendliness that seemed to glow from the man now. He put his arm around Eddie's shoulder and said, 'I am going to ask our beloved chief guest, Appa Achrekar, to address us now.'

'Two years ago, I had predicted that Eddie Coutinho would be the star pupil in the locality. I was wrong.'

Just by itself Appa's rabble-rouser voice would have echoed in the four corners of the CWD chawls. With the mike and speakers, it resounded like the voice of God Himself calling man to heed Him while there was still time.

'Eddie Coutinho is the finest pupil of the Sabha in the whole of Bombay state. Nobody in the past, not a single student, has got the grades he has got in every single subject. Gym, drill, physical exercises, martial arts, spiritual singing, lezhim, he's got the highest scores ever. As if all this were not enough, just a few minutes ago, he gave us a rendering of the Mahabharata, the likes of which I have never heard before. And all this in a language, our dearly beloved Marathi Maiboli, that he had not spoken till he joined our Sabha. When I heard him talk of Abhimanyu and the rain of arrows that fell upon that great hero in the very flower of youth, I said to myself, Eddie Coutinho is Abhimanyu brought back to life. There is no doubt in my mind that Eddie Coutinho is the reincarnation of not just Abhimanyu but of all our glorious Hindu traditions.

'In my seventy-five years of life I have not, I have to admit, ever been so moved. I had goose-flesh on my body.

'Eddie Coutinho, mark my words, for my prophecies have always come true, will be one of the great leaders of the Sabha. Our tradition and our future are safe in the hands of people like Eddie Coutinho.'

There was thunderous applause. In the distance, Eddie saw a dot. Actually, it was two dots, a big dot accompanied by a small one. The big dot seemed to cast a shadow on Eddie even from that distance. The shadow grew bigger by the second just as it had in the story of the prodigal son that Appa had told two years ago.

There's a time to dawdle and a time to run. Eddie knew that it was time to run for his life. He shot out but Lele Guruji's hand clamped him firmly on the shoulder.

'In appreciation of the extraordinary work Eddie Coutinho has done, we have had to create a special new award for him.'

The big dot was running now. The little dot had difficulty keeping up with it.

'He is our first Star of Hindustan.'

Even now there was time to escape. He jerked his shoulder and tried to push Lele Guruji's hand away. There she stood life-size, his mother Violet, and panting behind her was his sister, Pieta. As Lele Guruji steered him to Appa, Eddie caught a glimpse of Pieta trying to pull his mother away. There was dismay and sympathy in Pieta's eyes. Eddie loved her then as he had never loved anybody before. He knew that Pieta's gesture was futile and he loved her all the more for it.

'Strange, I thought I heard the words Eddie Coutinho reverberate in our chawl. Sewing night and day makes me feel giddy at times. I must be imagining things, I said. Then I heard it again and again and again. I looked out of the window trying to trace the source of the loudspeaker. How can it be, I said, it's a Hindu gathering.'

Appa's hand was not as steady as his voice. He was having trouble pinning the 22-carat gold medal on Eddie's shirt.

'I should have known better. That woman downstairs has performed black magic on him and sold him to Satan. But I won't rest till I've exorcized the devil even if it means taking him apart, limb from limb.'

Hurry, please hurry. What was the point, she was already on the dais, she was pushing people aside, now she had the medal in her hands and it was on a parabolic flight over the heads of the audience who watched it as if it were a wondrous talisman. And so it was. It was Lord Krishna's sudershan chakra flashing through the cosmos on an intergalactic mission. But Eddie knew that it had lost its homing instincts and would never come back.

And now Violet was hauling her prodigal son down the dais. Eddie's foot slipped, got caught in the jute matting that covered the steps and twisted, but that didn't stop her, she marched into the crowd and past them on to the road, her strides had become gargantuan, she seemed to be in a terrible rush, Eddie was no longer trying to keep pace with her, she had him by the wrist and she was never going to let go, passers-by and people in buses and cars and cabs stared at them and the girl running after them, with tears the size of the Kohinoor diamond, sobbing, 'Let him go, Mamma, please.' She turned the corner and was in the compound of St Sebastian's Church, another set of steps and they were inside, Father D'Souza was in the nave talking to some elderly woman, and Eddie was flung at the foot of the altar.

If he could have, Father D'Souza would have asked, 'What now?' Instead he said, 'What can I do for you, Mrs Coutinho?'

'Please carry on, Father. I do not wish to interrupt.' Violet folded her arms and stood intrusively, pointedly ignoring Father D'Souza's companion.

'It was nothing of consequence, really,' the elderly woman said a little too eagerly and backed away.

'Exorcize him,' Violet commanded the priest. The elderly woman left in a hurry. 'He's joined the people downstairs and become an idol worshipper.'

~

Everybody can excuse herself or himself and get away. Not me though. Why does she always come to me? She behaves as if there isn't any other priest in the parish. Father D'Souza sometimes wondered whether Violet Coutinho thought he was Eddie's father merely because he had been present at his birth. For every little thing—unfortunately for every big thing too—she marched into the church with her son. If he was not there, she came over to the school. And if he was not there either, she sent a peon to fetch him from his room in the priests' quarters. It didn't matter whether he was taking a class, talking to some other parent, hearing a confession or lying stone dead with overwork, she stood her ground. She stood politely enough. She had dignity and presence. But there was no way you could ignore her. As always, he knew she was on the premises long before he saw her. That strong palpable bouquet of unspoken grief and grievance preceded her. She was like a fine fish bone stuck between your teeth. There was no relief, you couldn't pay attention to anything else until you had attended to her.

What was it with her boy, always getting into trouble, doing things he wasn't supposed to do, asking questions to which he, Father D'Souza, had no answers. But the problem didn't end there. It was an odd sensation chastising Eddie, for he often made Father D'Souza feel as if he had victimized an innocent.

Father D'Souza listened to Violet's tale with growing alarm. He had to admit that the matter was more serious than life and death, for it was obvious that Eddie's immortal soul was in jeopardy. You had to give Violet credit. She was seized of the gravity of the situation and had acted with admirable dispatch to contain the damage.

'Are you telling me that your mother is lying? That you never said Hindu prayers?' The anger rose in him like red steam but again he had the impression that Eddie had forced a reversal of roles, leaving him with a sense of guilt.

'I did, but they meant nothing to me. I wanted to learn to use the wooden staff, both to attack and to defend. I like wrestling and I loved to hear the stories that Lele Guruji told.'

The instant he volunteered that last bit of information Eddie realized that he had crossed the taboo line and revealed what his mind had automatically screened out all these years.

'What kinds of stories?'

'Stories from the Mahabharata.'

'And?'

'Stories of Krishna.' Eddie remembered to drop the title Lord in the nick of time. 'Rama, Shankar, Ganesh, Indra, Shivaji, hundreds of stories.'

'What did I tell you? He has sold his soul and worshipped pagan gods.' Violet said this almost triumphantly.

'I didn't. I didn't.' Eddie was close to tears.

'Did it never occur to you that you were committing a heinous sin listening to these stories?'

'No, they were stories, just like any other stories. Even the Bible has stories. Lele Guruji told us those too.'

'How dare you compare the Bible with these idol-worshippers' tales? The Bible is the word of God, the one and only true God.'

'Those people say the Gita is the word of God.' With the stabbing pain of betrayal, Eddie realized that he was already referring to his former friends as those people.

'And you believe them?' Father D'Souza's wrath now knew no bounds. He looked at Violet. It was as if he needed her to corroborate and seal Eddie's guilt. 'Or are you going to believe me and your mother? And Jesus our Saviour who gave his life to save sinners like you?'

Eddie looked up at the statue of Jesus way above him at the back of the church. It had never occurred to him to betray this gentle Son of God whose suffering he could never bear to look at. Why then were his mother and Father D'Souza so angry with him and making such a terrible fuss?

'Do you know the price of worshipping anyone but our Lord God Jesus Christ? Excommunication.'

That word had been explained to Eddie several times. There was nothing worse that could happen to you. But he knew something worse than that word. It was the awful sound of it. That 'X' seemed to shut him out. It was like a sound-proof, one-way glass door. He could see everybody but they couldn't see him. They never would, though he was just an outstretched hand away from them. There was a finality about it that seemed to press down and crush the very essence of his life and asphyxiate him. It was an inflatable word that grew bigger and bigger. It spilled over and pushed out the moon and Mars and Venus and Jupiter and the sun and all the galaxies till there was no space left and then it squeezed him out over the edge.

Father D'Souza must have realized that Eddie did not

understand the full implications of the word. 'You know what that means?' He proceeded to give him a vivid exegesis which paradoxically shrank the word and brought it under control.

'Your soul will burn in hell forever.'

A sob escaped Eddie and then he couldn't stop crying for the sheer relief it gave him.

'Repent in front of our Lord and promise never to go to any other Hindu meeting and never to worship any other god but the true God, our Lord Jesus Christ.'

Eddie hesitated for a moment, wondering what was expected of him.

'Go down on your knees.' Father D'Souza pressed down on Eddie's shoulder till he sank to his knees; and then he retrieved for Jesus Christ a soul that He had never lost. 'Repent and promise. Or I'll excommunicate you from the house of God and the life hereafter.'

'I promise. I promise.' Eddie spoke with such fervour and conviction that even Father D'Souza was pleased.

'Promise to strangle and break the neck of that viper who was responsible for banishing us from paradise, Satan himself, every time he raises his head in your bosom.'

'I promise. I promise.'

'Promise to ask Mother Mary to intervene on your behalf with our Lord Jesus Christ and beg her to ask his forgiveness every day of your life.'

'I promise. I promise.'

'Now say a hundred Hail Marys, every day for a whole year. May the Lord find it in his heart to forgive you.'

'Yes, Father.'

'Rise my son.' Father D'Souza felt good. He had that rare sense of a job well done. He felt cleansed. He put his hand on Eddie's head as he rose.

'Is it true that Ravan, the boy who stays below us, killed my father?'

Father D'Souza had the fleeting thought that if he didn't withdraw his hand it would attach itself to Eddie's head as with a resinous glue and nothing but sawing it off at the arm would ever separate them. He wasn't taking any chances. He pulled his hand away harshly. You couldn't ever be off your guard with this boy. Even when you had just saved his soul and begun to trust him, he would spring a rotten question on you and drag you all the way down to perdition.

'Who told you that?'

'Mummy.'

Father D'Souza looked at Violet reproachfully. She stared back at him defiantly.

'It was an accident.'

Nine

'Ravan.'

Ravan rose. The disembodied voice came from behind him. He would recognize it long after he was dead. Prakash. Tyrant, terror and a youth of prodigious powers. Prakash was sixteen. He had plugged the fifth grade six times and finally caught up with Ravan's class. There was only one way to stay out of his orbit. Go and live on another planet, not the closer ones but Saturn or Jupiter. Or better still, pick another galactic system. Even the teachers left Prakash alone.

He wasn't particularly large or tall but to Ravan and his peers he appeared a colossus. They did his homework, bought cigarettes for him and wiped his four-by-two inch mirror on the seat of their shorts when he wished to comb his hair. He was the only one in the school who had a pair of closed shoes. They were made of buffalo hide but had the sheen of patent leather. Ravan (or whoever else was summoned first thing in the morning) wiped the dust off the top of his shoes, applied daubs of Kiwi shoe polish with his fingers, brushed them steadily for seven minutes—'lightly, you arsehole, this is delicate stuff, not your coarse hide—and then polished them again till the leather shone blindingly in the sunlight.

The fifth-grade students had no difficulty rendering these services willingly and with dispatch. The world, as Ravan well knew, was divided into slaves and slave-drivers. And then there were those who owned the slave-drivers. He was intelligent enough to realize that he would never be located on the same side of the fence as Prakash. But the source of Ravan's and his colleagues' awe lay elsewhere.

'Watch this,' Prakash had said six months back to seven of his slaves after class. The school building was deserted. Prakash presided sitting at the head of the staircase while the bonded labourers sat on the steps below. The boys fell silent. His eyes passed over and took in each individual face. What was he going to do? Swallow a sword? Ask them to rob a bank? He undid his fly and exposed his penis. There was nothing spectacular about it. Just like mine and Chandrakant's and everybody else's in class, thought Ravan. Prakash Sonavane began to stroke it gently. Is he trying to pee, I can do it without all this show.

It was odd. As Prakash stroked the length of his member, it grew in length. How did he do it? Ravan was mesmerized. It took a little time for him to register that it had also grown in body and width, frankly it had swollen monstrously as if Prakash was pumping air into it. Suddenly it went rigid. Its head looked dopey like the pictures of whales he had seen except that this thing had a vertical slit instead of a horizontal one. 'It's going to burst,' Ravan blurted in panic.

'It's a gun. See that hole, that's where the bullets come from.' He swung it wildly, then pointed it at Naresh. 'Shall I shoot?' Naresh cringed and shrank back. 'Does anybody have the guts to challenge me?' Ravan thought it was an absurd question. Not even in his most megalomaniacal dream would it occur to him to cross Prakash.

'You smirking, Ravan, you smirking at me?' Prakash grabbed hold of Ravan's hair and yanked him down. Ravan fought shy of the barrel of the gun but Prakash held him firmly. 'Open your mouth, you son of a bitch, or I'll blow your brains out.'

Ravan opened his mouth. Before he knew it, the gun had rammed into the back of his throat. It pressed into his windpipe and choked him. His gullet reacted violently to the presence of a foreign body and tried to regurgitate it but Prakash's hand continued to press his head forward. Ravan's knees began to give and his eyes bulged out dangerously. He heard Prakash's irritated voice. It seemed strangely muted. 'Close your mouth, asshole, close it.' Despite his fast-ebbing consciousness Ravan responded to the instructions and snapped his mouth shut. Prakash let out a cry of such intensity and urgency, it slapped Ravan out of the darkness descending upon him.

'Fuck, fuck, fuck you, you son of a bitch, you bit my cock off.' Prakash was nursing his genitals as if they were the last of a rare and fragile species while performing a frenetic dance. Ravan's classmates were in an uproar, rolling down the stairs. Ravan never forgave them.

The general mirth got to Ravan and he began to smile. Prakash looked at him. Ravan knew he was in trouble. Prakash brought Ravan's head down sharply and shoved his penis back into his mouth. 'All right, wise guy.' The place had fallen so silent, Ravan could hear the words like coins ringing on a metal floor. 'Close your mouth. Gently. And suck.' He pulled Ravan's head back and pushed it forward. 'In-Out. In-Out. In-Out.' The minutes passed. Ravan was close to tears. His jaw ached and his head was ready to split for lack of oxygen. He was discovering a whole new geography of pain down his spinal column. There was a skyward crick in his neck and it sang and zinged spottily across his back.

'Exhausted, asshole? Go on. Go on. Up. Down. And don't vary the pace.'

What was Prakash talking about? His head was in a fog which was emanating from between his eyes. What would the bullet do? Was there one bullet or many? Would it explode in his head? Would it traverse through and leave a hole with burnt edges and lodge itself into the rear wall?

Ravan felt Prakash's grip on his head slacken while his body tautened. His hands and legs twitched and jerked in an uncoordinated fashion. He leaned back, his thighs caught Ravan's head and squeezed it hard, went lax and then tightened again. Ravan surmised that Prakash was having a fit. Gangadhar Thate from the third floor in CWD Chawl No. 14 suffered from them. He would get them anywhere, on the staircase, in the toilet, on the playground. They came without warning and he collapsed on the spot. You had to rush and insert a stick or Yo-Yo between his teeth and hold a smashed onion, the sole of a shoe or an ammonia bottle over his nose.

Prakash was moaning now. Deep, long sighs. He was obviously in pain. Ravan tried to pull his head away. He wanted to put a notebook between Prakash's teeth but Prakash wouldn't let go of his hair. As a matter of fact he was pulling back and forth in a frenzied fashion. Suddenly he became inert and something leaked into Ravan's mouth. It was thick and sticky and sweet with an acidic after-taste. Sala, jerk, the swine had peed in his mouth. He spat it out. It was white and cloudy like gum and not even a mouthful. Couldn't be pee, what the hell was it?

'You shit. You spat it out?' Prakash was not only awake and wide alert, he was beside himself with rage. 'Don't you dare. Ever. Lick it. Lick it.'

Ravan stared at Prakash uncomprehendingly. He was willing to do almost anything for him but why drink pee. His line of thought was cut midway as Prakash caught him by the neck and pressed his head to the grey tiled floor.

'Lick, you asshole, lick. It's precious stuff, my seed. Within nine months you are going to have a baby. Everyone in our class is going to bear my sons. The girls from the Lady Sirur School will bear my daughters. Naresh, it's your turn tomorrow. You watched Ravan, so I won't have to teach you again.'

~

'Ravan.'

Was it his turn to service Prakash today? No, as far as he could remember, it was next Tuesday. So what did he want? You never could tell. His shoes were shimmering but that wouldn't dissuade Prakash from asking him to shine them again. Besides, there were times when he wanted to be sucked six or seven times a day.

He could ask for anything, just about anything, so long as it wasn't about the baby. As far as he was aware, and admittedly his knowledge in these matters was limited, only women delivered babies. But Prakash was no ordinary mortal. Did you see what he could do with his cock? Amazing, nobody but nobody he knew could pull that off. And anyway, whether men and boys could bear babies or not, he knew he was pregnant. He felt a heaviness in his belly, in the first four months he had thrown up frequently. There were days when his stomach stood out a mile and a half and Prakash himself had put his ear a little below his ribcage and felt and heard the baby turn.

'Where will it come from?' Ravan had asked him. 'From your navel, where else? It will tear open your stomach as the god Narasimha did. Your intestines will be flung on the floor, all two hundred and twenty yards of them. Wind them neatly the way your mother winds wool and put them back carefully. You'll bleed a lot, the whole floor will be wet, drink it up quickly and then breastfeed the baby. If I hear that you've been starving my child, I'll kill you.'

When was the baby coming? It was way past nine months.

Why, you may well ask, didn't Ravan spearhead a revolt against Prakash? He could have tossed Prakash with a flick of his wrist, made him turn seven continuous cartwheels in the air, broken his back, shoved his toe in his crotch and unmanned him for life. He could have… but the truth was a little less flamboyant. In time Ravan would become highly accomplished in tae kwon do. But right now it was only an academic discipline. You practised in class, at home, in the open playgrounds in the CWD chawls but it had nothing to do with real life. Even later when he understood that tae kwon do could be used defensively against bullies, local dadas and toughs, he would find it difficult, if not impossible, to translate his skills into an instant physical response. But that's still missing the point altogether. Ravan was not even twelve yet while Prakash was not just older but brutish, aggressive and vindictive. Whatever his physical dimensions he was a malevolent colossus.

Prakash ran towards Ravan and put his hand on Ravan's shoulder. What was wrong? Prakash never even walked up to anyone. He called, you ran. He had an odd look in his eyes. 'Is it true you killed Eddie Coutinho's father?'

This is the end. The absolute end. The final end. The last final end. There was no point asking how he'd found out. Obviously Eddie had told him. Prakash was going to make him pay for it, with his life, what else.

'And Gandhi? Mahatma Gandhi?' Ravan still didn't answer. 'Look at me. I heard Godse and you killed him.'

Chandrakant, Chandrakant Dixit, you were my friend, my closest friend. How could you do this to me?

'Boy, you're some guy. A real chhupa Rustum.' So, he was a murderer. The whole world but he knew about it. Ravan couldn't and wouldn't look at Prakash.

'I want you to kill my stepmother. I'll give you twenty rupees.'

~

It was now over two months since Prakash had made his request. It had not thrown Ravan. He wasn't even flabbergasted. He simply blanked it out of his mind. You could call it his best career move to date. It was also one of his most important lessons in life and commerce. Like the kernel of a fable or parable, it would stay buried in his mind but affect his actions. Perhaps even when he grew up he wouldn't be able to articulate the moral of the experience, but it wouldn't be the less potent or real for that. He understood that many things, if not everything in life, were for sale and had a price on them, especially the illicit, the immoral and evil. He also began to realize that tides can change, tables can turn, roles switch and those in power become supplicants.

Prakash misunderstood his silence. He raised the ante from twenty to fifty, then to seventy-five.

'Hundred and twenty-five,' he said, 'that's all the money I have.' More than the escalating price on Prakash's stepmother's head, Ravan was struck by the change in his voice. It was uncertain and insistent.

'I'll think about it.'

Ravan tried to avoid Prakash. He could feel his eyes on him from across the classroom during the next few weeks. Occasionally he came over and lingered politely.

'When are you going to do it?' He finally got hold of Ravan while they were on their way to the physical-training class in the school courtyard.

'I haven't said yes yet.'

'Please Ravan, I know the money's not enough but I'll get more, even if I have to steal it and pay you later.'

That was the first time Ravan looked Prakash in the face. His teeth were beginning to stain with the tobacco he chewed and smoked. The lock of hair he had trained so carefully to curl upon itself on his forehead had come undone. What had made Ravan think of him as a giant? He was taller and he shaved and he had a moustache, but he no longer loomed over Ravan like a calamity and there was not much in him to hold in awe. Ravan wouldn't dare say it to himself even now, but with the lower lip of his mouth perpetually hanging slack, Prakash looked a mutt. He had to concentrate hard and long to get the drift of the simplest things. He had room for only a couple of thoughts in his head at a time and any new idea made him ill-humoured and suspicious. Ravan wondered why it had taken him so many weeks since the day Prakash had broached the subject of his stepmother to feel a sense of release and relief. He was a little confused. Did the source of the power that Prakash had exercised reside in Prakash or in Ravan himself?

Life, that most hackneyed of teachers, but also the freshest, was about to teach Ravan another lesson. If you did not show curiosity and were patient, human beings would tell you their entire life-stories, spew out every single sour and rancid detail.

'You don't know my stepmother. I was a king before she came. My mother died two years after I was born and it's six or seven years since my sister got married. My father lived for me. What I said was law. Anything I wanted I got. The headmaster complained about my attendance and performance in school. My father didn't believe a word of what he said. I could do no wrong. The headmaster threatened to throw me out. My father said he would talk to the minister. I guess you don't know that my father works at the Secretariat. He's a peon in the Ministry of Education. I was the apple of my father's eye. Until she came into our lives.

'It was my mother's mother who arranged the whole thing. For years my father had refused to remarry. God knows they tried a dozen times every year. Then out of the blue this nineteen-year-old tart turns up, she's a third or fourth cousin of mine, flashes her teeth and makes eyes at my father and my father suddenly insists I need a new mother. She's done some black magic, I swear to you, I can't recognize my father. He puts dye in his hair and takes her to the movies at least twice a week, this man who couldn't bear to watch a film. As for me, he doesn't even remember he has a son. Hemlata this and Hemlata that, it's Hemlata morning, noon and night. Can't wait for me to go to sleep. Before it's ten-thirty he's busy picking up her sari. Doesn't get enough of it at night, so he's begun to take days off from work. A man who never in his entire career took a day off, not even when my mother died. Just cremated her, took a shower and went straight to work, the minister won't know where the files are, he said. Now the same man says the minister can look for the files himself if he needs them that badly, or the country can come to a standstill, he doesn't give a damn. Nobody's been as conscientious as I've been, he says, and all I've got to show for it is one measly watch they gave me after twenty-five years of service and that too stopped working a long time ago. High time I took it easy, he says, and you, you Prakash, get off your bloody arse. I'm not going to support you all your life, you fail this year and you're out, out of school and out of this house too. I know that bitch has been whispering in his ear, that's the reason he's been giving me a hard time. He says to me, you can take up a job and find a place of your own. And if you don't fancy that, too bad, four months is all you've got to shape up. And don't look at your mother, I'll smash your bloody face if I ever catch you eyeing her that way. Hemlata was telling me that you talk back to her and call her Lata. You watch your mouth, boy, if you want any teeth left in it. You'll call her Mother and touch her feet every morning. And the bitch stands there plaiting her hair and nodding her head and smiling sweetly at me.

'Do you understand the hell I must be going through? No child I know has ever been put through such torture. Save me, Ravan. Snuff that woman out.'

~

It was about a week after this overwrought confession that Rajeev Borade slipped a dirty crumpled envelope into Ravan's hand during the geography class. Ravan excused himself and went down to pee.

My dear Ravan,

Please cut off my father's left hand. He's a leftie. He hit me yesterday because I stole eight annas to go thrice on the merry-go-round and to buy ice-fruit at the Mahashivratri fair. Once he has no left hand, all he'll be able to do is wave his stub in the air when he wants to bash me up. And he'll lose his job too.

Am enclosing three rupees and seventy paise.

Yours gratefully,
Rajeev

~

Ravan buttoned up his shorts, left the lavatory and sat down on the lowest step of the staircase. He felt drained by the first intimations of the power of evil. It would be the source of his ethical ambivalence at many critical moments in later years. He had never been so confused in his life. Nothing had given him as much pain and as many nightmares as the discovery that he was a murderer. He had lost his sleep and he had lost weight. He was ashamed to walk among human beings for fear that they would recognize him for what he was: a parricide. A killer of not just an unborn baby's father but the killer, albeit part-killer, of the father of the nation.

Now all of a sudden everybody knew his past and instead of spitting on him and running away from his very shadow, they were seeking him out, asking him to commit the most terrible crimes and paying him cash, not on delivery but in advance. He felt a delirious sense of power. He also felt like throwing up.

Was this his vocation? Was he born with a career which he was too opaque to recognize? Should he give up school? There was clearly a lot of money in this business. His mother Parvati wouldn't have to slave all day and half the night. He could buy her a nice bed and place it on the other side of the room, opposite his father's.

~

The next morning when he was going home, Sudhir Salunke accosted him. He was a little incoherent and took a good deal of time to come to the point but the gist of what he said was clear enough. The landlord of Sudhir's chawl was threatening to evict his family because they hadn't been able to pay rent for the last seven months. Sudhir's father had told the landlord that he was about to get his job back but the landlord was adamant. Would Ravan please dispatch the man, name and address—Mr J.V. Sardesai, 49, Jamshedji Road, Nana Chowk. They could negotiate a price to be paid half in advance, half after commission of services.

The most memorable day in Ravan's new-found calling occurred a fortnight later. When he returned home from school, his mother rushed him into the kitchen and said in a hushed voice, 'There's a letter for you.'

'For me?' There was as much awe in Ravan's voice as in Parvati's. She handed him an envelope.

'I didn't want it to fall into his hands,' she said pointing in the direction of his father's bed.

Parvati gave him a knife to open the envelope but he decided to have his cup of tea and the snacks his mother always served him after school, first. He had not felt so important even when Prakash had approached him with his momentous request.

He wiped his hands on his shorts and sliding the knife into the sealed flap of the envelope, sliced it open.

'What does it say?' his mother asked before he unfolded the lined notepaper on which the letter was written.

'It's private.' Ravan had yet to read it. Parvati was taken aback by this unexpected answer. She looked at Ravan with new respect.

My dear Ravan,

My father beats my mother, me and my nine brothers and sisters every night. Yesterday he hit my mother with my cricket bat and broke open her forehead. We had to take her to hospital. The doctors gave her seven stitches and have kept her under observation.

Will you please help me and my family? God won't. He never hears any of my prayers. All of us will owe you an everlasting debt of gratitude if you get rid of our father. I would not ask you to do this if he thrashed just me and my brothers but I can't bear to see him hitting my mother. If we don't stop him now, he'll kill all of us. Last night he threatened to do just that when we said we wanted to take my mother to the hospital. He was in a bad temper this morning and bashed my oldest sister and stopped only when she fainted.

You need not fear about what will happen to all of us after his death. Half the time, my father does not go to work. When he does, he spends most of his money on drink. I'll take up a job somewhere. My two older sisters are already working as servants. We'll manage.

Please do something soon. You are a real saint.

Yours gratefully,
Ashok

P.S. Do not worry about money. My brothers and I will pay you every month all your life.

~

Subtly over the next few weeks, the centre of power in school shifted. Nobody kowtowed to Prakash any longer. He didn't seem to demand it either. He was now one of the boys. But while people began to treat Ravan with deference, it was all covert and never spelled out. Even when they came to ask him for favours, there was something furtive and clandestine about their requests. Most of them like Ashok Sane preferred to write.

'Ravan.' It was Prakash.

'Are you going to kill my stepmother or not? Or are you just so much hot air? And all those tales about your earlier murders nothing but lies?'

'Yelling won't get you anywhere. Neither will your impatience.'

'No more talk. Give me a fixed date.'

'Your stepmother, you yourself admitted, is doing black magic. The only antidote for black magic is stronger black magic. The stars have to be right and you have to perform very expensive rituals and ceremonies. All you've got is a piddling hundred and twenty-five rupees. One false move and her ghost will sit on your neck and drink your blood every night. If you are unhappy with the way I'm handling things, go and get somebody else to get rid of your stepmother.'

'I'm sorry, really sorry. I thought you were going to kill her with a knife or shoot her with bullets, the way you killed Gandhi. Now I understand, but please do it fast. I can't take it any more.'

Damn. He had escaped for the moment but what was he going to do? Couldn't God make him disappear? How was he going to face all these people? If he didn't deliver fast, they would turn on him and maybe lynch him. Every day for the past two months he had avoided confronting the two questions that needed urgent answers. How was he going to live up to all these people's expectations of him? How was he going to commit these dire acts? He couldn't for the life of him recall how he had terminated his first two victims.

'Run, Ravan, run.' Ashok Sane almost knocked Ravan down as he ran the length of the school corridor in search of him during the recess. Prakash's looking for you and...'

Too late. The rest of Ravan's class watched silently as Prakash Sonavane got his hands around Ravan's neck.

'I told you to kill my stepmother, not my father, you bastard.' He was crying like a child. His nose was running and he couldn't make up his mind whether to wipe it or throttle Ravan first. He wanted to speak. He had perforce to take his hanky out and blow his nose. 'I'm going to kill you. Give my father back to me. Or I'll kill you.' His hands were back at Ravan's throat.

'Do you want the black magic to kill you too?' Prakash withdrew his hands as if he had touched live electric wires. Ravan may not have known what black magic was or how it operated but he had no doubt in his mind that there was black magic in the world and that he was an old hand at it. How else could you explain the words that had escaped his lips just now? He certainly hadn't spoken them. He had never wished Prakash's father ill, let alone dead. He had never even wished any harm to Prakash's stepmother. And yet Prakash's old man was dead. All because of him. Did he need any more proof that he was a murderer?

Ten

❖

'I'll do as I please.'
'No, you won't.'
'It's my life.'
'No longer. You've got two children.'

Mother and daughter were not shouting at each other. It was the intense hostility in his mother's voice that had woken up Eddie.

'They are doing okay.'
'They would if their mother was all right.'
'Are you suggesting that I'm not right in the head?'
'You are a hard, bitter woman in whom all love has dried up.'
'What do you expect of a widow who has to work twelve to fourteen hours a day to feed her children, not to mention you.'
'You were a hard and bitter woman even when Victor was alive.'
'That's not true. I tried. I tried my best till the end.'
'He tried, not you. He tried to win you over in every way he could. He bought you pearls. That gold necklace you're wearing he bought you for giving him a daughter. He took you to the cinema, he tried taking you to dances but you pursed up your lips at everything.'

'You're lying.'

'You are lying to yourself, Violet. You never forgave him for marrying you.'

'Mummy, if you go on any more about the past, I'm going to stop talking to you.'

'I don't want to talk about the past. I'm trying to get you to live in the present.'

'By getting me married off again?'

'You are still young. There's no point denying your body. You need a husband.'

'I don't need anybody.'

'Your children need a father. He'll be firm but not inflexible like you. They can go to college instead of starting to work as soon as they finish school. He'll earn money as the man of the house should. You can take it easy and not work like a dog.'

'I don't mind working for my children.'

'All I'm asking you to do is to see Mr Furtado. If you don't like him, forget him. There will be many others.'

~

And I thought you were on our side. How could you do this to me, Granna? It was shameful the way Granna was carrying on, trying to get his mother to marry Machado, Furtado, Figuereido or someone as bad. What did they need a man for, they had got along fine without one for the last eleven years or so and would do so for the next hundred.

When he was a child he had two names. He was called Eddie at home and Poor Eddie by almost everybody outside. (Poor Eddie but never Poor Pieta. Not that he minded, but it struck him as a little odd, after all they shared the same father.) He surmised that he was poor because he had no father, and he did pretty well for himself out of his fatherless state. People, especially women, got a wet, emotional look in their eyes and went into their kitchens and got him something, usually a sweet, to eat. His mother whacked him a couple when she caught him polishing off these morsels of pity, but that didn't deter him from looking dolefully into the eyes of mothers whose children continued to have fathers.

Some time back, Mrs D'Costa gave him a shirt and a pair of shorts. He had a hunch that his mother would not approve of his latest acquisitions and hid them under the rest of his clothes in the bottom drawer. But nothing escaped her eyes and in no time at all she uncovered the culprit shirt and shorts. The ferocity and violence of her reaction left him breathless. She took it as a personal affront that Mrs D'Costa had presumed to gift him clothes. She threatened to throw him out of the house. He had not gone asking for the clothes but she called him a beggar and an emotional blackmailer and ordered him to take them back that very instant. He was about to leave with his head hanging in shame when, to his even greater horror, she decided to accompany him.

'It was indeed very kind of you to give your ninth child's hand-me-downs after they had seen service with your first eight,' she told Mrs D'Costa. 'I'm afraid you'll have to look for someone else to give them to or wait till you have your next one since we do not care to be the objects of your charity.'

Time had blunted people's memories. And even if they remembered that he was 'Poor' Eddie, it didn't often send them scurrying for a chocolate or marzipan.

He was not quite sure what role fathers played in families. His field sample was the thirty-nine other Catholic families who lived on his floor. Wherever there was a father, a living one, there seemed to be a hell of a lot of children and the mothers were pregnant round-the-clock. There was not a moment when a chorus of babies, half a million on his floor and a zillion lower down, was not raising alarms in all five continents of the earth. The Castellinos had seven, four girls and three boys, and Mrs Castellino perpetually walked with her hands clasped around her jutting belly. The Rozarios had three but they had been married only five years. The De Penhas had nine. He wasn't sure but it looked as if Mrs De Penha was beginning to show signs of another pregnancy. The record-holder was Mrs Aranha. She had eleven and you wouldn't believe it if you saw Mr Aranha, he was so old, wispy and forgetful. But he had got another baby in the works. The Correas had five, Pereiras six, Mirandas nine, Almeidas four, Rodriguezes seven. Eddie could have gone on in this fashion for another fifteen neighbours. At least twenty of them had grown-up children who would start making babies any moment now.

If he got a new father, the man would work and earn money and from what he gathered, his mother would stop working. He had no idea if there was much of a difference between what his mother earned and what the newcomer would make. It seemed doubtful if, apart from the switch in the role of breadwinner, there would be much more money coming in. The only other thing that seemed certain was that babies would start rolling in. Whatever extra the new man earned would be wiped out by the new mouths that would have to be fed. His mother, as a matter of fact, would have no alternative but to start working again. So much for his mother's life becoming easier. As to babies, that was a subject that Eddie wasn't even willing to contemplate. Did you see how the Da Cunha's Cyril popped out his yellow-brown, semi-solid shit? Celebrated his third birthday last week and yet did it standing, you won't believe it, he even did it while he walked. If you went to any of the homes on Eddie's floor, they always reeked of unformed milky shit and at any time there were at least fifteen to twenty-five cloth nappies strung up on clothes-lines criss-crossing the room and giving off a sick, moist smell. The latest child of that endless mother, Mrs Aranha, was unquestionably the most beautiful baby in the world, so beautiful that the usually circumspect and cautious Eddie had impulsively taken her in his arms and what do you think had happened? She had bobbed up and down and gurgled away happily while throwing up all over Eddie's shirt-front and shoulder.

And where were all those babies that his mother would inevitably have, going to sleep? Even more important, where was the Man going to sleep? In his mother's bed? Perish the thought. And what was this intruder, this destroyer of the Coutinho family's peace, to be called? Eddie could not, even in his thoughts, bring himself to call him by the name children use for the husbands of their mothers. And the brats? As it was, it took a superhuman effort to cope with that arch-nemesis of his life, his legitimate sister, Pieta. But these half-blood, half siblings of his, what was he to do with them? Was his mother going to ask him to rock them to sleep, clean their mess and wipe their butts, listen to them screaming all day long and all through the night, make baby-talk and entertain them while the lord and master of the house took his ease?

But perhaps the Man would not take his ease but raise Cain instead as a lot of the men in the CWD chawls did. There were many things that a displaced Goan male missed in Bombay: siestas, foreign goods (until Goa lost its colonial status and started, according to some, the process of assimilation, decline and fall into the Indian subcontinent), cashewnuts, mangoes, feni, dances, all-night revelry—but his sense of deprivation was most acute in the matter of booze. It was not as cheap as air, but the price of beer in Goa was the next-best thing to getting it free.

And there was no sin in it, whereas in Bombay and most of India it was undoubtedly one of the cardinal sins. Most Goan men continued to drink but their imbibing became as joyless as that of the rest of India's population. In Goa drinking was badinage and banter, good spirits, theatre, political and social commentary that encompassed everybody including the non-drinkers in its good cheer. In Bombay it was a lonely and solitary business, even when you sat with others. More like work than fun. It was an act of rebellion, perhaps the only one available. The men sat in speakeasies or occasionally brought the stuff home and drank it dutifully till they became boisterous, then morose and finally unconscious. Between maudlin and stuporous, it was touch and go. The men suddenly wanted to get even with the world and beat up all and sundry, including their wives.

Did the sought after stranger drink? And would he too, like Mr Sequeira, Mr Cardoz, Mr Pereira and so many others wallop Eddie and Pieta?

~

'He had taken a month's leave. He couldn't wait for me to get out of the house. I was never at home anyway.' It was difficult for Ravan to keep pace with Prakash's narrative. They were sitting on a bench in the garden on Mazagaon Hill. 'He moved my stuff and mattress into the common balcony. He wanted to hump her all the time. I could hear him struggling at nights trying to get it up. When things got unbearable he took it out on me but never her, never, though she was the cause of his failures and all our troubles. That night when he woke her up, she snapped at him: "Leave me alone, seven tractors won't be able to raise it. I don't know why I got married to an impotent old man." I could hear him whimpering and weeping early in the morning. How I thanked God that she was lying dead to the world and couldn't see this final defeat of my father. Throw her out, throw the bitch out, I kept saying to myself, and everything will be as it was.

'She was serving me dinner two days before he died, I don't know what got into his head, he kicked my thali. "Find some other place for yourself. Your mother has better things to do than wait on you hand and foot all day long. If I see you in this house after Sunday, I'll kill you." I was so flabbergasted, I didn't know what to say. "Where do you want me to go?" I finally managed to ask him. "Go to the Himalayas, walk into the sea for all I care. Eighteen years old and still in the sixth grade." "Seventeen, not eighteen," I yelled at him. Before I knew what was happening, he had slapped me for the first time in my entire life. "Don't you dare talk back to me. What difference does it make, you'll be twenty-six and still in the sixth grade." He said that in front of my stepmother. I felt bloody humiliated. She tried to intervene on my behalf, the bitch, but he wouldn't listen. She brought me another thali and cleaned up the mess on the floor. I sat there stunned but not stunned enough not to wish my father dead. I have never wished for anything so hard. I wanted him dead then and there. I saw a BEST bus lurch to the sixth floor of our building. It speeded towards him. The driver saw him screaming but he didn't veer away. My father ran for cover but the driver kept chasing him and knocked him down. Then he reversed and ran over him again and again and again. Nothing has given me as much pleasure as watching my father die.

'I blamed you for my father's death but knew all the while who was responsible for it. You had warned me about how delicate the whole black magic business is. No wonder everything went wrong. Do you know who the driver of the bus was? It was me. The black magic went wrong because I wished my father dead.'

Prakash always left Ravan exhausted—in the old days with the sheer physical effort Ravan had to put in, and in the last few months with this endless stream of words. It was not a stream, a stream is linear. Prakash's words piled themselves one on top of the other till they formed a heap that became a mountain. The mountain kept rising till it broke through the sky while it pressed down on Ravan until he couldn't breathe. He had lost Prakash several times. He couldn't understand why Prakash's father needed to mount his stepmother. What was supposed to rise? And why would he want to beat his own prick? But Ravan had learnt to turn off his curiosity and to hold his silence.

'I want that bitch dead, Ravan. Let her pay for her sins. If she hadn't come into our lives, my father and I wouldn't have fallen out. And he wouldn't have gone out of his mind wanting to sleep with her day and night. You better work your magic again. I'll pay you as much as you want once she's dead because all my father's money will come to me.

'Do it quick but let her suffer.'

Prakash's father's death, especially his blaming Ravan for it in public, had one peculiar effect. Ravan wasn't sure whether he was happy about it or distressed. The boys from his school stopped coming over with death wishes. They liked the idea of a hit man but only so long as he didn't kill anyone. Ravan had actually killed a classmate's, albeit an ex-tyrant's, father when he was supposed to have killed the stepmother. The boys treated Ravan with respect but were now clearly afraid of him and kept away. Ravan was relieved by this new development at first but not for long. He was surprised at how happy he felt when Prakash turned up at school after months and spoke to him.

'Can you undo something you've started, Ravan, something that is perhaps on the verge of completion?' Prakash's voice was trembling.

Ravan had got that faraway look in his eyes. He reverted to the stony silence of the sphinx. What did the bugger want now? Prakash was nothing but trouble, always one thing after another.

'Help me, Ravan, please help me. I've made a grievous error. My stepmother is a saint. Please don't kill her. I'll do anything you say, anything. Please, Ravan, please.'

Ravan looked away. He had no idea of how to respond to the metamorphosis of Satan to saint.

'Hell, what's the point of lying to you? You know everything anyway. Hemlata is no longer my stepmother. She and I are, oh what the hell, lovers. She's the most fantastic person I've ever met. I'm going to take up a job and then we're going to get married. Her parents want her to go back, her mother even came and stayed with us a month, but now there's no going back. It's not too late, is it, Ravan? Have you set things in motion that no one can take back?'

Ravan stuck to his silence.

'You have? Oh God what have I done? Please, Ravan, anything, absolutely anything.'

'I don't know. Almost impossible.' Again that other voice, the one that spoke through his mouth but had nothing to do with him.

'Try. Please try.'

'Can't say whether it will work. Cost you a lot of money.'

'Don't worry about money, that's the least of our problems. Just do it, that's all.'

The Prakash episode is good for one last platitude. Money promised is not money in hand.

Reputations, even unfounded ones, are prone to sudden deaths. It was doubtful if within a year or two, any of Ravan's classmates would remember his black-magical powers. Prakash never returned. Ravan heard that the minister under whom Prakash's father had worked had given Prakash a job and that his ex-stepmother, Hemlata, was pregnant.

Eleven

How was Eddie to recognize the Man who was about to change his life forever? Was he tall or short, did he have a limp, did he have thick dark eyebrows, was he fair, was he young or old? Maybe he had a squint and had to wear two-inch-thick lenses. Maybe he was hunchbacked. He dismissed that possibility instantly. Any man who aspired to his mother's hand would have to be good looking.

'Are you Mr Furtado?'

It was getting close to six. If he didn't act quickly the Man would slip through his fingers.

'What?'

'Mr Furtado? Are you Mr Furtado?'

Eddie was keeping a lookout for the gentleman at the corner of Chawl No. 17.

'Do I look like Mr Furtado?'

That was an odd question if he had ever heard one. Did Mr Furtado have his name spelt out on his forehead?

'I don't know.'

'Stupid bugger, don't waste my time.'

The man walked past Eddie and past Chawl No. 17. Eddie realized that the fellow was right. It was stupid of him to take a position at the corner of the building. The only way he could narrow his margin of error was to stand inside the building at the bottom of the stairs. It would be ideal if he positioned himself on his own floor, but Granna was certain to catch him and order him back into the house. She had forced Eddie to put on the white silk shirt and the deep blue trousers that he had worn at her grand-niece Judy's wedding. The trousers didn't quite reach his ankles and they were a little tight around the waist, but Granna, who usually indulged him, was adamant about this choice of garments. She even made him wear a burgundy bow.

'Sit on the bed next to your sister and don't fidget.' Sit next to Pieta, didn't Granna know that she was asking for trouble? Just look at Pieta. You would think Mr Furtado was coming to meet her. She wore a white blouse with puffed sleeves that were gathered with red ribbons and a tutu-like skirt made of sky-blue organza. Her pearly white shoes were topped by blue socks that matched the sheer organza. She had waist-length hair which she thought the Queen of Sheba would have envied. She left it loose and at the slightest pretext shook her head and let it swirl around.

He could have forgiven her anything (and there was much to forgive, according to him, her patronizing airs, her coming first in class in every subject) but the expression on her face. It made him violent. He wanted to scratch it out the way some boys in class ran their nails on the blackboard till everybody dug their fingers into their ears and begged them to stop. Those prissy lips pressing upon each other and that sunny, oh so sunny, holier-than-thou look in her eyes. Not just the eyes, her forehead, her mistily pink cheeks, the almost invisible pores in her flawless complexion, everything told you, 'Look at me. I'm better than you and everybody else you know. Kiss my feet. Now. Because if you don't, I may change my mind and you may never again get an opportunity to do so.' If it meant wiping out her life to wipe out that look, he was willing to do so.

He yanked at the red ribbon on her sleeve which disappeared under the white cloth and resurfaced every couple of centimetres.

Granna had disappeared inside the kitchen where Violet was changing from black cotton to black silk under duress; they could hear Granna insisting that she wear the pearl necklace Victor had given her. 'Granna, Mom, Eddie is tormenting me and has torn out the ribbon from my blouse and ruined my hair and is making it impossible for me to live with him under the same roof.'

How he loathed her at such moments. There was nothing, absolutely nothing, unpredictable about Miss Prim and Preening. Normally Pieta needed to call upon heaven and its Lord of hosts to get a response from Granna. Today things were different. Before she could complete her tirade, Granna had smartly whacked Eddie on his back. 'Not today, Eddie. Not a word to Pieta. And don't touch her. Sit still, do you hear me? And as for you, little Miss Muffet, one more word against your brother and I'll chop off your hair.'

Granna went in and Eddie sprang out of the open door. 'Granna, Eddie's run away though you had told him not to move.' He would have to deal with Pieta some other time, he had more urgent matters on hand. He took off his bow as he ran down the stairs. He would have liked to get into more sensible clothes but there was no time for that.

'Mr Furtado?' He had let five men enter Chawl No. 17 without springing the question on them. They were Hindus and he knew his mother was not about to marry one of them. He wondered how he could separate the Hindus from the Catholics with such assurance. It was not a question of dress. The majority of them wore the same clothes as Catholic men. It was certainly not because they didn't wear a cross on a chain, hardly any Catholic men wore them outside their shirts. Catholics spoke

English and not too many of the Hindus he knew did. But they didn't have to open their mouths for him to tell them apart. So what was it? Was 'Roman Catholic' written in large letters on his people's foreheads and 'Hindu' on theirs? Was it the way they walked or stood or the way they held themselves? Did religion make people look different? Or was it language? Because even among Hindus, he could tell a Gujarati from a Maharashtrian and a Punjabi from a Bengali. Did one's mother tongue leave a permanent mark on one, change the way one's face was set and alter the contours and lines of one's features?

He was intrigued by these questions but had no time for them just now. The rumpled man with an even more rumpled face whom he had just accosted was saying something.

'Which Furtados did you have in mind? The ones from Mhapsa are known as the cashew-kings of the East Indies. They own half of Mhapsa. Very upper crust, their voice carries weight even in Lisbon. The grandsons are a dead loss. Not a patch on their grandfather. He was the enterprising one. Ambitious, ruthless and devious. It was his eldest son, the current head of the family, who consolidated the empire, diversified, went into shipping and mining. His third son Joachim was with me in school, a real wastrel.'

'But are you Mr Furtado?' What was this weirdo talking about? Eddie had run out of patience.

'I guess you could say we are. I'm married to my third cousin. On her mother's side, they have some Furtado blood, not the Mhapsa Furtados, mind you, but the ones from Diu.'

Mother of God, he could have strangled the man. Was he never going to say whether he was Mr Furtado or not.

'Is your wife alive?'

'I resent that question, young man. I deeply resent it. Of course she is...'

There was another man fixing his tie on the first floor-landing. He wore a double-breasted suit with a herringbone pattern. His pallor was ashen. He had thinning hair which he was patting down at that moment. In three leaps Eddie was standing next to him. The suit hung loose on the man, he had obviously lost a lot of weight. He had transparent skin which was stretched thinner than that of an over-inflated balloon. Beads of perspiration stood out on his closely shaven upper lip and the lobes of his ears.

'Are you Mr Furtado?'

The man almost jumped with surprise. 'How did you know?'

'Going up to see Mrs Coutinho?'

'How do you know so much about me?'

Eddie looked around. This fellow was even more nervous than he was.

'Everybody knows.'

'Everybody? How? Have there been others before me?'

Shoot. How was he going to answer this one? He shrugged his shoulders.

'That many? How many?'

'I can't remember.'

'You've lost count? Mary, Mother of God, what am I getting into? Is this Coutinho woman, this Violet, a worldly woman?'

'What's worldly?'

Mr Furtado ignored Eddie's question.

'Does she have any boyfriends?'

The man's transparent fears struck some deep chord within Eddie. They fed his imagination and liberated him. He would have been surprised and hurt had anyone told him he was lying. Life was nothing but a series of possibilities. Why was only one chosen to be reality? Fiction was a fact that had not yet occurred but certainly could. (Would anyone have predicted a fortnight ago that the widow Violet would entertain the idea of getting married again?) By now Eddie's re-working of the truth had more to do with the artistic impulse than the thought of material gain.

He said, 'Lots. Sixty-seven.'

'How do you know the exact number?'

'Arre, everybody in the building knows.'

Eddie's blood tingled. He felt alert and buoyant. It was not merely the exhilaration of inventing a new mother that thrilled him. Instead of her being the boss and putting the brakes on him whenever she felt like it, he could now control her future and reshape her past. Her fate was in his hands. He was able to render Mr Furtado's suspicions prophetic and self-fulfilling.

'Oh,' said Mr Furtado. Eddie could see that it was taking some time for the information to sink in. 'Would you say then that she's a fast woman?'

Eddie didn't quite see his mother as a racing car but he liked the idea.

'Very fast.'

'They have parties?'

'No parties, sharties.' One of Granna's pet phrases came back to Eddie. 'Every day's a carnival.'

'Drinks?'

'Drinks, dance, music. All the neighbours complain but they don't listen.'

'Why don't they call the police?'

'What can the police do?'

'She's got them in her pocket too? Does she also drink?'

'Like a fish.' He saw his mother sprawled out like Mr Mendez in Room 63. Her eyes were glazed, the bottle in her hand empty and she was screaming, 'Sala, give me a drink. Who do you think is paying for it? Your father? I am. With my blood, sweat,' at this point Mr Mendez usually started to cry, 'and tears. See them? See?'

'Then why does she need a husband?'

'To earn money, what else? Granna said once you're there, Ma can take it easy.'

Alarms seemed to go off in Mr Furtado's parchment face. His eyes bulged and he became short of breath.

'Is she your mother?'

Shit, shit, shit, how could I have let that slip out.

'What?' He played for time.

'Why did you call her Ma?'

Eddie was now impatient with the man's obtuseness.

'Because I was repeating what Eddie's grandmother said.'

'What else did she say? I thought at least she would be a decent person.'

'What decent? Everybody in their house is a chor. She said that the children can go to college instead of working because you would look after them.'

'If those witches think they're going to get a slave by putting a ring on my finger, they're in for a surprise. I'm nobody's fool, you tell them that.'

'Yes, I will.'

'No, no. Not yet. What are her children like? Don't be shy. You can be quite frank with me.'

'The mother's a saint compared to the daughter.'

'How old is she?'

'Eleven.' Eddie paused for breath. 'Eat a biscuit, step out to play, come home five minutes late, she'll tattle about everything. She'll take two hours to wash her hair but you take more than five minutes for a bath and she'll scream her head off.'

'Spoilt rotten. And the boy?'

'Don't you want to hear more about Pieta?' He could have gone on for weeks.

'I think I've got the picture. Tell me about the boy.'

'The son's a devil. Even his mother says so. She's afraid of him.'

'Why's she afraid of the brat?'

'He lies all the time. Comes and goes as he likes.'

'That doesn't worry me. I'll straighten him out.'

This was too much for Eddie. He would have to put the fear of God into this man. 'He has a knife.'

Mr Furtado was not impressed.

'I saw him stab two people. Even threatened his mother.'

'I can handle the boy. He won't breathe without my permission. But his mother's a different story.'

Eddie was not about to give up.

'Eddie's going to buy a gun.'

'How do you know so much about them?'

'We are neighbours.'

'I really don't know how to thank you. Will you do me one last favour?'

What now? 'I don't know.'

'Don't tell anyone I was here.' Mr Furtado took out a five-rupee note and gave it to Eddie. 'Is that a promise?'

'Okay.' Eddie smiled.

Mr Furtado shook Eddie's hand.

'Thank you. You've been so helpful and I still don't know your name.'

'Eddie Coutinho.'

~

Shishupal.

He knew what Shishupal felt like when he had committed his quota of a hundred crimes. He could have gone down on his knees, wept and begged and apologized and sold himself and the next hundred generations of his children and their children as slaves but it was doubtful if that would have loosened Mr Furtado's grip on his wrist. Mr Furtado had thin long hands to match his body, the bones stuck out at the knuckles as if they had been broken. And though he was slight and had looked as if he was about to pass out a little while ago at the discovery of the infamy of the Coutinho family, he was a new man now. There was colour in his face, almost a rosy hue. He had got his breath back and though Eddie was a deadweight he was taking the steps three at a time.

There was no need to knock, the door was open. It was dark in the common passage and even darker inside. Mr Furtado groped for the electric bell and then rang a little too long. Eddie could see the trinity waiting inside the darkness. Not the Father, the Son and the Holy Ghost but his mother, Granna and Pieta. They sat still like Brahma, Vishnu and Shiva, who Lele Guruji said always sat at the very end of the sanctum sanctorum, the black garbha-griha of the temple. Shiva, the destroyer got up and came forward to perform the dance of death on Eddie's limp body. Granna was wearing a silk dress with red roses printed on it. She smiled but Eddie knew that the end of the universe was no cause for sorrow to Shiva.

'Come in, Mr Furtado. I'm so glad that Eddie came to receive you.'

Furtado stepped in but the blade-like grip of his fingers did not relax. 'You must forgive me for this delay. I was held up by none other than your grandson.'

'This is my daughter, Violet, and my granddaughter, Pieta. Won't you sit down, Mr Furtado?'

'It is my great misfortune that I have been introduced to the whole family by the wrong person. I owe you all the gravest apology.'

'Won't you sit down?'

'Not until I've revealed all and whipped this viper in the breast of your family till his skin and soul have fallen off in shame.'

'What did he do?' Violet's voice was low but steady.

'Ask him.'

As someone long dead, Eddie was incapable of speech.

'He lied. For half an hour, the half-hour that I was delayed, he told me the most deadly and dastardly lies about you, madam and you, his most revered grandmother and this innocent child.'

'My son never lies, Mr Furtado. It does not reflect well upon the listener that he stood and listened for a full thirty minutes to all manner of lies and stories.'

'I had no choice. He called you a fast woman and a loose one. He would have called you even worse names if I hadn't stopped him. He said I was to earn money while all of you lived off me.'

'I repeat, Mr Furtado, my son does not lie.'

Mr Furtado paled. He could not understand Violet. What was she saying? Was she trying to tell him that her son had told him the truth?

'Then you're a woman of loose morals and dubious character?'

'I would let you be the judge,'

～

The subject of Violet's marriage was closed for good after that. Eddie didn't know what to make of his mother. People were so unreliable. He waited for her to slap him, hit him with anything that came to hand, the stick with which she hung clothes on the clothes-line, her shoes, the broom. She didn't. Granna came to him and asked him, 'Did you say any of those things, Eddie?'

'Ma, that chapter is over. Whether he said anything or not is not the issue. What matters is that I made my children feel so insecure.'

He could never forgive his mother. He wanted to be shriven. She let him burn in his own hell.

Twelve

A Meditation on Neighbours

Depending on your point of view, there are some elementary or critical differences between the Catholics and Hindus in the CWD chawls. It would be unwise, however, to generalize and a little excessive to say that these differences separated all Catholics from Hindus in India.

Just a few examples will suffice to help you understand how irreconcilable the differences between the two communities in the CWD chawls were. Hindus bathe in the morning, Goan Catholics in the evening. Do not expose your vast ignorance in such delicate matters and scoff and say that this is an absurd or picayune non-issue. It is conceivable that the whites will go back to their countries of origin and leave the Americas to Amerindians and the IRA only marry the daughters of British policemen and the Croats and the Serbs share wives but it is unthinkable that Roman Catholic Goans and Hindus from the CWD chawls will sit together and hammer out a compromise which says, for instance, that all Hindus and Catholics will henceforth shower or rather have bucket baths in the afternoon or at midnight.

Hindus, at least those who had access to a little water, were hyperconscious about personal cleanliness. They bathed religiously or at least let the water wet them every day and even forced their poor gods to shower whether they were installed at home or in temples. Christians, on the other hand, didn't think that salvation and bathing were causally related.

Hindus ate betel nut and chewed paan and tobacco and spat with elan and abandon in the corners of staircases, on the road and, if you didn't watch out, streaked you an earthen red from double-decker bus windows. Hindus didn't think that spitting was peeing through the mouth. Catholics did. They didn't eat paan, and could not be faulted for indecent public acts.

Catholics ate beef and pork. Even non-vegetarian Hindus hardly ever did. Hindus went to free municipal schools, Catholics to schools run by priests and nuns. Hardly any of the Hindu boys went to college. And when they did, they got into some el cheapo place. Catholics went straight to heaven or rather its equivalent on earth, St Xavier's College, even if they got barely 45 or 50 per cent marks in the higher secondary exams.

Hindu women wore saris, Catholic women dresses except on special occasions, when they switched to saris. At home Hindu men moved about 'shamelessly' in striped underpants or pyjamas. It was normal for Hindu men to roll up their vests almost to the armpits like Ravan's father and expose their flat, nascent or pot bellies when relaxing at home. Since their banishment from Paradise, Catholic men were shy of exhibiting their midriffs. And if they did, they didn't do things halfway, they didn't wear anything on top.

It was of course religion that was the source of all the differences between the two communities. Hindus went to temples as and when they felt like it. Catholics, one and all, went to mass on Sundays. For Ravan, it was Sundays that separated Hindus from Catholics. Run-of-the-mill, routine weekdays, when everybody went to work or school, were shared by both communities in equal measure. But, on Sundays, God turned His back on the Hindus. Ravan had not expected such discrimination, out and out partiality, and injustice from God.

What did the Hindu men do on that day of rest? They got up late, took their morning tea and breakfast in an easy chair in the corridor, read the papers while scratching or aimlessly fiddling with their dongs. Around 9.30 or 10 a.m., unshaven and unbathed, they got into loose striped pyjamas, made of the same cloth as their underpants, put on a shirt over them and went to the bazaar with a tote-bag to buy mutton and fish. (The word for mutton and fish among many of the Hindus was, tellingly enough, bazaar. While women did all the other household shopping, bazaar was macho and the prerogative of men.) The Sunday trip for 'bazaar' was the one domestic chore the man of the house performed. Often he took the youngest boy with him, perhaps as an initiation and training for later life. The arguments and occasional fights with the fisherwomen were always more acrimonious than those with the butchers who were men. Lunch at 2.30 p.m. after a late bath. Then a long siesta. Eventless evenings since there was no TV in those days, unless your father decided to take the family to the garden or the beach at Chowpatty. That's it, a lazy, lacklustre end to the week.

On the fifth floor, it was a different story. It was as if the whole of the Catholic community was going to a wedding between 6 and 11 a.m. If you belonged to the older generation, a freshly cleaned and ironed shirt, woollen trousers and shining shoes were not enough. A tie and a jacket were de rigueur. Some of the people from below might call it a fashion parade but they were just envious. Would you go to see your boss in shabby clothes? God was Chairman and MD of the world. You obviously took the trouble to dress up for the occasion. Nylon and polyester had not invaded the country yet, so women wore cotton or silk dresses, with puffed, raglan or full-length sleeves copied from foreign magazines. They covered their heads in church but only after they had permed, curled or back-combed their hair. Ravan had a vague recollection that somebody in his chawl had said that only women of loose character wore lipstick and other make-up.

He wished that all women were loose and wore nail-polish, mascara, eyeshadow, rouge and that fantastic microscopic stuff that transformed their eyelids into starry, twinkling skies. If you had any doubt that they belonged to a superior race, all you had to do was look at their arms and legs. They were hairless and shiny and smooth like Kwality's coffee ice-cream. Ravan could lick them all day long. But that was not all. On rare occasions, some Catholic women sheathed their legs in sheer silk. However, if Ravan had been asked to define the essential difference between Hindu and Catholic women, he would have told you without a moment's hesitation that Hindu women were flat-footed, or rather, wore the most boring, flat sandals whereas the feet of the women above almost never touched the ground. It was a mystery how they kept their balance on four- or five-inch heels. He wanted to lie down and ask those women to walk all over him and stab his heart with their stilettoes.

Inconceivable for a Hindu to go to a temple without bathing and you might hear snide comments about the cleanliness of Catholics and why the women from the top storeys had to wear Tata's Eau de Cologne or some foreign perfume that kept Ravan awake at nights and lingered in his memory for years. Their children were just as handsomely turned out, especially the girls. Eddie's sister Pieta's blue chiffon dress had so many pleats that when she pirouetted, and she always made it a point to do so, the whole skirt filled out and rose up to reveal coordinated blue bloomers.

Add fine, upright and doting grandparents, multiply them a few hundred times, and you'll begin to get a faint idea of the impact the Catholic families had on those below as they walked down the stairs and out of the chawls, greeted each other and proceeded as one single, quiet and dignified community to Saint Sebastian's Church.

If the folks from the lower storeys felt left out or a trifle envious, they made it a point to never mention it. It wasn't as if they didn't have religious occasions when the whole community got together and celebrated. Gangadhar Tilak, the shrewd and implacable freedom fighter from Maharashtra, had transformed the Ganapati festival into a public and political event since pre-Independence times, with the image of the elephant-headed god installed in every lane and alley. But even at such times, there was never any discipline informing their actions. Perhaps it is too late to impose it now.

Fortunately it did not occur to members of either community to wonder whether their faith, culture and mores were superior. They took it for granted. It was a happy coincidence that both sides shared the conviction that they were the chosen people. It did not cross the minds of most Hindus that barring exceptions, they were responsible for Catholicism in India. The outcastes of Hinduism, the untouchables, who fell beyond the pale of the caste system had ample reason to convert to Catholicism. The caste-Hindus, as a matter of fact, left them no choice. As sub-humans they were little better than slaves.

In the eyes of Jesus Christ and his energetic missionaries, the new converts were equal to any man or woman, at least to any other Indian. The new religion not only gave them self-respect and dignity but educated them and offered them a chance to work at any profession they fancied. Bread, or the Western concept of bread, was both the motive and symbol for conversion. If you broke bread with a Christian or drank from a well where a devious Christian missionary was bruited to have thrown a slice of bread, you were tainted for life and excommunicated from Hinduism.

The recent converts had no memory of their past unless they came from the higher castes. Jesus Christ and the new faith notwithstanding, the former Brahmins did not forget, nor would they allow anyone else to, that they were the highest of the high. They ensured the purity of their stock and maintained their exclusive status by marrying other Brahmin-Catholics and occasionally the expatriate grandees of Portugal.

Along with religion, the other great divider in the CWD chawls was language. Often, the one got confused with the other. Hindus spoke Marathi, Catholics, English. Konkani was still very much the lingua franca in the Goan home but outside the house, the younger people communicated almost entirely in English.

English was the thorn in the side of the Hindus. Its absence was their cross, their humiliation and the source of their life-long inferiority and inadequacy. It was a severely debilitating, if not fatal, lack that was not acknowledged, spoken of or articulated. It was the great leveller. It gave caste-Hindus a taste of their own medicine. It made them feel like untouchables. It also turned the tables. The former outcastes could now look down upon their Hindu neighbours.

Perhaps Dr Ambedkar was wrong to convert millions of his untouchable brethren to Buddhism. He should have converted them to English. That would really have stood the caste-Hindu world on its head. Roman Catholic missionaries were seized of the power of English long before the rest of the population caught on. Outside Goa, they abandoned Portuguese and took the English tongue almost as seriously as their faith. They went on a spree and opened English-medium schools and colleges across the country.

'Chhya men, he's a dutty bugger. Tree times I told him don't climb the tree to look at my sas. Leave my sas alone, men. I asked him 'gain and again but he din listen, so I gave him a hit, straight on the face like. De bugger began to cry like a baby, men. He begged me like but I din listen. I told him, you look at my sas, and I'll break your bones and balls.' Goan English is easy to mimic and an easy target for well-educated and affluent Bombayites. It is burlesqued in plays, reviews and films. Such niceties and caricature are lost on the Hindus from the CWD chawls. Ask any one of them, in an unguarded moment and he'll tell you that he would give his right hand, make it his left, to be able to speak like the people from the top floor. Because there are only two kinds of people in the world. Those who have English and those who don't. Those who have English are the haves, and those who don't, are the have-nots.

How could you possibly grasp the meaning and value of English if you spoke it before you were toilet-trained or had a place reserved for you in an English-medium school? English is a mantra, a maha-mantra. It is an 'open sesame' that doesn't open mere doors, it opens up new worlds and allows you to cross over from one universe to another.

English makes you tall. If you know English, you can wear a 'suit-boot', do an electrician's course or take a diploma, in radio and refrigeration technology. You can become a chef at the Taj Mahal Hotel or a steno at Hindustan Lever, even a purser with Air India or Pan Am. If you know English and someone steps on your foot, you can say to him, 'Bastard, can't you see?' You can talk like a foreigner. Sit down in a local train and hold a best-seller like *Peyton Place* in front of your eyes and even read it. If you know English, you can ask a girl for a dance. You can lean Eileen Alva against the locked door of the terrace and press against her, squeeze her boobs and kiss her on the mouth, put your tongue inside it while slipping your hand under her dress.

Language is leverage. Not a very original or revolutionary perception really. Our ancestors had grasped the principle two or three thousand years ago. The word for culture and tradition was sanskriti. Those who spoke Sanskrit had sanskriti. What about the rest of the folks? Well, what about them, they spoke Pali or some such dialect and ate crow. Did they have any choice in the matter?

There is only one difference between then and now. Sanskrit was the language of the gods, thirty-three million gods and of Parameshwar or Everlasting God (our great great grandfathers were certainly aware of the difference between small-time, easy-come, easy-go gods and the Big One) and of Brahmins. As go-betweens, middle-men, spiritual hustlers and keepers of our deities, Brahmins had exclusive and total rights to God. Since they coined the words and phrases, they called themselves Brahmin or the people who know Brahman or God. Dynaneshwar, the boy saint who finished his life's work by age twenty-one and bid goodbye to the world, may have caused a few hiccups when he translated the Bhagawad Gita and wrote a commentary on it in the 13th century in a local and young language called Marathi, but that didn't lessen our grudging respect and admiration for the learning, erudition and culture of the Brahmins. But Goan Catholics were not even Brahmins. They had not learnt the Puranas by heart nor discoursed on the Upanishads, nor had they preserved and perpetuated our culture. And yet without in any way earning it but doing what they so aptly call 'bugger all' they had English on their tongue. Just like that.

The fact is there is no justice on earth.

~

There is one other difference between the Hindus and the Catholics. Or at least there was at that time. Hindu boys and girls and their parents saw Hindi movies. Catholics wouldn't dream of it. They went to English films. It was the kind of difference that would take Ravan and Eddie further apart than they already were.

At the end of the fifties, Ravan's life took on a new colour and complexion. It changed the landscape of his mind and the way he viewed the world more deeply and pervasively than any revolution or traumatic experience could have.

Vivekanand met Ramakrishna Paramhansa, Mephistopheles found Faust, the Buddha sat under a pipal tree and gained enlightenment, the Virgin Mary woke from a deep sleep with an immaculate conception, Ravan saw *Dil Deke Dekho*.

It was Subhash Vachnani's birthday and he was taking the entire 5.30 a.m. tae kwon do class to a movie at Broadway cinema. He would have liked Mr Billimoria to come along but Mr Billimoria was more snooty than the Catholics and would never deign to see a Hindi film. And anyway he had classes in the evening.

Ravan was no friend of Subhash's but certain privileges accrued to all members of the tae kwon do fraternity and Subhash's mother was not one to stint on a few balcony tickets and chocolate ice-creams and packets of popcorn because some of the boys did not belong to their social milieu or were not in Subhash's inner circle of friends.

Dil Deke Dekho was not Ravan's first film. At the yearly Ganapati festival, they always showed at least one film as part of the celebrations. During municipal elections, some of the candidates hired a projector and showed some ancient film on the main road after 9 p.m. The film would keep breaking off, the speakers would crackle and flutter with every treble note and sometimes the projector would pack up halfway but it was unthinkable for anyone from Mazagaon not to be there for a free show. Ravan had seen *Mela* with the young Dilip Kumar as the hero. He had fallen asleep during the second reel though he was deeply impressed by the villain Jeevan who spouted letters from the English alphabet as if they were full-fledged words. The cobras and other snakes in the mythological *Naag Panchami* had kept him awake through the movie and through the next ten nights for fear that one of them would turn up in his bed. There were a few others, but he had forgotten them.

Then came *Dil Deke Dekho*. No English translation will do justice to the alliteration, pacing or ellipsis of the Hindi. 'Give your heart away' is the closest one can get to the meaning.

Most Hindi commercial films in those days were love stories but they were sad and woebegone. And even if they weren't tragic, their heroes and heroines were mature adults. *Dil Deke Dekho* was revolutionary. It was about youngsters, teenagers.

A Not So Short and Utterly Unnecessary History of Romantic Comedies in Hindi Films in the 1950s and 60s

Dil Deke Dekho started a trend that is revived every few years in Indian cinema. It was the brainchild of Subodh Mukherjee, an old pro from the world of Hindi cinema who had decided to make films under his own banner called Filmalaya. Filmalaya was meant to be a film institute, not just a production company.

Filmalaya would train young people to be actors, actresses, directors, music directors, scriptwriters, cinematographers and technicians in its own school and then give them breaks in its own films.

Dil Deke Dekho was everything Mukherjee had promised. Barring its hero and director, it featured unknowns in their late teens or early twenties.

Mukherjee was taking an enormous gamble handing the job of music director, and that too of an out and out musical, to a newcomer and he compounded the risk by giving it to a girl who was very likely the first woman music director in Hindi films.

Director Nasir Hussein and hero Shammi Kapoor were the only veterans in the film.

Let's pause a minute here and survey the contribution of Hussein and Kapoor to Hindi cinema. Commercial Hindi cinema was rarely expected to make sense, and to its credit it never pretended to, either. Hussein made the same film over and over again. He mostly kept clear of social relevance, neo-realism and family dramas. His films were romantic comedies. He had a light touch and he kept the intermittent plot moving with music, romance and masala. The masala could be anything: suspense, smugglers, comedy, mystery, children and parents separated by the machinations of villains.

For the longest time, the music and stars in Hussein's films played a major role in giving him hit after hit. They said he had a special feel for music. Maybe he was just lucky in the music directors he chose. But the magic was bound to pall at some time and it did. Not because the next generation of film-makers had anything new to say or said it differently. No, they just imitated him better than he could.

The one thing nobody could do was imitate his star, Shammi Kapoor. He was one of a kind, a phenomenon. He came from a family of thespians.

Shammi Kapoor was the second of three sons. His older brother, Raj Kapoor, joined his father's theatre company, moved to films and became a matinee idol. Within a short time he established his own film production company. He was Charlie Chaplin, Frank Capra and Vittorio de Sica all rolled into one.

As a director, he had a superlative instinct for the box office. Along with his critics and audiences, he confused worthy themes and profound shallowness with social commitment and artistic cinema. He played the same character, Raju, in almost all his films. He was the eternal hobo or vagabond with a heart suppurating with emotion; a naïf and waif among the corrupt and the rapacious who brought about a change of heart even among hardened criminals and walked away with the heroine. He was the clown and the joker who made the whole world laugh while concealing his own sorrow.

Raj Kapoor rolled up the cuffs of his trousers and appropriated the mantle of Charlie Chaplin in India. It was a smart move. It effectively shut up his critics. Questioning him meant questioning the great Chaplin. His humour, if you could call it that, was elementary and jejune. Devoid of Chaplin's powers of sharp observation, irony, and visual and verbal wit, he improved upon his shortcomings: the soft sentiment and the easy tear.

Shammi Kapoor grew up in the shadow of his flamboyantly successful older brother and joined the world of films when he was barely twenty. He was a tall, athletic man with a swashbuckling Errol Flynn moustache. Try as he might, his star wouldn't rise and flop followed flop.

One day he took off his moustache and his career took off. Is there a nexus between the two? Who is to say, we are talking about Hindi commercial movies here. Overnight with *Tumsa Nahin Dekha,* Shammi became a cult figure. Nasir Hussein and he were made for each other. Shammi rarely ventured into serious or social films. He didn't have the sensitive or romantic good looks of his brother Raj Kapoor. He had an unfinished face as if someone had lost interest while working on its lines, bones and structure and had never got back to it. An unlikely face for romantic comedies, so Shammi Kapoor changed the nature and content of the form itself. The romantic heroes of Hindi films before him were soft, shy, tentative or intense. They were gentle and appealed to genteel, middle-class audiences, especially women. Shammi Kapoor was not just the exact opposite, he was unthinkable and inconceivable till he happened.

One of his later films was called *Junglee.* That's what he was, wild and uncouth. He was not a conscious actor but he had instinctively carved out his own niche. The older generation of cinema viewers shunned him and the critics were superior and found his antics tasteless and risible. But his market was the young people, the working classes and the lower stalls. They went berserk when he appeared on the screen. Short of throwing coins and notes at him, a practice which was reserved only for nautch girl sequences, they showed their appreciation in every other way. They hollered, whistled and interspersed catcalls with raw, bawdy comments.

Cinema and not religion had become the opium of the masses after the country won independence and Shammi Kapoor gave the people of the smaller cities and towns a high that no other celluloid hero could.

Shammi seemed to suggest that it was all right to work in a restaurant or a band and not belong to the hoity toity classes. You could still make it and get the girl. What he had was a total lack of self-consciousness. He was uninhibited and utterly indifferent to making an ass of himself. He didn't give a centipede's shit about how absurd you thought he was. Quite the contrary. He rejoiced in the knowledge and cocked a snook at you and went on to perform even more ridiculous capers.

His clarion call was an apt and symbolic one though chosen without any conscious sense of irony. It was a 'yaa-hooo'. It echoed in theatre halls and wherever he went. He could never sit still. He was perpetual motion and distortion. He had a putty face and his ears, nose, throat, eyes and lips seemed to be interchangeable. He was slim, boneless and made of polyurethane foam. He turned and twisted upon himself, tied himself in knots and undid them all in the same breath. He could not say a simple yes or no, much less a full sentence without going into a series of contortions, raising and wrinkling his brows, pulling a face, dropping a shoulder, running his hand over his slicked-back hair.

Shammi never needed a pretext to be outlandish but he really came into his own in song sequences and his films were strewn with them. He threw a tantrum in mid-air, he landed on his butt and thrashed his legs. He flung his head back, he yelled 'yaa-hooo', he rolled in the snow, he went stiff as a flamenco dancer, he sank to his knees, he dislocated and fractured his body in a dozen places. He walked mincingly, dropped in a dead faint, his narrow mouth went all over his face—all in the course of one song.

Indian critics never tire of saying that Raj Kapoor was the ultimate showman. His brother Shammi may be underrated but he was no side-show either.

~

When the lights went out, Ravan saw a houri, an apsara, a celestial creature in black and white of incredible beauty and vivacity. He was hard put to understand how such a rarefied and refined aesthetic experience could induce such painful tightness and tension in his groin. He would have been horrified if anyone had opined that her thick lips gave the impression that they were just a trace out of synch with the words she spoke or that the slacks she wore only helped to emphasize the magnificence of her hips. How could anybody be so gross about a creature so ethereal? His dilemma was altogether different: would Neeta, the heroine of the movie who was so mischievous, carefree and adorable, fall in love with the hero or would the villain get her? But if Neeta rocked the earth under Ravan's feet, the hero Raju swept him off his feet at gale winds of 700 m.p.h. Raju was a musician, a singer who played the drums. He had hands that could caress the drums, turn them into flurries of rain or avalanches of intricate rhythms that rolled in, wave upon wave and dispersed as a fine mist of sound.

He was a rascal, a real badmash who could do no wrong and he had a hundred tricks up his sleeve. He was a one-man fancy dress competition and changed personalities, accents and his dress so fast that nobody, not even Neeta, realized he was the same person. He was a magician in a goatee one minute, a fat old mullah with a beard that reached to his belly and a tummy that extended a yard ahead of him, the next. He was so funny and such fun and so handsome, Ravan decided to adopt him as an older brother.

For a moment there, things looked extremely dicey and Ravan had some anxious moments. It was like this: Raju had been separated from his mother since childhood. Now the villain had convinced the mother that he was her long-lost son, Raju. It was so complicated even Ravan couldn't always get it straight. And then by chance, imagine, what fantastic luck, the real mother and the real son were standing face to face but oh God they didn't know it and Ravan bit his fingernails almost to the knuckles and nearly shouted, Raju, Raju that's your mother, the real, actual, long-lost mother you've been pining for.

The audience including his classmates went bananas when there was a song. They knew every word and they sang every word while keeping perfect time by clapping their hands. Ravan sat back in his chair in a state of rigor mortis. They had forgotten to close his eyes and mouth before he died. He had the sensation that he was breathing the songs, swallowing mouthfuls of them. He felt them going down his throat. Both the sound and visual flow entered directly into his bloodstream and lit him up. His body had become transparent, the veins and arteries in it glowing brightly like the filament in an electric bulb. He dared not move for fear that the spell would break. There was little doubt in his mind that he was in heaven. His five senses had got together and created a sixth one that had to be divine. His whole body, every pore in it and every hair, was standing on end playing the songs. He became weightless. He lost all awareness of his body. He was no longer a medium for iridescence. He was light and joy and they were the same thing.

~

The next day Ravan asked his mother for two rupees to see *Dil Deke Dekho*.

His mother could not contain her astonishment. 'But you saw the filim yesterday.'

'I need to see it again. It's important.'

'No way. Who's going to do your homework?'

'If not today, how about Sunday? I'll finish all my school work on Saturday.' He used patience and restraint with this woman who seemed incapable of understanding the momentous nature of his request.

'Is your father going to shell out the money so you can see the same filim again and again?'

'How about on the first when all the customers have paid you?' Ravan endeavoured to accommodate his mother and keep open the pathways for a mutually acceptable solution.

'Mention that filim once more and I'm going to whack you. Why don't you open your books instead and study? Came forty-third in the class last time and you still want to see a filim, not any filim but the same one you saw yesterday. If you are that keen on going to the cinema, come among the first ten in your next exam. I'll take you to see the filim myself, that's a promise.'

Ravan smiled. He felt that the hopes and expectations of human beings should be rooted, however tenuously, in reality. Stand among the first ten in class? Might as well expect him to climb Mount Everest or be Tarzan. After that day he did not broach the matter of DDD again. First he sold his books, one after another. Next, he took money from Parvati without asking or telling her. When that was used up, he considered taking money from his father's stash at the bottom of the papad tin but decided against it. His normally inert father could fly off the handle without warning. It was best to steer clear of him. Ravan sold one of his mother's gold earrings. If the need had arisen, he would have undone the clasp of the mangalsutra from around her neck while she slept, and pawned it. Luckily, *Dil Deke Dekho* was taken off after celebrating a silver jubilee and Parvatibai's mangalsutra stayed around her neck.

In all, Ravan saw *Dil Deke Dekho* seventeen times. And there was nothing Parvati could do to stop her son who had turned into a full-fledged thief overnight. She whipped him across his back, caned him and hit him with her shoes; she scratched him with her nails. She singed his calf with burning coal, almost cracked his kneecap with a rolling pin. Ravan passed out. Parvati kept him without food and water for two days. The beatings exhausted her. She felt faint and giddy. She told him regularly that he was going to be the cause of her death.

'If you stop pounding me, you won't die.' Ravan ventured to tell her this a couple of times, but his counsel had unfortunate consequences.

'Here my blood is rising and you've got the gall to give me advice?' Even a truncated ailment sounded so much more dire and desperate in English. With renewed zeal she returned to her task. She fell upon him with the strength of eleven elephants. Six to box and bash him and invent new modes of pulverizing him. Three to call upon her parents, her recumbent husband, Sai Baba and any other baba and guru she could recall, upon God in all his incarnations and to scream murder until she went black and blue in the face and lost her voice. The last two to sigh and moan in a ghastly manner. Parvatibai was a tigress, no, she was the goddess who rode the tigress in her most malevolent avatar. From time to time she would call out the name of her son whom she had so recently mangled and almost mutilated. 'Ravanya, ayyayyayy-ayya, just see what you've done to me. There's not a bone left in my body that's not broken and bruised. Are you listening, you wretch? Don't you have any feelings for your poor mother?' Again that sky-rending ayyayyayyayya. 'Don't just lie there, press my body.' Shameless Ravan. He complied. He massaged, kneaded and soothed his mother's hurting and aching body.

At the best of times, there's nothing private in a chawl. Within a matter of weeks, Parvatibai had become the most public figure in Mazagaon. She felt trapped between her unrepentant son and her own daily atrocities. She dreaded the thought of going out and showing her face to the world. She was willing to put in as much effort as necessary to discipline Ravan and bring him back to the straight and narrow. But Ravan's mute forbearance wore her down. All her life she had assumed that persistent endeavour was always followed by success. She now realized she was wrong.

Moments after Ravan had undergone third-degree corporal punishment, he would break into song. He had always been more than a mere bathroom singer but DDD turned him into a crooner with professional ambitions. He practised songs from DDD all day and part of the night till Shankar-rao sat up in bed and in a dangerously low voice asked Ravan to shut up.

Ravan was both singer and unappeasable critic. If he was unhappy with the rendering of a particular phrase, he sang it a couple of thousand times. His neighbours lost patience and threatened to call the police or slit his voice-box. Ravan carried on undeterred. His mother was too worn out to respond to his ceaseless musical outpourings. What infuriated her more than anything was the fact that despite her dour resolve to have nothing but violent converse with her son, she would on occasion catch herself humming cluelessly along with Ravan.

To punish Ravan and to teach him a lesson, Parvati refused to replace the textbooks he had sold. Ravan spent the following year in the same grade. He did not deny that he had taken the money or sold the earring. Parvati said repeatedly that her son was beyond redemption. If he had become a thief and highway robber at such an early age, can you imagine what the future held for him? She became aphoristic and prescient. 'Coming events cast their shadows. Mark my words, you'll become a dacoit and spend a lifetime behind bars.' Who can talk of the future with any certainty? But since an event of the magnitude of DDD did not occur again till he grew up and started working, Ravan did not feel the need to indulge further in petty or other larceny at home or abroad.

Thirteen

✦✦✦

Ravan and Eddie were not twins. Ravan did not wince with pain if Eddie was hurt. Eddie's thirst was not quenched when Ravan drank five glasses of water. If one studied, the other did not pass his exams. Later on, when one copulated, the other did not have an orgasm.

Let alone blood brothers, they were not even stepbrothers. Eddie and Ravan's lives ran parallel, that's all. And there is no greater distance on earth than that which separates parallel lines, even if they almost touch each other. One city, one chawl, two floors, two cultures, two languages, two religions and the enmity of two women separated them. How could their paths possibly meet?

It was music that brought Rani Roopmati and Baz Bahadur together. The paths of Baiju and India's greatest singer, Tansen, crossed because of music. And music it was which made Laila and Majnu, the legendary lovers, immortal. The music from *Dil Deke Dekho* should have bound Ravan and Eddie for ever and ever. But Eddie went to see *Rock Around the Clock* and the reconciliation between our mighty heroes was jinxed once again.

Fear not, my friends. This is a Hindi film story. Even if it's written in English, it is not bound by the petty logic and quibbling of the colonizer's tongue. Even and odd dates fall on the same day here and parallel lines which should meet only at the horizon criss-cross each other merrily in our universe (or Bollywood as it's called). But patience, for it is not to be yet, not yet. Who knows, perhaps not in this book at all, but in the next one.

~

That Saturday evening, Paul Monteiro was going to take his girlfriend Crystal to *Rock Around the Clock*. Just as Paul was about to leave home at five-thirty, his father, the one and only Catholic freedom fighter from the CWD chawls, began to get shooting pains in the stomach. The doctor, Sylvester Carvalho, who had been a classmate of Paul's father before he abandoned school to join the struggle for independence, asked the patient, 'What the fuck were you doing all this while, Paul?' There was the usual confusion and neither Paul Senior nor Junior attempted to answer since each thought the question was addressed to the other. 'I'm talking to both of you. I've told you a hundred times to change your son's name. One would think there's just one name in the English language.'

'His name's Mohan. What am I to do if nobody calls him by his Indian name?'

'Stop groaning like a horse. I want to know why you didn't call me earlier. What about you, didn't you know that your father was very ill and in such pain that no normal human being could bear it?'

~

It was unfashionable in those days to give a vernacular name to a Catholic child. But then Paul Monteiro was an odd bird. He had called his son Mohan after the father of the nation, Mohandas Karamchand Gandhi, whose band of non-violent fighters he had joined in his youth, despite his parents' threat to disown him. The name Mohan did not take hold. The Catholics from the CWD chawls called Paul's son Paul.

It was impossible for both the Catholic community and clergy to understand how a Catholic boy from a Catholic school could have been drawn to a toothless Hindu leader in a dhoti to the point of giving up his education and meagre inheritance. But Paul Senior had not stopped at that. His best friend was another freedom fighter, Ravan's neighbour Mr Dixit, who had revealed that Ravan was an active partner in Gandhi's murder. They were not just 'bum chums' to use Paul Monteiro Senior's phrase, they were in and out of each other's houses, dined with each other often, exchanged plates of sweets and savouries at Diwali and Christmas and what was even more exasperating, sang old Saigal and Punkaj Mullick Hindi-film songs. There were other more unforgiveable crimes Paul Senior had committed. He lost all control over himself when any CWD Catholic supported the Portuguese presence in Goa after 1947. He spread absurd stories that but for accident, Vasco da Gama might have landed in Calcutta or in Thailand and that all the Goans would then be Hindus and worshipping idols.

~

'He didn't say a word. How was I to know?'

'Do you realize how serious the situation is? He's got a burst appendix. If he's not moved to hospital immediately and operated upon...'

'I thought the pain would go away.' The blood drained from Paul Monteiro's face.

'It will. It usually does after a person dies.' Senior was moaning so melodramatically by now that his son began to laugh.

'Like hell he's going to die. He's just pretending to be sick. The bugger wouldn't leave Mama alone till one thirty or two at night. She said, "Not now. Paul's not asleep yet." "So what," he says, "I'm not trying to make out with somebody else's wife, am I?" Isn't that the truth, Ma?'

'Shut up, Paul.' Paul's mother went as red as the crimson bindi on her forehead at her son's revelations. 'Grown-up man like you, still don't know how to talk in front of your Doctor Uncle?'

'Arre, what's the matter? Don't pretend you're a saint, Ma. You were just giving Daddy a hard time, so he would get even more excited. Speak up, Daddy, what were you up to last night?'

'Paul, you bastard.' He couldn't control his laughter and that made the pain worse.

'Sala, if Mama's alone in the house for one minute, the bugger latches the door and grabs her.'

Paul's breathing had become uneven and he was sweating unnaturally but that didn't dampen his spirits. He loved to hear his son praise his libido and sexual prowess.

Their neighbours found it difficult to understand the camaraderie between father and son. It was uncouth to suggest that a mother had sexual characteristics and needs. Her gender was mother and nothing more. Besides, even in families where relations between children and parents were friendly and open, there were unspoken but sharply drawn boundaries. Paul and Paul were culpable on two counts. They broke the code and gave other people's children all kinds of ideas. What if their children became familiar and started to talk in a similar vein?

'That's because you never give us a chance,' said Paul Senior trying to massage his swollen stomach down to its normal size. 'Any time Crystal's here, even if she's here a minute, this bugger's hand is missing. You don't have to look far for it. It's under her slip. Take my word for it, he'll disappear altogether when he gets married. Inside his wife's dress. All of him. True or not?'

Paul's father didn't get to hear the answer to his question. He opened his mouth to laugh at his joke and became unconscious.

~

Paul Junior was his parents' only child. His mother should have been in *The Guinness Book of Records*. According to conservative estimates she had had seventeen miscarriages. After her marriage she had never had to use sanitary towels. She was pregnant every three or four months. Within eleven weeks on the outside, the foetus would say goodbye and begin to drip stickily. The day she dropped the foetus, she got pregnant again. In the old days, Paul's mother would lie in bed at home or in a hospital without turning on her side or moving a centimetre. Doctors, alternative medicine, Mount Mary, novenas, potions and lotions, black and blessed threads tied around her wrist or waist, talismans, even gurus and babas thanks to her fecund Hindu friend, Mrs Dixit... she had tried everything. To no avail.

One day she said to her husband when he woke up, 'Think of a number.'

'What for?' Paul asked her.

'Never mind.'

Seven days she asked her husband the same question. His answer did not vary. On the eighth day he lost his temper.

'Sala, seven times I've asked you what the hell for but...'

'Seven times. Thank you for the number, Paul.'

He had no idea what she was thanking him for but she smiled so beatifically, he pulled her skirt down right there.

Days, weeks and months passed. Nothing changed.

She became pregnant. She bled. After the sixth miscarriage, Paul's father lost heart. He couldn't figure out whether it was his fault or his wife's. Did God will it so or was it fate? He went to see his classmate Dr Sylvester Carvalho. 'Why should you worry, Paul? You do your job. Keep trying.'

'De fuck. What do you think this is, a cycle pump or my prick? I try and I try but all my wife's got to show for it is hot air.'

'That's nonsense, Paul. Your wife gets pregnant like clockwork.'

'I don't want a clock,' Paul screamed at him. 'I want a baby.'

~

Men, as women well know but will wisely not admit, are at best sprinters. When it comes to that marathon called life, it's the members of the weaker sex who have staying power. Paul Monteiro's wife Yolanda didn't throw up her hands because the odds were against her, she merely tried a little harder.

'Once, just once. Only once,' Paul's wife begged him every day. She would wake him at odd hours, play with him, kiss him, sing him songs, rub her breasts against him, lick his earlobes. To no avail. Neither the man nor his member responded.

'Don't give up Paul. Please don't give up.' That did it. Paul Monteiro, freedom fighter, Gandhi's non-violent disciple, indefatigable copulator, enlightened Roman Catholic from Goa and ceaseless aspirant to fatherhood, lost his head and lit into his wife. 'Fuck off. Can't you leave me alone.' Even as he was hitting his beloved Yolanda, he began to cry.

'Forgive me, Yolanda, forgive me,' he sobbed and wept and coughed and choked. His wife was unnerved by the violence of his repentance.

'What shall I forgive? You were right. I've importuned you and pestered you every hour of the day for weeks. I wouldn't listen. Even God would have lost patience.'

That would have reassured the devil himself but Paul walked in the path of Gandhi and non-violence. He had been beaten with hard wooden police batons that had no give, his head had been broken open and his kidneys damaged permanently, he had been dragged by the hair for sixty yards and then kicked in the face. His self-control had been tried to the very limits when British police officers and their native underlings had brutally manhandled women, and yet he had not retaliated because Christ, and Gandhi, asked him to turn the other cheek. And now, because of an unborn foetus which was a drop-out way before it had entered the world, he had beaten his uncomplaining and loyal wife. He was staggered by the discovery of the repressed and pent-up violence in him. Everything that he stood for and had fought for was destroyed by that one random action. He knew that if it could happen once, it could happen again. Hadn't Adam fallen for all mankind? Was it necessary for everyone else to continue to fall? It was humiliating to know that he was no better than others.

His mood changed. The self-loathing in his lower lip was replaced by a dour resolve. It was unsettling to look into his eyes. They had reached a point of no return. He got up and went into the kitchen. He picked up the big cleaver in his left hand and placed his right arm on the wooden cutting block so worn out with use, there was a trough in it.

'More violence?' His wife Yolanda was standing at the door in the partition that separated the kitchen from the living area.

Paul Monteiro came as close to hating a living organism as he would in his entire life. 'What do you want me to do then?'

'Lie with me.'

That was one thing Paul Monteiro could not bring himself to do.

Four months had long passed and yet Yolanda Monteiro's stomach stayed flat. It was a subject of grave concern in the CWD chawls. Paul's mother may not have given birth to a single child yet, but her sheer persistence and state of chronic pregnancy had become symbolic of fertility in the chawls.

It is difficult, if not impossible to appreciate the dimensions of the crisis that gripped the CWD chawls then. Paul's mother had been spotted buying Sirona sanitary towels. It was certain that something terrible was going to happen. The residents of the CWD chawls were still divided, but for the first time in living memory, the division was not along religious lines. One group defended Paul, the other spoke up for his wife.

'How much longer do you want him to keep trying? Keeping that woman pregnant is a round-the-clock, round-the-year job. What do you expect, a Qutab Minar after all these years? He's worn it out till it's disappeared.'

'It's she who should be exhausted. All he does is clamber on to her. She is the one who has to do the bearing and the losing.'

Prayers were said for Mrs Monteiro in every home in the CWD chawls. On the thirteenth of September, for the fifth month running, Paul's mother got out of the house in the morning. Oh God, please, not to the Happy Family Chemist's, please. But everyone's worst fears came true. The Sirona pack was wrapped in newspaper but she might as well have strung the twelve napkins into a garland and worn them around her neck. Paul's father who was Mr Nonstop Cheerful all these years had begun to look gaunt. He was almost uncivil now and would not respond to a greeting if he could avoid it. His low spirits and moodiness had not affected his wife's sunny temperament so far. Some kind of immense faith kept her happy and smiling. But the dry and barren fifth month changed her too. She lost colour and seemed to be plunging into a depression. Even the inimical tension that had kept the husband and wife going disappeared. They had lost all interest in each other and life.

Then one day what should not have happened, happened. While he was rejoining the broken yarn on the power-loom at the Jeejibhoy Spinning and Weaving Mills, a centimetre-long, black ant slipped in where no decent ant should. Paul Monteiro tried to ignore its gentle explorations, but the creature continued to tickle him. He squirmed and wriggled as it wandered around. Then, for a full three-quarters of a minute he stood transfixed to the ground. What his hands chanced upon was a living miracle. His shy, withdrawn and almost non-existent prick had grown into the mother of all hard-ons. He left the yarn from the loom hanging loose and abandoned the bobbin that slapped against his eardrum twice every second and walked away.

He walked fast without hurrying. A big black ant is neither necessary nor sufficient cause. Psychoanalysts and novelists need reasons. Life subsists on excuses and pretexts. Paul's problem was to extend the duration of the miracle. He had not moved his hands. They held on tightly to the living miracle and warmed it in broad daylight and in the heavy traffic. It was difficult to climb on to a local train without support, but Paul Monteiro picked up his leg from the knee and stepped in. He got off at Byculla and started walking in the direction of the taxi-stand when he realized his folly. He would need at least one hand to open the cab door and would then have to fish out the money from his wallet. It was two-thirty in the afternoon. The sun was still almost overhead. His shirt, armpits and face were soaked in sweat. From Byculla to Mazagaon, Paul's father-to-be looked straight ahead and ignored the stares and salacious remarks of passers-by. He was tempted to take long strides. He controlled himself. He walked at a steady pace till he reached the chawls. Others may have laughed and scoffed at him. Not the people from the chawls. They knew he was carrying a lamp. A slight breeze, a false step and the flame would die.

On the third floor there was a crisis. Only he and his God knew the depth of his despair at that moment. It occurred to him that the manhood he had preserved and protected for forty-five minutes could vanish with the same celerity with which it had appeared. He stood still while that thought played havoc with him. He felt he had slipped into an air pocket. The soles of his feet opened up and all his substance was sucked out. He was flung from one wall of the pocket to the other and yet he kept falling. But he was a strong and wilful man. It would take more than atmospheric turbulence to rock him. He exhaled slowly for a long time, then took a deep breath and climbed the last two floors.

'Shut the door,' he said.

Yolanda Monteiro became pregnant for the seventh time. Seven, the magic number. Consequence: Paul Junior.

~

'Peritonitis has already set in. There's a chance that he might survive if he's operated upon right now. But I'm not guaranteeing anything.' Dr Carvalho looked grim. Mrs Monteiro was wiping Paul Senior's forehead. She wasn't going to permit herself to work out the implications of what the doctor had said. Even the dead had more colour than her husband.

Paul Junior had stood in the queue at the Strand cinema for four and a half hours on Tuesday morning to buy tickets for *Rock Around the Clock*. He had not expected his father to bear him such ill-will and enmity as to prevent him from going to the movie.

'Why don't you operate tomorrow, Doctor Uncle? It's a Sunday. You can take the whole day if you want.'

'Stop wasting time, you fool, unless you want to see your father die in front of your eyes. I'll call for an ambulance and arrange for the surgeon. You and your friends carry Paul down the stairs. That way we'll save time. Be very careful. No jolts.'

'I'll walk.' A small voice spoke up. It came from the dead man. Paul's heart jumped up in joy.

'Sure. I'm sure you can walk to Masina Hospital.' Dr Carvalho spoke with uncalled-for sarcasm.

'See, nothing's the matter with him,' Paul said. 'Nothing that won't wait till tomorrow.'

The ghost sat up. He put his foot down and raised himself. Doctor Carvalho watched him with interest. He knew when Paul Senior's legs would give and had his hands ready to hold him.

'Another word from father or son and I'm going home.'

~

Paul's wife put his head on her lap while their son closed the door of the ambulance. There was a crowd of people gathered in a semi-circle behind it. An ambulance and its seriously ill or dying patient and its retinue of weeping relatives was classic theatre. The chawlwallahs were connoisseurs of drama and wouldn't miss it for the world. If pressed, they would have had to confess that the Monteiro show was not up to scratch. Short on emotion, small cast and that doctor was in the damnedest hurry. Even Eddie who was at the head of the crowd was disappointed.

The ambulance stopped. There was hope. There was reason to believe the show was going to come back to life. Maybe Paul Senior had kicked the bucket. Maybe Mrs Monteiro would break down now. The doors opened and Paul Junior looked out. A hundred people were difficult to focus on. They might as well not be there. His eyes hunted for a familiar face but could not prise one out. That idiot Eddie was smiling and waving as if Paul and his parents were going to Kashmir on a holiday.

'Eddie.'

Eddie ran forward.

'Go and tell Crystal that I won't be picking her up for the movie because my father's seriously ill. Tell her we are going to Masina Hospital.'

Eddie wanted to tell him to go jump, he had better things to do than tramp down to Ballard Estate and meet Crystal. And anyway he couldn't, even if he wanted to. His mother had asked him to buy two pounds of onions and one anna's worth of ginger and was expecting him fifteen minutes ago.

'Here, take this.'

'What's it?' Eddie had stepped back, ready to make a run for it.

'Tickets, stupid. Tickets for *Rock Around the Clock*.'

Eddie couldn't believe his good fortune. There was bound to be a catch.

'Sell the other ticket and bring the money back.'

'Shut the bloody door or I'll throw you out,' Dr Carvalho was screaming.

Before Eddie could ask, 'What about the bus-fare?' the doors of the ambulance closed and it whizzed off. Eddie decided not to think of the whacking he would get at night, the complaints to Father Agnello D'Souza the next morning after mass, Father D'Souza's turned-down mouth and hopeless face silently wondering what terrible mischief Eddie had been up to while speaking bitterly to him of the afterlife, and what lay in wait for him.

He had recently learnt the f... word. He didn't know what it meant but it reflected his frame of mind. 'F... it,' he said and caught a moving bus. 'Mother-fucker,' the conductor asked him, 'do you want to die?'

Eddie handed him the money and said, 'Two pounds of onions.'

~

Thousands of people had laid siege to the Strand cinema. It had become one of the holiest shrines in the city of Bombay. It would take another hour and a half or two for Eddie to become a devotee. The Lord God of one, two, three o'clock, four o'clock, rock; five, six, seven o'clock, eight o'clock, rock; nine, ten, eleven o'clock, twelve o'clock, rock; we're gonna rock around the clock had not yet taken possession of Eddie's soul to the exclusion of all else.

Time and again Eddie crashed against the impenetrable mass of people and fell back. Even the greatest military formations have chinks. The trick is to find them. In Eddie's case the chink found him. Someone asked him, 'Extra?' Before he could understand the implications of the question, thirty-three people fell upon him from all sides. His mother, Granna and sister would have to recover his dismembered body from the morgue at J.J. Hospital. When Eddie rose from underneath the stampede, he was devoid of a shoe along with its sock, the collar of his shirt, two buttons of his fly and Crystal's ticket.

There is no rational answer to how Eddie managed to salvage one ticket from the maelstrom, when both had been laminated into a single indivisible entity by sweat and heat. It should have been possible to tell who had made away with Crystal's ticket once he got into the theatre and had been shown to his seat. He tried asking both his neighbours for reimbursement of the ticket. One shoved his face away and the other said, 'Bugger off.'

Eddie was incensed by his own helplessness. Zap zap, wham bam, kaboom, Eddie wanted to let loose his raging anger the way Captain Marvel and Superman did in the comic books. But that's one good thing about life: willy-nilly you become wise to the ways of the world. Captain Marvel and Superman had underlined the same truth. If you wanted to pick a fight, make sure it was with a weaker adversary. Eddie swallowed his pride and sat quietly smouldering in his seat.

The main picture started and Eddie forgot all, his neighbours, Father D'Souza, his family, his dead father, his homework, the terrible fate that awaited him. What was going on on the screen would make him forget to eat, drink, sleep and breathe. And if you could forget to breathe, you could forget the very name of God. No wonder so many state legislatures in the United States wanted to ban the work of Satan which Bill Haley and his Comets, Elvis Presley, Chuck Berry, Jerry Lee Lewis, Gene Vincent and all the other godless people called rock'n' roll. A controversy raged amongst clergymen and decent lay folk across India whether or not *Rock Around the Clock* should be declared enemy number one in Catholic Journals, and any Catholic who saw it despite the proscription, excommunicated.

It was difficult to decide what was worse: the events on the screen or those in the aisles of the theatre. The primitive rhythms and gods of Africa had flown across continents and invaded the Strand cinema. The young men and women in the theatre were obviously possessed by the most dank and evil spirits. They had regressed God knows how many millennia to their tribal origins. They had gone wild. Stark raving mad. They danced besottedly. They would be tearing their clothes off next and fornicating like reptiles right there to the bumping, grinding and libidinous rhythms emanating from the screen.

Eddie had never witnessed such pandemonium before. For some time he watched the proceedings on the screen and in the aisles with a half-open mouth and ripped open eyes that would never again close. Then his hands and legs and arms began to twitch as if electrocuted. They had severed their connections with his body and gained a life of their own. He tried to hold himself still but to no avail. He was no longer his own creature. The witch-doctors and shamans and the dark forces of the earth had taken charge of him. In a fourteen-inch circle, Eddie managed to perform what seasoned dancers could not have on a 320×320 foot stage.

The plywood bottom of his seat broke and Eddie's chin cracked on the back of the seat in front of him. His brains, sinuses, eyes and tonsils crashed into each other and could not be unscrambled. He felt his chin. Apart from a three-inch gash and exposed bone and a permanent cavity where his former brain had resided, there was no injury whatsoever.

Eddie had no alternative now but to step on to the floor. 'Giddiup ding dong, giddiup,' the whole auditorium rocked on its feet and clapped as if the audience had been training all its life for that one song. There were about a hundred couples dancing in the aisles and in the space between the screen and the seats. Eddie didn't have a partner but he made such a song and dance all on his own that the other couples drew back grudgingly. At first he was nothing but a pesky twerp whom the men would have happily pushed out but for their girlfriends who were more patronizing and willing to watch the little boy's antics for a while. Eddie had two things going for him. He didn't know how to dance and he equated his body completely with the music. He let go. He didn't just dance with his legs; his kidneys, liver, fingers, tendons, pancreas, bronchi, throat, chin, buttocks, everything responded to the music and danced.

He was coming out of a particularly frenetic phase when he saw a young woman in a dress with red, blue and green stripes alternating with white, leave her partner. She was unconscious of what she was doing and seemed only to be waiting for a cue to enter the magic web he had been weaving. She slid in. A single finger welded the girl to him. He spun her all the way till she was nestling against him for an instant and then let go of her. She uncoiled. The edge of her skirt undulated and touched him. He felt the blade of a knife run under the entire length of his skin.

Now even a finger did not join them and yet they wound and unwound in each other's arms. They had become mind readers though they had not set eyes on each other before. Their bodies were yin and yang, exact opposites that drew them together and repelled them.

Now Bill Haley was belting out *See You Later, Alligator*. Eddie had not thought much of him when he first saw him on screen. He was a pudgy, slightly crosseyed fellow with a swirl of hair slicked carefully on to his forehead. One of his eyes was somewhat volatile and kept wandering away from the other. But then he started singing and Eddie thought he was the handsomest man he had seen. He wanted to wear the same clothes Haley had on, black trousers and shiny jacket with a lame or velvet lapel, frilled shirt buttoned at the collar, and of course the very same hairstyle. Come to think of it, he thought the eyes rather charming now. There was no question in his mind, he wanted to be Bill Haley now and forever.

He got into the bus and realized that he had no money. The conductor called him all kinds of names and stopped the bus to make him get off. He didn't mind walking. The girl's skirt brushed against him. In the Bombay heat and night, he shivered a little.

Fourteen

Parvatibai may have made prophetic pronouncements about her son's career (as with all prophecies the point is not whether they come true or not, but whether people believe the dark and dour prognostications of the soothsayer) but on the level of self-preservation alone it would have been more profitable if she had spent the same time and effort on her husband and divined what he and the future held in store for her family. Frankly, she did not need to examine his horoscope or palm, the tea-leaves at the bottom of his teacup or the entrails of sacrificial animals, or measure the shadow of her husband at the first light of dawn. All she needed to do and didn't, was to pick up clues and signals, and there were plenty of them, and interpret them. For instance on a Tuesday, four months ago, he changed the parting of his hair. When the thin plaited leather bridge of his Kolhapuri chappals gave way, instead of picking up the shoe in his hand and bringing it home for Parvatibai to get repaired, he took it to the cobbler himself.

He had shown other signs of independence and initiative. In the last three weeks he had shaved seven times which was some kind of record for him since he normally shaved once every fortnight. As usual his objective, at least the immediate one, was clear. The intention was not to erase the stubble on his chin and cheek, it was to gouge out the top layer if not the second one of his skin. He did a fairly good job of it and a Hindusthan blade assisted him considerably in the task. It was a dual purpose blade. Cut-and-paste artists from advertising agencies broke it into tiny jagged pieces and cut art card, poster paper, bromides, box board and mountboard into the sizes they wanted or impaled individual typeset letters or words on a point and carried out proof-corrections in artworks according to the proofreader's or copy-writer's instructions. It was also, as you have already learnt, used for shaving.

Economics alone would not account for Shankar-rao's use of this particular brand of blade. Parvatibai was willing to buy him an imported 7 O'Clock or Gillette steel. They were a little more expensive but they lasted longer and they didn't disfigure the face as systematically as Hindusthan blades did. Perhaps the appeal of the Indian blade was an aesthetic one. After a good, clean shave, Shankar-rao had, on an average, seventeen tiny bits of *Bittambatmi* stuck all over his face and throat. The newspaper fragments absorbed the blood as it clotted. When he took them off, the nicks opened and his face once again looked like the scene of a bloody miniature battle. Shankar-rao avoided drinking water after a shave for fear of springing leaks and the water flowing out like a fountain from his throat.

The writing on the wall should have been clear by then even to a blind man or woman, but even if it was not, there was one sign no one could have missed. On two occasions Shankar-rao had effectively shut up Ravan's warbling. What he did was so unusual, it should have silenced all the people of the CWD chawls. He sang two phrases of one of the songs from DDD repeatedly as he lay doubled up facing the wall on the bed and when he traipsed to the toilet at the end of the corridor on his floor. Parvatibai did not notice this or if she did, she did not pay any heed to the signs of turbulence and catastrophe ahead. What else can one say but that she had it coming to her?

~

Parvati's and Ravan's torture sessions came to an abrupt end one evening. His father, Shankar-rao, had gone to buy his tabloid, *Bittambatmi,* and had come back two and a half hours later with his sister. Parvatibai was sitting on the floor slicing cabbage on a willi at a speed that made her hand almost invisible. She must have been among the last ten women in Bombay, if not the whole of Maharashtra, who still used this traditional gadget without turning her fingers, palms and hands into ready-to-eat, raw mincemeat. It had a serrated disc sticking out at the end of a steel crescent with which she grated coconut but she had flipped back the curved knife which normally rested with its blade facing down on a wooden platform and was shredding the cabbage to fine confetti. Ravan, who was not having much success with his homework in history since he had no books, not even a maths book to refer to, looked up at his father in wonderment.

'Sister?' Parvatibai asked her husband as she continued to slice the cabbage for the next day's lunch, 'you never had a sister.'

Shankar-rao smiled and threw up his hands. 'Seeing is believing. There she is in flesh and blood. Father had a mistress and this is the fruit of that relationship,'

'I will not contest the truth or otherwise of that statement.' Parvatibai lost her concentration and cut her finger for the first time in all these years on the willi. The blood ran all over the green flakes of the cabbage but she was not aware of it. 'There's a young boy here and I would appreciate it if you spared us the details of the lady's antecedents.'

'Have it your way. She's here to stay.'

Parvatibai caught hold of Ravan's wrist and tried to drag him into the kitchen. He was transfixed. His eyes had lost all lateral motion. He would not be able to close his mouth in this life or the ones that would ineluctably follow for a Hindu. His father was a magician, a miracle worker. He had shoved his hand into an invisible hat and pulled out not a white dove, or a rabbit or a string of flamboyantly coloured scarves but a live woman, not just any woman but a sister. The door to the past was always locked. But his father had a key to it. A past that must have stretched to a time when Ravan was not born. Who could tell, tomorrow or a month later he might bring back a brother, his brother's children or a grandmother. It would be terrific to have children of his own age to play with. He could show Chandrakant Dixit and his classmates that they were welcome to leave him out of their games because he had lots of friends of his own.

What he yearned for most was a grandmother. He had seen Eddie's 'Granna' and how she pampered and shielded him and told him stories sitting at the top of the stairs on the fifth floor. For a brief while, Ravan too had had a family. He had never felt as secure and happy and wanted as the time when Shobhan and her folks had adopted him. He wasn't going to miss them any more. He had an aunt now. It would take time to get to know her but that was OK. She would play carrom with him and buy him schoolbooks. She was wearing kumkum and a mangalsutra and would very likely have sons or daughters as old as Ravan. And even if she didn't, she could start now. Just think of it, that silent, empty and uncommunicative house of his was going to come alive. It would be bubbling with laughter, there would be long conversations, arguments, disagreements, the children would throw tantrums, he would set his jaws tightly one upon the other, flatten his lips till they were a razor-thin slit and quieten them with just one disapproving look.

His mother jerked his hand hard. What was the matter with her? He knew that she never allowed her lunch and dinner customers to step inside the house. Whatever converse there was between them, it was always outside in the common passage. But this was his aunt, his own father's sister. Could she not make her feel welcome? The fact was his mother was an unsociable person, all work and no play had killed all feeling in her. Do surgery on her and instead of a heart, you would find a stone. What was wrong with sitting down in this room? He always did. It wasn't as if his father and aunt had something private to discuss. And even if they had, they had all the time in the world. Hadn't his father just said she was here to stay? Ravan rose unwillingly, his head was turned back and his eyes were still fixed on his aunt. And then it happened. He was astounded, delighted and speechless. His aunt winked at him.

That night Parvatibai made her first false move. She would regret it bitterly, she would curse herself, swear mutely at her shortsightedness and the calamitous consequences that followed from it but there was no undoing what she had done. She spread both Ravan's and her own mattress inside in the kitchen. She liked to go to sleep early since she had to get up by five and start cooking. By quarter to ten she had switched off the light in the kitchen and was dozing within five minutes. Ravan was restive because although he was still in his own home, he had never before slept in the kitchen.

She didn't know what time it was but she was suddenly woken up. Her husband's sister was panting, screeching, screaming, slapping Shankar-rao, egging him on, instructing him about what she wanted done where, sighing, moaning, biting his ear hard so that he was hollering and hopping. She encouraged him with strings of abuse that the people from Sawantwadi and Ratnagiri in Konkan use continually as endearments or for emphasis and occasionally in deadly earnest. They were sharp, sonorous, brief word-pictures that had more immediacy than the real thing. She called him mother- and sister-fucker, a whore-son, pimp, arse-buggerer, pederast, cunt-licker, father-fucker and then became highly creative in the extensions and variations of her sexual imagery. A horse's prick in your mother's gash, tie a knot in your member and whip me with it, your sister's dash dash is wide enough to accommodate a rhino and have room left. At this point Parvati made her second wrong move. Instead of letting sleeping dogs lie, at least for that night, the scatological exuberance of her husband's sister induced panic and horror in her. She did not think of her son as an innocent or a nascent Buddha who needed to be shielded from the facts of life but she was of the belief that his sex-education, especially that of a more arcane and erudite variety, should be left for a maturer day.

Her concern for her son was doubtless valid but her fears at that particular moment were unfounded. A little observation and quiet reflection would have revealed that Master Ravan Pawar was dead to the world and not likely to be resurrected except under the gravest and the most frightful provocation. Unfortunately this was readily available in the state that Parvatibai was in. 'Get up. Can you hear?' she whispered urgently to him. 'What can you hear? Tell me every word. No, I don't want to hear. Most certainly I don't want you to hear.' In a rush of maternal protective instincts she gathered Ravan to herself. Her stupendous breastworks, one on either side of his face, should not only have dampened but drowned all terrestrial and extra-terrestrial sound. They did. They also almost smothered Ravan to death. The boy had been woken up without due preparation and preliminaries and then asphyxiated in a sustained fashion. The more he fought for air, the more Parvati was convinced that he was savouring the martial calls and counter-calls that issued forth from the next room and passed unhindered through the thin plywood partition that rose three-quarters of the way to the ceiling.

In one last-ditch effort, Ravan flung his mother aside and reeled drunkenly from lack of oxygen. He was sure he was hallucinating. A woman was crying out aloud: on your mark, get set, charge, attack, onward ho. The voice that followed these exhortations was unmistakable. His father, that staid, tepid, and immovable object which had been a part of Ravan's landscape and furniture since childhood, was vociferously sounding the war-cry of the. Hindus: Har Har Mahadev. Har Har Mahadev. Kill, kill, kill. Fierce and fatal battle was joined by Ravan's aunt and father. His own mother, the usually sane and solid Parvatibai, was rushing around like a demented woman. She clasped her hands around Ravan's ears. In the adjoining room, his father's sister was whimpering and wheedling for more. She yelled and begged in a rhythmic chant that was hypnotic: don't stop, don't stop, go on, go on you mother... that dread word from which Parvati wanted to shield her son stayed incomplete. 'Oh no, don't tell me. You coward, you've admitted defeat even before knowing which way the battle would go.' Parvatibai had now packed Ravan's ears with cottonwool and was tying a wet sari that she had pulled down from the clothes-line like a turban around his head. The first two swirls went around Ravan's ears but the next one covered his nose.

'Stop it, Ma.' He tried to push his mother away. 'Stop it, you are suffocating me.'

Parvati lifted the twisted cloth from over his nose but continued to swathe him. She was in far too much of a hurry and the loops kept slipping down to Ravan's neck as she drew them tight. It hit Ravan then that his mother was going to strangle him. He yanked the sari out of her hands.

'Give it back to me.' Parvatibai closed in on Ravan threateningly. For some reason both of them were talking in whispers. Ravan retreated till he was up against the door of the room. Suddenly there was an eerie silence. The scuffle and battle-cries from the next room had ceased. Parvati stood undecided, then went to the plywood wall and put her ear against it.

What was wrong with his father, Ravan wondered. Had he not after all these years had the good fortune of rediscovering his sister? Why had he brought her home if all they were going to do was swear at each other and fight murderously? And what was the matter with his aunt? He didn't even know her name yet. His father was the most lethargic man he had ever known. How and why had she provoked him to the point where he was willing to kill her? There was not a sound from outside. Were they both wounded and bleeding or were they already dead?

Parvati opened the door stealthily and before Ravan realized what was happening covered his eyes, pushed him into the outside room, and without looking right or left, unlatched the front door, shoved him out and down the staircase.

'Please don't kill me, Ma, please don't,' Ravan thirteen and a half going on fourteen was bleating now. But his heartless mother didn't let go of him. He could hear his aunt laughing uncontrollably.

'Poor Ravan,' she said and slapped his father. Parvati and Ravan were on the second floor close to the Sarang home but Shankar-rao and his sister were still in splits. At the bottom of the stairs, Parvati unmasked her son and flung the sari over her right shoulder. Ravan was trembling but she ignored him.

'Let's go for a walk,' she told him and started walking.

'What for?'

'Because I say so.'

'You go, I'm going back home to sleep.'

'Don't even try it,' she said coldly. 'I'll break your leg right here and now.'

He didn't need to look at her. He didn't disbelieve her words. They walked up to the park on Mazagaon Hill where Prakash and Ravan had sat. The gate was locked. Parvati picked up her sari, climbed over and sat on a bench. Ravan avoided her and lay down on another. Strange and cosmic cataclysms and violent upheavals were under way. He looked at his mother and knew that he had lost her. She didn't want him any more. All those months when she had pounded him to a fine powder because he had sold her earring to see *Dil Deke Dekho*, or even before that when he had discovered that he was a murderer, he had not once got the feeling that she wanted to be rid of him. Now he knew his time had come. He didn't mind that, even though he had pleaded with her not to kill him. What he couldn't bear was to see her sitting with her head in her hands. He would have liked to smash her face to avoid seeing the despair in her eyes. His mother, his own indomitable, unvanquishable, never-say-die mother, who stood between him and the perils of the world, his first and final resort, she would not look at him or acknowledge him. He would protect and preserve her, fight the armies of the night and the gods of daylight and shield her from whatever evil had befallen her. But she had woven such an impenetrable wall of hopelessness around herself, he found her unapproachable. Ravan had no idea how long he had been asleep when his mother came and woke him up.

The next morning, around ten o'clock, after Ravan had gone to school, Shankar-rao came into the kitchen and said he and his sister wanted coffee and some snacks. Parvatibai made two cups of tea and took them to the front room. She spoke softly but her voice had Ravan's tremor of last night. Tea will be at seven in the morning. Lunch is at eleven. Tea and biscuits or savouries at four and dinner at eight. Ravan and I will go for a walk from nine to ten-fifteen. Whatever brother and sister wish to do at that time, is your private affair. When we get back I expect the door to be unlatched and the two of you asleep.'

Shankar-rao tossed his shoulders. 'We'll do what we please and…' His sister put her hand on his arm and said, 'That's OK. We'll be sleeping by the time you get back.'

∽

The woman saw Ravan staring at her and ignored him. She sat up, the pallu of her sari fell on the bed. She did not pick it up and replace it on her left shoulder. She had a witching smile that fluctuated around her dimples. Her right leg disengaged itself and came down over the edge of the bed. It ran back and forth over a man's torso.

He had almost flung his school bag on the floor when he realized he had walked into the wrong house. He stepped back. Couldn't be Eddie's place. That woman on the bed in the red sari and green blouse, with her leg pulled up and the back of her head resting on the palms of her hands was not Violet, her mother or Pieta. She had a kumkum dot on her forehead and paan in her mouth which had painted her lips an earthen red. Where the hell was he? Sleepwalking in broad daylight as always, wake up Ravan Pawar. Must be the Jadhav residence on the third floor. Unless of course he had stepped into Chawl No. 16 or 21.

Ravan was turning around to leave when he glanced down. His father Shankar-rao was lying on the paper-thin mattress on which Ravan had slept all his life. The woman pulled up her sari, scratched her right calf lazily and let the sari down. How could he possibly have forgotten his aunt of last night? Were there some things so terrible that the mind wiped them out instantly?

Ravan stood undecided for a moment and then ran out of the building. He did not stop till he was out of breath and his feet would carry him no further. Mr Billimoria, his tae kwon do teacher, was used to seeing him turn up at any time in the evening even though he was officially enrolled for the early morning class. He usually entrusted Ravan with the job of supervising the warming-up exercises for the junior section.

'You OK?' he asked Ravan during a break in the exercises. Ravan nodded his head. He still hadn't got his breath back. 'You don't look it.'

Mr Billimoria continued with the class. After ten minutes he gave up.

'In India we believe in paying for shoddy work in the hope that others will ignore our own third-rate stuff.' His voice rose suddenly. 'But you are not in India. This patch of 20 yards is Billimoria land. I don't pay you, you pay me and yet it hurts my eyes, my whole being hurts like hell to watch your antics here. I'm considering doubling your fees but that won't relieve the agony of watching grasshoppers picking their wooden legs to pee all over me.' He paused and looked distastefully at his pupils. 'Ravan,' he did not take his eyes off his recalcitrant students, 'it seems impossible for me to humiliate these monumental Henry Moore Stones and bronzes. Perhaps you may be foolhardy enough to take this class and demonstrate that what we are attempting here is ensemble choreography and not private twitching.'

Ravan did as he was bidden but he had the feeling that while the class was particularly lackadaisical that day, his teacher was also making it a pretext to reach out to him. Ravan's pupils were older than him but he was not awed by them. He could have put the group through their paces blindfolded and yet picked out the slightest discrepancy or laxness. He was his master's younger version and therefore unable to suffer clumsiness but he was far more patient than Mr Billimoria.

'Good work, Ravan,' Mr Billimoria told him at the end of the day, 'but your heart's not in it today.'

Was an answer expected of him? What could he say since he didn't know what the matter with him was.

'Good night, Ravan.'

'Good night, sir.'

Ravan locked up and gave the keys to Mr Billimoria. He pretended to walk away but after Mr Billimoria had disappeared, he went back and sat on the steps of the tae kwon do gym. It was dark. The lights in the surrounding buildings had come on at least an hour and a half ago. The vast grounds of St Theresa's School were empty. The stumps and the bails on the cricket field had been removed and the netting used for practice sessions looked like a prison abandoned by its jailbirds.

Ravan recalled his physics teacher enunciating the laws of thermodynamics. It seemed that whether you converted matter to heat, or heat or electricity to another form of energy, the equations stayed constant. There may be loss of energy or heat in the process of conversion but everything remained within the universe. What did that mean? Were the waves that Mr Billimoria had created when he was demonstrating the poetry of tae kwon do on Ravan's first encounter with that martial art form still dispersing, reacting and ricocheting against other previous or newer waves in the atmosphere? What had happened to the energy and sound-waves of the 'ghati' with which Mr Billimoria had addressed him? Had they left an impress on the air that would last to the end of time? Could it be recovered? Was there really no history to energy? Were the past and the future in the present? Was death a passage of one form of energy into another? He had no idea where these thoughts were leading or what he was trying to get at. He wasn't quite sure why he was hovering at the edge of questions about the nature and purpose of life.

He could not decipher the hieroglyphics of the events of late noon that day in his house. Why should a single night turn his world upside down? What was the bond between a son and his father? Ravan felt he was as attached to the chair or fan in his house as he was to his father. That back which he had turned upon the world and Ravan many, many years ago did not give any purchase to Ravan. What had they done with his mother? Had they driven her out? Was he finally an orphan? If aloneness was the same as being on your own and shut out, then despite the rock and citadel and strength of his mother, he had always been an orphan. It was not an alien sensation, certainly nothing to get worked up about. It was like being born with a bodily defect. Either you combated it and got around it or you ignored it as Shobhan did. So why did he think that the earth had slipped from under his feet and he was marooned in space?

Who was going to look after his mother? There were no rewards in life for doing a good job, supporting your family single-handed, bringing up your healthy husband and school-going son and working close to sixteen hours a day. You could be thrown out at any moment. Were the roles of husband and wife spelt out when two people got married? When two parties came together was it mandatory that one was subordinate to the other?

Even between a victimizer and victim there was always a sense of belonging, need and bonding. What last night or that leg which rowed across his father's body like a paddle in water made plain to him was that he was no longer marginal or peripheral to the scheme of things; he was irrelevant. When it was possible at some future date to retrieve the past by unscrambling the air, there would be no trace of him.

Where was he planning to go? Why was he always asking questions when he did not have the answer to anything. He had heard of boys who ran away from home and joined the circus. There were stories of mendicants who lured runaways or lost children to some distant place and trained them to pick pockets or beg or shine shoes. He could always take a train and go to Delhi, Madras or Hyderabad. But what was the use? If the police caught him wandering around at night, they would worm his address out of him and take him back to his father and the new tenant. Someone tapped him on his shoulder.

'Let's go home, Ravan.'

'Can't we go some place else, Ma? Take a room and supply food to your customers from there?'

'We could but we need to pay a big pagdee, fifteen or twenty thousand rupees before anyone will rent a room to us.'

His mother held his hand in hers, something she rarely did these days. 'Besides why should we look for another place when we already have a home. That place is yours and mine, Ravan. Don't let anybody tell you any different.'

~

'Ma, the second button on my shirt's gone.'

'Give it to me.' His aunt caught hold of his shirt-tail as he was going to the kitchen. 'I'll stitch it for you.' He tried to pull it away from her. She didn't let go.

'You would like it to tear, wouldn't you, so you won't have to go to school?'

'That's not true. I like school.'

'Sure. That's why you fail in every test.'

'How do you know that?'

'You have only red marks in your notebooks.'

'I still like to go to school.'

'Lots of girls waiting for you there, is it?' His father's sister had slowly drawn the shirt out as if she were pulling in a line with a fish at the end of it.

'Chhhya. No girls in our school.' She pulled out the sewing box from under the bed. 'Sit down, don't hover over me and make me nervous while I thread the needle.'

He looked at her while she sewed the button. She was a source of endless wonder to him. After tea in the mornings she put several plastic clips in her hair. When she took them out, believe it or not, her hair had waves running through it. Often she left a comb in her hair. She took a bath late and wandered around with just a blouse and petticoat.

'Please wear a sari,' Parvati had told her. 'There's a young boy in the house.' What he had to do with his aunt's sari was a mystery to him. She had laughed at his mother. 'And ruin the crease of my sari? You've got to be joking. Besides, don't shelter your son so much, Parvatibai. It's time he was exposed to the facts of life.'

'Let me be the judge of that,' his mother said sharply. 'Everything in due time.'

Come evening, his father's sister powdered her face, wore an ironed sari and then put on lipstick. Her lips were thin but she made them look wide and full painting them broadly and reshaping them. She had a wooden vanity case that was inlaid with exquisite brass vines, leaves, flowers and fruits. If she wanted to get at coloured powders and pastes, rouge, mascara, eyeshadow, kohl, Snow, foundation and cold creams stored in tiny compartments and boxes in the inner recesses, she lifted the whole lid and laid it back. But if she wanted to look at herself or put the red tika on her forehead, she flipped half the lid back and stood the mirror on the inside at an angle. She spent hours squeezing blackheads from her face, plucking her eyebrows or just gazing at herself.

She gave him his shirt.

'Do you know my name, Ravan?'

He shook his head. 'Don't you want to know?' She had a way of thrusting her chest out from time to time which left him confused and a little uncomfortable though he couldn't say why.

'I asked you a question.'

'Yes.'

'Yes what?'

'Yes, I would like to know your name.'

She caught hold of his hand. 'Are you sure?'

'Yes.'

She pricked his index finger with the needle in her hand.

'Ouch,' Ravan yelled in surprise. 'Why did you do that?'

'To tell you my name.'

She pressed the tip of his finger hard till a big drop of blood gathered on it. His yelp had brought Parvatibai out. She stood in the door to the kitchen. He tried to withdraw his hand but his aunt held it fast. He had the odd feeling that she was doing it deliberately to provoke his mother.

'The name's Lalee. I'm the red running in your veins. I'm the red of the lipstick and the red of the paan I chew. I'm the red in the sky at the Gateway of India as night is about to fall.' She put his finger in her mouth and sucked it.

He squirmed with an embarrassment that was mixed with a strange undercurrent of pleasure.

'Let go of my hand.' He was sure his mother was watching him.

'I'm Lalee,' his aunt whispered, 'and you are my lal. Do you know the meaning of lal?'

'It means red.'

'Yes but in Hindi it also means son.'

Ravan jerked his finger away and slipped into his shirt with an excessive show of haste.

'See? You are Lalee's lal.'

'I'm not your son.'

She squeezed his finger again, much harder this time. The drop of blood returned.

~

'I need money,' Shankar-rao came into the kitchen one day and told Parvati. 'My expenses have gone up. I have a sister to look after. I'll need at least ten rupees a day.'

Parvati Pawar. It had crossed her mind since that Thursday over a month ago when her husband had brought home his sister, to break Shankar-rao's left leg, then the right; the left hand, then the right; to rip open his stomach, remove his intestines and use them as a rope for her and Ravan to climb out of the window and down to the bottom of CWD Chawl No. 17 and never to return; to pick up the wooden bat with which the maid beat the dirt and the life out of clothes and split open Shankar-rao's head, no, change that, she would have liked to treat her husband's head as her sari, or Ravan's shirt and shorts or any piece of cloth and work on it all day and all night for weeks till there was no wood left in the bat. She had had other thoughts, some less violent but more malevolent than others. She had always known that she had two children and of the two Ravan was the older.

She did not have high or low expectations of life; she did not think of her lot as a good, bad or indifferent hand that fate had dealt her. Life was a given, you did your best which in Parvati's case meant her damnedest best and that was that. She would not admit it because the honesty of admission could often mean that you had given up, but sometimes in the middle of her recent sleepless nights she was unable to lift her hand or turn on her side or sit up because her husband's last move had broken her spine and spirit. Was it because Shankar-rao had thrown down a card that she had never seen before? Yes and no. It certainly had not occurred to her that her husband would wilfully destroy his home and so wantonly confuse their son. She had no truck with what Shankar-rao did outside his home but what was Ravan going to tell his friends or anyone who asked about the visitor? That she was his aunt? Chawl No. 17 and every other chawl in the CWD complex knew by now of Shankar-rao's sister. Parvati's own customers would enquire after her, start a conversation with her and linger at the door. All the neighbours starting from the children sniggered and smirked when they referred to the aunt and the women gloated over what they considered Parvati's much-deserved comeuppance. That was all right with her. She could take it and like all scandals, this one too would lose its novelty and be forgotten.

Men and women carry on with each other. They always have and are not about to discontinue one-night stands, flings and affairs. Their neighbours might be incensed, their sense of morality deeply offended but that was natural. If you lived in a chawl, maybe it was the same almost anywhere else, you had to reinforce each other's hypocrisy. It was bound to rile them that Shankar-rao, and not they, had got himself a companion and was brazen enough to install her at home. You had to hand it to Shankar-rao. He had been prone to disappear at night occasionally, and sometimes when he had gone to pick up the newspaper, he had stayed away for an hour or so. But that was the extent of his contact with the outside world. He didn't have a job and he was not flush with money. Parvati didn't remember too clearly what he looked like but never mind who his sister was, or where she came from, he had got her and the other men in the neighbourhood were envious that they hadn't. But what was Ravan going to make of the woman, his father and his mother? Most of all, himself? She believed that like it or not, children inherit the sins and practices of their parents. Mind you, she was not even touching upon the nocturnal shenanigans of her husband and the woman.

Parvatibai had no imagination or rather she had no time to indulge the flights and options that a febrile imagination offers. The words surprise or astonishment are of course inadequate to describe her reaction to the newcomer but that was not what got her down. If she felt defeated before she had a chance to retaliate, it was because she had no idea how to react. Like Ravan and all the other pigheaded optimists of this earth she suspected that there was a right and effective response to any situation but it continued to elude her. Without breast-beating or self-pity, she had asked herself what she could do. She had not considered physical disfigurement of her husband as a deterrent in a raffish moment of light-heartedness. She knew that she would do almost anything to protect and save her home and her son, within what she considered reasonable limits. What did she consider reasonable? Shankar-rao was physically stronger than her but she could take him unawares. As a consequence she could be thrown into jail and Ravan would very likely be out on the street. Violence was no solution just as taking her case to the courts wasn't. She didn't have the money to hire a lawyer. Besides she didn't think men, which is what judges were, would listen favourably to her dilemma. Appeal to the finer instincts of the sister? She didn't think that there was much fineness there anyway. And she was never in two minds about one fact: the intruder was blameless. If Shankar-rao was so hell-bent on being made a sucker, who but a saint or a fool would resist taking advantage of him? Would someone please tell her, she was willing to pay him or her for the advice, how to get that woman out of the house? Her husband wanted ten rupees a day, that was three hundred rupees a month. Give or take some, that was about the size of her monthly profit margin.

Parvati answered her husband in her usual level voice. 'We don't make that kind of money. If you need more money, the only alternative is to take up a job.'

Parvatibai was much mistaken. There were other alternatives.

~

Two mothers? One for bread and butter and one for jam? Lalee's lal, he liked the sound of that phrase. I too am red, Ravan thought. Red as the stop signal at the traffic lights. Red as the loincloths of the boys in the Sabha gymnasium, red as a parrot's beak, red as, red as... he ran out of reds. He hated going out every night for a walk but that was because of his mother, not his aunt. He had not heard his father and aunt fight after that first day.

'Lal' his aunt called him. There was something funny about the way she sat. It made him feel furtive and he had to turn his eyes away. She always sat with her legs spread apart. But it was not just that. He would not have said this aloud or even to himself but there was something about the way she carried herself, stood with her hands on her hips, talked, pulled up her sari, walked or just looked at you that made him feel uncomfortable. He recalled how Shobhan's sister, Tara, adjusted her body-movements, the lilt of her behind, the tension in her neck, the way she threw her pallu over her shoulder or flicked her tongue over her lips when she was eating sherbet or ice-cream but it was always for the benefit of her boyfriend, Shahaji Kadam. It was the same with the girls from the top floors, their come-ons were directed at specific people. With his Aunt Lalee almost anything that moved got the same treatment. She was never really relaxed. Even her involuntary habits had a studied element to them. You were always aware that she knew that you were watching, and was doing whatever she was to provoke you or to make it a point to tell you that she was not doing it for you but for somebody else.

'How's your finger, Lal?'

'Which finger?'

'You've already forgotten? The one that was bleeding.'

'Oh that? That was weeks ago. It's fine.'

'What a shame. If it was bleeding, I could have sucked it and painted my mouth red.'

'Yuck, I can't stand the smell of blood.'

'I love it. I'm a vampire. Come here.'

'Not if you are going to pierce a needle into my finger.'

'Can't bear just a little pain for your Lalee, Lal?'

Red as, red as what that song said, lal lal gal. Red as cheeks.

'Come here, you beastly little boy.'

He loved the names she called him and all the nonsensical epithets she used. He sat down next to her on the floor. In the daytime she sat on the durry while Shankar-rao got the bed, but at night it was the reverse. He didn't feel shy or awkward because his mother wasn't around. She was out very often these days. What she did was fill the tiffin boxes by four o'clock, leave them just inside the door, serve tea to his father, aunt and him and then stay out till 8 o'clock at night.

'What?'

'I've got something for you but if you don't want it, forget it.'

'For me?'

'Haven't you got a present ever before?'

'Sure. Ma buys me my school uniform at the start of the year. When I was a good boy she used to buy me all my schoolbooks. And she buys me clothes for Diwali.'

'Those things are not presents, silly. Books and uniforms are things you need. Presents are given just like that. For no reason at all except that it may be someone's birthday or marriage. Or because you love someone and feel like showing that love.'

She pulled out a box wrapped in brown paper from the space she had appropriated for herself under the bed and handed it to him.

'I can't take it.'

'Why?' She almost screamed at him. 'Why?'

He was cowed down by the anger in her voice. He stared at the floor and answered softly.

'I've got nothing to give you.'

That elicited an even more unexpected response. She drew him close and kissed him on the cheek. She was delighted that he looked more surprised and pleased than she had expected. She kissed him on the lips. He went red.

'Lal lal gal. Look how red your cheeks are. Maybe you've got red wine in them. Gifts are not a tit-for-tat competition. Open your present. Quick.'

He tried to peel the tape off carefully so that the brown paper would not tear. Aunt Lalee was not so patient. She stuck her nail into the paper and ripped it. He opened the box. He had never seen, heard of or imagined a shirt so red. And yet right there in front of his eyes folded immaculately inside the box was a red so beautiful he wouldn't dare to wear it for fear of creasing or dirtying it.

'For me?'

'No. Your Aunt Lalee's going to wear it. Stop wasting time. Let's see how it looks on you.'

She made Ravan take off his school shirt and wear the new one. Oh, the smell of a new shirt. He kept sniffing at it.

'Only dogs do that, Ravan. Smell their armpits, their coats, between their legs. Stand up straight and let me button you up. Look at you, you look like a red prince. Ravishing. All the women in the chawls are going to leave their husbands and throw themselves at your feet. You can't afford to reject a single one because she'll instantly commit suicide.'

'What absolute nonsense.' Ravan smiled shyly. He had not got so much attention from his mother as far back as he could remember.

'You call it nonsense? If the sight of you drives your Aunt Lalee plain crazy, can you imagine what must happen to mere mortals like the women in these chawls? Star material, Ravan, sheer star material. One of these days a film director's going to be passing this way and he's going to spot you by chance. That's the end. We'll never get to see you again. You'll be the new Shammi Kapoor, Dev Anand, Dilip Kumar, Rajendra Kumar. You won't look at us. People will mob you. The only way we'll get to see you is on the screen.'

'Take off that shirt.' His mother was at the door.

Ravan wasn't quite sure how, but he knew he had betrayed his mother. Why couldn't she have come a little later and allowed him to enjoy his moment of glory. She was such a spoilsport. How long had she been standing there watching him? Had she heard everything? His Aunt Lalee had such a way with words. She made even the most far-fetched things seem real. But when she talked about Shammi Kapoor, she touched something deep within him, a sacred and devout spot where the flame of adoration burnt eternally. Shammi Kapoor, his hero from *Dil Deke Dekho*, the man, he could even be a god, for whose sake he had committed a theft that had deprived him of his schoolbooks and earned him his mother's rage and thrashings.

Just a couple of minutes before, his Aunt Lalee had conjured up a vision of him, Ravan, as the greatest star of all. His movie was being premiered, there were hundreds of thousands of people mobbing him outside the Broadway theatre (he would have preferred Liberty but he had not seen it, not even from outside and couldn't incorporate it into his vision), people from the CWD chawls were screaming his name but he couldn't hear them because there was nobody in that crowd who wasn't chanting Ravan, Ravan. He saw his Aunt Lalee for a second but the mob was cradling him on the tips of their raised hands and passing him on straight into the theatre. Shammi Kapoor and Asha Parekh were waiting inside. They touched his feet and then hugged him. 'Ravan,' they said, 'we were big stars and we had swollen heads. But you've brought us to our senses. You are the greatest. You are our master and we are your slaves.' He would have liked to exchange a few words with them but the audience was clapping and hollering for him. As he was propelled into the auditorium, Shammi Kapoor called out to him, 'Ravan, one request, one request from your greatest fan. Please honour it. I'll be indebted to you all my life. Your red shirt.'

Ravan started to unbutton his shirt. He stopped and said, 'No, I won't take it off. You are jealous of my friendship with Aunt Lalee. In all these years you've never given me a gift. Aunt Lalee's been here for barely three or four months and already she's given me a shirt. Not an ordinary shirt but a red one, the colour of Aunt Lalee.'

His mother went into the kitchen. If she was angry, disappointed or let down by her one and only son, she did not show it. Aunt Lalee drew out a small ball of cotton from her vanity case and then a brocade purse whose plastic gold thread was tarnished to a dirty black. Inside were ranged ten tiny glass bottles with glass stoppers. Aunt Lalee examined each bottle individually and then opened one. A heavy, stupefying perfume emanated from it. His aunt tilted the bottle gently and wet the cotton. A relentless wave of nausea started to build inside Ravan. His head reeled and his legs felt like butter on a hot day. The vapours from the bottle filled his head and glazed his eyes. Lalee rubbed the cotton swab on Ravan's wrist and then behind the ears. Ravan blacked out. He was hit by a tidal wave. A 400 m.p.h. sneeze threw Ravan up in the air. His head jerked and his limbs were flung in all directions.

Aunt Lalee's purse shot up in slow motion. Ravan was still dancing up there in mid-air. A series of rapid-fire sneezes would not allow him to touch the ground. The purse started to lose height. With the precision of a practiced football player, Ravan headed the purse once more into space. It rose, it lurched, it emptied its contents. The bottles disengaged themselves. They tinkled like crystal in a chandelier and splintered on the floor. Ravan's red shirt was now wet with ten overpowering perfumes. The fit of sneezing was, if such a thing was possible, much worse than before.

'You... you... you,' it took a while for his father's sister to find her rhythm, 'you shit, you arsehole, fool.' She lit into Ravan with the flat of her hand, her fist and knee. 'Do you know how much those attars cost? And those priceless bottles?'

'Don't raise your hand against my son again,' Parvatibai interrupted Ravan's dismemberment, 'ever.'

'Can you see what your stupid son has done? Is your bloody father going to replace the perfumes or the perfume bottles?'

'The poor man's long dead. And even if I could, I wouldn't. As for my son I wonder why you were trying to win him over. A little too young for you, I would think.'

Parvatibai had to admit that that was uncalled for. She could not quite fathom Shankar-rao's sister's relationship with Ravan. Of course she was playing him against his mother, but there was more to it. Ravan, Parvatibai sometimes got the feeling, was her only human spot.

Parvatibai unbuttoned Ravan's shirt and got him out of it. 'Put on your shoes and sweep the floor. Make sure you collect even the tiniest fragment. Then mop the floor and have a bath.' She turned her attention to her husband who was wearing his latest acquisition: an expression of false bravado on his face. 'I want to have a word with you. Inside.'

'She and I have no secrets,' Shankar-rao parried and looked at his sister for approval. 'Say what you want in front of her.'

'You may share all you have with her but I don't think I care to humiliate you in front of her.'

Shankar-rao's face fell. He went into the kitchen.

'Where is the stove?'

'What stove?'

'The third primus stove.'

'Oh that.'

'Yes, oh that.' Parvati did not lose her patience.

'We wanted to eat some fish and she wanted to buy Ravan a gift but there was no money in the tin under the papads.'

'So you sold that stove I bought just two months ago?' There was a crack of disbelief running through Parvati's voice. 'Do you know how much these industrial stoves cost? How do you expect me to cook for fifty people without it?'

'Don't make a drama of it. Besides we didn't sell it, we just pawned it.'

'How am I going to get it redeemed?'

'You'll think of something.' Shankar-rao was pleased with his sense of sarcasm. 'You always do.'

'You sell one more thing from this house,' Parvati walked to the other stove on which the lentils were bubbling, removed the steaming lid with her bare fingers and dipped the big ladle in it, 'and I'll throw this dal at you.'

'Like hell you will.'

'Try me. Try me now.'

Shankar-rao stopped smiling.

~

In the past five or six weeks, Parvatibai had taken to going to the temple regularly. She prayed with an intensity that must have intimidated the gods. In mythical times they were often caught in a bind. Overwhelmed by the unswerving and relentless force of an ardent disciple's devotion, they were compelled to part with boons. Soon a time came when the devotee's powers posed a threat to the world order and the gods themselves. Desperate and fighting for survival, the gods resorted to dubious, unorthodox and underhand methods—subterfuges, sex, not to mention foul play—to regain the upper hand. Parvati's was a strange and perhaps misplaced prayer. She appealed to the goodness, reason and sense of fair-play in the gods. She forgot her surroundings and would not have returned home in time but for the fact that the temple-doors shut at 7.30 at night.

There were a couple of things preying on her mind: she had to get her husband's sister out once and for all, at almost any cost. The reasons were obvious enough. Her son was at extreme risk. The woman was a drain on the limited finances of the house. The outsider's presence also made Parvati realize something about herself. Parvati discovered to her surprise that she actually resented the loss of her independence and freedom. She earned her living. She had, she thought, earned the right to make her own decisions. But there was something which was even more pressing than these matters. What would she do if instead of one intruder, there were two? All that hyperactivity on the bed was bound to bear fruit. She had nothing against the unborn child. But she didn't want him in her house and she didn't want to support him. It really boiled down to one thing: the woman had to go, she had no idea how, though. If she did, why was she having to importune the gods? The folks up there, however, seemed a little unresponsive. Perhaps they had finally learnt a lesson. Mankind was nothing but trouble. Let them sort out their own affairs. Frankly, gods though they might be, they had enough problems of their own.

Someone she met at the temple told her about an Ananta Baba, a holy man of such powers that he could alter destiny and fate. Parvati was by nature and belief down to earth. She was not favourably disposed towards middlemen and intermediaries. God was a personal matter. The greatest of saints like Dnyaneshwar, Kabir and Tukaram had always maintained that when you could approach the top guy, there was little point in going to the underlings.

But desperate times call for desperate measures. Despite her reservations, Parvatibai visited Ananta Baba on four or five occasions. He was a good man, at least he did not ask for money or payment in kind. He listened patiently to her, gave her a black thread which was blessed and did not say whether things would improve or not.

What was the framework in which the celestials functioned? Wasn't there a time-frame within which alone intervention and aid had meaning? After all what was the point of succour if the person was beyond help? Was it possible that the gods who lived outside time did not comprehend the concept of time and its finality for mortals? One thing was certain: far from any help or assistance coming Parvati's way, matters had deteriorated to a point where her livelihood was threatened. Shankar-rao was a fool and that was that. It was his sister who was a conundrum. Parvatibai was of the belief that the key to human beings was self-interest. She was beginning to realize that she was wrong. Self-interest would have dictated that the least the new woman would do was preserve the status quo. Where else in Bombay could she get a roof over her head, three meals and non-stop service, all of them for free? And yet all that Shankar-rao's sister seemed interested in doing was destroying Parvati's home. Where would that leave her? She too would be out on the road but that obvious consideration did not figure in her thinking.

Parvatibai had heard that the gods visit trials and travails upon mankind to test them. Test what? Their faith, their loyalty, their fortitude, their capacity for suffering? She thought that this was what rotten parents did: they did not know how to handle their impotence and rage against their partners, fate or the world and so beat their children and said it was for their own good. She had no idea what good ensued from piling hardship upon hardship, evil and torture. If watching people lose heart, break down and squirm, gave the gods pleasure, then they were stranger than men and women. Whatever the truth of the matter, Parvatibai knew that she could not afford to leave the house for such long periods from now onwards. If she had had any choice, she would not have left home even to go shopping for vegetables, rice and other necessities.

The next morning Parvati got up an hour earlier than usual since she had to make do with two stoves instead of three. She went out after the lunch boxes had been collected. One earring was already with the pawnbroker. She gave him the second one and redeemed the stove. On her way back she tried to wrestle with a marketing dilemma: should she raise the price of her lunches and dinners by two rupees a month? Just a month before Shankar-rao had brought his sister home, her clients had raised hell and threatened to take their business to somebody else when she had increased the price of the meals. Would the traffic bear the strain of one more price-hike? It was dicey. At the very minimum, anywhere between five to ten customers would abandon her. Would the gains offset losses? Even if they did, which she doubted very much, she would not get to see the money. As soon as Shankar-rao and his sister heard Parvatibai telling her customers that their meal-ticket was going to cost more, they were bound to want to buy an imported American car like the winged one in which she had seen Raj Kapoor drive past, or a bungalow on Juhu beach. No, she would either have to say goodbye to her earrings or wait for a windfall to repossess them.

Fifteen

❖

'What have you gone and done to yourself, son?' Father Agnello D'Souza crossed himself and asked Eddie the question in alarm.

'Yes, your son. I haven't begun to tell you the brave and magnificent deeds of your son yet.'

'My son?' Father D'Souza stepped back in even greater alarm. Soft black silk slithered on his skin. Eddie's father's eyes were fixed on him. The next moment he would raise his right hand from the coffin and point it at him. I need some clarifications here, Father. Is it true Eddie is your son? Not mine? I need an answer, Father. Now. Unless I get to the bottom of this affair, my soul won't be able to rest in peace. 'Lord God, Jesus Christ, you are my witness,' the tremulous words finally escaped him, 'Eddie's not my son. Why do you say such terrible and untrue things? What will people say if they heard you?'

'Don't get me wrong, Father.' Violet Coutinho laid a gentle hand on his shoulder to pacify the overexcited priest. Burning coal. Atomic radiation. A leper's hand. Father Agnello drew back even further. Taken aback by his reaction, Violet opened the floodgates on Eddie.

'This, it's this boy who's ruined my whole life, destroyed my peace of mind. I sent him to get onions last evening at 5.30. He returned at 10.45 without the onions or the money. And in this condition, if you please. Not a word of explanation either.'

'I tried, but you locked the door on me,'

'Don't you dare say a word, shameless boy. God knows what he was up to, Father. Please help me, Father. I don't think I can bear it any more.'

'You said that the last time too.' Father Agnello was going to get his pound of flesh today but Violet was determined to have the last word.

'That's because you never straighten him out.'

~

Violet had not taken Eddie into the house the previous night. And she played the same trick she had when Mr Furtado had dragged him upstairs. She had a heart of stone, this woman who claimed to be his mother. Which mother would torture her son, her very own son, in such a terrible fashion? The same stony silence, except that it weighed on him even more this time. Talk of suffering, what did she know about it? No one had stopped talking to her. Starving him was bad enough but to starve herself, Pieta and Granna, only she could have thought of that. (Correct that. He hoped Pieta would starve herself to death.) She alone could be that diabolical. Why couldn't she be like any other mother and give him a drubbing? Let both her hands and mouth have free play till she felt better. See, he was not thinking of himself or of his own self-interest. He was concerned about her, he wanted to ease her pain. He had always had her welfare at heart. Why couldn't she at least occasionally reciprocate? When he couldn't take his mother's silence any longer, he did something he knew he shouldn't, but always did.

He spoke to his sister in a whisper through the barred window. 'What's the matter with Mamma?'

'What's the matter with Mamma?' The words came back amplified a million times over. 'You should know. It's because of you that she's lost her sleep and peace. She hasn't eaten and neither have Granna and I. At least they are old. But I'm young and growing and I need all the proteins and vitamins I can get.'

On some other occasion, Eddie would have cut her tongue out with a pair of scissors and thrown it to the crows. Or better still, wrung her neck with his bare hands. But today all he wanted was to become an ant or worm and disappear between the stone tiles of the floor. His sister had declaimed her piece to all of Mazagaon and yet his mother continued to darn the dress she wore to church as if unaware that he had returned, and she had locked him out. All the neighbours opened their doors and inspected Eddie's condition at this late hour. Their children tried to talk to him but they were told to go back to sleep. He asked Sybil Pereira whether he could sleep at her place but before she could answer, Pieta had once again woken up the dead.

'Don't you dare interfere, Sybil. Think of my mother who works night and day to feed this boy. Her eyes have become so weak, she can't thread a needle any more.' She found the word she was looking for and raised her decibel level. 'She's devastated by his conduct.'

You had to hand it to her. She may have been a parakeet but no mere bird could have matched the tremulous quiver in her voice. When his mother complained, Eddie had no problems going deaf. But, when Pieta reproduced her mother's speech verbatim, she put so much feeling into it, that even Eddie loathed the boy who put his mother through such agony.

They didn't eat that night. The kerosene stove was not lit

the next morning and nobody got breakfast before going to church.

It finally began to dawn on Eddie that his mother had changed her strategy totally. She was not going to raise her hand against him. A new Violet was in the making. Long-suffering, hardworking, forbearing and selfless, the essence of her personality was going to be extreme martyrdom. He would have to bear her like an ache that would not go away. He was right without knowing it. Nobody can match the sanctimonious cruelty of martyrs.

~

Father Agnello D'Souza was solemn and dour. He took off his specs to glare at Eddie. 'Come inside.'

'Why?'

'For confession.'

'I confessed last Thursday, don't you remember?'

'Don't argue. Get in.'

'Must I?' Eddie asked his mother. She looked away. Pieta pressed her lips together and said a thin 'yes'. Eddie's lips moved soundlessly.

'Mamma,' Pieta yelped as if some stranger had unzipped her dress on a crowded road, 'he called me a bitch.'

'Shush now,' Violet shut her up.

'Go, my child.' Granna put her hand on Eddie's head. 'Tell the priest whatever you did last night and beg forgiveness of God. Both you and your mother will feel lighter and better.'

~

There was a high, dark and arching quiet in the church. Beams of light descended from the skylights and froze whatever was in their path. An ancient woman sat under one of the spotlights. She had broken out of time and the cycle of life and death. She sat alone with her God. The small shrunken body on its knees was more still than a graven image. Her head was bent forward and the light caught in her silver hair hung over her head like a nimbus. The pomegranate beads in her rosary dripped steadily without her arthritic fingers moving.

Far away, above the altar, Jesus Christ continued to haemorrhage silently. His head hung limply to the right. Eddie understood that this was a clay Christ. But each time he looked at him, he had an intense urge to pry out the nails in his hands and feet and bring him down. Sometimes at night he spent hours struggling with those nails. Exhausted, he would try to pull Jesus off, instead of the nails. One of these days, the nails would stay where they were and Jesus would come crashing down on him.

'Do you have any idea of the consequences of your actions? You are so young and yet how you've hurt your father and mother. Ever thought of that? That was no slip of the tongue, I meant your father. Even if he's not here, he's watching you constantly. Let alone your parents, do you realize how you are torturing our Lord Jesus? Even a single sin, a single sinful thought can cause him unbearable pain and open his wounds again. He has to bleed again and again to wash your sins.' A livid Father D'Souza narrated the far-reaching effects of Eddie's crimes to him in a hoarse whisper.

Eddie was not particularly disturbed by the pain he was causing his parents. His father was beyond his imagination and hence incapable of feeling pain. He had seen his father's photograph at home but found it difficult to believe this man was once made of flesh and blood. And even if he was, he could neither relate to him, nor did he want to. If his father had had the slightest feeling or sympathy, he would not have allowed Eddie to starve last night and this morning. As for his mother, they were quits. He was giving her as hard a time as she was giving him. Frankly, he thought she was having a better time of it than he was. But he became terribly restive at the thought that Jesus's wounds were bleeding again because of him. He wanted to break open the hard crust which had formed over the long and throbbing lesion under his chin by hitting it against the back of the bench in front of him. He would keep on bashing his head till the gash reopened and he washed Jesus clean with his blood.

While Eddie's motives and intentions were mostly laudable, he was wise enough to appreciate that it is easier to bear someone else's pain—even if that someone else was God himself—than one's own. For hundreds of years they had left the Son of God hanging on the cross and now Father D'Souza had the temerity to suggest that he was responsible for Jesus's sufferings. In a fit of temper, Eddie asked, 'Then why don't you bring him down and bandage his wounds?'

The blood receded from Father Agnello's face. He was speechless. It was such a simple and logical thought, it could only have come from the Prince of Darkness, Lucifer himself.

'Eddie,' he thundered. The old woman kneeling at the front of the church looked back at them startled. 'How dare you blaspheme in the house of the Lord?' He caught hold of Eddie's neck and forced him to his knees. 'Father, please forgive this worthless boy. He's thoughtless.' But even as he begged the Lord, that ghastly suggestion Eddie had made entwined itself around his mind. Satan's coils seemed to feed his anger but he kept a hold on his voice. 'Where did you go yesterday? Which gang of scoundrels and rascals were you with? Have you seen yourself in the mirror? No decent boy would be seen like this.'

'I didn't want to come. Mummy forced me to.' Eddie was cowed down by now. He didn't believe his own words. 'I wasn't with any gang. Twenty people, no forty, surrounded me and attacked me.'

'Stop it. What do you take me for, a babe in the woods who's still being fed milk through a dropper? If you don't want to tell the truth, at least don't tell lies.'

Eddie looked at him in despair and amazement. 'I'm telling you the truth. I swear to you.'

'Get out. Swearing falsely in the holy of holies, our own Mother Church? Have you no shame? Fifteen or thirty people fell upon you. As if you were carrying gold bricks on your person. I am kind and gentle but not a fool. Leave the church. I can't bear to see your mother suffer. Otherwise I would not have seen your black face again. Why are you staring at me? I said get out.'

Having decided that Eddie was trying to stare him down, Father D'Souza tried to outstare him. It was an uneven contest. Eddie's mind had stopped functioning. He continued to gaze blankly at Father D'Souza. Father D'Souza took short, large breaths in an attempt to keep his eyes open. He put pressure on his eye muscles to widen his eyes as much as possible. That made him look more outraged than he was. Am I overreacting? What if he is telling the truth? Is the boy being defiant or am I imagining things? And suppose it is not Lucifer wound round him but Jesus trying to reach him?

The wretched boy was a scoundrel, no two ways about that. Father D'Souza blinked.

~

Eddie was on the last step leading out of the church when Father D'Souza spoke to him again. 'If there is a little shame left in your heart, come for confession in the evening and beg the Lord's forgiveness.'

There were still a few young couples and four or five families talking to each other in the large compound of the church. But Eddie's mother, sister and Granna were not among them. He felt forsaken. Was it possible that even the woman who had caused him such wordless pain and agony had lost interest in him? He felt dead, formless and empty. Entire galaxies could have traversed through him unhindered. He was touched by the terrible loneliness of the Son of God.

Some blows are such that it takes years for the wounds to appear. There is no greater loneliness on earth than when someone turns his back on you. The loneliness of death, misunderstanding, distance, separation and irreconcilable differences cannot match it. But the aloneness that even Jesus could not bear was the loneliness of being forgotten.

Jesus was Lord God. The only Son of our Father. God sent him down to cleanse the sins of mankind. The nailed Christ broke down once, just once. 'Father, Father, why hast thou forsaken me.' What was he trying to say? After all Christ was all-knowing and knew God's plan for him. How could he speak his mind? How could he reveal that God had not deserted him but that he had completely slipped out of God's mind? How else can you explain a father abandoning his only son to suffer such terrible pain and suffering and loneliness?

~

'So, what did Father D'Souza have to say about your unforgivable conduct?' Since nobody else was willing to ask, Pieta took it upon herself to enquire of Eddie. His mother gripped the primus stove firmly in her left hand and with her right she pumped air rapidly into its brass belly. The chill blue flower above the burner blossomed in a rush. And along with it the flaring hiss that would drill into your brain long after you were asleep, long after you were dead. Violet put the pot of beef stew on the stove. Eddie felt relieved. Granna was grating a coconut. Eddie picked up a pinch of snow-white fluff and put it in his mouth and said softly to Pieta, 'Father D'Souza said your sister Pieta is such a sweet girl, kick her in the butt at least five times a day without fail.'

He had an innocent and ingenuous smile on his face. Pieta leaned forward to hear his whispered message. She planted her nails in Eddie's face and tried to scratch him but Eddie wouldn't hold still. 'Ma, did you hear what Eddie said? He said that Father Agnello told him Pieta is such a sweet girl, kick her in the butt at least five times a day without fail.'

Violet gave Eddie a searing look and incinerated him. The silence continued. She was not willing to make peace. Granna said, 'Enough now, Eddie. Get out of those torn clothes and take a bath. And you, Pieta, if you tattle on your brother once more, I'll not give you that piece of silk I bought for your birthday.'

Pieta was aghast. Here was the criminal standing next to her in person. Instead of banishing him for life, though come to think of it a public hanging in the CWD grounds would have been more apposite, Granna, her very own grandmother, had insulted her. She was sure now that rank injustice and unfairness would be her lot in life.

'I'm leaving. See if I step into this house ever again.'

Granna and her mother ignored her. Eddie was the only one who was sympathetic and had kind words for her though he mimed rather than spoke them. Go, my pet, go. Leave this instant, his hands and expression suggested, don't ever come back. These people don't deserve you. Pieta was in a fix. She certainly did not want to acquiesce in her brother's wishes. And yet it was a matter of honour, now that she had spoken. Who was worse, her mother and Granna who had taken the news of her impending departure so calmly or her rogue brother who continued to encourage her magnanimously in her proposed course of action? Her resolve, however, was shaken only for an instant. She walked to the door and lifted the latch decisively. She opened the door and looked back. She was not the tallest in the house but she managed to look down on her family. Her gaze passed over her brother, Granna and then Violet.

'I'm leaving. We'll not meet again. I'm going to commit suicide. I'm going to leap into the creek. Perhaps I'll lie across the rail tracks and the local train will make three equal parts of me. One for Eddie, one for Ma and one for Granna. I do not bear a grudge against any of you. It is not your fault. You are incapable of appreciating me. You won't know my value till I die. You must learn to take care of each other since I'll no longer be here. If you repent and grieve for me, try not to weep too much. It will be too late.'

Eddie watched his sister in awe. His admiration for her at this moment was boundless. He was not sure that he had followed all the metaphysical ramifications of her speech but he was staggered by the audacity and reach of her imagination. He saw the three parts her body had been cut into. Head and legs on either side, torso in the middle. One for Ma, one for Granna and one for me, she had said. Which one do I get? He was enthralled and overcome by Pieta's inspired acting. He had not seen the likes of it before. Truth to tell, if you had called it acting, he would have called you a fool. When it's truer than true, how can you possibly call it acting?

Pieta guessed that she had floored her brother Eddie. Two more heart-rending emotional sentences and the fellow would sob his heart out. When she said her last 'goodbye' softly, he would be on his knees, begging her forgiveness and mumbling distractedly, 'Never, never again will I say such awful things to you, please don't go, please, I'll do anything you want, just change your mind.' But Pieta's sights were set on greater things, infinitely greater things. She was going to make her mother and Granna cry till they got hiccups. Revenge, sweet revenge. Let mother and daughter break down and plead, let them bring the building down with their tears and sorrow, lesser hearts would crack but not hers, she was not going to pay any heed to them. That train was heading straight for her. The driver saw her. He blew the horn. He put his entire weight on the brakes. Too late. Nothing was going to be of any use now. All she needed to do was take her father's name. Victor Coutinho. The Papa she had never had or had had only for a year. He was the only one in this world who would understand what she had been through. I'm now going to him forever. That said, her mother would crumble. She would pursue her on peeling, bloody knees and hold Pieta in her arms and rock her till she fell asleep. She knew all the dialogue and action by heart. But before she delivered the fell blow, she would have to prepare the ground a little, draw out the last drop of emotion. 'You may take my ruler and eraser, Eddie. My doll Cecilia I leave to Aunt Grace's Ruth. The perfume which John Uncle got me from Madagascar and which I've used only twice so far I leave to you, Mamma. Whenever you apply it, even when you merely open the bottle, you'll remember your one and only daughter, Pieta. And to Granna, I bequeath the polka-dotted red and white silk,' Pieta was not one to shy from the full weight of irony, 'with which she was going to make me a dress. Make a blouse in my memory with it and wear it to church every Sunday.'

Not just her audience, Pieta herself was wrung out by the elegiac quality of her peroration. But her shameless and heartless

Granna destroyed the tragic effect she had so meticulously and painstakingly built. A stone would have melted and wept. Instead Pieta's grandmother cracked up. Not a soft snigger or a smile that hovered between the lips and the cheeks, either. A full, immoderate and villainous ha ha ha till the tears flowed from her eyes. And even then she continued to laugh.

Pieta was filled with loathing and disgust. She felt such boundless pity for herself, she forgot her climactic and masterly final stroke. She did not want to spend another minute in this house with its worthless people. She walked out but not without slamming the door hard.

'Pieta, Pieta I was wrong. Please forgive me. Honestly I am sorry,' Pieta kept walking down the staircase despite Granna's words. When she reached the second floor she craned her neck and looked up. She waited till her grandmother was just fifteen steps behind her, then she set out determinedly to die.

Eddie's sorrows were of a different order. He drew the curtains and sat on the stool with rotting legs in the tiny area in the kitchen where the family bathed. The first mug of cold water on his body and back, and his courage caved in. How was he to face the evening? How was he to present his black face, his black sins and his black soul to Father Agnello D'Souza? And yet, if his problems had ended there; he would have considered himself lucky. His worries and fears were legion. It was no state secret that he had committed horrendous and unmentionable crimes. Why else would Father Agnello be so enraged? But he could not for the life of him guess what they were or give them names. He had tried to speak the truth this morning but it was plain that that was not going to be enough. He was more than willing to confess before God. But he was beginning to understand just how low he had fallen: he did not even know what his crime was.

As he finished his bath, the sizzling blue flame in the primus stove turned yellow and leapt almost to the ceiling. His mother tried to pierce the micron hole at the bottom of the burner with a primus pin, gauge number four. But she couldn't locate it and, even when she did, the carbon particle or speck of dust that had lodged itself there would not budge. He wondered why the flames did not engulf him and put an end to his misery. The pin went in and the stove began to breathe freely.

He had been fasting since last night. It was one-thirty in the afternoon and he was ravenous. But when he sat at the table, he couldn't get a single morsel down. Though Pieta's attempts at suicide had not met with success, the atmosphere at the dining-table was funereal. Granna had caught up with Pieta outside their chawl. Pieta had put up heroic resistance and performed a stunning one-woman show in technicolour and stereophonic sound without the aid of loudspeakers. 'I will not return, not on my life. Everybody mollycoddles and pampers Eddie. I am a stepdaughter in my own house. Let go my hand or I'll miss the 12.47. After that there isn't a fast train till 3.30. And without a fast brain, there won't be clean cuts and three even parts.'

She said she could hear her father calling her. Her timing was slightly off, her throat was sore and her voice was hoarse with all that screaming and weeping and her mother wasn't there but she knew that everyone in the CWD chawls was her audience, even that villain Ravan was watching spellbound. She took a deep breath and said that devastating piece about her father, how he alone knew her value and how she was now going to be with him forever. Not just the very old and the womenfolk but strong young men who had not shed tears for many years wept like babes at Pieta's monstrously sad tale and its tragic end. Not just men and women and children but even the inert and cold brick buildings of the CWD complex cried their hearts out.

Suddenly, Pieta's mother was at the window. A six-syllable streak of lightning without thunder fell to the earth. 'Pieta, come on up.' When Pieta came home Violet slapped her. Pieta's head swivelled a hundred and eighty degrees. Violet repeated the gesture. Pieta's head returned to its normal position.

It was a red-letter day. A day that would go down in history. A day that Eddie had prayed for fervently for many years. God had answered his prayers with a generosity that would have converted a hardcore atheist. For the first time in living memory, his mother had hit Pieta. But the fates must surely be sourpusses and spoilsports. How else could you explain Eddie's failure to take an interest in the proceedings? He did not jump for joy. He did not take his friends out for a night on the town. He did not declare the next day a national holiday. Instead, he lay in a state of hopelessness. He was in a tunnel and there was no light at the end of it because there was no end to the tunnel.

For the hundredth time today, he went over all that had transpired between 5.30 p.m. yesterday and 10.30 a.m. this morning. But the voice which should have shrieked in his heart and told him the difference between right and wrong, and which Father D'Souza said was the compass on the ocean of life, had gone dead. Or to be more precise, God's voice or his conscience was malfunctioning and could not tell him where he had gone wrong. He considered praying, but what was the point? It was clear that God had lost interest in Eddie and forgotten him.

It was a Sunday but Violet's sewing machine was not idle. There was a bird in it which was condemned to peck mechanically at the same loop of thread all its life. It was a sound that was sewn into the lining of Eddie's brain. Whether he was in class, in the playing field, in the cinema theatre, the bird was always pecking away at his brain. But it was also a soothing sound.

It was the sound of sleep for Eddie. All his living years he had dozed off at night while his mother was still working. Today was one day when that soporific was not going to work. The cares of the world were nothing compared to his problems on this black Sunday.

At a quarter to five Granna woke him up for a cup of tea. He looked at the clock on the wall, checked the time with his grandmother and got into his Sunday clothes and shoes and combed his hair in a frantic hurry. Only a callous sinner like him could have lost consciousness and slept during one of the worst crises of his life.

'Where are you going in such a rush?' Granna asked him. His mother had not yet broken her vow of silence.

'For confession.' Eddie was out of the door.

'But I thought you confessed this morning?'

'Father Agnello wanted me to come in the evening.'

~

The sinners stood in two rows. There was no knowing which line would end up at Father Agnello's booth. Seven in one queue, nine in the other. Eddie opted to start his penance before confession. The longer he waited, the longer he would suffer. And if he suffered, Jesus might just possibly take pity on him, and, instead of Father Agnello, he could relate his litany of sins to Father Constantine. He joined the longer queue.

He was second in line. He suddenly had a premonition that this would lead to Father Agnello. He changed queues and went all the way to the back. He was number eleven now. Was it not possible to be absolved before confession?

It was his turn now. He tried to peep through the latticed window behind which the emissary of God sat in his black box.

He pressed his nose, he twisted his neck, narrowed his eyes, but the darkness did not yield its secret. He would have disregarded the woman behind who was getting impatient, but the priest inside cleared his throat twice, knocked his elbow against the wooden partition and emitted a 'huh?' to nudge the sinner. Eddie's throat went dry and his tongue became immobile.

The voice of God's proxy thundered at him in a stage whisper, 'Stop fidgeting, Eddie, and wasting my time. Start your confession.'

Oh God, I trusted you, I really did. I changed queues, stood that much longer. I suffered and what do I get for all my troubles? Father Agnello. Is there no fair play left in the world? Eddie put his neck on the block.

'Forgive me, Father, for I have sinned. My last confession was on Thursday.'

'Stop mumbling.'

'Ma sent me to get onions last evening but I didn't get them.'

'Why?'

'Paul Monteiro asked me to go to Crystal's home and tell her that his father was seriously ill and was being taken to Masina Hospital.'

'Did you?'

'Yes.'

'Then? Do you expect me to prompt you after every word?'

'No, Father.'

'Speak up. I haven't got all day.'

'I went to see *Rock Around the Clock*.'

'What?'

'Rock Around the Clock.'

'I heard you. How dare you go to see a film that the Church has not approved of yet and may very likely never do?'

'I didn't know it was not approved, Father.'

'Don't you read the *Good Samaritan,* our school journal? It says so clearly in it.'

'Paul gave me the tickets. He should've known.' Got away this time.

'Ignorance is no excuse in the eyes of the law, Eddie. But we'll come to that later. What happened then? The truth, Eddie, nothing but the truth. Watching a film won't deprive you of half your collar and shirt buttons. And make you filthy as a gutter rat.'

'That Ravan has a gang, Father. They call themselves the Mazagaon Mawalis. Their members always make fun of us. They insult our mothers and sisters. When we go to school they throw orange peels and rotten eggs at us. On Friday night I sent a message to Ravan. I said, "Sala, if you've got guts, come and meet us face to face. We'll have a fight to the death on Saturday evening. Our gangs will meet at the playground next to the Railway Colony." He said okay. I immediately got our gang ready and prepared for the fight. Santan Almeida is my deputy chief. Roger, Peter, John are the other members.'

'What's the name of your gang?'

'Do or Die Devils. We fought for an hour and a half. They were nine, we were five. But we fought like lions and saved the honour of the top floors. Peter got scared and wanted to run but I stopped him. You see this wound under my chin, Ravan hit me with an iron pipe. He tore my collar too. Then I lost control. I punched him so hard I broke the bridge of his nose. He cried and he cried. He touched my feet and begged me to stop. He said, "Please stop, Eddie. Please. You and your Devils have won, the Mawalis have lost." But I didn't listen. I asked him whether they would chase after our women. He said, "Never." I said if he ever touched our women, I'd break his legs.'

Eddie felt spent after that fight. He wiped his mouth and waited to hear the penance Father Agnello would give him.

'Huh.'

Eddie didn't have the courage to disappoint Father Agnello.

'Then we went to Cafe Light of Iran and ordered five Cokes. I ordered two plates of mutton samosas for the gang. You know where you get the best non-veg samosas in Bombay? Light of Iran. But be there before six or they're over. Then I ordered two more plates. We polished them off but then I realized I had no money. Boy, did we run for our lives. The waiter and the Irani just stood by and watched us disappear.'

'Huh.'

More? What more did Father Agnello want? Eddie had already ransacked his memory for plots from all the comic books he had read. Mutt and Jeff, Archie, Roy Rogers. He added whatever tit-bits he remembered from the conversations of older boys and his friends but even that was not enough. He had to fall back on his own resources and imagination now and concoct his own masala. How many more terrible things could he have done in just one evening? But there was no end to Father Agnello's appetite. Nothing was going to satisfy him and Eddie feared he would still be here when the church reopened for six o'clock mass the next morning.

'We slipped into the railway quarters. Lots of Anglo girls decked in nylons and jewellery and solid high heels were going to meet their boyfriends because it was Saturday evening. We watched them.'

Over and out. Eddie stopped. But Father Agnello was not going to give up till he had got to the bottom of Eddie's dirty mind. His silence lay there with its jaws open.

'The staircases in the Railway Colony have fretted wooden lattices from which you can see everything.'

'See what?'

Kiss me again. What does he think people look at from under a staircase? Eddie explained the mysteries of staircase watching patiently.

'See what they're wearing.'

'You don't have to stand under a staircase to see what dresses they're wearing.'

Give me a break.

'Not dresses. To see what they're wearing under them. Two of the girls had flowers on their panties. They were twins. Do you know how fantastic white daisies look on blue? Sala, Peter has no taste. He preferred the sister with the yellow daisies on red. He was really hot. Those girls were standing at the stairwell two storeys above us and he was stretching his hand to touch their panties. What would have happened if their boyfriends had seen us? Can you imagine? They would have peeled our hides off. We are not going to take Peter out again with us. The bugger gets excited and it's difficult to control him. As it is, half the fun's gone these days. Hardly anybody goes out without panties any more. What's the point of craning your neck for hours and getting a terrible crick, all for nothing? It's become boring since Mr Johnson was transferred to Bhusaval.'

'What about Mr Johnson?'

Father Agnello was really dumb. You had to explain every single thing to him. 'What about him? The trouble was that Mrs Johnson had to go with him to Bhusaval. Sometimes, when she wanted to get cigarettes from the shop at the corner and she was wearing a thick dress, she wouldn't wear a slip or anything else. That was too much. We would scramble on top of each other to peer inside.' Eddie sighed.

'Verily, Eddie, you have sinned.' The volcano in Father Agnello now began to erupt with a vengeance. Wave upon hot wave of lava engulfed Eddie. 'You are so young and yet look at the number of your sins. It is conceivable, at least theoretically, to forgive all those sins after the person who has committed them repents from the heart. But you have such a criminal mind, you've fallen so low and your soul is so warped that you've been reciting this interminable litany of sins with a great sense of pride. There's not an iota of regret or repentance in your mind, heart or soul. Instead of feeling ashamed, you have been waxing eloquent and showing of. I do not know if you are the son of man or the son of Satan.'

Oh, what relief. Eddie's labours had finally borne fruit. Father Agnello was no longer asking for more details. Eddie's crimes had been identified and he was about to be punished. He was beside himself with joy. He could not believe his luck. He tore the dark velvet burgundy curtain behind the confessional and rolled at Father Agnello's feet.

Eddie's violent reaction caught both Father Agnello and the people queuing up for confession off guard. Father Agnello did not know what Eddie was up to. The others, those just beginning to gather for six o'clock mass, watched Eddie with apprehension. One of them rushed forward and tried to pick Eddie up. 'Someone call a doctor. The boy's having an epileptic fit.' Father Agnello waved him away.

'I was wrong, Father Agnello, I've sinned most terribly. As God is my witness, I'll never again do what I did in the past. Punish me, Father, punish me any way you want.'

What was Father Agnello D'Souza to make of Eddie's unorthodox repentance? Was the boy up to one of his usual tricks? Perhaps. But it was also possible that God had smitten the child and his grief was real. If that was the case, he, Father Agnello D'Souza, would be committing the sin of presumption.

Who was he to question the ways and wisdom of God? 'Save me, Father. Save me. I am caught in the quicksands of sin. Give me your hand and help me up, Father. I beg you, Father.'

That Sunday would be etched forever on Father D'Souza's soul. When he was next sinking in the slough of despond, he would remind himself of the golden Sunday when God wrought a sea-change in a wicked and incorrigible sinner. He suspected that God had chosen Eddie deliberately to warn him of the sin of arrogance. No one, but no one, was beyond the pale of forgiveness. No man was so fallen that he could not be raised to heaven and the embrace of God Almighty. How he had gone astray, he, who should have known better. His pride had prevented him from seeing the work of God in this child. How else could he explain what the boy had said about Jesus? It was still a highly explosive thought and he wouldn't mention it to anyone but praise be to the Lord God and his son Jesus. How shall I thank you Lord for retrieving this prostrate child from the claws of Satan and for chastising me?

The prostrate child was having a field day. The dams of repentance had burst and there was no staunching them. All his pent-up anger and grief and grievances against his mother, all the terrors of the previous night and of this afternoon were being washed clean in this deluge of weeping.

'Get up, Eddie, get up, my son.' Weeping tears of gratitude, Father D'Souza bent down and ran his fingers through Eddie's curly hair.

'Not unless you forgive me, Father.'

'My forgiveness is of little import, Eddie.' Father Agnello smiled. 'I myself would not put too much faith in it. But God has forgiven you, Eddie. I know that His heart is filled with joy to see your great sorrow and repentance. For a sinner who exerts himself and disowns the devil is dearer to our Lord than a man to whom virtue comes easily. Rise, my son.'

'Not until you tell me what penance I must do.'

'Say twenty Hail Marys every day and pray that you will always walk in the shadow of God.'

At this, all the men and women who had watched the transformation of Eddie that evening fell to their knees and said: 'Amen'. The next Sunday Eddie asked Father Agnello's permission to pass the plate after mass. Father Agnello was delighted.

'Of course, you may. You must help me in the work of the Church from now on.'

During the Eucharist, Eddie passed the golden plate on either side of the nave. It was a full house. The Sunday morning nine o'clock mass always was. On the collection plate, coins made a racket. Notes landed without a sound. Saint Sebastian's was a poor parish. Mostly the plate rang out. Four- or eight-anna coins at the most. Two eight-anna coins so far. One from Mr Figuereido and another from Mrs Pereira. In the second row from the rear, Mr Rodrigues, the sole owner of the Happy Family Chemist, sat with his eyes closed in prayer. Eddie had to rattle the coins twice to break his reverie. Mr Rodrigues opened his eyes. He drew back his jacket and took out his wallet from the rear pocket of his trousers. He picked out a five-rupee note and set it on the plate.

'I don't have that much change.'

'I don't want any,' Mr Rodrigues said and went back to his prayers.

~

On the Tuesday after he had borrowed Mr Rodrigues' fiver, Eddie skipped school after lunch. He had done his homework. Advance bookings for the following week at cinema houses in Bombay started on Tuesdays. It took him four hours to get to the window. He got three one-rupee-five-anna tickets for the one o'clock show the following Monday. The Monday after, he was back at the Strand. He sold two of the tickets in the black market for five rupees each. With the third ticket he saw *Rock Around the Clock*. This time, nobody tore his shirt collar.

He was back next Tuesday with ten rupees. He bought three tickets for the following Friday, three for Monday and one for Tuesday, all for the one o'clock show. On Friday and Monday he saw the film again and sold the extras. On Tuesday, he booked for the coming week and saw the film yet again.

On Saturday morning Eddie was back at church. He prayed to God and thanked him from his heart. He got up and went to the charity box. He caught hold of the lock and pulled at it a couple of times.

'What are you doing?' Father D'Souza's voice caught him redhanded. Eddie looked back quietly and met Father Agnello's eyes. 'Giving God what belongs to God.' He turned and coaxed seven one-rupee notes down the slit of the charity box. Father D'Souza suspected that Eddie had said something profound, but he didn't quite know what it was, and he didn't want to let on that it had gone over his head.

Eddie discovered that he had a scalper's mind. He was good at arithmetic and had a feel for what the market would bear. On two occasions he got ten rupees per ticket. Young men who wanted to impress their girlfriends but hadn't stood in queues for the advance booking were always more desperate to see the film than others. He also had an instinctive sense of when the market was falling and cut his losses quickly. Perhaps the black market was Eddie's metier. From scalping he could have graduated to smuggling. The sky was the limit here. Silver, gold, transistor radios, nylon and polyester saris and dress materials, cameras, record players, TVs, the market was wide open and growing. But there were two problems. The first was that Eddie believed rock'n' roll was his vocation and not illicit trafficking. The other was a minor mishap.

Sixteen

Aunt Lalee and Ravan had long since made up. Ravan was not going to hold it against her that she had lost her temper and thrashed him. After all, he had to admit that he had gone overboard with that tae kwon do demonstration on the attar bottles. Besides it was not possible to nurse a grudge against this aunt who was so worldly-wise and knew so much more about life than either of his parents or anybody in the chawls. She had a host of rich friends. She had been driven around in cars, stayed in palatial houses where the beds were round and the size of his home. She had smoked cigarettes, been to a film studio where she had watched Raj Kapoor shooting with Nargis for some film called *Aah* and had been asked by the dance director whether she would take part in a dance sequence. She had politely refused. She had standards, she said. Ravan didn't quite know what she meant. Did Raj Kapoor, the dance director and Hindi films not have standards? Were her standards better or theirs? But he had said, 'Yes, of course,' and nodded his head vigorously.

'If I had taken that role, I would have been a heroine today, with my smile, my musical voice, my looks and, needless to say, my exceptional figure.' Ravan was not about to dispute such fundamental truths though he had some reservations about the gaps in Aunt Lalee's teeth and her voice which tended to be a trifle affected and high-pitched but maybe that was the way women in high circles spoke. As to looks, she certainly stood out, with that trick of her hips which seemed to tell you to follow her, the angled elbow and the hand at her waist and the sari pallu always falling down, but he had to confess that while his mother was not his favourite person these past few months, his father's sister was not in the same league as Parvatibai. Aunt Lalee certainly was more casual about her figure. There was an invitation and challenge in her eyes to check out the goods. Ravan was getting curious about female anatomy of late and tended to linger in the kitchen when his aunt was having a bath because she didn't draw the curtain all the way and came out with a wet sari draped lazily around her but his mother always yelled at him and asked him to get the hell out before he was able to get a clear picture of the Red One's topography.

Was he expected to affirm what Aunt Lalee was saying or comment or improve upon it? That was one good thing about her. She was not really interested in anybody else except when she wanted something. Ravan was struck by the curious observation he had just made. He had not meant to be unkind but if there was any truth in his perception, he would have to find out how he could possibly satisfy any of his aunt's needs. Sure he was at her beck and call but so was his father. He too ran down to get paan and betel nut for her, have her saris pressed by the man in Chawl No. 21, buy a Roger's carbonated ginger for her when she had indigestion or see her off at the bus-stop on Thursdays which was the day she visited her mother whom no one had seen.

What did she want of him? Why was she cultivating him? A month ago she had taken him to the Gateway of India for a boat ride. Ravan had dipped his hand in the water. If they kept going in a straight line, the wake of their boat could reach all the way to

America. His history teacher had said that the Elephanta island which the boatman was pointing to must have been a thriving Hindu outpost and had some very fine caves and rock-carvings. The Portuguese had come there four or five hundred years ago across four thousand miles. Imagine touching the same water and being in the same sea as them. Was Vasco da Gama in that lot? What clothes had they worn? They were Catholics just like Eddie. Wouldn't it be wonderful if he could take over the wheel and pay a return visit to Portugal? They wouldn't believe their eyes. 'Indian boy-captain lands on Portuguese coast' the headlines would scream. If he hadn't already decided to follow in the footsteps of Raju from *Dil Deke Dekho,* he would have joined the navy and travelled all over the world like Vasco da Gama and Columbus.

In Praise of Audacities
or
The Shortest Survey Ever of the Portuguese Adventure in the Old World
(Skip it if you want and move on with the story.)

Mario de Lima Leitao. Henrique de Meneses. Jorge de Almeida. Alfonso Lopes de Sequeira. Garcia de Noronha. Francisco Antonio da Veiga Cabral da Camara Pimentel. Bernando Jose Maria da Silveira e Lorena. Luis de Mendonca Furtado e Albuquerque. Wake up at four in the morning, finish your ablutions, face the east and chant these marvellous names. Their wondrous sonority is as elevating as that of a Sanskrit shloka. Open the Bombay or Goa telephone directory and you'll find that the names have got drastically shortened. The poetry of chains of names and place-names has been severely cut down to D'Sa, Da Cunha, Saldanha and Mascarenhas. And yet they are among the last reminders and vestiges of a civilization that has left the shores of India. Whatever the injustices of colonial conquest and rule, fortunately one can still be beguiled and entranced by the beauty and lilt of an alien language and its culture. Who were these strange men—and they were almost all only men—with strange names who dared to cross unknown and unmapped seas, voyage for months over four thousand miles of dangerous and stormy oceans to come to India?

In 1494, John II of Portugal and Ferdinand of Spain signed the treaty of Tordesillas under the aegis of Pope Alexander VI, one of the most dubious Borgias and popes in history. Their rapacity, greed and avarice were no more and no less than that of any other European or Asian potentate of the 15th century. What was staggering was the sweep, megalomania and intemperateness of their appetites. Columbus had just crossed the Atlantic and discovered America for Ferdinand and Isabella of Spain, though to his dying day he did not give up his obstinate belief that he had found a new sea-route to Asia. (It would take another 200 years, 1726 to be precise, for the West to realize that Asia and America were not joined together in the region of the Bering Straits.) The two kings, however, did not aspire merely to the 'new world', they wanted the whole world. There was not much of a difference between the earth and a cake. They divided it. The earth was still Ptolemaic and flat then. Portugal took all lands and, even more critically, all the seas east of a line running between longitude 30 and 20, 370 leagues west of Cape Verde. Whatever was west of that line went to Spain.

The Portuguese half of the earth was a happy but academic concept until Vasco da Gama went round the Cape of Good Hope and landed in India in 1498. The division of the abstract spoils then began to have concrete implications. Immediately after the discovery of the sea passage to India, Dom Manuel I of Portugal appropriated the title 'Lord of the Conquest, Navigation and Commerce of Ethiopia, Arabia, Persia and of India'. The

Portuguese Crown had encapsulated its aims with astonishing clarity and articulation.

If the Portuguese king was the self-proclaimed Lord of the Sea in Asia, it followed logically that he was entitled to control all sea trade in Asia, and for that purpose police the coastline and the seas as well. In Europe as in Asia until then, the seas and oceans were free-trade zones open to all. It may have come as a bit of a surprise to Middle Eastern, Indian and East Asian sovereigns, seafarers and merchants that the Portuguese had walked away with the Indian Ocean. The Portuguese were among the first empire builders to teach us that it is always prudent not to consult those whose interests are likely to be damaged the most by your actions, a lesson that was learnt well over the centuries by Hitler and Stalin when they divided Poland or when America enunciated the Monroe Doctrine.

Talk of audacities, talk of originality of thought, talk of sheer gall, no one could beat the Portuguese. They reinvented the ancient concept that the right of ownership belonged to the one who made the first claim. It was a marvellous idea. Only the Portuguese Crown could trade in spice to Europe or between eastern ports within Asia. No one except those licensed by the Portuguese could ply the waters. No private trade even by the Portuguese, at least that was the official position.

The procedure was this: a trading ship got a pass or *cartaz* for a small fee from the Portuguese which stated the destination, nature of the cargo, name of the captain and crew strength. The money, however, was in the customs duties. A ship was under obligation to call at a Portuguese port both on its way to and back from its destination. No *cartaz* meant that the ship could be confiscated and its crew killed or sent to the galleys. Even a *cartaz* was not enough if the conditions were not fully met. You could not build or maintain a fort as the Sultan of Gujarat was to discover at Surat, unless it was approved by the Portuguese Viceroy. In return your ships were given protection against piracy. When the threat from the freebooters became more serious, the Portuguese organized convoys of trading ships guarded by an official fleet. The customs duties in Goa on an average amounted to 60 per cent of Goa's total revenue collection in the 16th century. In the rest of the empire it was close to 65 per cent.

We have jumped the gun. Commerce was the last stage of the Portuguese King's title. What preceded it was conquest and navigation. By 1511, the Portuguese had taken Malacca in southeast Asia. Hormuz at the mouth of the Persian Gulf followed in 1515. At various points in time the Portuguese had outposts in Mombassa and Mozambique in Africa, Macao, Macassar in the South China Sea and as far as Nagasaki in Japan, not to mention Brazil in the Americas, to name only a few. On the western littoral of India they had forts at Diu, Surat, Daman, Bassein, Bombay, Goa, Honavar, Bhatkal, Mangalore, Cannanore, Calicut, Cochin, Quilon and in Colombo in Ceylon. A remarkable spread by any standards, but extraordinary considering the times and the fact that Portugal was such a poor and small country and that its exchequer was almost always broke.

There could of course be no exploration or conquest without navigation. Portuguese ships were among the finest in the world. In the early 1640s, John Chandler, the British Consul at Lisbon wrote: 'As for the nine Portuguese galleons they are well appointed ships, as hardly cannot be seen better, the less of them about 800 tons, and three of them about 1,000—all exceedingly well mounted with artillery.' Both Lisbon and Goa, as also Bassein and Cochin, were major shipbuilding centres. King John IV of Portugal was so impressed with ships built in Indo-Portuguese shipyards, he considered using the *Sao Laurenco* as the flagship of the High Seas Fleet. While the master shipwrights were Portuguese, the carpenters, dock-workers and ordinary shipwrights were all Indian.

The Portuguese landed in Bombay in 1509. Like many an invader they felt compelled to make a show of strength at the outset. 'Our men captured many cows and some blacks who were hiding among the bushes, and of whom the good were kept and the rest were killed.' What happened to these good black Bombayites? Were they kept as indentured labourers or turned into slaves? The second seems unlikely but the question is not irrelevant. In 1434, the Portuguese imported the first African slaves to Lisbon. By 1448, they had grasped the economic dimensions of this branch of trade and set up a slaving centre on the African coast. But it was only in the 18th century that the slave-trade became a major growth industry. By then the initiative had passed from the Portuguese, Spanish and Dutch to the French and English.

But to get back to India: In the sixteenth century, the seven islands of Bombay were nominally under the Sultans of Gujarat. It was Sultan Bahadur Shah who made over the islands, and Bassein on the mainland, to the Portuguese king in return for Portuguese aid against the Mughals. It is suspected that the only help he may have received was a push off a Portuguese ship at Surat that drowned him.

You could rent an island in Bombay from the King of Portugal for eighty-five pounds per year. The first man to rent an island in Bombay from the King of Portugal was a fine botanist and honorary court physician called Garcia da Orta. Mazagaon, where Ravan and Eddie were born, was one of the seven islands acquired by the Portuguese. Mazagaon, scholars would have us believe, is a mutation of 'machha-gram' or fishing village. Try thinking of an island that does not go in for fishing. Perhaps the simple Marathi translation of Mazagaon tells us more about the pride that the early inhabitants felt for the place: my village. As a Portuguese settlement, Mazagaon was famed for its mango orchards. They must have been truly magic trees for they bore fruit twice a year, once at the height of summer in May which is the normal mango season on the west coast of India, and once in late December. In 1572, the King of Portugal gifted the district of Mazagaon in perpetuity to the de Souza e Lima family who built a house known in its various incarnations as Belvedere, Mazagaon House or Mark House. White-washed regularly, the house served as a landmark for vessels coming into the harbour.

Bombay remained a Portuguese colony for over a hundred years. Then, in 1662, hoping for a major political and military alliance, the Portuguese royal house arranged the marriage of Catherine of Braganza to Charles II of England. Part of her dowry was Bombay, which the British East India Company had been eyeing for a while. The contract notwithstanding, the Portuguese in India were loath to let go of Bombay. A month before it was finally ceded to the British, the Viceroy of Goa, Antonio de Mello de Castro wrote to the Portuguese monarch in astonishingly clairvoyant words: 'I confess at the feet of your majesty that only the obedience I owe to your majesty as a vassal could have forced me to this deed.... I foresee the great trouble that from this neighbourhood will result to the Portuguese and that India will be lost on the same day on which the English nation is settled in Bombay.'

It is difficult to keep nostalgia and yearning at bay when talking of Bombay a bare twenty or thirty years ago. Extend that to fifty or seventy years and one has entered a time-warp when the romance and beauty of Bombay were at par with that of any city that has grown up next to the sea. If you looked east from Mazagaon Hill where Ravan sat listening to Prakash's tirade against his father, you could have seen Portuguese merchantmen from a hundred and fifty years ago proceeding in a leisurely fashion to Elephanta island. (The Portuguese named the island after the stone elephant outside the caves. They also indulged in some exuberant target practice on the magnificent Maheshmurti and other carvings inside.) Mazagaon Hill itself is said to be the site where the first Portuguese to settle in Mazagaon, the Jesuits, built a chapel and a monastery. Perhaps that is the reason why the Mazagaon-Byculla belt has a heavier concentration of

Roman Catholics and more parochial schools per square foot than anywhere.else in Bombay.

The green and the woods of Mazagaon have long since disappeared. The rich and the chic abandoned Mazagaon close to a hundred years ago and moved to Peddar Road, Breach Candy and to Malabar Hill, a sibling of the hills at Mazagaon and Cumballa. The port and the docks of Bombay have crowded out both the land and the easy and leisurely pace of Mazagaon. You can glimpse the older island culture in some of the by-lanes but the Mazagaon of Eddie and Ravan was a dusty, hectic and grey place of warehouses, shipping godowns and round-the-clock trucks moving newly arrived cargo into the hinterland. Mazagaon Hill was partially knocked down in 1864 by British railway engineers to make room for the harbour railway line, the fish market and the Electricity Board.

In 1530, Goa was formally declared the capital of not just Portuguese India but of its entire eastern empire, and became the focal point for Portuguese commercial, political and missionary forays into the East. On paper and by letters-patent the Viceroy of 'Golden Goa' was omnipotent, second only to the King himself. He had the power to make war and peace with 'the kings and rulers of India and of other regions outside it'. The King promised 'to confirm and fulfil exactly' any truce or peace treaty the Viceroy may negotiate 'as if it had been done by myself in person, and agreed and signed in my presence'. The Viceroy however was aware that, notwithstanding the royal sanction for all his acts, the Crown was capable of overruling him and there was, in theory at least, the possibility of a judicial investigation at the end of his tenure.

Apart from monetary, commercial and territorial gains, colonial India and the empire had other uses. Illegitimate sons and second, third, fourth and fifth sons whom primogeniture made redundant and jobless saw a future and a fortune in the colonies. Poor relations, needy friends and servants all tagged along with viceroys, governors and other overseas officials in the hope of a government post. The only ones who got left behind were wives. From 1505 to 1961, Portuguese India had 128 governors and viceroys. Of these only a handful brought their wives with them. There was as a matter of fact a good deal of intermarrying between the colonizers and the conquered.

Rivalry between those who married and stayed in India and those who returned to Portugal was often sharp and acrimonious. The former, known as *Indiaticos,* came lower than the latter, called *Reinos,* in the pecking order in the colonies. Barring some exceptions, most governors and viceroys were chosen from Portuguese nobility in Portugal.

The rivalry between *Reinos* and *Indiaticos* was just as strongly operative in the religious orders as in the laity. Dom Alfonso Mendes of the Society of Jesus was of the view that 'very few individuals should be admitted to the Society here, because all our ills originate with this rabble, since they have very little learning and a great deal of envy and hatred against those of us who come from Europe.' The sentiment, needless to say, was strongly reciprocated.

Everybody starting from the viceroy to the lowliest Portuguese official traded on the side or openly. Their salaries could not support them and there were often fortunes to be made by overseas as well as interport trade. The goods and destinations changed, what remained constant was commerce. Textiles, beads, pepper, cinnamon, saltpetre, rice and other foodstuffs from India were exchanged for ivory, gold-dust, ebony, hardwoods, silver, seed-pearls, horses, dates and anything for which there was a market. Often the Portuguese went into partnership with local merchants. The Goa economy, it is said, was dominated by Gujarati vanias and Saraswat brahmins.

The history of Portuguese settlements, it is often remarked, is the history of Jesuit settlements. This is obviously an exaggeration—there were other dedicated orders like the

Franciscans and Dominicans, besides the Jesuits, not to mention the work of fine and intrepid sailors, admirals and great governors and bureaucrats—but there is a grain of truth in the statement. The Church Militant did not just battle and convert the heretic Hindu, Muslim and pagan countries and peoples which it colonized, it helped preserve Portuguese authority in India when it was seriously threatened.

God and Mammon were, if not the same, at least interchangeable. The brotherhood of Jesuits often interpreted the care of souls to mean an engagement with the full spectrum of life to promote the faith. They were custodians of Crown funds, ran the Royal Hospital in Goa, became moneylenders, supervised the minting of coins and looked after the fortifications at Diu, Chaul and other places, traded in sugar, slaves, livestock from their own plantations in Brazil, and even cast cannons at a pinch. To quote C.R. Boxer: 'Their economic activities were therefore far greater than those of either the Dutch or the English East India Companies, which are sometimes termed the first multinationals.'

The Portuguese left India many years ago. But one of their legacies continues to be among the most powerful agents moulding young minds in the country: the hundreds of schools and colleges run by Jesuits, Franciscans and other clerical orders, including the school Eddie went to.

Within two hundred years of their arrival, the Portuguese had lost most of their colonies in Asia and Africa to the Dutch and the British. There were numerous reasons for this but the most important was that the Portuguese were hopelessly overextended. The wonder is not that such a far-flung empire petered out, but that it survived for so long when at no time were there more than 10,000 Portuguese in the colonies, including Brazil. Why did the British not throw out the Portuguese from Goa and the French from Pondicherry? Was there much profit left for the

Portuguese in staying on in Goa? Salazar, the Portuguese strong man and dictator, must have seen the writing on the wall in 1947 when the British left India. But he hung on to Goa and painted Nehru into a villain when the Indian Prime Minister decided to liberate it.

Strange word, liberation. Did the majority of the people of Goa want to be liberated? They had not asked the Portuguese to occupy their land and rule over them 400 years ago. But they were realists and they had invested three to four centuries in the service of the new masters. A great many had converted to the colonizer's religion and married Portuguese soldiers, bureaucrats, traders and professionals. The Portuguese were 'family'. The language of business and the medium of instruction in schools was Portuguese. Now overnight they were being asked to disown family, sever connections with their patrons, give up their distinctive identity and lose themselves in a landmass a hundred times the size of Portugal and among 350 million Hindus and Muslims, and were told that this was liberation. They felt a sense of loss, nostalgia, upheaval... something that the rest of India was oblivious of.

And yet there were many staunch freedom fighters, both Catholic and Hindu, in the colonies of Goa, Diu and Daman. They wanted to be united with their motherland and often went to jail for it. In 1961 they got what they had fought for.

Now, thirty-five years after the departure of the Portuguese, there's talk of setting up a Portuguese TV channel in Goa. The new colonizers, as we are all learning, are not countries but multinationals and satellite TV.

~

'Will you take me to Elephanta?'
'Now?' Ravan's aunt asked a bit alarmed.
'No, one of these days, to see the carvings in the caves.'

'I don't care for carvings and such stuff. I have a better idea. Let's have a picnic there.'

'Really?' Wasn't his aunt amazing?

'What's so special about a picnic? Stick with me, Mr Ravan Pawar, and I'll take you to Kashmir on a fifteen-day picnic.'

'Kashmir,' Ravan gasped and almost fell into the water. All the boys from the chawls including the ones from the top floors went to their 'native place' in the summer holidays. All except Ravan, that is, since he did not have grandparents. Of course, any other relatives would have done too. Parvati had a sister and a couple of cousins whom they could have visited. She refused to have anything to do with them. She did not want her sister and cousins to know that she had a good-for-nothing husband and secondly, once you visited someone, they had the right to pay you a return visit and Parvati had neither the money nor the time to look after them. When Ravan was young, one of the cousins had written to say that he and his family of seven were planning to come across to Bombay during the Diwali vacation and could they stay with Shankar-rao and her? She had written back in some haste to say that it would have been wonderful to have them but what a pity they hadn't come during the last Diwali holidays as next week they were moving to Jamshedpur since her husband Shankar-rao had got a job there.

'Sure. I've been to Kashmir. Dal Lake and Nishat Baag in Jammu and Pahalgam. What's Kashmir, we'll travel all over India.'

Ravan looked at his aunt with awe. Two men were staring at her with eyes that seemed to be unbuttoning her blouse. She smiled back, Ravan wasn't quite sure whether it was at them or at him. He didn't care. He was going to make up for all those years of deprivation. And he was not about to go to some piddling town like Sawantwadi or Roha or even Poona but to that paradise which they called the Switzerland of India.

Aunt Lalee might want a hundred things from him but he had nothing to give her. So there was nothing to worry about. And yet he was ill at ease in her presence. He could not get rid of the feeling that he had become the battleground where the two women in his home fought a pitched but silent war.

~

'I would like to have either mutton or fish from tomorrow at least once a day,' Aunt Lalee told his mother. It had escaped him that the two women had hardly exchanged a word till now. His mother had not even realized that Aunt Lalee was addressing her. 'I said I would like to have mutton or fish at meals from tomorrow.'

'You talking to me?' Parvati asked bewildered.

'Who else? Does that dolt of a husband of yours do the cooking here that I should ask him?'

Parvatibai smiled self-deprecatingly. 'We would all like to eat mutton and fish once in a while but where's the money to come from?'

This time around Parvatibai took care not to advise her husband to take up a job to keep his sister happy nor did she tell Ravan to stay where he was when Aunt Lalee got up in a huff and said, 'Let's go, Ravan. We'll go and have an omelette at the Light of Iran Cafe.'

The same thought seemed to have struck mother and son: had another stove disappeared from the home or was it the fan? It couldn't be Parvatibai's eight gold bangles or her grandmother's gold necklace which for reasons unknown to her was traditionally called a garland of shoes in Marathi, since she had left both these items with one of her most trusted friends at the Byculla market. The fan was whirring away and all three stoves were cooking the evening meal.

'Are you coming, Ravan Pawar, or shall I go and eat the omelette on my own?'

~

Ravan had seen the Light of Iran Cafe almost since the day he first opened his eyes but had never been inside. How could he? You needed money to enter these places and he never had any, not even to go to the dingy fish place called Kal Bhairav. Seeing a place from outside and sitting inside ordering some preternatural delicacy were experiences that had nothing in common. It was an exquisite moment of heightened superciliousness. Within seconds Ravan had become a cad and a snob. He looked at people walking past on the road and felt infinite pity for them.

The tables had heavy wooden legs and marble tops yellowed from the tannin of millions of cups of tea. The wooden chairs had spindly legs and backs and plywood bottoms painted deep black going on chocolate. The walls were covered with glass paintings interspersed with mirrors. A morose king of Iran with heavy moustaches and even heavier crown and a cape that reached to his ankles sat on a throne while his plump queen stood behind him with a thin smile, one hand resting on the back of the throne and the other on the shoulder of the erect and prissily sour-faced crown prince. There were sylvan scenes of harrowingly beautiful damsels with fair complexions and flowing robes filling pitchers of water at the stream; forests with gentle waterfalls and peacocks; finally a princess with long golden tresses leaning over to kiss the forehead of a scantily dressed prince lying either dead or unconscious. The paint behind the glass in some of the paintings had begun to peel and it was disconcerting to see a hole in the queen's fur or the discoloration in the princess's hair, which made it look as if rats had been nibbling at it. Under the mirrors were instructions to the customers in English. They were arranged in pairs. 'Don't put feet on chair or table. Trust in God.'; 'Don't talk to strangers. Don't comb hair in front of mirror.'; 'Beware of pickpockets. No outside eatables allowed.'; 'I lent money and made a friend, I asked for it back and won an enemy. No credit.' But Ravan was not about to quibble about strange juxtapositions or a little worn paint when the place was magnificent.

The waiter brought two masala omelettes and a plate heaped with neatly cut slices of bread. The oil was still fizzing over the yellow surface and the aroma filled Ravan with a heady sense of expectation. He was grateful that he was not born a cripple, without a nose and a stomach and was able to enjoy these celestial aromas. A pronged instrument and knife had been placed next to the plates. Aunt Lalee struggled to cut the omelette with that strange spoon and knife but it jumped out. Ravan tore at his with his fingers and ate in a daze. The omelette was as thin as crepe, the oil a trifle rancid and his mother's omelettes were fatter and far more tasty but they could not compete with the thought, thrill and ambience of eating out. As if all this were not very heaven, Aunt Lalee ordered a Coca Cola for him and a cup of tea for herself. The Coke bottle was sweating on the outside and cold as liquid ice inside.

He felt his throat turn transparent as he sucked up the frozen fluid. It was sweet and bitter and he hoped that the bottle was bottomless and he could keep drinking from it till the breath went out of his body. He made a racket sucking the bottle dry and then the straw till its sides collapsed upon themselves.

'Why don't you wring the bottle, there's bound to be some drops left in it,' Aunt Lalee suggested to him. He was about to when he realized that she had got up.

~

Shankar-rao sat up to drink the tea that Parvatibai brought him.

'I'll go to the market and be back within an hour and a half,' Parvatibai told him. He had no idea why she was volunteering this information when all these years she had left without a word. She took the large, folded tote bags from the hook on the back of the door, then stopped and put her foot on the chair.

'This anklet's a nuisance,' she muttered almost to herself. 'The sari keeps getting caught in it.'

She placed the bags down on the floor and bent down to adjust the anklet. The sari must have got deeply entangled for it took her some time to free it. The delicacy of her fingers and the curve of the anklet around her firmly moulded ankle bone were all the more appealing because she was so unconscious of the grace and sensuousness of her gestures. Look at her, she was stooping down, those two lifebuoys at her breast bobbing up and down ever so gently and yet her sari had not drifted off her shoulder.

She looked up and saw her husband staring at her. She picked up the tote bags and left.

When she got back the doors were locked. That was unusual. Everybody in the chawls left the doors open for cross ventilation. She knocked. Nobody answered. She knocked again. The silence continued. Were brother and sister engaged in intimate converse? If so, where was Ravan? She relaxed when she saw that the window into the common corridor was open. How naive could she be? As if those two gave a damn or could be trusted to behave themselves just because the window was open or Ravan was in the house. She walked over to the barred window and drew the curtain aside. Shankar-rao, his sister and Ravan were smirking and trying to suppress their laughter.

'Ravan, open the door.'

'Stay where you are, Ravan,' Aunt Lalee said.

'Ravan, please open the door. I need to make preparations for tomorrow's meal.'

Ravan fidgeted. Surely a red shirt, a trip to Elephanta and an omelette and Coke could not, he thought, make him betray his mother. He was wrong. Even without the prospect of a visit to the blue mountains and the shimmering lakes of Kashmir, he would have turned his back on his mother. There are, he would find out, few thrills greater than stabbing someone you had loved without thought and without restraint all your living years. He stole a glance at his mother and then sat with his head between his knees. A hot wind of guilt singed the back of his neck.

'Even your son has abandoned you, Parvatibai.' Aunt Lalee sliced betel nut into micro-fine slivers with her nut-cracker, put three quarters of them in her mouth and slipped the rest into Ravan's hand. She picked up her pallu and held it uncertainly, not quite knowing what to do with it and then flung it over her shoulder. She walked over to the window. 'Have you come to some kind of decision about non-vegetarian dishes for your husband's sister?'

'I would be happy to, if I had that kind of money.'

'Do you want to starve the baby that's growing inside me?'

'What do you want me to do?'

'Why don't you take on some more customers, raise the price of the meals, take up some extra work.'

'You can't get customers overnight. But even if I could, I can't handle any more single-handed. And we'll need to buy more vessels and more stoves. Will you help?'

'While I'm in the family way?' Lalee seemed deeply offended.

'All the women in the chawls work till the day they deliver. They say it makes the delivery easy.'

'I'm not one of your women from the chawls. I'm used to a better lifestyle than this wretched place offers. Anyway it's up to you. You want to come in, you have to do what I tell you.'

Parvatibai took a long time to answer. 'I'll do as you say.'

There was mutton, fish or shrimps for lunch in Shankar-rao's sister's plate twice a week. Parvatibai took care to cook Lalee's special food when Ravan was at school. Shankar-rao was the one who suffered the most. The smell of the non-vegetarian food was overpowering and his stomach rumbled and rioted. He asked Parvati to give him just a little bit, a mere taste of it. She said, 'Ask your sister.'

'May I?' he asked Lalee.

'What for? Are you pregnant?'

~

One afternoon when Ravan came back from school, he hung around the kitchen as if he had something on his mind. In the good old days Parvati would have administered a straightforward emetic like, 'Out with it. What's the problem?' or a deliberately distorted one, 'So, your teacher's asked you to stand outside the class for the next seven days because you didn't do your homework?'

'What rubbish, you don't know a damn thing.'

Either way, the effect would be the same. Ravan would unburden himself for half an hour or so while Parvati pottered around. Most of the time the absolution would be in the confession itself, but sometimes Ravan would get angry and ask her, 'What's the point of my going into this long spiel if all you've got to say is "huh, huh" every five minutes.'

'If I give you advice, are you going to follow it?' That would shut Ravan up till the next occasion when he had something urgent to impart.

Their relationship was a little strained now, at least from the son's side, but Parvati was certain that if she carried on in a business-as-usual manner, things were bound to come to a boil and her son would spill whatever was bothering him. Ravan went through his routine. He stuck his hand in the sliced cabbage. Parvati said, 'Stop it.' Soon he was playing with the uncooked rice soaking in water in a pan. She cracked his knuckles with the rolling pin.

'Can't you sit still?'

'Where are Dada and Aunt Lalee?'

'They didn't tell me but they were talking about seeing some filim.'

'Ma…' He seemed to be having trouble getting to the point today. 'Ma…'

'I'm here Ravan.' Parvati smiled. 'I'm afraid I'm going to be here whether I'm wanted or not.'

'Am I going to have a sister, Ma?'

'I don't know. It could be a brother.'

'Who is the father?'

'Your father.'

'No, it's not, it's not,' Ravan yelled lunatically. 'You are lying. I know you are. I hate you. I hate you.'

'That's enough, Ravan.'

Why was he screaming? A tantrum wasn't going to change anything. There was a bad taste in his mouth. It had, he was sure, something to do with growing up. He hadn't just lied to others, he was willing to practise deceit and prevarication upon himself. Hadn't he known from day one that his father and Aunt Lalee were carrying on? He found it puzzling that he had gone to such lengths to sustain the pretence when the concerned parties hadn't given a hoot.

'I would prefer a sister. Eddie has one. What shall we call her?'

'That's up to them, your father and his sister.'

'I wish they would ask me. I would call her Neeta like the heroine in *Dil Deke Dekho*.'

Ravan seemed to have run out of steam. Parvati had the feeling that Ravan's long preamble had nothing to do with the intent of his visit.

'Shall I get rid of her?'

Parvatibai looked uncomprehending.

'Not the baby. Aunt Lalee.'

~

Shankar-rao and Lalee got back by seven o'clock.

'Where's Master Ravan?' Lalee asked Parvatibai.

'Practising tae lando or whatever they call it, with his teacher, I guess.'

Lalee switched on the ceiling fan. 'How come there's no breeze? Is the electricity off?' She looked up and saw a hook on the ceiling instead of the fan. 'Where the fuck is the fan? Parvati!' She was screaming now. 'Parvati.'

'Yes?'

'Don't say yes. What did you do with the fan, you bitch?'

'Sold it.'

'What?' Lalee asked hysterically. 'Whatever for, you stupid woman?'

'You said you wanted mutton and fish.'

'What's that got to do with the fan?'

'It paid for the food.'

'Look what you've gone and done.' Shankar-rao was beside himself with rage. 'We'll have to suffer because you wanted some fancy stuff for yourself.'

'Don't you worry, I'll make that bitch get the fan back if it's the last thing I do. Get it back, you hear, get it back.'

'I'll try,' Parvati said meekly, 'but then you won't get your fish and mutton.'

'Fuck the mutton and fish.' There was a nasty edge to her voice. 'Have the fan fixed.'

~

On Thursday after Lalee left around 11 o'clock, Parvati took a bath and was fastening her blouse, one hook at a time, when Shankar-rao came in to have a glass of water. Parvati turned her back on her husband and tried to get the remaining two top hooks into their loops. Shankar-rao put his glass on the floor, went over to where his wife stood, and put his arms around Parvatibai. He had his hands full.

'What will your sister say?' Parvatibai asked gently.

Shankar-rao went to the copper pot in which the drinking water was stored. He drank half a glass and stopped. He seemed to have resolved something of importance and urgency in his mind. He put the glass down and came back to Parvatibai. He held her tight. This time his wife did not resist.

War. Not the make-believe, playful variety that Shankar-rao and his sister had indulged in on the night that woman moved into Parvatibai's home but the real thing. Parvati was clear in her mind that there would be no quarter, no mercy, and she would take no casualties. No holds barred and it would be a fight until one of the parties was routed. She knew that she didn't stand a chance in a head-on confrontation. She would fight a war of attrition, employ guile, deceit and guerrilla tactics. She would retreat, admit defeat, cringe, grovel, collapse, beg, suffer any ignominy her enemy was pleased to inflict upon her. But she would not give up.

What then was the difference between her and the other women? None. Except that she had not started this war. It had been thrust upon her. She was fighting for her home, her son and for herself. She had discovered that when you are ranged against devious and evil people who will stoop to anything and stop at nothing, you must be willing to confront the injustice and evil in you. You may pretend or even believe in high-mindedness and the victory of light over darkness but there is no escaping the fact that you too will soil your hands, be brutalized, debased and demeaned. Was it worth it? It is a valid and relevant question but you may ask it only after you've won.

Winning itself was going to be a complex and fraught affair for she could not vanquish the enemy without winning one of them over. And here was the trickiest part: which enemy had ever been asked to restore, perhaps even invent, her husband and rival's self-esteem and confidence?

Shankar-rao was a hungry tiger. He had no time for foreplay. He took possession of the room, annexed the chawls, ascended the walls and paced the ceiling impatiently, leapt down, mauled and pushed aside whatever stood in his way. He was ravenous and he would brook no delay. He would rip his prey and eat her flesh, bones and all. Then suddenly without prior notice, the very intensity of his rage and lust seemed to sap his energies. He looked distraught and distressed and in need of help. Parvatibai invoked the name of the god of war, the one with the third eye who destroys to create a new order. Har Har Mahadev. Shiv, Shankar, Mahadev, they were all names of the same god, her own husband's namesake. It was an irony that did not escape her. Even when she was warring with Shankar, she had to take his name before battle could be joined. Unlike her rival, there was no soundtrack to Parvati's combat. She was a frogwoman, a commando who had to slip into enemy territory, lodge the explosive charges carefully, check the contact, start the clock ticking and then run for cover. Without stealth and guile, frantic excitement and impatience would get the better of Shankar-rao. Even now he was raring to go. If she couldn't slow him down, Parvatibai was certain, all would be lost. He tried to tear her blouse open. Fortunately all that overwrought haste made him clumsy.

'Easy, easy. We've got the whole day ahead of us,' Parvatibai told her husband.

'Have we?'

'Ravan comes back from school at four.'

Parvati had taken off her blouse now. Shankar-rao was trying desperately to swallow his wife's right breast in one gulp while undoing the knot of her petticoat. She took hold of his hand firmly, exhaled and pulled her stomach in and slipped it inside her petticoat. Shankar-rao's hand was trapped between her belly and the string of her petticoat. If only she could distract him for a while, maybe, just maybe... But he was in no mood to listen. He had to enter her now, now before it was all over. She guided his hand to the crevice. It gave him pause. She let him explore her. A strange thought entered his mind: could it be possible that giving pleasure was one of the most erotic things a human being was capable of?

Even then, they had a long way to go. If he had his way he would have forced his fist inside her. She undid her petticoat and put her palm on the back of his wrist. She stroked his hand slowly, very slowly till he calmed down and echoed her rhythms.

Suddenly he was in a hurry again. He was out of his trousers and beating at the gates. She was sure he was not going to make it. She took his member in her hand and almost broke it in two.

'What are you doing?' Shankar-rao screamed.

'Trust me.'

He cooled down then though he was wary of her. She led him inside her. He was growing frisky again. Parvatibai clamped down on him, the muscles of her vagina held him in a vice. He could neither move forward nor withdraw. He felt trapped and became frenetic. It was as if someone had caught hold of his throat and was squeezing it till the life had ebbed out of him. He was gasping. What was she doing? He had suspected foul play earlier but like a fool had not done anything about it. He was going to pay dearly for being such a credulous, trusting idiot. She was going to mutilate him. She was going to shut off the blood supply. His thing would go blue, then black, atrophy and fall off altogether, never to rise again.

'Please,' he was sobbing now, 'let go of it. Please, I beg you. It's the only one I have. Not replaceable, you know. Please. I'll do anything you want. I'll get rid of her. Tomorrow, tonight, now, as soon as she returns.'

Parvatibai did not reduce the pressure for a long time. Slowly, he quietened down. Parvati relaxed. Shankar-rao was pleased to find that he had become the bobbin shuttling back and forth, back and forth, in a power loom. He kept going at an even pace. Afterwards he lay next to her for a long time. He would never know how tense Parvatibai had been and how much she had riding on this single event.

~

When she got back, Lalee sat down on the floor with Parvatibai, peeled off the tough strands from the sides of the green beans and threw them into a large brass vessel. 'That was clever, very clever, Parvatibai.'

Parvati looked up in alarm. Oh God, had that stupid husband of hers told this woman that he had exercised his conjugal rights thrice today. How could he have, he hadn't had a moment alone with his sister since she had returned. 'I'll say one thing for you, Parvati. You've got spunk. You had me fooled with that business of the fan. Your delightful husband Shankar was only too happy to jump down my throat since he didn't get to taste the meat and the fish you cooked for me. I didn't pursue the matter because I didn't want Shankar-rao's or Ravan's evil eye to fall on the food they couldn't have and on my baby.' She clutched her stomach protectively and paused for effect. 'But I owe it to you to give you a word of warning. Nobody humiliates me and gets away with it. See this talisman? My mother and I went to a tantric and he gave it to me. He said that it will, come what may, drive you and your s...' she checked herself since Ravan was listening intently, 'you certainly, out of this house before my son is born. This place is going to be mine. I'm going to employ a few cooks who'll make food for hundreds of people. I'm going to be rich, Parvati, filthy rich. When you want a job, come and ask me. I might think about it, though considering the quality of the food you cook, I wouldn't give you a job even in an orphanage.'

~

There were times when Ravan suspected that Aunt Lalee was genuinely fond of him. Every once in a while she took him out to Malabar Hill or for a meal as she was doing today. He wasn't quite sure why he had gone off her. Was it the comments of the boys in the chawls? They cracked the same third-rate joke every day. Whose turn is it today with Aunt Lalee? Your father's or yours? He had been foolish enough to suggest once that it was their father's turn. Hooray, that will make our father's day. Can we join in too? Mr Tamhane, the clerk from the Metropolitan Court, smiled his thin sticky smile and asked Ravan how his father's whore was. He had looked it up in the dictionary and was pleased that dirty Mr Tamhane was wrong. His aunt was certainly not 'proffering sexual favours for monetary considerations'. There was something, about dictionaries, at least the Marathi ones that he knew of, which intimidated and put off Ravan. You went to look up a difficult word and they usually explained it with ten other difficult ones, especially if it had anything to do with sex. Mr Tamhane had of course not stopped there. Is your father the pimp and your mother the madam? Are they planning to expand the business, get a whole stableful of girls to keep young Miss Lalee company? Or is your mother going to turn tricks. I'll bet she'll attract more business than your Aunt Lalee. But I must insert a word of caution here. These are, as you are well aware, residential premises. Carrying on corporal commerce here is against the law. I'm afraid one of these days I'll perforce have to inform the police department of Lalee's red-light activities.' Mr Tamhane must have found his own words hilarious for he cackled dryly and then began to cough. Ravan thought he was finished but Tamhane said after he had stopped coughing, 'Are they married?'

'Who?'

'Lalee and your father? Because if they are, there's very likely a case for bigamy there.'

'Don't be absurd, they are brother and sister.'

'That would make it incest.'

Most of the families in Chawl No. 17 though had forbidden their children to have anything to do with the Pawar household on the fourth floor. Ravan's home was invariably referred to as that House of Sin.

Ravan was used to people saying nasty things behind his back and to his face. But this was different. He was acutely embarrassed by the things they were saying about his aunt and yet he also knew that whoever spoke disparagingly about her, and almost everybody did, also exhibited an obsessive and prurient curiosity about her. He thought this was the first time people were jealous of his father. 'What's the bugger got that I haven't?' A man, whom he had never spoken to, from Chawl No. 3 asked him, 'Women must find good-for-nothings far more attractive than simple people who have to work for a living.'

Aunt Lalee was no longer news. She had been with them for close to ten months now, but he also knew that just the fact of her going down the stairs or standing at the bus-stop created waves. He liked that. Aunt Lalee was a circus. There was always excitement wherever she was. He knew she was unreliable and would disown anyone without a moment's thought so long as there was something to be gained from the act or simply because she was bored. He thought he had used the word 'disown' by chance. Maybe not. It was a word that would never occur to his mother. He had blithely disowned her but that didn't make any difference to her. She may have been disappointed and hurt but once she had accepted you, there was no going back. She would speak her mind in no uncertain terms but she would stand by you. Look at his father, she should have thrown the man out years ago. In the past few months, Ravan had a difficult time stopping himself from wringing his father's neck. He was so patently thoughtless, childish and selfish. Ravan could not understand why his mother didn't poison him. But the answer was always clear: you don't disown people, come what may. Ravan had a strange insight about himself then. He could be bought, his price was not very high either. Yet he had to be able to live with himself. When Aunt Lalee humiliated his mother, he could not.

Besides he was sure he understood his aunt's game plan now. She was certainly planning to throw his mother and him out of the house. It wouldn't be long before his father too was evicted and Aunt Lalee took over the place.

～

Something big must be in the offing. No omelette and Coke today. The bribe was a full-fledged deluxe biryani with curd and salad. Ravan went at it systematically. No hurry, Ravan, no hurry at all.

'I don't know how to tell you this, Aunt Lalee,' Ravan stumbled over his words in a dither of embarrassment and guilt.

'Speak up man. There are no secrets between us. Vomit it all out. Don't hold back anything. That's the secret of life. Anything you want to do, might as well do it full-bloodedly. I always say, you want to fart, go ahead and do it loudly. Get pleasure out of it. Why else should you do it.'

Despite so much encouragement, Ravan was slow and diffident to start. 'I know black magic.'

'No kidding.'

Ravan nodded his head to stress and affirm what he had just said. He realized that Aunt Lalee didn't know whether to believe him or not, more likely not, and she was just indulging him.

'What kind of black magic?'

'You know Eddie, the one who told my friends that Ravan's Aunt Lalee is a whore? I killed his father.'

'Good for him and bully for you, Ravan. I'm glad nobody can call Lalee names in front of you. Is that all?'

'I killed Prakash's father, the boy who used to terrorize our school students and teachers, I killed his father.'

'Why?'

'He asked me to.'

'And why did you kill Eddie's father?'

'He was making eyes at my mother.'

'And pray when did you kill him? Last week?' She was getting into the spirit of things now, ribbing him, making an ass of him and enjoying it hugely though something about his face and manner bothered her. He couldn't seem to see how ridiculous he was, telling such bizarre tales. He had an expressionless face and his voice was deadpan as if not he but someone else was talking through him.

'I killed him when I was eleven months old and Eddie was still in his mother's womb.'

'What marvellous stories you invent, Ravan. I'm impressed, really I am.'

'You can ask Eddie's mother.'

'Why would I want to do that?' Aunt Lalee looked a trifle disturbed by Ravan's monotonous persistence.

'Just to make sure that I'm not lying.'

'What difference does it make whether you are or not?'

Ravan shrugged his shoulders. He would leave it to his aunt to decide. 'Here are letters from the boys from my school asking me to do black magic on people who had been bothering them. They also talk about payment, how much cash down and how much they would pay on completion of the job.'

The smile had disappeared from Aunt Lalee's face. Ravan untied the string of the packet and carefully took out the notes and letters. There were at least fifteen of them. They had aged with the passage of time and had an authentic look to them. Ravan pushed them towards his aunt.

'You read them.'

Ravan ate his biryani with a spoon and through mouthfuls of fried Basmati rice, mutton cooked just right, crisp, burnt onions sprinkled on top, lightly fried raisins and cashewnuts, he read from the letters without a trace of feeling for the writers, for the payments offered, or their victims.

Aunt Lalee became progressively more restless. After the seventh letter she asked him to stop. 'What are you trying to tell me? That you'll bump your mother off if I pay the right price?' Ravan shook his head. 'What's the right price?' Aunt Lalee had missed the movement of his head. Ravan stared at the food and again shook his head. 'You won't charge me or you won't kill your mother?'

'Neither,' Ravan said slowly, almost reluctantly.

'So why the hell are you telling me all this?'

She was suddenly silent, her eyes narrowed in an effort to sort out the tangle in her mind, then they opened in horror, perhaps even a little bit of fear.

'Why, you little twerp, are you trying to tell me while eating biryani at my expense,' she flung the stainless steel plate at him, fortunately he had almost finished, 'that you are going to do black magic on me and kill me?' Ravan nodded. The plate was on the floor and Aunt Lalee had him by the throat. 'And to think that I brought you here to break the good news to you first. I'll kill you, you shit.' She would have too but the Irani owner and the waiter rushed to separate them.

'How can you do that to a young, defenceless boy?' the old fat Irani, wearing pyjamas that didn't reach his ankles, asked Lalee.

'No child this, he is a bloody murderer. He wants to kill me.'

'Talk sense, how can a boy his age do that?'

'Ask him. He says he committed his first murder when he was one year old.'

'And you believe him? I don't care if he killed someone when he was in your womb....'

'This shit is not my son.'

'Then what are you doing with him? Have you kidnapped him?' Before Ravan could say yes, Aunt Lalee paid the bill and got out. She had one last question for Ravan as they headed back home. 'If you are going to kill me with your black magic, why not do it instead of telling me about it?'

'I thought I owed it to you,' he echoed his aunt's words to his mother.

'Listen you jerk, listen carefully. You touch one hair of mine and I'll make you a cripple but won't let you die. You follow, you toad, I'm talking to you. Did you hear?'

Ravan nodded his head and then said gloomily, 'But you'll be dead before that.'

'Don't say it, you evil boy. And to think that I bought you the shirt you are wearing, took you to Apollo Bunder and bought you omelette and biryani with my own money.'

'My mother's money.'

~

When they got to the house, Lalee went inside and changed her sari. If she took pains and painted her face with half the things from her vanity case, she looked like the disgruntled queen of a tiny kingdom who's fallen out of favour but is a queen nevertheless. All that make-up couldn't cover the fine lines stretching from her eyes to the temples and the slackness around her mouth but she was wearing one of Parvatibai's rich Narayanpethi saris in traditional peacock blue with a border and pallu of a vibrant and violent yellow and that seemed to make her look old-world and aristocratic. Ravan saw his father standing at the mirror trying to figure out how to knot his tie. He was wearing his one and only suit. It was a little crumpled and outdated but Shankar-rao hadn't gained any weight despite his sybaritic lifestyle and it didn't fit him too badly. He was beaming and followed Lalee everywhere with his eyes. What were they up to? Were they going to Kashmir or leaving India for ever?

Lalee was in a great mood. She held Shankar-rao's hand and said, 'Don't we look like a picture? Parvatibai you must take out our nazar. Don't want the evil eye to fall upon us today of all days. Ravan, wear your party clothes. The shirt's fine but change into those swank white trousers I bought for you. Parvatibai, we need you to look good too. You are, after all, the elder wife. Change and then I'll touch your feet and ask for your blessings.'

Ravan marvelled at all this finery and festivity. Were these the same people he had known for years? Look at the jewellery Aunt Lalee was wearing and Shankar-rao's parrot green suit, white shoes and the red tie that was held in place by the same kind of knot with which he tied his striped underwear.

'What's the occasion? Where are we going?'

Lalee's mood had undergone a transformation. She had forgotten Ravan's dark threat and her own grip around his neck. She was smiling and the gold of her triple chain flashed in his eyes. 'Oh, look at us. We were so excited, we forgot to tell you both. We are getting married. Right here. A nice private wedding. The bhatjee should be here any minute. Tomorrow we'll leave for a honeymoon. Won't that be nice? Mother and son can have a little quiet time while we are away.'

Parvati knew when she was beaten. All of the sister's ploys had one thing in common. She liked to keep everybody off balance. Parvatibai had tried hard to guess her moves in advance but she had missed the most obvious one. She had been outmanoeuvred and all counter-moves were now futile. The game was over.

'How long will you be gone?' Ravan asked.

'Three weeks, four weeks, who knows? The world's a big place. Don't think I've forgotten about Kashmir though. On that trip it'll be just you and me, nobody else.'

The priest knocked and entered. He made preparations for the sacred fire.

'Only four people? Why? A wedding is a celebration, not a secret. Who is the young man?'

'That's Ravan,' Lalee told him.

'A trifle young, wouldn't you say, to be getting married to you even if it's one of those new-fangled things called a love marriage.'

'Please put on your spectacles instead of making a fool of yourself. This is my groom.' Lalee was sharp with the priest. 'Not that silly boy.'

'Ah good, now you look like the right age for a bride and bridegroom.' He was a friendly, loquacious priest. He didn't take offence at Lalee's tone and he was not put out by his own muddling. He worked quickly like someone who enjoyed what he was doing and had had lots of practice.

'And who's the lady and the boy whom I mistook for someone else?'

'He's my son.' Parvati intervened and let her husband's sister off the hook.

'And where's his father?'

'He's out of...' Lalee started to say but Ravan was pointing to Shankar-rao.

'So that's your father and you are his son. So you must be a widower,' the priest said in his bemused way. 'Very progressive of you Laleebai to marry a widower.'

Lalee smiled with all her twenty-six teeth. In the synthetic and ersatz genre of smiles, this was certainly one of the most disarming and friendly. 'Shouldn't we get down to business?'

'Yes of course, I like a bride who's in a hurry. They are so much more lively. And how did your first wife die, Shankar-rao? Cancer, TB, a woman's illness? I hope you didn't set fire to her because she didn't bring you enough money and a scooter and fridge.' He laughed heartily. 'No offence meant. It's just that we come across more and more of these cases as the years pass. You still haven't told me who the beautiful young woman standing shyly next to the boy is?'

Lalee said, 'A guest' and Shankar-rao, 'My wife.'

It was a bit confusing for the bhatjee but he was a patient man with a sunny temperament.

'Shouldn't we hurry or we'll miss the auspicious time of the muhurat.'

'You leave that to me. Once I unravel these crossed signals, we'll be sailing along. I'll explain every word and especially all the major concepts that are so integral to the way our religion looks at marriage in plain Marathi, even if I recite in Sanskrit first.'

Seven minutes later he had packed his bag. 'You ought to be ashamed of yourselves. And if you are not worried about criminal consequences, what about me? The police would certainly haul me to jail for aiding and abetting a crime. And what's wrong with your first wife? She is surely far more lovely than this new one. She is certainly far more cultured. And you, madam, why are you being party to this crime instead of speaking up.'

'They are not in a frame of mind to listen to me.'

'You can get the police.' He thought that over. 'Maybe not. You still a need a place to stay?'

'Get out. We'll get another bhatjee who'll be more sensible.'

Lalee, as always, had the last word.

~

The marriage was postponed. It shouldn't have been difficult to locate an indigent priest in a city like Bombay who would marry two people in a hurry. Frankly you could get anyone you wanted just so long as you made sure that Parvati and Ravan were not around.

On Sunday morning Eddie and his family were returning from church when 'that woman from Ravan's house' accosted Violet.

'Madam,' she said in Marathi, 'may I have a word with you?'

Between sewing and house-keeping, Violet did not have time to keep abreast of events or gossip and hence, unlike Eddie, did not know whom she was talking to.

'Please excuse me,' Violet told Lalee in her uncertain vernacular, 'but my charity is reserved for my home, and when I can afford it, the church.'

'I have not come for charity.' Lalee was aggrieved that anyone should think that she lived off charity.

Violet was thrown off balance. Surely she should have been more observant and realized that a woman who wore lipstick would not be begging.

'Please make it brief. I have to cut and sew an engagement dress for a client by this afternoon.'

'I wanted to make enquiries about a certain Master Ravan who I believe...'

'I do not wish to sully my tongue with that abominable name. Do you know him? Because if you do, I will not have any converse with you.'

What a question, Eddie thought. Only his mother would not know that Lalee was Ravan's aunt. He shook his head frantically but Violet was not aware of him.

'No friend of mine, I assure you.'

'Beware of him. He killed my husband. But there are worse things in life than that evil boy. If he doesn't get you, his mother surely will.'

A few weeks later, Parvatibai and Ravan were returning from one of their nocturnal walks. Parvatibai had begun to enjoy them. It was the only peaceful time of the day and walking made her feel well and whether anyone would give it credence or not, it gave her a sense of freedom, a time she could call her own. Usually Ravan raced her up the stairs but today one of his classmates from the third floor wanted a carrom partner.

'May I, Ma?'

'Twenty minutes, not more.'

'Thirty.'

'You heard me the first time. You have school tomorrow.'

She was glad she was alone when she arrived at her house. Shankar-rao and his sister were engaged in a dialogue that seemed to strain the limits of imagination.

'Now get into bed and give me a good time.' Lalee's voice was honey and soft fire.

There was no response from Shankar-rao. 'Come baby. If you won't give me a good time, I'll give you one. Not just a good time, the time of your life. I'll do things you wouldn't dream of. Once I do them, you'll never be able to sleep again.'

'Parvati and Ravan will be back. Let me sleep.'

'You come here,' she screamed at him, 'did you hear what I said. Come here and fuck me. I want that child.'

Shankar-rao's reply was curt. 'Go fuck yourself. You are never going to be pregnant.'

Parvati knocked and entered and put off the lights.

Had she brought all those troubles upon herself and her innocent child? Getting to be a young man now and hardly innocent after his meeting with Aunt Lalee. She excused herself in the middle of the act, went into the kitchen and brought out the willi with which she had been cutting cabbage on the day Shankar-rao had brought his sister home. She sat astride her husband. He had been too engrossed in foreplay to react to Parvati's sudden departure. He tried to grasp Parvati's breasts in the palms of his hands. It was sheer torture. His eyes closed and he mooed at his good fortune. Lalee was lascivious and her face, manners and posture suggested undiscovered worlds of lechery and pleasure but she was mostly a cock-teaser and nothing more except on the rare days when she needed urgent satisfaction. He increasingly had the feeling that at heart she was bored with sex. In the last few months except that one occasion when Parvati had walked in, it was always, you want it, go ahead, work at it, just so long as you don't expect me to stop combing my hair, or chewing aniseed or just plain sleeping. He would get so frantic wanting her, he usually mistimed and that made her nasty and bitchy. Besides she had loose, semi-solid boobs. Even the slightest movement and they tended to become unstable and go in the most unexpected directions. Didn't even qualify as medium-sized. Now look at these. These weren't pomegranates, they weren't giant watermelons, they were cannon balls. No, what he had in his hands was the earth, one in each hand. Stupendous, his hands couldn't support them for more than a minute. They got exhausted holding up the crystal globes and dropped them. Mom, Dad just come and look at these monster jackfruits from my personal garden. Yeaaaaahhhhhh, if this isn't paradise....

He felt something sharp at his Adam's apple. For some stupid reason, Parvati had decided to blabber in the midst of his sacred trance, nothing short of a profound mystical experience. But he was Shankar, the Lord of Destruction, he was going to open his third eye and burn her tongue to ashes; just the tongue, no no no no no no, not those two wonders of the world. Never, what did you take him for? A fool? Wouldn't allow that third eye to touch the bells of heaven. Nothing could match them, they were priceless. He opened his eyes and his magnificent erection collapsed. It was not even semi-solid, it was a vanishing species, it evaporated, there was a void where it had stood so magnificently. Nothing, the primal emptiness. But there were even more urgent calamities and crises to be dealt with. The crescent blade of the willi had settled like the thin fine line of a thread on his neck. Parvati held the wooden handle casually with her whip hand.

'Please,' tears rolled down from Shankar-rao's eyes, 'please don't kill me. I'll do anything you want, anything. I'll go back to work. I beg of you. Spare me. I was wrong. I should never have got her. I'll get Lalee to pay for her stay and meals and the stoves.'

'Will you shut up and listen to me?'

He shut up.

'You may have sex with me, once or twice a week. But only when Ravan is in school or at his lai tando classes.'

Does she need to slit my throat to tell me this? 'Will you please take the willi away?'

'I'm not finished. If your sister ever shows up here, I'll kill you.' She pressed the blade down a little with her thumb. A red crescent began welling up all around his throat. 'If you bring another woman to this house, I'll kill you.' She pressed the knife edge down a little further. 'If you ever sell any of the goods in our house, stoves, fans, beds, vessels, anything, I'll kill you.'

'It's hurting.' A tear slid down his left cheek. Several others followed. 'Please don't kill me. I'm your husband.'

'Then behave like one. And like the father of a boy who needs to be set a good example. Don't get your tarts and mistresses here. This is our home, not a whore-house. Do I make myself clear?'

He was crying now, oddly enough only from his left eye.

'I want an answer: a yes or a no.'

'Yes. Anything you say.'

'You may finish making love to me.'

Life is not a victory, Parvati thought, it's a hard-won compromise. She picked up Shankar-rao's lifeless hands and placed them where they had been.

Seventeen

Rock Around the Clock ran at the Strand for seventeen or maybe nineteen weeks. Eddie should have seen it over fifty times if he had averaged three shows a week. But due to certain unforeseen circumstances he saw it only fourteen times. On Tuesday, he was doing his routine, sidling up behind men who looked lost and were asking for extras. He chanted his mantra in quick short bursts: 'One-rupee-five-anna tickets for five rupees. One-rupee-five-anna tickets for five rupees.' The latter half of that last word was to prove prophetic. A midnight blue shadow fell across the road and a hard, calloused hand clamped down on Eddie's arm. The intention was not to cut off the flow of blood, it was to break the arm. It belonged to a policeman. The only presence of mind that Eddie could muster in that moment of crisis was to pee in his pants.

The other scalpers continued to work undisturbed. With a little experience Eddie could have resolved matters on the spot. The policeman too realized his mistake a little too late. The criminal's wet pants and the combination of 'Sorry, sorry' with 'I didn't do anything, I swear, I didn't do anything' had gathered a substantial crowd. One or two people half-heartedly said, 'Let him go, he's still a child,' but Eddie's dripping shorts changed the focus and made everybody laugh. It became, unfortunately, a matter of the policeman's honour and professional dignity.

It was 2.45 p.m. by the time the policeman and Eddie reached St Sebastian's School. The peon sensed the gravity of the occasion. He got Father Agnello out of his eleventh grade algebra class.

'What is it?' Father Agnello asked him impatiently.

The peon was cryptic. 'Come and see for yourself.'

Father Agnello made a sour face but followed the peon obediently.

'You want a kick in your butt? You trying to make an ass of me?' The policeman asked Eddie when he saw Father D'Souza.

Eddie didn't look up.

'Is this the man?' There was horror and a glimmer of prurient recognition on the policeman's face. Eddie nodded his head.

'This boy says you are his father.'

'That's true. Everybody calls me Father.'

'Real father or that kind of father?' The policeman directed the question at Eddie. He was leering and his voice had become offensively familiar. He had always known that these priests were not to be trusted. Pretending to be celibates all their lives. Sure, so long as they could have as many flings as they wanted on the side.

Eddie looked a long time at Father Agnello D'Souza but wouldn't speak.

'Eddie, behave yourself. What seems to be the problem, havaldar? What's the meaning of a policeman bringing you to me in the middle of a class, Eddie? And what's that evil smell coming from you?'

'Take charge of your son. Call yourself a priest and yet fathering children all over the place. Should be ashamed of yourself. Like father, like son. No wonder your brat was selling tickets in the black at Strand.'

'Whose son, whose father?' A vein in Father Agnello's temple was throbbing dangerously and his face had gone red. His voice was thinner than a screech. 'What did you tell this policeman?' It was Father Agnello's turn to grab Eddie's arm now even as he made a superhuman effort not to do violence to the boy-Satan in front of him.

'I told him what Ma said that Sunday. You are my father.'

Poor Father Agnello. He was beginning to fear this boy. What was his purpose, meaning and role in life? Was he the eye God kept on him? Or was he the living and breathing flesh and blood of the devil?

This time instead of Violet calling upon Father Agnello, the priest summoned her.

'Mrs Coutinho, I'm at my wit's end. He's selling film tickets on the black market and telling the police that I'm his father. What should I do with him?'

'Don't ask me, Father,' Violet told Father D'Souza while pointedly ignoring her son, 'I'm only a woman and his mother.'

'What does that mean?' Father D'Souza was greatly perplexed by Violet's answer. Had the woman lost her senses or had he lost touch with reality altogether?

'Starve him. Break his legs. Drown him.'

There was, the priest had to admit, much merit in Violet's suggestions but as a man of God, Father Agnello D'Souza could not take such extreme measures against Eddie. Instead he caned Eddie and had him report to him at every recess between classes. But the adamantine rigour had gone out of Father D'Souza's wrath and punishments. His spirit was broken. Had the boy been telling the truth the first time when he said that he had gone to see *Rock Around the Clock?* Then what about Ravan and the Mazagaon Mawalis and the rest of his confession?

Was there no longer such a thing as truth?

~

After the *Rock Around the Clock* episode, Father Agnello and Eddie crossed swords only once before Eddie left school. Eddie had just learnt to masturbate. Some of his friends had taken to the practice with the diligence, devotion and single-mindedness needed to fulfil the most difficult and exhausting of vows. At times they would waste their manhood six or seven times running. Of course they were aware that playing with oneself was not just the despoiling of the body but a cardinal sin. It is open to debate whether the boys would have indulged indefatigably in such handiwork if their elders had not proscribed it. Like hundreds of thousands of their peers, they compared the width, length and peak flows of their dicks and ranked their manhood on a daily basis.

It would take another fifteen to twenty years for the Spanish word 'macho' to become a commonplace in English. Till that time, English had not taken cognizance of two factors about sex: the public nature or aspect of intercourse and its innate competitiveness. The people from the lower storeys of the CWD chawls did not feel this inadequacy. They understood that there are always dimensions of valour to the male principle. Men are brave and courageous even when they merely lie in bed. Which is why in Sanskrit, Marathi and the other local tongues, man's sticky emanations and seed are called virya or 'heroism'. Men are heroic inside the vagina, in wet dreams, quickies or in love.

~

That day Joachim Correa had got a page from *Playboy*. In those days, *Playboy*, too, had a strong sense of shame. It may have been a sex magazine but it knew what was decent and what was obscene. It was Hugh Hefner who established the law—which he himself would break later—that the region around the female organ is as unblemished as a mirror.

It is impossible to guess how many normal and healthy repressed Indians (there aren't any other kind, or at least weren't in British and early post-colonial India) went into shock when they discovered that their women had hair in places other than their heads.

Perhaps Eddie too would be traumatized later in life at the sight of the real thing. For the moment, he merely raised his right pinky in class, and the geography teacher, Mr Sequeira, who believed that physical needs took precedence over intellectual edification, granted him permission to evacuate his bladder. There was a titter among Eddie's friends but Eddie kept a straight face and walked to the toilets. He latched the door and faced it since the sun was streaming in from the window at the back. He took out the picture from *Playboy* from his right pocket while unbuttoning his shorts and roughly pushing aside his briefs with his left hand. He unfolded the page with both hands. He was careful not to damage it, many others were to get their pleasure yet. Bloody hell, instead of naked female flesh, there were three columns of printed matter. That bastard Errol, he had played the same trick on him two weeks earlier and passed on a page from some trigonometry book. He would fix the bugger after school. Or was it Joachim's idea this time? He unlatched the door and was about to leave when he saw the black and white picture on the other side.

The name in a delicate black typeface under the right hand corner of the picture read Anita Ekberg. A vertical fold ran over her left breast and a horizontal one bisected her navel. Since she had turned her head sharply to the left you could see only her right profile. She sat a little cramped, her right leg folded under her left. Her belly-button was a soft blur on her stark white complexion. She had drawn her shoulders and hands tightly behind her, and the tension between the breasts and her body was so finely distributed that there wasn't a millimetre of slack. Her left nipple stood out like a faded doorbell. On the taut column of her neck stood the solitary flower of her ear. Her hair was pulled back and tied in a ponytail. There was not a shadow of self-consciousness on her body or face. But she refused to raise her head and look at Eddie.

Eddie had heard of Anita Ekberg because of her stupendous breasts. But he did not feel any sexual attraction for her now that she was seated before him. He stared at the picture for a little over five minutes. He had held the pictures of many nude women in his hands during the last few months, but the reaction this picture evoked in him was a little strange. Even though his body refused to respond to Ekberg, watching her gave him a quiet sense of happiness and pleasure. His eyes felt good. The undercurrent of guilt that laced his bouts of sexual turbulence was absent today. A stillness and peace descended upon him.

The dirty toilet bowl, the rusty chain of the flush tank, the walls with graffiti effaced by the censoring hand of the Father Prefect, the smell of ammonia that had accrued over decades... he forgot his environs. Like a star that was turning to ashes, the light from Anita Ekberg flowed soft and unfocused. She looked insubstantial. He guessed intuitively that the mystery of her beauty lay in that light. Not just in the picture, even if she had been sitting in front of him in person he would not have dared touch her. In the deepest recesses of her beauty there was the chill of an iceberg. She was made of flint or marble. The breath of life could never touch her. She was only a stone sculpture.

Eddie folded the picture and put Anita Ekberg in his pocket. He was about to button up his fly when he heard Joachim's voice from the next toilet. 'How's it going Eddie? Isn't Anita something else? I've broken all records today. Jerked off eight, I swear to you, eight times with Anita today. Soon as you are through, I'll start again.'

Eddie felt a sudden rush of envy. What the hell, why am I wasting my life?

'Joachim,' he hollered loudly.

Joachim was terrified. 'Eddie, talk softly, you bastard.' But Eddie was not to be stopped and sang out, 'Little boy, little boy, what are you holding in your hand? Is it a bat and ball, or your cock standing tall?'

Joachim threw all caution to the winds. 'Yes sir, yes sir, my prick is for one and for all. It's at your beck and call.'

Eddie looked up a few moments after the door opened. His eyes were locked into Father Agnello's. Damn, he had forgotten to relatch the door.

'What are you doing, Eddie?'

It maddened Eddie when Father Agnello refused to see what was in front of his eyes and pretended ignorance.

'As if you didn't do it.'

The blood drained out of Father Agnello's face.

Eddie tore the picture in a rush and pulled the chain several times. A part of Anita Ekberg's thigh stuck to the wall of the toilet bowl and would not be flushed down.

Eighteen

✦

'No.' Parvati had her back to Ravan.
'Please, Ma,' he begged of her.
'No.'

Since the business of *Dil Deke Dekho,* his mother's vocabulary seemed to have shrunk to that one word. 'Come on, Ma. Tomorrow's Sankrant, the only day in the year everybody flies kites. Chandrakant's got a dozen, the Gokhale boys have fifteen among the three of them. Even that boy from upstairs, Eddie, he's got six. I'm just asking for one kite and a bit of manja.'

'No, you learn to pass your exams. Then maybe I'll buy you a kite.'

At least she no longer expected him to, come within the first ten.

'You don't buy me books, how do you expect me to pass?'
'Where's my gold earring?'

He gave up. It was a long time since he had pawned his mother's gold earring. Parvati had paid the shopkeeper and redeemed it but any time Ravan wanted something, she demanded that he return it. He didn't hold it against her. He had stolen it and he would have to pay for the theft all his life. It would have been the easiest thing for him to snitch an eight-anna coin from his mother's purse and buy the kite, but the thought did not occur to him.

He was not about to walk out of his home because his mother had refused him some money. But her continuous nos had begun to get him down. A walk and a bit of fresh air might help him forget the kite. He was on the main road adjoining the compound of the CWD chawls when he realized that wandering around in this area was not such a good idea. Every grocer, cycle shop, chemist and even the corner Irani restaurant was selling kites and manja so sharp it would cut not just kite strings but bystanders' throats.

If he had his way, he would make manja at home as Syed Ali from the adjoining Rafiya Manzil did. Syed Ali was the king of kite-cutters. He prepared a special glue with exotic dyes, mixed microscopic glass in it, ran thousands of yards of thread through it and then hung it up to dry. A couple of days later, he wound the red, blue, green, yellow, violet threads around wooden phirkis. It was deadly stuff. If your manja barely brushed against Syed Ali's you could say goodbye to your kite. It would float in the air with its remnant of thread, all the tension and purpose gone out of it till it sank to street level. Suddenly seven or eight kids would appear from nowhere, weave in and out of the traffic and chase the drunken kite. Three or four pairs of hands would rise to grab the coloured paper diamond and more often than not rip it apart.

Ravan heard a voice calling his name. By the time he came out of his reverie and saw her at the Shyamjeebhai Valji Patel Grocer's shop, it was a little too late. There wasn't time to cross over to the other pavement as he had done for years now. She smiled that same gentle, uncertain smile. He wondered if the limp had got worse. There was a rent in the black pouch over her foot which had been repaired with coarse white twine. She tugged at the folds of her sari at her waist and tried to pull it down a little to cover the offensive obsidian at the end of her leg. It was obvious she had been to the market. She was carrying cloth bags jammed with vegetables, tea and dal in both her hands.

'How are you, Ravan?' Shobhan asked.

'OK,' Ravan muttered.

'You've grown so tall. Tara was right. In a few years you'll look like a film star.'

Ravan avoided her eyes and concentrated on the glass bangles on her right forearm. Her cotton sari with soft flowers printed on it was worn out in places but darned with such care and finesse that only close scrutiny revealed the repair work.

'What were you going to buy?' she asked Ravan.

'Nothing.'

'How silly of me. What else would you buy today but kites?'

Ravan wasn't about to tell her that his mother had refused to give him money for the kites.

'Give me six kites,' Shobhan told the grocer.

What did she think about behind that tranquil face of hers? Whatever the provocation, she never clenched her jaws, swore or got angry. Did she watch everything from a distance, as if even her own life was happening to someone else? Nobody could see it but instead of a face, she wore a mask. No, Ravan wanted to rephrase that. What he and everybody else saw was the mask, not what went on inside. That's why ten or twenty years from now, he couldn't think beyond that, she would look just the same.

'Here. These are for you.'

Ravan did not want to take them but could not believe his good fortune. He held them lightly. 'Will you fly them for me, high up in the sky above all the others?'

He did not answer her.

'Will you?'

He nodded his head.

'Tomorrow is Sankrant. A good day to renew friendships, isn't it? Such a long time since I said to anyone: tilgul ghya ani godgod bola. Will you have dinner with us tomorrow?'

Ravan looked uncomfortable.

'For old times' sake. Tara will be happy to see you.'

Why did it take him so long to answer her when he wanted to hold her hands and face and say yes, yes, yes.

'Okay.'

'Seven-thirty sharp? By that time it will be dark and you won't be able to fly kites any more. We'll play not-at-home.' A shadow crossed her face. Ravan thought of the last time they had played cards. 'Or we can play carrom. Or just talk. We've got so much catching up to do.'

They could have walked back to the chawl together but Ravan said he had some errands to run. He was about to walk away when her hand brushed his. 'Thank you, Ravan.' He withdrew his hand sharply. Why should she thank him when it was he who ought to have expressed his happiness and gratitude. He couldn't figure out his awkwardness and why he was behaving in such an uncouth manner.

~

He was on all fours looking for a place under the steel bed to store the kites safely till the next morning when Parvatibai came out of the kitchen. Her first reaction was to check whether her earrings and bangles were still on her person. She went back to the kitchen and looked into her pantry drawer. Her wallet was still there. She opened it and counted the notes, five tenners, one fiver and a two-rupee note. Fifty-seven rupees, nothing missing there. She didn't recall exactly how many coins had been in the change pocket but they felt right. She came out. Ravan had arranged the kites carefully above the steel trunk under the bed and was winding the manja around the wooden reel.

'I thought I told you not to buy kites this year.'

'You didn't expend that many words on me. You merely said "no" to giving me money.'

'Where did you steal the money to buy the kites?'

'You've already checked and found that no money's been stolen from your wallet and all your golden goods are intact.'

'Don't act smart and don't give me so much lip. Have you taken to stealing money from outsiders now? If you have, I'll personally hand you over to the police and make sure you go to jail. Answer me.'

'I didn't steal any money.'

'Oh! So the grocer and the Irani are standing outside and distributing kites for free on the eve of Sankrant?'

'Shobhan gave them to me.'

'You asked her?' She was livid now. 'Don't you have any shame? Bet you told her what an ogre and a harridan your mother is.'

'She and the entire CWD block already know that,' and before Parvatibai could interrupt him, 'just as they are perfectly aware that your son is a hopeless criminal. No. I didn't reveal any family secrets and I didn't beg her to give me kites. She gave them to me of her own free will.'

'She is a fool.' Parvatibai was still smouldering but did not know what more to say. 'Poor Shobhan. She must have spent a small fortune from the little she saves. She has no money to buy a new shoe for her foot.' Parvatibai went back to the kitchen and came out again. 'I should have given you the money.'

~

That night Ravan had a dream. It was Sankrant. There were at least a hundred youngsters and adults on the terrace of CWD Chawl No. 17 flying kites. The terraces of all the buildings in Mazagaon were just as full. There were people standing in the open space where he used to attend the Sabha meetings. The battle for the skies was raging. There were terrible brawls and clashes between kites. The kite-king Syed Ali a.k.a. the Butcher was living up to his deadly name. What everybody was witnessing was a massacre, pure and simple. Seven, sometimes even nine or ten, kites besieged Syed Ali's single warrior. They ran circles around it, used every feint and trick in the book, chased it, led it astray but Syed Ali's post-office red kite with its black death's head and crossed bones emblem was a wily one. It acted dumb and seemed to cower, then with a casual sleight of hand turned the tables on them. Just as they were zeroing in on the kill, it slipped out from under and let them get inextricably entangled with each other. It pulled away from them and ascended rapidly. Then like a cobra bending over to administer the kiss of death, it swooped down and ever so gracefully nicked all seven or nine of them where they had tied themselves into one big knot. Soon there was nobody left in the sky but Syed Ali's killer-kite. It was prancing and preening now, taking mincing steps one minute and sweeping the horizon the next to reaffirm its supremacy. It was a superb show, that victory dance. The death's head leapt and froze, it somersaulted, zig zagged and shivered, it arched like a rainbow, drooped, then shot up gloriously.

It would have continued its triumphal march but for a tiny speck in the sky. Syed Ali's kite was not about to rest on its laurels. Its mission was to police the heavens and smash any pretender, would-be usurper or riff-raff who thought that it could carve out a small principality while Big Brother was not looking. The speck had turned into a happy-go-lucky, ne'er-a-care-in-the-world daredevil of a kite. It was free-wheeling, blithely unaware of the shadow of the grim reaper racing over the buildings of Mazagaon. Perhaps Syed Ali's mass murderer may have spared the little newcomer if it had paid its respects, acknowledged its sovereignty and fawned sheepishly around it. But to ignore it, or worse, not even be aware of it, that was heresy. It went for the cheeky tyke.

The string of the kite was in the hands of none other than the child Ravan. He was barely a year old. He held the wooden phirki almost vertically so that his dark yellow kite could unwind the green manja at a blurry speed as it rose like an impatient sun in the morning sky. But its days were clearly numbered. The butcher had traversed half the earth and waited discreetly for its prey to come within its ambit. The people on the streets and the terraces were yelling and screaming now. 'Look out, look out. Beware, Syed Ali's out to get you. Run. Fly.' But the child Ravan was so engrossed in the beauty and grace of his kite, he did not hear the warnings and screams. The death's head was upon his kite now. It bent over, went round the green manja and came full-circle. It was a stranglehold, the ultimate vice that would snuff out the upstart. Something strange happened then. At the very last minute Ravan noticed the deadly predator. He realized that this was no time to reason with the intruder. It was do or die. He flicked his finger and yanked the manja. Oh foolish audacity and suicidal temerity, the crowds down below sighed, and waited for the little kite to be cut off from its umbilical cord. Syed Ali must have felt the same way. With the supreme modesty of one who is about to crush an insignificant opponent he pulled his kite away. The death's head turned turtle, wavered, lost its moorings and took a kamikaze dive. Slowly, almost unwillingly, Syed Ali of the demon-manja, the serial-killer of Mazagaon sank ignominiously to the ground.

There was a shout of jubilation from the crowd. They hugged each other, went mad with happiness and danced in the streets till someone looked up and lost his power of speech. They followed his gaze and saw the most incredible sight of their lives. The square yellow sun on a green leash was climbing crazily to the meridian and with it the child Ravan. Kite and child had taken off from the terrace, Ravan hanging on to the handles of the reel, and were speeding across the heavens. A hush fell upon the world. They would not look up any more because they did not want to see Ravan hurtle down to his death. Some people ran into their homes and brought out mattresses to cushion his fall but there was no way of predicting the path of his descent. Then they heard bubbling laughter. They looked up. They couldn't believe their eyes. There was an expression of such beatitude and ethereal joy on Ravan's face, he looked like a celestial creature. Perhaps he was the child of a god and goddess, and as the mouse was the vehicle of Lord Ganesh and the bull of Shiva, the kite was Ravan's.

Air was his element and he seemed to float in it effortlessly. He was laughing all the way. He felt the sky racing to meet him. He opened his arms to embrace it. Now he was going to fall, he didn't even have the support of the phirki. Nothing of the sort happened. He floated weightlessly in the air. He grasped the reel again and became a trapeze artist doing cartwheels in the air, leaping, swinging a full 360 degrees on the arms of the phirki. He waved out to the people below. The breeze caught in his hair and ruffled it. The earth was rapidly receding from his vision. He turned his right foot at an angle as if it was a rudder and moved port-wards. There, he could touch the moon now. It was cold to the touch and round like a silver lollipop. He licked it. There was no doubt in his mind, he was eating the food of the gods. His next stop was the sun.

He slipped it under his armpit. He would never be in the dark again and he could always play ball with it. He was about to crash into the sky. It swivelled and tilted dangerously. Would it crack and splinter into a billion pieces? He did not want to break a single thing in this beautiful universe. He needn't have worried. The sky opened up and let him in. And then it came to him. He was one with the world because all things, stars and earthly creatures, trees and mud, lizards and air, sky and water were all made of the same substance. He closed his eyes and could feel a shower of stars passing through his body. He threw his head back and closed his eyes. He had never been so happy in his life.

~

The next morning he was on the terrace by 7.30. The sky was already a dense patchwork of bright coloured checkers. They swayed and luxuriated like miniature sailboats suspended in the air. Ravan sat on the floor and carefully measured out the exact points along the length of the kite where he would need to pierce holes on either side of the thin bamboo backbone. Now came the tricky part. You threaded the holes and tied knots so that if you held the apex of the triangle of thread with the kite as its base, the kite would balance perfectly. He tested his handiwork again and again. A slight imbalance and the kite would nosedive to the ground and break in the middle. Now he tied the kite to the manja on the phirki and slung it over the edge of the parapet. He took Shobhan's name for she had said fly them for me and pulled the kite up. The first tug was the most important. It usually decided whether the kite would take off or needed some more adjustments. The kite lifted on a light current of air and started climbing.

The essence of kite-flying for Ravan as well as everybody else in Mazagaon was the aerial skirmish, the bellicose scrapping and the lethal dog-fights. You used all your cunning, guile and skill to scalp the kites of your friends and foes. Frankly, there were no friends on Sankrant. Every kite other than yours was the enemy. If you wanted to survive, you went for the kill. No mercy. Ravan seemed to have misplaced his aggression for the day. He avoided the other kites. Shobhan had wanted him to fly his kite higher than everybody else's and that's just what he was going to do. Get away from this madding crowd and land up at the pole star. Who knows, I might take flight once again, become a bird, circle the sun, trespass into the Milky Way, saunter around Jupiter and on my way back meet Martians. From the corner of his eye, he saw an aubergine patch stealing in on his red and blue. He yanked sharply at his kite, swerved it to the right and continued to fly it out of harm's way. But the airborne missile was bent on a fight and tracked his kite down. Damn, who was out to get him so early in the day? It was difficult to locate his enemy in that vast crowd on the terrace but he identified him soon enough. Eddie. Ravan, even after all these years, could not understand his neighbour's single-minded animosity. He decided to lose altitude rapidly and give Eddie the slip. But Eddie's aubergine combat aircraft continued in hot pursuit. On any other day Ravan would have said, 'You want a scrap, Eddie? You've got it.' Not today. All he wanted was to coast along lazily. But Eddie followed him throughout the day like his shadow and nemesis.

Sometime in the afternoon Syed Ali noticed Eddie strutting around and gloating, 'Kati patang, kati patang. Watch out, Ravan, here's your fourth kite gone.' But that was not to be. The kite-killer of Mazagaon thought it was time to teach Eddie a lesson. Nobody beats Syed Ali except in dreams. Like everybody else Eddie had to eat his words. Ravan felt no sense of elation or satisfaction. He was merely relieved to be left alone.

The sun was spilling blood onto the horizon. The sky was anchored to the earth with thousands of coloured strings. Ravan had been down to his home just twice in the entire day, once to drink water and the next time to pee. If there had been slaughter all day long, there was no sign of it now barring the swollen red river in the sky. An exhausted quiet had settled on the terraces of Mazagaon. Ravan was on his last kite. Its flaming orange stood steadfast in the still air. At one end of the terrace a few boys were exchanging notes about how many kites they had downed and what devious and heroic strategies they had used.

His kite was darkening now. There was a slight wind blowing and it rocked from side to side as if it was putting itself to sleep. If you had a long enough string, would a kite reach all the way to the moon? He wound the manja and brought his kite down. He was exhausted, happy and famished.

~

He bathed, put on a washed and ironed shirt and shorts, combed his hair and sat down.

'You must be dying of hunger,' Parvati said to him. 'Come, I'll serve you dinner.'

'I'm not feeling hungry.'

'Must be all that sun.' There was concern in Parvati's voice. 'But you can't go to bed on an empty stomach. I'll make you some buttermilk.'

'No.' He got up and had three glasses of water.

'Are you angry with me?'

It was an odd question coming from his mother. 'Why would I be angry with you?'

'Because I didn't buy the kites for you.'

'No,' he answered matter-of-factly, 'I'm not.'

There were boundaries of affection that Parvati would not cross. Neither she nor her son would be able to handle it.

'If you change your mind later, it's all right. Even if it's twelve o'clock, I'll warm up the food for you,'

He got out his notebook and started working on algebraic equations. The door was open as all doors in a chawl are till the time you go to sleep and sometimes even after that. He waited for the sound of Shobhan's footsteps, one firm and the other a little muted and hesitant.

'Why haven't you come, Ravan? We are all waiting for you. I've made shrikhand for you.' She would smile and take his hand and drag him to her house. Shobhan did not smile with her mouth but with her eyes and it was one of the most beautiful sights in the world.

He wanted so much to go to the Sarang house. He wanted to be with those nine sisters but most of all with Shobhan. He would do anything to wipe out all those intervening years when he had turned his back on them and kept the memory of the pool of blood under Tara at bay.

He lay in bed and waited for her to come and get him even after it was past one at night.

Nineteen

❖

It was five o'clock in the morning and Eddie was still fast asleep. A right index finger jabbed him hard between his ribs and stayed jabbed. He turned over. The finger was now boring into his back and would soon penetrate his heart and come out on the other side. He was familiar with the phrase heart attack but he had not imagined that he would be the recipient of one at so early an age. It took a colossal effort to open his eyes. It was worse than a heart attack. It was the silent one, the one who had severed all diplomatic and hostile relations with him. Mother. Violet was standing like a statue of justice that he had seen in some film. Her left hand was raised and in it instead of the scales of justice, she held an empty bottle of milk. On the previous morning he had skipped this chore altogether and made straight for the terrace at five-thirty. Granna, Violet and Pieta, not to mention Eddie himself, had gone without tea and milk the whole day. Life without tea was inconceivable for Granna. She said it leaked into her joints, warmed, and then thawed them out. After the third cup, she came to life and was mobile, though a little arthritically, for the whole day. As for Mother, Ma, Mamma, nowadays just an insistently intrusive blank, tea was not an addiction. It was fuel. Without it, the sewing machine could not work. On the 14th of January, the day Hindus called

Sankrant, the sewing machine lay idle all day long. Without hourly tea and tannin, Violet's body rebelled and went into withdrawal symptoms. It occurred to her during the course of the day that she should climb one flight of stairs, go up to the terrace, get hold of her son and heave the boy over the parapet. But she was a woman of self-control and discipline. Besides she was not talking to her son.

The much scratched and colourless half-litre bottle glinted dully over Eddie's head. Would she drop it or smash his head in with it. He grabbed the bottle and got up. It took him a while to locate the rupee coin his mother had left on the dining-table. He was at the staircase. Mother of God, he had forgotten to put on his shirt. He went back, fought his way into an old shirt and slammed the door behind him. There was always a shortage of milk at the Aarey Dairy milk booth. If he didn't hurry, there would be none left and even Granna would stop talking to him. He was leaping, flying down the stairs, colliding into Ravan in his tae kwon do uniform, each making space for the other and yet continuing to race down fast fast fast. They stopped. The bottle fell from Eddie's hand and he screamed and screamed and clung to Ravan. And Ravan swayed but didn't let go of Eddie.

They butted and burrowed blindly into each other; buried their heads into the cavities they had scooped out from one another's breasts. They had closed their eyes. They could not and would not look without. The world was shut out once and forever. They were sufficient unto one another. Great and uncontrollable tremors shot through and ravaged them, and tried to break them asunder. But they had become the double helix that entwines the very essence of our lives. The bonding of fear is greater than the throb and embrace of sex, illicit passion or love. They were a circle, a completeness that would not brook intrusion or interruption. Only mortal enemies could trust each other so wholly, without suspicion and without thought of consequence. They had witnessed the betrayal of life in the early morning light and earned their wings as adults. Perhaps this is what it means to be born again or twice-born. You are now initiated and may consciously and deliberately, of your own free-will, break a promise to yourself or others, stab someone in the back, let others down, inflict pain or suffering, be the initiator and perpetrator of hurt and guilt.

Somebody was hanging from an old iron hook in one of the beams of the second-floor ceiling. The sun was rising behind her. The youngest son of the Deshmukhs, one-year-old Susheel, was leaning on the fallen stool, holding on to her feet and trying to stand up. He couldn't manage it and flopped down. The body rocked back and forth gently. This time the sari did not hide the black pouch with the crude white cross-stitching on it.

There were people gathering on the stairs now. Eddie's mother looked in disbelief at her son hugging Ravan.

'I didn't do it,' Ravan told her. 'I swear I didn't.' But there wasn't much conviction in his voice. It was a long time before Violet moved. She bent down and collected the broken pieces of glass and put them in a corner. She picked up Susheel Deshmukh who had begun to cry and returned him to his mother. Then she took Eddie firmly by the hand and whisked him away. She was not about to let her son get close to the murderer of her husband.

Epilogue

The matriculation exam in those days was after the eleventh grade. Like a lot of other students from municipal and not-so-fancy parochial schools, Ravan and Eddie never went past the tenth grade. There were scenes, bitter fights, Shankar-rao turned his back upon the proceedings but Violet broke her vow of stubborn 'no comment'. The boys were threatened with eviction, told repeatedly not to follow in the infamous footsteps of 'the other boy' and made to reappear for the tenth-grade exams. But the education of Ravan and Eddie, at least the formal academic variety, was over. Whatever the hopes and ambitions of their mothers, the two boys had minds of their own and the cussedness to disregard their mothers' wishes. They were going to be bandleaders. Eddie was going to follow in the footsteps of Bill Haley, Gene Vincent and Elvis Presley. Raju, the hero from *Dil Deke Dekho,* was Ravan's role-model. He would sing and play the drums and blow the horn just as his hero had done. He kept an open mind. A girlfriend and a job as musician on the hotel circuit were a must. But who knew, he might even join the movies and become a hero.

What was the world out there for if not to conquer? Coming home a little late one evening, Ravan was taken aback to see Eddie working out with a staff. It was a beautiful sight and Ravan lingered despite himself. For some reason, he was sure that Eddie was performing for his sake. What Eddie held in his hands was not a wooden staff or a bamboo pole. It was greased lightning, it was a liquid rod, a swirling and unravelling instrument of infinite danger and grace. The staff was in front of him, over his head, behind him, weaving in and out and around him. It seemed unconnected to his body and his hand. It had taken on a life of its own. He advanced, he fought the armies of twilight, he turned somersaults in the air, he retreated and sprang back.

It was too much for Ravan. His hands and arms uncoiled. He went rigid. His body became a series of planes and angles in motion. It was as if he was gathering momentum. He made tentative probes, drew back. He circled his quarry trying to intuit a way to enter the shifting magnetic field that Eddie kept generating around himself. Then with a flying leap he was in. They were in perfect harmony, intersecting each other's orbits in a Pythagorean paradise. It was a duet. Two volatile martial arts in a state of continuous equilibrium. Two warriors and two life-long enemies locked in the ritual of battle.